Praise for *Book of Lost Threads*

'In this highly engaging and compassionate novel, [Tess Evans] successfully realises her evident ambition to salute the bravery of the small souls of this world.' *The Age*

'... charming, full of tenderness and compassion and gentle humour ...' *Adelaide Advertiser*

'All their stories are told with skilful flashbacks, and a warm understanding of hopes, dreams and kindness. Make friends with these special people.' *Woman's Day*

'There is genuine care, concern and love between the four main characters and when each of their problems comes to a head they all band together in support ... a strong and intricate plot ...' *Good Reading*

'... wonderfully written, creating a complexity and sense of place that makes this journey toward redemption an enjoyable one.' *Bookseller & Publisher*

'Evans wants to show the best of humanity ... *Book of Lost Threads* deserves to be enjoyed by many readers.' *Sydney Morning Herald*

'There are many layers to this engaging debut—all expertly woven together. One to pass on to your friends.' *Who Weekly*

BOOK of LOST THREADS

TESS EVANS

ALLEN&UNWIN

This edition published in 2011
First published in 2010

Allen & Unwin
83 Alexander Street
Crows Nest NSW 2065
Australia
Phone: (61 2) 8425 0100
Fax: (61 2) 9906 2218
Email: info@allenandunwin.com
Web: www.allenandunwin.com

Cataloguing-in-Publication details are available
from the National Library of Australia
www.trove.nla.gov.au

ISBN 978 1 74237 612 7

Text design by Emily O'Neill
Set in Adobe Caslon by Post Pre-press Group, Australia

Printed and bound in Australia by Griffin Press

20 19 18 17 16 15 14 13

MIX
Paper from
responsible sources
FSC® C009448
www.fsc.org

The paper in this book is FSC® certified.
FSC® promotes environmentally responsible,
socially beneficial and economically viable
management of the world's forests.

18773479
BKCB EVAN (REL)

Dedicated to my father, Colin Websdale,
a great dad and a great lover of books.

Rebirth us with Wisdom, as
we are knitted once again
back into wholeness.
—From 'Ariadne's Blessing', Janet Bristow, 1998

Others also there are who perished unknown; their sacrifice is not
forgotten, and their names, though lost to us, are written in the
Books of God.
—Inscription from the Shrine in the Scottish War Memorial.
Reproduced with the permission of the Trustees of the
Scottish War Memorial, Edinburgh.

I

Moss and Finn

'HELLO. DOES MICHAEL CLANCY LIVE here?'

Silence. The door between them remained shut.

'Michael Clancy. Michael *Finbar* Clancy?'

'Who's asking?'

'Moss—Miranda. Miranda Sinclair.'

Moss wasn't a spiteful person in general, but in later moments of honest self-appraisal, she had to admit that spite was one of the less savoury elements in her decision to seek out Michael Clancy. She had nurtured this ignoble spite for months. It had walked with her up the path to his house, stuck like some disgusting mess to her shoe. And it was directed at Linsey. Linsey, who loved her. Amy's softness offered no resistance and Moss needed hard edges on which to hone this uncharacteristic desire for revenge.

She had checked the timetable when she bought her ticket. The journey from Melbourne usually took just over two hours, but that day the train was delayed at Fosters Creek for nearly an hour, which meant that Moss missed the connecting bus. It was close to eight by the time she arrived, tired, cold and hungry, wishing she'd never come. Never come and never heard of Michael Finbar Clancy. Amy had warned her: *He won't want to know.* But she'd come anyway.

The chill rain numbed her face as she half-sprinted in the direction indicated by the driver. She stopped in front of a shabby weatherboard house, alive to the tension that crawled over her scalp; alive to the tingling root of every hair.

There was no knocker and she felt around in vain for a bell, finally rapping, louder than necessary, on the glass panel.

'Hello. Does Michael Clancy live here?'

Silence.

'Michael Clancy. Michael *Finbar* Clancy?'

There was a reluctant scraping sound as the door opened a niggardly few centimetres and a soft, uncertain voice squeezed its way through. 'Who's asking?'

'Moss—Miranda. Miranda Sinclair.'

The sliver of light from inside revealed four surprisingly neat fingers.

'I don't know any Mirandas.' The fingers withdrew and the door began to close but not before Moss managed to wedge her foot in the gap.

'Please. I've come all the way from Melbourne. It's freezing out here—not to mention the rain.'

On the other side of the door, Finn was at a loss. Visitors were rare. Especially after dark. He considered his options. He could close the door and that would be that. He could continue to talk through the crack. Or he could simply let her in. The second option seemed safest. The first was rude and the third was risky. It meant asserting some authority, though. Not really his forte. His mind searched for something to say and caught at the tail of her plea.

'It's been raining since lunchtime,' he said.

'And it's still raining and I'm soaked. Please. Just let me in so I can talk to you.'

A pause. 'What do you want?' he asked warily. 'I'll let you in if you tell me.' Regretting these words even as he spoke.

'I just need to talk to you. I can't shout it through the door. You knew my mother once. She told me all about you.' Moss was overstating the case, certain that Finn couldn't possibly know anything about what her mother might have told her.

'*All* about me? Who is she then—God Almighty herself?' Finn's uneasy chuckle erupted into an embarrassing snort.

'Please. Just let me in.' There were tears in her voice.

He applied his eye to the crack. A small figure was huddled under the inadequate shelter of the narrow verandah. 'Alright. You can come in for a bit.' A grudging invitation at best.

The door scraped open to reveal a petite young woman— in her early twenties, maybe; a sodden waif with dark hair plastered in tendrils around her urchin face. Her japara was soaked, and he was dismayed to see that she was shivering. He knew then that he had no choice. Noting with a sinking heart her ominously large backpack, he stepped aside to let her in.

'You're wet through. Take off your coat and come and sit here by the stove.' He led her down a dimly lit corridor to a large kitchen where he indicated an armchair clumsily draped with a purple chenille bedspread. 'I'll put on the kettle. Are you hungry?'

She nodded and Finn busied himself around the kitchen, making a pot of strong black tea and cutting two thick slices of bread which he tried to ram into the toaster. Muttering curses at the recalcitrant bread, he shaved off the excess crusts. It was still a snug fit. 'There,' he said, pleased. 'It won't take a minute now.'

His guest sat obediently by the large wood-fired stove, warming her hands and looking curiously at Finn and then hungrily at the toaster. Finn had the hunched shoulders of a man uncomfortable with his height; with his long thin legs and narrow face he looked for all the world like an apologetic stork. *Excuse me*, she could hear him murmur at stork meetings and stork functions, *do you mind if I sit here, in this seat at the back?* And there he would sit looking morosely at the more successful storks, the better dressed storks, the richer storks, the whole *network* of storks as they mingled and discussed storkly issues with a confidence, a conviction that he could only wonder at.

The toaster, struggling to expel its burden, gave a kind of *whummph* that was the signal for Finn to perform an extraction and proceed to the generous application of butter.

'Jam? Honey? I'm out of Vegemite, I'm afraid.' He looked at Miranda with eyes so blue, so kind, that she burst into tears. 'If I'd known you were coming I would have got some Vegemite,' he said, bewildered at her extreme reaction to its absence. He hovered over her, flapping his hands, making little soothing noises.

'Honey's fine,' she sniffled. 'I'm just cold and tired.'

His grin was unpractised. 'Honey it is then.' He indicated for her to come and sit at the table and poured tea into two mugs. 'Now,' he said, stirring his tea nervously. 'What shall I call you? Miranda's nice, but it is a bit of a mouthful.'

'You're telling me.' She smiled suddenly. 'Wait till you hear my full name—Miranda Ophelia Sinclair. There's a mouthful for you. I hardly ever get called Miranda. Everyone calls me Moss. It's from—'

'From your initials. Very clever. A good solution.' He looked at her with something like admiration. 'Moss is a very good solution.'

'Mother Linsey doesn't think so. She used to insist on calling me Miranda and I would refuse to answer and we'd go on like that for hours. Days, sometimes. But in the end, on my thirteenth birthday, she gave me a book, some sheet music and a new beach towel and promised to call me Moss from then on. It was a good birthday. Even her card said *Happy Birthday, Moss.* Mother Amy only called me Miranda when she was mad at me about something.'

Finn's alarm had returned when he heard the name Linsey. 'You said before that your mother knows me,' he said. 'What's her name? Where do I know her from?'

Moss licked honey from her fingers and stole a look at his face. Now the moment had come, panic constricted her throat. The bravado with which she had set out had been washed away with the rain. She swallowed painfully. 'Amy,' she mumbled. 'Her name is Amy Sinclair. You knew her from before I was born.'

Finn slopped his tea as he set down the mug. 'Amy Sinclair . . . Amy and Linsey.' He stood up abruptly and fussed with the kettle. It was so long ago. The person he was then no longer existed. What was he supposed to say to this . . . this *interloper* who had materialised on his doorstep? Crouching down on his haunches, he poked at the fire and looked at her covertly from under his eyebrows. She was obviously waiting for him to say something. He frowned. There was something not quite right . . . What was it? It came to him suddenly.

'Obviously you didn't turn out according to plan,' he observed in what he hoped was a normal voice. 'What did Linsey have to say about that?'

Moss flinched. Despite Linsey's assurances to the contrary, she had always believed she was a disappointment and here at last was confirmation. She'd been right all along. Her resentment was justified. Her pain was real. She looked straight at Finn, her tone carefully neutral.

'She left just before my fifteenth birthday. Mum says it was for the best.'

'Possibly . . . Possibly . . .'

Finn lapsed again into silence. What more could he say? He saw that the fire was burning low, and with some relief escaped out the back door, muttering that he needed to get more wood. He grabbed his tobacco pouch on the way out and stood on the back verandah, rolling a cigarette. Shielding the flame he lit up and drew deeply, his mind a kaleidoscope of shifting images—a tall blonde woman, a small dark woman, a rose garden. Gilt chairs. A glass jar . . .

Moss was grateful for time in which to compose herself and looked curiously around the room. Considering the outside of the house with its sagging verandah and peeling paint, inside it was, well—*cosy*. The kitchen was warmed by the wood-fired stove where the large black kettle bubbled and steamed on the hob. On the mantelpiece above, a sturdy little clock measured the minutes with an uncompromising tick. The table, piled at one end with newspapers, was old and heavy, with a slight depression in the middle from years of scrubbing. None of the chairs matched. Two were padded dining chairs, one with worn green velvet upholstery, the other with a brocade of doubtful pattern and hue. The sideboard, probably quite handsome in its day, retained some of its former dignity if little of its original surface. It had what antique dealers call *patina*—years of patina, she guessed. On every inch of its shelves, glasses jostled with plates, bowls and mugs, and books teetered in ziggurat formation among cooking utensils, pens, pencils, notebooks and a self-important orange ashtray. A steel spike speared an alarming amount of what were probably bills, and a brave little jar of wild violets sat precariously but hopefully on the edge of it all. The walls, roughly plastered, were a cheerful if streaky yellow, and several tattered art posters were affixed with what must have been whole rolls of sticky tape. They were bold and colourful. Matisse? It didn't matter; she felt comfortable here. Living with Amy, Moss was used to clutter. She closed her eyes for a moment, starting guiltily when she heard Finn stamp his feet on the backdoor mat as he returned with an armload of wood.

'Still raining,' he said. Perhaps if he ignored those wounded eyes, she would go away and leave him be. She had breached his first line of defence and he felt besieged. Rightly aggrieved. At all costs, they mustn't continue where they'd left off. Change the topic of conversation—to what? Anything. Anything but Amy and Linsey.

He sat down, not sure what to do with his hands. 'I understand what you were saying about being called Moss. I like people to call me Finn—for Finbar, you know. Your mother, and my mother too, for that matter, called me Michael, but he was an archangel, you see—not me at all.' His tone became judicial. 'Now, you might well point out that Saint Finbar was a bishop. And that's certainly true. From Cork, he was. But most of his life was spent in a monastery. Did you know he was even a hermit at one time? You can see that's more me than an archangel. I just shortened Finbar to Finn. It's easier.' Having completed his story Finn sat back, hoping his diversion had been successful.

Moss was defeated. She was warm now, and tired. So tired that her head was sinking under its own weight. Fearing that Finn would continue to babble about bishops and angels, she decided to take the initiative.

'Look, I know it's a bit of a cheek, but can I doss down in front of the fire? It's too late to find somewhere else to stay and I brought a sleeping bag and a blow-up mattress. I won't be any trouble. You can send me away in the morning, if you want. I guess we both need time to think before we, you know, talk properly.' Did he understand her meaning? she wondered, both hoping and fearing that he did.

Despite the abruptness of her request, Finn was relieved, on two counts. There was no accommodation to be had in town now that it was past closing time at the pub, and he couldn't simply send a young woman away into the night. Regardless of why she had come, he was now responsible for her safety, at least in the short term. There was also his realisation that his

Finbar story had seriously depleted his fund of small talk. The only things left to say were too big to approach tonight.

'Good idea,' he said. 'Let's call it a night. Bathroom's through there.' He put the covers on the stove top and ensured that the back door was secure. Picking up the orange ashtray, he headed off down the short corridor, but hesitated at his bedroom door. 'Um . . . goodnight, then, Moss.'

'Goodnight, Finn.'

Finn sat on the edge of his bed and rolled another cigarette. He was trying to give up yet again and was down to four a day. His routine had always included a cigarette before bedtime and he often smoked in bed even though he knew it was dangerous. But tonight he sat upright while he drew in the acrid smoke. With someone else in the house, his carelessness could have serious consequences. Abstracted, he smoked his second and then third cigarette before climbing into bed. His sleep was fitful and he struggled to keep at bay the dreams that drew him back to the house with the rose garden, back to the house where Amy and Linsey had greeted him with so much hope, all those years ago.

2

Michael, Amy and Linsey

WHEN FINN WAS STILL MICHAEL, his stork-features were not at all evident. At twenty-two, he was tall and supple in the way of an athlete or dancer, or even an archangel, and his thick blond hair bore no trace of corrosive yellow. It was white-blond, a Viking blond that matched his deep blue seafaring eyes. Further blessed, he was one of the brightest in his year at university, where he was majoring in pure maths.

Women found him variously handsome, gorgeous, scrumptious, sexy, funny, clever, attentive, charming: infinitely attractive, in fact. They loved his hard, lean body, the silver-gilt halo of his hair, his kind, vulnerable blue eyes. But despite his undoubted good looks and charm, he had an air of innocence that turned the minds of his female acquaintances to dark thoughts of passion, seduction, and, in some extreme cases, corruption. Every one of them wanted to see lust in those dark blue depths and Michael, who was nowhere near as innocent as he seemed, was happy to oblige. Strangely enough, as he moved easily from one conquest to the next, he left behind very little resentment. Disappointment, yes. But very little resentment.

As none of them actually fell in love with him (or he with them), it seemed only fair to share him around. Most of his women eventually went on to marry lesser but more accessible men. Of the remainder, two never married: one entered a convent, and the other disappeared into the black hole of the Murdoch newspaper empire from whence she later emerged as a waspish commentator on other people's sex lives.

The problem with all this female attention was a lack of ready cash to fund his exploits. Michael had a bursary that paid for his books, his scientific calculator and some of his rent, and to supplement this, four nights a week he stacked supermarket shelves for twelve dollars an hour, earning just enough cash to cover the rest of his living expenses. As a consequence, he often had to leave his paramours alone in their beds as he dived into his clothes and hurried to rendezvous with laundry detergent, baked beans, tomato sauce, Tim Tam biscuits and bonus-sized bottles of Coke. There was no doubt that money was short, but somehow he always found a way.

'Hey, Phil, can you lend us a couple of dollars?' he asked his housemate one day.

Phil looked up from his newspaper. 'Pushing your luck, mate. I only have six dollars fifty till I'm paid and you still owe me twenty bucks from last week.'

'Is that a yes or a no?' Michael had a happy knack of ignoring what he didn't want to hear. Getting no reply, he began to compile a shortlist of those he hadn't borrowed from recently. The list was very short indeed. He was close to despair when Phil came over with his newspaper. It was the official student publication, *Vox Discipuli*.

'Get a look at this, Mike. A job made just for you. Listen: *Part-time position. Earn up to $10,000. Applications are invited from males between the ages of twenty-two and thirty. They must be tall and fair, in good health and with an exceptionally high IQ. Special skill in science or maths preferred. Please send CV, academic transcript and two recent photographs (full-length and head shot) to PO Box OIV, GPO, Melbourne. Applications close 24 June.* There! What do you reckon? Up to ten thousand dollars, it says. *Ten thousand dollars*, mate.'

Michael looked at the advertisement. 'What do you reckon you'd have to do? It doesn't say here.'

'Model?'

'Why would they need an academic transcript?'

'Call boy? For super-intelligent females?'

'I could be their man.'

'It might be ASIO, wanting you to seduce enemy scientists.'

'Dangerous blonde Russian babes. Just my type.'

'Go for it, brother.'

So it was that a few days later, Michael found himself knocking on the door of a very nice house in a very nice suburb. He had received a letter inviting him for an interview and he presented himself punctually.

The door was answered by a serious-looking young woman in jeans and a neat T-shirt. She was petite, but her voice was that of a much bigger woman: the sort of voice that usually issues from a broad chest; the sort of voice that suggests confidence and authority. He was startled to hear it coming from such a small frame.

'Michael Clancy? I'm Linsey Brookes. Come in.'

Linsey led him into a small sitting room and he lowered himself gingerly into one of the elegant little chairs as she dashed away down the hall, telling him she wouldn't be long. He tried to lean back in the chair, but it was impossible to sit any way but straight. He looked around, trying to ignore the gilt curlicues abrading his spine. What struck him most about the room was its order—its uncompromising symmetry, its matching fabrics, its clear preference for right angles. It was a room that strove to keep you in your place and it rigidly resisted Michael's sudden desire to move the coffee table to a forty-five-degree angle—or, better still, seventeen degrees. Squirming like a schoolboy in the frost of its disapproval, he wished he had worn a subversive red shirt just for the joy of alarming its smug colour scheme and prim furniture. By the time Linsey returned, he was feeling resentful and sullen.

'Follow me,' she said, and led him to a dining room where another woman sat with her head bent over some papers she was reading. Linsey indicated a chair, and Michael found himself sitting opposite the two women. It didn't quite feel like a job interview—but then he didn't have much experience to go by.

Linsey introduced the other woman as Amy Sinclair. He realised now she was somewhat older than him—*Around thirty*, he estimated. *But what an incredible . . .*

Amy stood to greet him, taking his hand in cool fingers. Like Michael, she was tall and blonde with blue eyes fringed by impossibly dark lashes. Her face was heart-shaped and her mouth generous. He stole a glance at her breasts. Two perfect curves rose from her soft V-necked sweater. *Things are looking up*, Michael reflected, reluctantly adjusting his gaze to the table and what he realised was his résumé.

'I see you're an Aquarian,' Amy noted, glancing at the résumé. 'That's a good start.'

Linsey frowned. 'But hardly a clincher, Amy.' She turned to Michael. 'You seem to meet most of our requirements, but can you be discreet?'

'Absolutely.'

'And reliable? Are you reliable?'

'Discreet and reliable. That's me. Anyone will tell you.'

'Unfortunately, we don't have the luxury of being able to ask anyone. Your academic and work records seem to speak for your reliability, and you were on time today. Discretion, now. That's another thing altogether.' Her dark brows, winged at the outer tips, swooped together. 'Can you give us an example of your ability to be discreet?'

Michael was unsettled by Linsey's keen stare. He gained some time by moving his chair closer to the table and folding his arms thoughtfully. Then he brightened. 'I never discuss the girls I sleep with.' This was true. He felt a strange delicacy about discussing his conquests, a courtesy not returned to him by the conquests themselves, who never tired of discussing him.

Linsey smiled grimly. 'Unusually discreet, for a man,' she said. 'Tell me, are your parents and grandparents still alive?'

'My parents are, but I only have one grandparent.'

'And how did the others, er, die?'

'You want to know how my grandparents died? What sort of job is this?'

Linsey looked severely over her pointed little nose. 'You can leave now if you wish. When we have satisfied ourselves as to your suitability, we'll explain further.'

Amy said nothing, but managed to look both charming and concerned.

What did I have to lose? Michael asked Phil later. *Nothing at all, mate,* said Phil.

Michael explained that his maternal grandparents had been killed in a train crash in India. 'They liked to travel,' he said, noting the approving nods. His father's father had died recently, at the age of seventy-five. 'Lung cancer. He was a smoker.'

'You don't smoke, do you? We don't want a smoker.'

Michael told his first lie. 'No. Never seen the sense in it,' he replied, shaking his head. 'What with Grandad and all.'

'Do your parents keep good health? No chronic illnesses or allergies?'

The second lie was easy. Phil had coached him on this point. With job interviews, you tell 'em what they want to hear. 'Nope. Both disgustingly healthy.' His mother's asthma was hardly worth mentioning, so he didn't.

'Thank you, Mr Clancy. We'll be in touch in the next few days.'

That night, Michael and Phil speculated over a bottle of rough red. Two bottles, in fact. The best theory they could come up with was that he was to be part of some sort of scientific experiment.

'No, it makes sense, mate,' Phil argued. They had already agreed that this was the best explanation, but Phil had reached the stage of drunkenness where he sensed that the brilliance of his logic was best demonstrated by reiteration. He counted off on his fingers. 'You have to agree, mate: one, there's the health questions, b, there's the academic stuff, and four, there's the . . . other stuff.'

'You're so right, mate.'

Three days later a call came from Linsey. 'You are the successful candidate,' she announced. 'Can you come and see us again? We have a proposition to put to you.'

'Cool. They're going to proposition you,' Phil chortled gleefully.

'I'd better wear my red shirt then,' said Michael. 'They might as well know what they're getting.'

As before, Linsey answered the door. This time she took him straight into the dining room, where Amy was sitting with a third woman.

Linsey nodded in her direction. 'Our lawyer, Sally Grainger. Sally, this is Michael Clancy.'

'Lawyer?' Michael felt at a distinct disadvantage.

Sally, plump and middle-aged, looked more like his Aunty Joan than a lawyer. To complete the impression, she smiled reassuringly, her small eyes almost disappearing as she squinted at him through her reading glasses. 'Don't worry, Michael. You can certainly have your own lawyer. In fact, I strongly advise that you do.'

'We'll pay, of course,' said Amy hastily. 'All expenses will be paid.' Her smile was accompanied by the most charming of dimples, and Michael, who had half-risen from his seat, sat down abruptly.

'I think it's time you told me what this is all about.' He frowned, hoping he sounded more resolute than he felt.

Sally and Amy smiled. Linsey tapped impatient fingers on the table. 'Sally? It's best you explain as we agreed.'

'I hope you understand that what I'm about to tell you is strictly confidential.'

Michael nodded, but this clearly wasn't enough.

'I must have your word. This will be a verbal contract until the formal one is signed.'

'You can trust me,' he replied. 'I give you my word.' And he meant it. Michael Clancy didn't give his word lightly.

'Very well. Amy and Linsey, as you have probably guessed, are in a lesbian relationship.'

Michael hadn't guessed or even suspected, but he nodded gravely, one part of his brain trying to remember if there were signs he had missed. The other part continued to listen to Sally who was explaining in her brisk lawyer's voice.

'They want a child, but don't want a man—how can I put it?—too intimately involved in the process. In short, they hope to become pregnant with your sperm, using artificial insemination.'

'Oh,' said Michael. Then again, 'oh,' followed by an 'um'.

The lawyer slid a document out of the folder in front of her and continued: 'A contract has already been drawn up. You supply the sperm at the time Amy is ovulating. You must do this for at least ten cycles in the next twelve months. For this, you will be remunerated: five hundred dollars each month with an additional five thousand dollars if a pregnancy occurs. You will sign an agreement not to have any contact with the child, and for their part, Amy and Linsey will forgo any call on you for financial or emotional support.' She sat back and Michael became aware of three pairs of eyes looking at him.

He gaped a bit.

'This is all contingent upon the quality and motility of your sperm,' Sally added. 'We would need you to go to a doctor of our choice to verify that you're fertile.'

'Um,' he said again. 'No strings? I mean, I don't want a child. Not really cut out to be a father.'

'No strings,' confirmed Linsey as she turned to Amy with an intimate smile.

Good grief, Michael thought. *How can I have missed something so obvious?*

Linsey was explaining further. 'We decided that we wanted the child to be the best she possibly can be, so it was clear from the start that Amy would be the birth mother.' She gestured towards Amy and her voice took on a quality Michael hadn't heard before. 'She's so beautiful. I wanted to ensure, as much as possible, that our child will have her blonde beauty and stature.' She waved a hand as Amy began to protest. 'No. I don't want a short plain woman like me. One in the family is more than enough.' She turned back to Michael. 'Amy is a musician, so I decided that a father with a scientific mind would broaden the skills base. Our child will be as close to perfect as we can make her.' Her thin face was alight.

Michael coughed. 'What if it's a—you know, a boy?'

'All the more reason he should be tall,' was Linsey's enigmatic reply.

'We just want a baby,' Amy said gently. 'We'll love it, boy or girl. And don't worry: we have four brothers between us. There are two grandfathers. He'd have plenty of male role models. We're not harpies, you know.' She smiled hopefully. 'Can you help us, Michael?'

In those days Michael was inclined to quick decisions. What could be the harm? It was a pity the process wasn't going to be a bit more normal, he thought, but he had a healthy libido and it wouldn't be too difficult to produce the required sperm. Besides, he was skint.

'Give me a couple of days to look at the contract,' he said, 'and I'll get back to you.'

He did look at the contract. Just to make sure he would not be encumbered with a child. It all seemed so easy. The next day he phoned the house, where the women were waiting anxiously for his call. 'I'll do it,' he said.

Three weeks later, he found himself following Linsey into a room at the top of the stairs.

She looked at him severely. 'Here's the . . . receptacle.' She held a jar between thumb and forefinger. 'I bought some magazines I thought might help. Just call when you're done and I'll come and collect the jar.'

Finn had first discovered masturbation at the age of thirteen and by now considered himself something of an expert. Taking a moment to recover from his embarrassment, he looked at the magazines and imagined poor Linsey, all beaky disapproval, having to purchase them. It almost distracted him, but this was a job, and he did it with single-minded efficiency.

Having completed the task, he called to Linsey. 'See your-self out,' she said and handed him an envelope, which he had the decency not to open until he was in his car. Five hundred dollars. And it was as easy as that.

Michael was a man of his word. He fobbed off Phil by telling him that he was taking part in a secret drug-testing pro-gram for a pharmaceutical company. This was a good cover as he had conscientiously given up booze and cigarettes for the duration and told everyone that this was part of the parameters of the experiment. It was also necessary, he explained, to have a beeper so that he could be called on the instant he was needed. This was a bit harder to justify, but his vagueness was put down to the secrecy of the tests. So when the beeper sounded during lectures, in the student canteen or at the pub, he was able to go without too many questions being asked. Amy's monthly cycle impinged on the ease of his sex life, but the regularity of her periods enabled him to ensure that he was never called while in another woman's bed.

Six cycles went by. He was quite happy about this. After all, it was five hundred dollars per cycle. On his seventh visit, however, Linsey was out and it was Amy who answered the door. She looked wan and seemed thinner than the last time he'd seen her.

'Are you okay?' he asked with some concern.

Amy's dimple had almost disappeared. 'I'm fine. Really,' she said. 'It's all a bit of a strain. Linsey's so determined to have this baby and I feel I'm letting her down.' To his horror, he saw that she was blinking away tears.

'I'll do my best,' he promised and immediately felt foolish.

He closed the door. The job took a little longer in this frame of mind.

'Good luck,' he said as he handed her the jar. And felt even more foolish.

'Tenth time lucky, maybe,' he said two and a half months later when Linsey rang to tell him that they were still unsuccessful.

The next time he was summoned, Linsey greeted him as usual, though he was conscious of Amy hovering in the background. He went to head up the stairs but Linsey motioned him into the sitting room, where he sat down on one of the gilt chairs. The two women sat on the edge of the sofa, facing him.

'As you're aware, this is the last time for you to . . . assist us,' Linsey began. 'You've been as good as your word and we appreciate that, don't we, Amy?' Amy nodded, started to speak and then fell silent.

'We had researched the matter extensively before we enlisted you,' Linsey told him, 'but we're starting to think there may be something wrong with our—what would you call it?— our *technique*. Consequently . . .' Her skin was taut over sharp cheekbones, and dark smudges shadowed her eyes. 'Consequently, we were wondering if more . . . *conventional* methods might not be required.'

Michael felt a surge of elation. Of course he wasn't averse to having sex with a beautiful woman—but it was more than that. While he had accepted the terms of the job and done his duty, as it were, he nonetheless harboured a nagging resentment that this beautiful woman didn't want to have sex with him. In this role there was an affront to his manhood that he had chosen to ignore in his eagerness for the remuneration. He had taken their money, and done what they asked, but now an ugly thought came unbidden: *Let's see how she feels after having sex with a real man.* Immediately ashamed, he pushed the thought aside.

'Fine,' he said gravely. 'I understand. Do you mean now?'

'Now is the right time,' Amy aspirated the words. He could hardly hear her.

She looked down as Linsey put an arm around her. 'I know it's asking a lot, darling,' Linsey murmured into her hair, 'but we know it may be the only way. We've nearly run out of money.'

Michael took Amy's hand and felt the tension that ran down her arm to her fingertips. 'Come on,' he said. 'I'm not a monster.'

But in the end, he couldn't do it. At the bedroom door he saw hopeless jealousy transform Linsey's carefully disciplined features. Amy was even worse. She was actually trembling. Michael was a generous, considerate lover: it was one reason why so many women were attracted to him. Looking at Amy, intuiting her distress, he felt like a brute.

'Tell you what,' he said as Linsey turned away. 'Tell you what. Let's keep the thing going as it has been for another couple of months before we, you know, take drastic action. I won't expect payment after today.'

He felt their relief wash over him like a flood.

'Thank you, Michael. You're a good man,' said Linsey with simple grace. Amy just smiled. Her dimple had returned.

So the arrangement continued as before until, several months later, he received a phone call.

'We're pregnant,' they sang into the phone. 'Michael, we're pregnant.'

Two days later there was a cheque for five thousand dollars in the mail. A note was attached saying that they were grateful and wished him well, and as the contract stated, he would neither see nor hear from them again.

But even as he breathed a sigh of relief, Michael couldn't help feeling just a little cheated.

3

Amy, Linsey and Moss

FOR AMY AND LINSEY, THE disappointment that had followed Michael's visit each month only compounded their delight when a pregnancy was finally confirmed. The two women looked at each other in awe at what they had achieved.

'We've done it,' Linsey breathed.

'With a little help from Michael,' Amy giggled.

The two women had first met when Amy went to work as a temp at the Melbourne University Faculty of Commerce, where Linsey was a lecturer in economics. On Amy's first day, Linsey burst into the secretary's office, her brusque instructions arrested mid-speech by the sight of the unfamiliar young woman behind the desk.

'When I saw you,' an enchanted Linsey later told Amy, 'I thought of summer—of peaches and honey and lazy blue skies.'

What she actually said at the time was: 'I need these by—um . . .'

Amy looked up from her typing. 'I'm just a temp,' she said. 'You'll have to show me what you want.' And she moved over with a gesture of invitation to come to her side of the desk, where Linsey bent over the manuscript with fierce concentration, trying to ignore the drifting perfume and faint female odour that arose from the seated woman.

For the two weeks that Amy spent at the university, Linsey was distracted. She of fierce efficiency became quiet and absentminded. She worked like a fury on her lecture notes just so she could take them to Amy to format and copy. She replaced her uniform T-shirt with business shirts of crisp white cotton or cream silk. She washed her cap of shining brown hair every night and even tried fluffing it out a bit around her face. She thought constantly of Amy—dreamily imagined intimate dinners, films, concerts—but spoke to her only about work.

On Amy's last day, Linsey was miserable. Confident and outspoken in a professional milieu, she was painfully shy socially.

So it was Amy who made the first move. 'Are you free for a drink after work?' she asked when Linsey came to collect her photocopying. 'Yes? I'll see you at Gerry's around five then.'

At work, Linsey had never made any secret of her sexuality, but she wasn't sure about Amy's. They hadn't developed a friendship or even an acquaintance in the time they had worked together, so to be asked out for a drink seemed like a good sign. But maybe Amy just wanted a reference, or to sound Linsey out about any permanent positions that might be coming up? These questions ran through poor Linsey's head as she shredded her paper napkin in the twilight of Gerry's wine bar.

'I'm sorry,' Amy said breathlessly as she sat down in the chair opposite. 'I was held up while they filled in the agency forms.'

Linsey smiled, hoping her relief wasn't too evident.

'Not a problem. What will you have to drink?'

And so this ordinary, even banal conversation set in train the relationship that, with the help of Michael Finbar Clancy, would produce Miranda Ophelia Sinclair.

But whole oceans would pass under the bridge before these two—now known as Finn and Moss—would finally meet.

Amy, Linsey learned that night, came from a Methodist working-class family. She had three brothers, one an insurance assessor and the other two public servants. Her father was a train driver and her mother worked part-time at the local doctor's surgery.

'They're good people,' Amy told Linsey over a second glass of wine, 'but not the sort to approve of . . . unconventional lifestyles. That's why I haven't told them.'

'My parents try to be open-minded, but I know they're really disappointed in me.' A shadow of pain passed over Linsey's face. 'I have a brother and a sister. They try to understand. They're quite supportive, really, but you can't help knowing that they have to make an effort.'

Both women were silent, each lost for a moment in her own private sorrow.

Later, over dinner, Amy told Linsey about her music. 'I go to classes,' she confided. 'It gives me somewhere to practise. Our house is pretty small and there's nowhere to go to escape the sound of the TV. I know it's ridiculous still living at home at my age—I've moved out a couple of times, but it hasn't worked out. I moved back a few months ago.' She shrugged. 'Just haven't got around to finding another place yet.'

'What made you decide on the harp?' Linsey was enjoying a vision of Amy, in a deep-blue silk gown, playing her harp, looking for all the world like one of God's own angels. She was already planning to offer her spare room as a practice studio.

'Well, there was this old lady next door. I used to do bits and pieces for her, you know, shopping and such. Mum wouldn't let me take any money from her, so she offered to teach me the harp instead. When she moved into a nursing home, she gave the harp to me. Mrs Hirschfield, her name was. A nice old lady. She always wore a black velvet band around her hair, like a little girl.'

Linsey lived in a fine old house left to her by her Aunt Shirley, the widow of 'Flash Jack' Mitchell, the extruded-plastic-pipe magnate. Of course Aunt Shirley never called him 'Flash Jack'. She always referred to him as 'dear-John-God-rest-his-soul'. And well she might. He left her over two million dollars and no children to share it with. After a short period of mourning, Aunt Shirley blonded her greying hair and dedicated herself to spending the lot. *I'm sure it's what dear-John-God-rest-his-soul would have wanted*, she explained prettily as she watched the roulette wheel spin. Fortunately for Linsey, however, Aunt Shirley died of food poisoning after eating some dodgy oysters in Marrakech, leaving her niece with a very nice house, a red MGB and a comfortable number of blue-chip shares.

Two weeks after their dinner, it was to this house that Linsey welcomed Amy as they extracted the harp from Amy's battered Corolla. If she winced a little at the drink bottles, fast-food cartons, magazines, tissues and indeterminate articles of clothing strewn carelessly around the small car, Linsey was hardly aware of it, so pleased was she to play benefactor.

'You can use this,' she said, opening the door to a small well-lit room, sparsely furnished with two ladder-backed chairs, a small table and a music stand. She was particularly pleased with the music stand, which she'd found at a local antiques market. She smiled at Amy and her wide-armed gesture seemed to take in the whole house. 'I hope this is suitable. You're welcome to come at any time.'

Amy was delighted, of course, and took Linsey at her word. Linsey often came into the small music room and stood quietly by the door as Amy played. She looked so graceful and serious as she stroked and plucked the strings, and Linsey gratefully drank in the serenity that seemed to enfold both music and musician. Often, though, she would find Amy just sitting, hands folded in her lap, looking dreamily out onto the garden.

'Play some more,' Linsey would say, and receive a smile of surpassing sweetness as Amy obediently returned to her music.

It wasn't long before Amy began to stay the night, and gradually evidence of her claim on the house appeared in scattered items of clothing, sheet music, makeup, and long blonde hairs in the bathroom. Grumbling a little, Linsey would restore the house to its normal order, but each time Amy returned, chaos followed. It was only in comparison to Linsey's pathological neatness that such a strong word as 'chaos' could be used to describe Amy's cheerful mess. But one day, when a stressed Linsey flung this word (and a good many others) at the untidy Amy, it provided not only the cause of their first quarrel but, oddly enough, the catalyst for Amy to move in permanently. Following her impatient outburst, Linsey watched in horror as her lover's blue eyes filled with tears and her sensuous mouth trembled.

'I'm sorry,' said Amy with an air of dignified grievance. 'I'll just get my harp and music. I won't bother you again.'

Appalled at the thought of losing her, Linsey petted and cajoled, wept and apologised, until Amy allowed her to kiss away the tears and lead her to the bedroom.

Lying in the quiet embrace that follows passion, Linsey turned and looked at her lover. 'Don't go tomorrow,' she said simply. 'Stay with me. I love you.'

Amy kissed the tense mouth and delicately traced its perimeter with her finger. 'I love you too, Linny. I have to go tomorrow, but if you really want me, I'll be back. As soon as I can, I promise. I just need to organise my things.'

It took nearly two weeks, but Linsey finally found herself being introduced to the Sinclair family as Amy's housemate.

'Linsey's a bit scared, living alone in such a big house,' Amy explained. 'The rent's very cheap and I can practise my harp as often as I want.' She hugged her doubtful father. Her mother, usually undemonstrative, squeezed Amy's shoulder as she helped her load the last box into the car.

'You can always come home if it doesn't work out,' she said. 'Although she seems like a nice young woman. Here, I made you some almond biscuits. You always say they're your favourite.'

Amy hugged her mother as she took the biscuit tin. She noticed it was the one with Edinburgh Castle on the lid.

She and her brothers used to make up stories about that castle. Her mother had already given her some towels and sheets (single-bed), but the tin and the biscuits came laden with obligation and love. She ate all the biscuits herself; it would have felt like a betrayal to share them with Linsey.

Before meeting Linsey, Amy had drifted in and out of relationships without ever becoming emotionally engaged. Her tendency to prattle masked an essential inertness that allowed her life to ebb and flow at the will of others. Good-natured but mentally and emotionally lazy, she relied on beauty and charm to smooth the creases from her life, and when thwarted, her natural response was a passive aggression that drove its target to tears of frustration. Curiously, at this stage she often simply gave in, as though even witnessing such passion was more than she could be bothered with.

In Linsey, Amy found stability and a generous wholeheartedness lacking in her other relationships. She liked being admired not just for her beauty but for her talent. It wasn't inertia that made her stay. In a world where sexual norms would brook no divergence, Amy was uncertain of who she was. And it was with Linsey she felt valued.

They settled into a life of pleasant domesticity until one deceptively bland evening when Linsey came home from visiting her sister, Felicity, who had recently given birth to her second child.

'You should have seen her, Amy. She has this little round face with a funny pointy chin. I swear she smiled at me. Felicity says it's just wind, but she was looking straight at me. And Toby calls her Pippa. He can't say Phillipa.' Linsey sat down and continued: 'I really didn't want to hand her back. Look, I stopped at Baby World on the way home and bought her this.' She scrabbled in her bag and produced a tiny navy-blue voile dress.

At the sight of the dress, Amy became interested. 'Gorgeous, Linny. I might get her a little hat to match. What do you think?' And they spent a pleasant half-hour discussing baby clothes and their favourite childhood books and toys.

In the days that followed, Linsey's amorphous need for love took shape. A tiny phantom hand gripped her finger and drew her on to seek information, which she diligently garnered before making her approach. Was she insane to risk this relationship to further a dream that she wasn't sure Amy would share? She wasn't blind to her partner's faults and knew that a child would encroach upon Amy's fundamental lassitude. On the other hand, she hoped—no, *knew*—that a child would bring them closer together, would provide the key to the store of love Amy surely possessed.

One evening, Amy sat languidly on the verandah, sipping a glass of wine. She was in one of her pensive moods, staring out at the summer rain that plashed softly on the warm earth and spangled the velvety petals of Aunt Shirley's roses. Linsey poured herself a glass of wine and hesitated before sitting down beside her.

'I love summer storms,' Amy said. 'It's worth putting up with the heat just to smell the ozone.' She lifted her head and took in a theatrical breath, but Linsey was lost in her own thoughts. For once, Amy noticed. 'You seem a bit preoccupied, Linny. Is something the matter?'

'No—well, yes. In a way.' Now the time had come, Linsey was not sure how to begin. 'I've been, um, thinking.' And she plunged once more into silence, twisting her glass and picking imaginary specks from her sleeve.

'Come on, Linny. What's up?' Amy affected a childlike whine, tugging at Linsey's sleeve. 'Tell me. Tell me.'

Linsey put down her glass and grasped the other woman's shoulders, turning her so that they were face to face. 'Look at me, Amy. I need you to be serious. Serious—and completely honest.'

'Of course. You're not sick, are you, Linny?' She sounded frightened.

Linsey took a moment to savour the thought that Amy cared. 'No. I'm fine,' she said. 'I want to ask you something. Amy, what would you say to the idea of having a baby?'

'Who? Who's having a baby?'

'Us, Amy. What would you say to the idea of us having a baby?'

'Us? How?'

'We could try to adopt,' Linsey explained, 'but they won't accept applications from same-sex couples.'

Amy giggled as she took another sip of wine. 'So it looks like we'll have to steal one. I think that's against the law too.'

Linsey had prepared for this moment. 'There's another way.' Amy was shocked. 'No, Amy. Not that. We can arrange for artificial insemination. It does work. That's how Margaret and Kris conceived.' She looked at the other woman, trying to gauge her reaction. 'What do you say?'

Amy was dumbfounded. Surprised to discover that she

wasn't averse to the idea; she just needed time for the thought to grow.

'This is a bit sudden, isn't it, Linny?' She held up her glass. 'Another drink please, darling: I need to think.'

The women sat in silence, each following her own train of thought. It was several days before Linsey got her answer. All that time, Amy was preoccupied, spending much of her spare time on the verandah or in the music room, looking out onto the garden. Meanwhile, Linsey prowled and fretted, tidied and swept, dusted and polished, weeded and pruned, until she was quite exhausted. She knew better than to harass Amy, who, as always, moved at her own unhurried pace.

Amy had always liked children. Babies smiled and cooed at her and her nephews and nieces jostled for her attention. She absently stroked her stomach. Imagined it stretched, rounded. Imagined her breasts dripping milk. She sat on the verandah and tasted the late summer, the teeming life of the sunlit garden: lush green lawns, full-blown roses, fragrant lavender and slow, fat, murmurous honey bees. Slightly intoxicated by sensory excess, she felt her body soften in welcome to her imaginary child. Cupping her breasts in her hands, she resolved to speak to Linsey that night.

A moment later she stiffened in dismay, jolted from her reverie by a sudden thought. What if Linsey wanted to carry the child? She had as much right. Would she, Amy, feel the same way if she were not to be the birth mother? She wasn't sure that she would. If they were to have a child, it had to be a child of her body, the body she knew was ripe and waiting.

That night, over dinner, she asked the question. 'Linny, if

we have this child, who'd be the birth mother?' A small knot of panic formed in Amy's throat, and her words had to push their way out through constricted airways.

On this matter, Linsey had never had any doubt. 'You, of course, darling. We want our baby to be as beautiful and talented as we can make her.' She looked at the other woman. 'Is that what you want? I mean, if you decide you don't . . .'

Amy felt the tension drain from her body. 'A baby would be wonderful,' she replied. 'Really, I want to carry the baby, Linny. The answer is *yes* . . .'

Linsey left her place and knelt beside Amy's chair, hugging her tearfully. 'Just leave the details to me. Darling, darling Amy. I'm so happy.' And she even giggled a little. 'Listen, I have a plan.'

Amy settled back to listen. Linsey was a very good planner.

'We'll advertise in *Vox Discipuli*,' Linsey told her. 'Offer money. That should find the target market.'

Target market. Odd language, Amy thought briefly.

Linsey would always look back on the period of Amy's pregnancy as the happiest of their lives together. After a passing nod to morning sickness, Amy bloomed. Her skin glowed, her dimple deepened and her hair shone. As her belly rounded, she lay on the sun-lounge, sleepy-eyed and full of promise, with a kind of tawny, feline grace that reminded Linsey of the great cats of Africa.

'But without the claws.' She laughed as she stroked the burgeoning belly. And Amy laughed with her. At the time, neither of them understood the ferocity at the heart of a mother's love.

Linsey fussed, of course. And Amy cooperated amiably with the exercise and diet regime that Linsey devised from the many books she'd acquired on the subject of pregnancy and childbirth.

As the pregnancy unfolded, their families, knowingly or unknowingly, participated in the fiction of the two women as housemates. Amy's mother, Kathy, was very impressed with Linsey's devotion to her pregnant daughter. 'Linsey's so good to her,' she said to Linsey's mother. 'I don't know what she would have done without her.'

'I don't believe it's such a great burden,' the other woman replied drily, watching her daughter pour the coffee.

'Still, I wish she'd tell us who the father is.' Kathy was mortified at the thought of her daughter as an unmarried mother, let alone the issue of a one-night stand. She still had faint hopes of a wedding.

'I doubt that will happen,' Meredith Brookes replied. 'I doubt that very much indeed.'

Amy gave birth to an eight-pound baby girl with huge, fathomless eyes and a thatch of dark hair that stood straight up, giving her a look of mild shock.

'Funny little thing. She looks surprised by the world,' Linsey said as she held her daughter close. 'Amy, I love you both so much.'

'Me too,' murmured a sleepy Amy.

If the pregnancy had been a time of happiness for Linsey, the birth was a time of such fierce and overwhelming joy that she could scarcely breathe for the wonder of it. She vowed that this child would be loved and cared for, that she would have the best education, the best start in life of any child who had ever lived. She plunged into motherhood with an intense, controlling passion. Her emotional extravagance was all the more tragic in that she had no natural facility with children and didn't understand how to translate her love into language that a child could understand. By contrast, while Linsey devoured books on childcare, Amy's love flowed with her milk and she sang little nonsense songs and played with her baby's toes.

Linsey was godmother when Miranda Ophelia was christened in the cream brick Uniting church where her birth mother had gone to Sunday school. Amy's single status was met with some disapproval by the congregation. *She always was a bit flighty*, they sniffed as they sipped their tea. *She's lucky to have found such a fine person to be godmother.* Kathy had broadcast Linsey's merit throughout the parish, innocently placing her where a father might more usually be found.

Linsey's family were puzzled by the thought of a christening. Her brother, Robert, was happy to go along without question, but Felicity couldn't resist. 'You're not even a Christian, Lins,' she said. 'What's this all about?'

But Linsey knew exactly what she was about. Amy, as birth mother, had a legitimate title, a legitimate claim for recognition as the baby's mother. 'Being godmother gives me some small public connection with Miranda,' Linsey said simply.

Felicity put an arm around her sister's thin shoulders. 'You know best, Lins.'

When Moss awoke, the kitchen was still dark, but, try as she might, she couldn't go back to sleep. The air mattress had deflated and her hipbone was uncomfortably sharp against the floor. She turned onto her back. She plumped the pillow. She listened to the rain drumming on the roof. Finally, she sat up and clasped her knees, wondering what Linsey would say if she knew where she was.

Her earliest memory was of a day at the beach. She must have been three or four. Her mothers were each holding a hand and swinging her over the waves. She was giggling and squealing until her hand slipped from Amy's grasp and suddenly she was choking on a mouthful of water. Linsey was scooping her up and Moss felt the fear that rippled along the encircling arms. Coughing up the last of the water, she squirmed to escape.

'Mummy Amy,' she called. 'Mummy Amy.'

Linsey released her abruptly. 'Here. You take her,' she said, pushing the child into Amy's arms. 'And for God's sake, try to be a bit more careful in future.'

Had her own actions helped push Linsey away? This thought had always made her uneasy. The night she was rushed to hospital with asthma, for instance. It was Linsey who bundled her up so decisively and confronted the triage nurse, ensuring that not a moment was wasted.

Moss remembered waking up in the narrow cot, the nebuliser over her face, to find a dark figure watching over her. It was Linsey, her hand threaded through the bars of the cot and resting lightly on her own.

'Where's Mummy? Where's Mummy?' Moss clawed at the mask, dislodging it.

Linsey's voice was soothing. 'It's okay, Miranda. I'm here.'

'I want Mummy *Amy*.' As Moss's wail filled the sleeping ward, Linsey tried frantically to calm her.

'Mummy Amy's just gone to get a coffee. She won't be long, now. Shh, Miranda. You'll wake the other children. Look, you've started to wheeze again.' Linsey struggled to replace the nebuliser but Moss continued to wheeze and wail until Amy came hurrying back. Her mothers changed places at her bedside while a nurse dealt with the nebuliser.

'Thank God you're back, Amy.' Linsey sounded really frightened. 'That awful wheeze . . .'

Why had she acted in that way? Moss now wondered. Small children are said to sometimes favour one parent, then the other, but Moss had always favoured Amy. She *had* loved Linsey, but always felt she had to measure up, whereas with Amy, she felt she had nothing to prove.

One way and another, Moss had had a singular upbringing. Until she started school, she hadn't realised that there was something odd about her family. She knew of at least two other children who didn't seem to have fathers and it had never occurred to her that there was anything remarkable about having two mothers.

She was still in first grade when, walking home from school one day, she was confronted by three older boys who shattered her simple view of the world. She was with Zoe and Michelle, her two best friends. They were nice friends, she remembered. It was a nice day and they were talking about—she couldn't remember what, but it was funny. They were giggling, smothering their giggles behind grubby fingers, doubled over with secret laughter. She did remember that—that and a little cloud, shaped like her granny's Staffie, Geordie. The three friends crossed the road at the lights and began to skip across the park. They were nearly at the other side when three fourth-grade boys leaped out from the bushes in front of them.

'M'randa's mother's a lezzo!' they chanted. 'M'randa's mother's a lezzo!'

The little girls moved closer together. Puzzled, Zoe and Michelle looked at each other and then at Moss, who was equally puzzled but on the defensive. The trouble was, she wasn't sure whether it was Amy or Linsey she had to defend.

'Which mother?' she challenged.

The boys feigned paroxysms of laughter, snorting and guffawing, punching each other with delight. 'Which mother! Did you hear what she said? Which mother!'

The little girls took the opportunity to flee.

'Lezzos,' her tormentors called out after her. 'Lezzos.'

Moss burst through the door and flung herself at Amy. 'David Hynes and the other boys said you and Mummy Linsey are lizards,' she sobbed.

Twenty-three-year-old Moss slid down into her sleeping bag and remembered Linsey's distressed indignation and the embrace of Amy's soft arms as her mothers attempted to explain their relationship to a little girl struggling with matters beyond her comprehension. She had finally found comfort in one certainty. 'I knew you weren't lizards,' she told them firmly. 'David's a stupid idiot.'

Kids like me have it so much easier today, Moss thought. *It was so unfair. They were good parents, both of them.*

Yes, she loved them both, but there was a stillness, a placidity, in Amy that made her seem somehow safer. As she matured, Moss became aware that Linsey was all angles and energy, and she saw how Amy's slow, slovenly beauty drove her partner to a distraction of love and fury. In many ways Moss was like Linsey, but despite that, or because of it, the child gravitated to Amy. As a consequence, she too experienced Linsey's sharpness and often felt she had fallen short. In her childish way, Moss tried to please, tidying her bedroom, for instance, only for Linsey to cluck over the books she'd pushed under the bed, or flick at the dust she'd failed to see on the dressing-table.

'Miranda, is it too much to ask that you put a little effort into your room? Go back and do it properly.'

And if Amy didn't come to her rescue, Moss would sulkily comply.

She tried hard at school, but soon discovered that she wasn't the prodigy Linsey believed she ought to be. Despite her best efforts, the As were elusive and Cs more common than Bs. With the exception of music, at which she excelled, *Miranda tries hard* was the best she could hope for on her school reports.

Linsey was neither cruel nor ignorant. She knew that a child who is trying and only achieving Bs and Cs is worthy of praise, possibly even more so than the gifted A student. But Moss always ran first to Amy with her report and sheltered there from the frown of disappointment she sensed rather than saw as Linsey scanned her meagre achievements. It mattered little that this was always followed by: *Good girl. Maybe better next time.* Moss didn't want to be a good girl. She wanted to be a smart girl. A clever girl. A girl of whom Mummy Linsey could be proud.

'To think your father was a mathematician,' Linsey once said, shaking her head over the results of a maths test. Moss was instantly alert.

'Linsey . . .' Amy's voice was laden with warning.

Moss had filed that snippet away. It was all she knew of her father, and she never dared to ask for more until much later.

The last of the rain spattered like gravel on her father's tin roof, and Moss became aware of the stirring of a new day. A cock crowed in the distance and the window shape emerged, a faint luminosity on the opposite wall. She thought of the morning when Linsey (she was just Linsey, by then; the 'mother' tag had stuck only to Amy) had come into her room to say goodbye. The noises then were city noises, but the dawn window glow was the same.

She had heard the door open and saw Linsey's dark shape materialise beside her bed. Amy, a much larger woman, always moved on cat-feet, but Linsey, who barely cast a shadow, was inclined to stomp and crash about in her nervous haste. That morning, though, she was like a wraith. Moss felt a hand linger on her cheek and smelled the familiar musky hand cream. A kiss like a breath, a whispered *I love you*, and she was gone.

Moss saw her young self lying still, hands clenched, averting her eyes from the void she now sensed in the house. Linsey had always been there for her. There was a strength in her mother Linsey that made Moss feel safe. Linsey had always discussed things seriously with her, showing her the kind of respect one would show to an equal. Moss didn't appreciate this approach as a child, but with adolescence she began to value it more. Now Linsey was gone. Bereft, Moss continued to lie stiffly in her bed until she heard Amy pad down the hall. Jumping out of bed and flinging herself at the pyjama-clad figure, she cried out in real fear: 'Mum! Mum! Don't you go too!'

Amy gathered her in. 'Of course I won't go. You know that. Linsey will come back to see you. You can visit her like we said. She's your mum too, remember. Don't cry, sweetheart. I'm here.' She smoothed the tangled brown hair. 'We talked about it, Miranda—you said you understood.'

They had talked about it, but Moss hadn't wanted to listen. For a long time she had tried to ignore the obvious fact that her two mothers were growing apart. Now she couldn't ignore it any more. On the contrary, she clung to it as the best explanation for Linsey's departure and never allowed herself to explore the other, more disturbing possibility that she, Moss, might be the real reason that Linsey left them.

By that time, Amy was a plump, untidy woman in her early forties, with sleepy blue eyes and a slow, tantalising smile. The dimple gave her a girlish air and her skin remained remarkably fine. She had never fulfilled her early promise as a musician— but perhaps she never was very good, her grown daughter thought suddenly. Linsey was always so careful to speak well of Amy.

These thoughts were only contributing to her wakefulness. Moss returned her head to the pillow, trying to make her mind blank. She was beginning to drift off to sleep when she became aware of a soft footfall and saw Finn's unfamiliar shape as he crept into the kitchen. She didn't stir, but watched as he paused at the table for a moment before opening the door and disappearing into the half-light outside. She heard the gate squeak and then silence. The birds had momentarily ceased their morning song. She wriggled deeper into her sleeping bag. She was so tired.

The next thing she heard was the sound of the back door opening again. It was now full daylight, and a watery sun lit the figure of Finn as he stooped to pass beneath the low lintel.

She sat up, running her fingers through her tangled hair. 'Hello, Finn. What time is it?'

Finn looked startled, as though he had not expected to find her still there. He pointed to the alarm clock on the mantelpiece, put a plastic shopping bag on the table and continued on down the hall. It was seven fifty. Moss climbed out of her sleeping bag and went into the bathroom. There was a striped towel on the handbasin with the name MOSS written on card with a magic marker. She turned on the shower and waited. Tepid water flowed sluggishly from the old-fashioned showerhead, and she found that she needed to duck and weave to get wet, washing herself in sections. Her shower was understandably short, and she was grateful for the roughness of the towel that warmed her a little with its friction.

When she arrived back in the kitchen Finn had lit the fire and was once more engaged in stuffing bread into the toaster. 'I got Vegemite,' he said with a shy smile, indicating the jar. 'And some cheese. For lunch.' He returned his attention to the toaster and lapsed into silence.

'I'll make the tea if you like,' Moss offered. Finn took down a canister from the mismatched assortment lined up beside the clock, then nodded towards the teapot with its colourful knitted cosy. Moss was puzzled. Puzzled and hurt—he wasn't making any effort to speak to her, and she began to feel like the intruder she undoubtedly was. The kettle boiled, and soon two steaming mugs of tea joined the wedges of toast which Finn had liberally coated with Vegemite.

'You found the towel, then?' Finn, unused to visitors, had been inordinately proud that he'd thought of the towel. 'It just came to me,' he said. 'The idea of the towel.' He looked at her hopefully.

'Just the thing,' Moss said. 'Thank you.' She couldn't work him out. Was he a bit—well, *simple*? Hadn't he been a mathematician? A brilliant one, from what she'd learnt. Perhaps he was just absentminded. Genius tended to be that way—at least in popular folklore. She bit thoughtfully on her toast and suppressed a grimace. For some reason Finn thought she liked Vegemite. Still, she ate her toast without complaint: she needed time and didn't want to offend him.

The salty taste of the Vegemite was sharp on her tongue, and as she and Finn carefully chewed their toast, the sound of crunching mingled with the ticking of the clock. Neither of them spoke until Moss poured them both a second mug of tea. She could wait no longer. Her plan had been to let Finn broach the subject, but his silence was resolute.

'You do know who I am, don't you?'

'What year were you born?'

'Nineteen eighty-three.'

'Your mother was Amy Sinclair? Partner of Linsey Brookes?'

Moss felt a sudden wave of nausea. *Dear God, don't let me*

vomit. Not now. She forced herself to breathe slowly, deeply, before replying. 'Yes. Amy and Linsey—my mothers.'

'Then you must be my daughter.'

And he just sat there, sipping his tea.

Moss had pictured this moment quite differently. This was when her father was supposed to open his arms wide and hold her for the first time. She had even imagined the roughness of his whiskers against her cheek. They would both cry a little and then laugh, and he would look at her with wonder and regret. Instead, he went on relentlessly sipping his tea. She tried to read his face but it was blank. Even the kindness she had recognised last night had been erased. *Say something*, she begged silently. *Please.*

But Finn was struggling. He had lived alone for so long that he found even small talk a challenge. Last night, before sleep claimed him, he had tried to cobble together some thoughts, some words that might at least be adequate. *I'm so happy to meet you at last.* That was patently untrue and Finn was a bad liar. *I've often thought about you.* Also untrue. And dangerous. It might make her think she was welcome. The last thing he wanted was another person in his life. Why was she here, anyway? *Keep the conversation as neutral as possible*, he advised himself.

'How did you find me?' he asked.

Moss swallowed her disappointment. 'Maths,' she said. 'I followed the maths trail.'

A few months ago, while looking through some of Amy's sheet music, she'd come upon the contract that had brought her into being. It was typical of Amy to be careless with such an important document. Her mother snatched it away, but not before Moss had seen the name: Michael Finbar Clancy. So, as she explained to Finn, at that point she had both his name and his profession. Fortunately, Michael was a prolific writer in his years as an academic, and had been making quite a name for himself in probability theory. Her search was temporarily frustrated when, after a few years of regular publication, his name suddenly disappeared from the learned journals. It seemed he had vanished without a trace, but by then Moss's initial curiosity had hardened into resolve. She saw that he'd written quite a few of the articles with a Philip Cousins who was now Associate Professor of Mathematics at Monash University. It was Phil who told her where to find Michael Clancy.

'He's changed a lot,' he warned her.

'I never knew him, so it won't matter to me,' she replied with a shrug. 'As I said, I'm only looking him up because my family used to know his family, and Granny would like to get in touch.' She was surprised at her own glibness.

Finn was appalled to learn how easy it was to find him and angry with Phil for revealing his whereabouts. 'So old Phil keeps track of me, does he? Never could mind his own business.' Seeing the hurt on Moss's face, he continued more gently. 'So what started you looking?'

'The contract. I found the contract.' Moss was being evasive. In fact, she couldn't really articulate her motives because she didn't fully understand them, preferring to sidle up and consider them obliquely. Initially, there was the simple fact that she was different. None of the children she knew had two mothers. The teasing at school had ebbed and flowed as the bullies and their satellites were diverted by newer victims. In primary school it was masculine, sporadic and almost ritualistic. 'Lezzos!' the boys would shout, and Moss would run to the shelter of the girls' toilets. Her friends would then cluck and cluster around, enjoying the drama. The little girls were not sure what 'lezzos' were, but knew they had to band together against the boys.

At high school, though, the girls were the predators, in particular the pretty queen bee, Jessica, who tormented her with such refined subtlety that Moss longed for the predictable cruelty of the boy gangs. The other girls milled around behind Jessica and her three cronies. It was better than being out front in the firing line. Moss met the taunts stoically but wept secretly in her room at home. By this stage she had no friends and spent lunchtimes in the library.

In childish desperation, Moss decided to buy Jessica a present, hoping to win a reprieve from the bullying. She saved up her pocket money until there was enough to buy what all the girls in her class coveted—a Magnetique Supa Gloss lipstick. She agonised over the colour and told the salesgirl it was for her big sister who was blonde and blue-eyed. She had it gift-wrapped, and the next day she waited until home time, edging up to Jessica as they rounded the corner from the school.

'I've got something for you. A present.'

Jessica raised her eyebrows as she took the parcel. 'A present? Let's see. Come over here, everyone. Miranda's given me a present.'

When her audience was large enough, she struck. 'Yeech! A lipstick! She's a lezzo like her mothers. Yeech! She wants a big red kiss.' And amid screams of laughter and exclamations of revulsion from the other girls she grabbed Moss's tiny breasts and kissed her full on the lips. 'Where else do you want to be kissed, Lezzo?' she asked with a sly smile at her audience. 'Come on, girls, who's next?'

Moss turned to run, but her arms were pinioned. The crowd began to slink away, but not before two more girls had kissed her and another squeezed her breasts painfully. Then Jessica opened the lipstick and wrote something on her victim's forehead, before stepping back to admire her handiwork.

'Quick! Miss Webb's coming.' The remaining girls melted away as the teacher turned the corner. She stopped and put her arm around the weeping girl who was rubbing a red smear on her forehead.

'Miranda, what on earth's the matter?' Her eyes narrowed. 'Was it Jessica?'

'It's nothing, Miss Webb,' Moss gasped between sobs. 'I just don't feel well.'

For several days, Moss was granted a reprieve. With Miss Webb hovering protectively in the background, Jessica lay low. Pale and peaky, Moss crept into class and scurried to the library in her breaks. The other girls kept their distance, and Moss felt sick and hollow and somehow dirty. She was ashamed of her mothers and ashamed of herself for feeling that way.

These thoughts were too painful to leave lying around unattended. She might come upon them at just the wrong moment and they would trip her up, sending her sprawling helplessly as the contents of her head poured out into the unforgiving sunshine. Her face became watchful and grim, the effort to control her feelings begetting a stubborn will for survival. Moss was only thirteen and felt an aching need to protect her mothers. Nevertheless, action was required.

'I have to change schools,' she announced abruptly one night at dinner. 'The teachers are picking on me.'

Her mothers looked at her with concern. 'Picking on you? The teachers? Which teachers?'

'All of them. They hate me.' And she burst into tears. The two women looked at each other as she jumped to her feet, knocking over her water glass.

'I'll go,' said Amy, and went off to her daughter's room, where she tapped on the door. Ignoring Moss's 'Go away,' she entered and sat on the bed beside the sobbing girl, who finally blurted out the whole story. Amy sat stroking her daughter's hair until her sobs subsided and her breathing became deep and even. She pulled up the covers and went back down to the dining room, unaware that Moss, who had been feigning sleep, had padded down after her and was listening at the door.

'She's being picked on because of us,' Amy told Linsey.

'Those little bitches. I could kill them! With my bare hands.'

'She wants to start afresh at Bradfield and . . .'

Linsey's voice was dry. 'I think I can see where this is going.'

'I'm sorry, Linny. She doesn't want the new school to know she has two mothers.'

'Well then. I'll have to become her aunty,' Linsey said bleakly.

'We can discuss that later.' Moss heard the pity in Amy's voice. 'It could be me—the aunt, I mean.'

Linsey's words were brisk but her voice was husky. 'Don't be absurd, Amy. Of course it will be me.'

At thirteen, Moss had little notion of what this offer might have cost Linsey. At the time, her predominant emotion was relief. Only in later years had she come to realise that, in all her relationships, Linsey had always been the lover. For Linsey, the beloved always came first.

Six years after Linsey's departure, when Moss turned twenty-one, Amy had finally told her about the odd circumstances of her conception. She was startled by the truth; while understanding her mothers' relationship, she had assumed that Amy had conceived in the usual way. She had had no inkling that they'd taken so much trouble to find the right father.

'All you need to know is that he was a good man, but the agreement was that he play no further part in our lives. We must respect that, Miranda.' Amy still called her Miranda when she needed to impress her with the seriousness of the matter at hand.

'I didn't make any agreement,' Moss retorted. 'What if I want to meet him?' She had a sudden moment of comprehension. 'I suppose this was all Linsey's bright idea.'

'Well, it was Linsey's . . .' Amy began.

'I knew it. I knew she never thought I was good enough. She tried to make me something I'm not, and I wasn't and somehow I'm to blame. She *experimented* with me.' She stopped and glared at Amy, who was processing this convoluted speech. 'You know what I mean.'

Amy opened her mouth to protest, but gave up and shrugged inwardly instead. She didn't want to get involved in a dispute between these two passionate souls. It was true Linsey expected a very different child from the one Moss had been. Besides, while their separation was reasonably amicable, old wounds still festered in Amy's breast. *No-one could ever measure up to Linsey's absurd standards*, she thought petulantly. *And that's a fact.*

But Moss brooded. If Linsey had a particular child in mind—a child who was beautiful like Amy and clever like her father—she, Moss, was obviously a disappointment. She glared at her reflection in the mirror. She was clearly not the tall, clever, blue-eyed blonde of Linsey's imagining. Small of stature, she had the wiry brown hair and gamine features of her Grandmother Sinclair. Her saving grace was her blue eyes, darker than Amy's but with the same long lashes. Aside from this, she saw herself as a failed experiment. Not to Amy, of course. Moss had always been sure of Amy's love and approval but perversely valued her praise less than the exacting Linsey's. Now, mortified to discover that she was a designer baby gone wrong, she realised she could never live up to Linsey's standards so there was no point in continuing to try. She felt a terrible hollow in her sense of herself. She needed to lash out. Place the blame squarely where it belonged. She would confront Linsey and then cut herself off from her entirely. After that, she'd find another parent—her father—to take her place.

That'll put paid to all her schemes, she reflected with spiteful satisfaction.

Privy to only some of her daughter's thoughts, Amy, while not encouraging her, did nothing to intervene. She did point out wryly that Moss was sounding just like Linsey, but her daughter failed to see the irony. She had carried out her plan and now, two years later, here she was, drinking tea with the man Linsey had chosen to be her father.

And he seemed totally unaware of the magnitude, the abiding significance, of this moment.

4

Finn and a girl called Amber-Lee

Though Finn continued to stare at Moss in silence, he was far from indifferent. Words assembled in his head and, just as they began to make sense, rearranged themselves in a new configuration. It was like some sort of folk dance where the dancers' positions kept changing in a flurry of colour and ribbons, leaving the onlooker puzzled and a little queasy. He continued to lift the mug to his lips, unaware it was empty. Moss looked back at him, expectation in the dark blue eyes that were so like his own. So like his mother's. And his grandfather's too, he recalled.

Moss was not used to silence. 'I'd like to stay for a few days,' she said tentatively. 'We could maybe . . . get to know each other a bit?'

Finn felt a sort of panic and tried to slow his breathing. 'Your mothers and I had an agreement. My name was to be kept out of—of *things*.' He saw her flinch and looked down, shame burning two red patches across his cheekbones. 'I'm sorry, Moss,' he mumbled. 'It's just that I'm used to being alone and this has come out of the blue. I . . .'

Finn paused. What *did* he want? He looked at the girl's face. His *daughter*. He turned the word over in his mouth. Absorbed its unfamiliar taste and texture. What did he owe her? Did he owe her anything at all? She was his in only the most technical sense. He tested himself for some emotional connection and found only bewilderment. Bewilderment—overlaid with his natural reticence. It suited him to be alone. He liked it— relished it, in fact. Was that all? Was that all there was to him? He probed deeper and found curiosity. Just a little, but it was there. Who was she? How had she turned out?

He cleared his throat. 'I—it's like this.' He stopped again. If he was curious about her, she must be curious about him. What sort of man did she think she was dealing with? What sort of father did she deserve? *Not one like me*, he thought miserably. *I'm sure she's done nothing to deserve a father like me.* She'd gone to a lot of trouble to find him, though. His thoughts completed the circle. If he owed her anything, it was the truth. He started again.

'It's like this. I'll tell you a few things about myself. If you still want to stay, you can. Just for a few days.' He blew out his cheeks unhappily. 'You won't find me great company, and after you know my story . . .'

They moved closer to the fire and Moss tucked her feet up, hugging her knees. She remembered this was exactly how she used to sit when she was waiting for Amy or Linsey to read her a bedtime story.

'I guess you know how Amy became pregnant,' he began and looked relieved when she nodded. 'Well, after the phone call to say we were successful, I felt a bit sad that I'd never see the baby, but to be honest—and we have to be honest with each other, Moss—the feeling passed and I more or less forgot. No, I didn't forget, it was just a—a *fragment* of my life with no special significance.' His smile was tentative, placating.

Moss was hurt, but her face remained impassive. She had often wondered about her father, but only lately dared to ask. For one thing, she didn't want to hurt her mothers, but on a deeper level, she feared rejection. When Finn referred to her as a fragment of his life, she began to taste that fear and clenched her teeth in misery.

Disconcerted by her rigid expression, Finn played for time. 'They seemed like good women. They treated you well?'

'Very well,' she snapped. 'They were my parents, remember.'

'Yes. Yes. Of course they were,' he mused. 'I was just a—a *tool*. No pun intended.' He interrupted himself hastily as he saw her faint grin. He grinned back. 'It was a strange situation, Moss . . . I hope I haven't . . .'

'No. It's okay. Go on.'

As he continued, his hesitancy gradually dissipated. This was, after all, a story he had told himself and Father Jerome many, many times.

'I left uni with a PhD in maths and then went on to do some research on probability.' She nodded impatiently. 'Not exactly riveting for your average punter, but I found it fascinating. After a few years, I was offered a research fellowship at Oxford. I was there for five years and then came back to Melbourne.'

Moss nodded again. She'd gleaned this much from the publications.

'I came back because of a woman I was seeing. She was one of my post-grad students, another Australian. Her student visa expired and she decided to move back home. I sounded out a few Aussie universities and landed a job at Melbourne—my old stamping ground. Different from Oxford, you know. Not as well funded, but it's got some top academics.

'To cut a long story short, this woman met someone else. I was furious. Well, you can imagine . . . I'd given up my post at Oxford because I thought we had some sort of future together, and within six months she was off to South Africa with a structural engineer.' For the first time since Moss had met him, he raised his voice. 'Have you ever met a structural engineer? No? You don't know how lucky you are. They're the most boring people. And think they're God's gift. What would they do without maths? That's what I'd like to know. The mathematicians do all the groundwork and the engineers take all the credit with their flashy bridges and—and *stuff.*'

Moss was a bit taken aback. It had never occurred to her that structural engineers could be so venal. There was a whole world out there where such declarations might be considered odd, but here, in Finn's kitchen, she found herself cheering for the mathematicians.

'Go on,' she encouraged. 'What happened then?'

'Well, life became a bit *complicated*. For some reason, I never had much trouble finding a woman. You'd be surprised how many women are interested in maths,' he added quite guilelessly.

Not so very surprised, Moss thought as she looked at his dark blue eyes and hollow, high-boned cheeks. Despite his bad haircut and daggy green jumper, her father had a sort of wistful charm and vestiges of a physical beauty long since disregarded.

Finn continued. 'Annetta—that was this woman's name— she was special, I really thought she was the one. Should've known better. Anyway, I'd always been a drinker. Especially during my student days.' He grinned despite himself. 'I remember Linsey insisting I give up the booze while I was ah . . . *employed* by her. Kept my word, too. Even though she'd never have known.' Finn looked at Moss expectantly.

She was beginning to read him. 'I'm glad, Finn,' she responded. 'I'd hate to have been born an alcoholic.' She wasn't sure that this was an issue, but was eager to please.

'Yeah. I smoked a bit of pot, too. Just a joint with friends every now and then.' He patted his pockets. 'I need a bit of Dutch courage for this next bit. Do you mind if I smoke? Tobacco, I mean. I've given up pot. And alcohol too, for that matter. Another one of Linsey's prohibitions,' he added, indicating the cigarette that he rolled with practised fingers.

'One night, I'd smoked a couple of joints with some friends and was feeling, you know, pretty happy. Then, just after they left, I get this phone call from Annetta. She couldn't even tell me face to face. *I'm leaving*, she says. *I'm sorry*, she says. *I'm going to South Africa with Pieter Langeveldt. I'll get my things tomorrow when you're at work.*

'I just put down the phone and poured a whisky. It was like I was watching myself from the ceiling or somewhere. I remember thinking, *I'll feel this tomorrow*. Then I had another whisky and decided I'd go over to Pieter's place. If she was there, I'd talk her out of going with him. If she wasn't there, I'd punch Pieter in the nose. It seemed like such a brilliant plan at the time. Win–win, I think they call it.

'So I jumped in the car and headed off for Langeveldt's. He was only a few blocks away. I could have walked. Should have walked. But I didn't. And that's how my life changed.' Finn drew hard on his cigarette. The ash was perilously long and Moss began to understand how his jumper had come to be punctuated with all those little black holes. She stared at the cigarette because she couldn't bear to look at his face.

His voice was flat now. 'Just around the corner from Pieter's, a girl ran out in front of the car. I didn't see her until it was too late.' He inhaled slowly—a long, painful breath. 'I can still hear the thud. It's an awful sound, Moss—the sound of a body hitting a car.' The ash fell but they both ignored it. 'She landed in the path of a truck. People came running. I got out of my car, but they pulled me back. Then I saw a shoe. It was lying there as though she'd just kicked it off. The sole was all worn down. I remember thinking, *I'd better get the shoe. She'll wonder what happened to it.* But a policeman put it in a plastic bag. Did I tell you? The sole was worn right through.'

Finn blew out his cheeks again. 'Do you mind if I stop for a bit? We'll do the dishes.' When he didn't move, Moss got up and refilled the teapot before running some water into the sink and washing their plates. She moved delicately, fearing to disturb her father who was sitting, knees apart, hands dangling between them. His head was turned to the fire and he was shaking it slightly, as if trying to dislodge something.

'Finn? I've made us a nice strong cup of tea. Don't let it get cold now.' She was his daughter but she sounded like his mother.

Finn came and sat at the table. 'I'll finish the story tomorrow,' he said, suddenly aware that this would mean she was staying another night. 'Tell me some more about yourself. What do you do?'

This was the very question she'd dreaded since dropping out of her course.

'Why, Moss?' an exasperated Amy had asked, over and over. 'You know Linsey put aside the money so you could continue with your singing lessons. We were all so happy when you were accepted into the Conservatorium. You were doing so well.' Such persistence was unusual for Amy.

'If I'm not speaking to Linsey, I've got no right to take her money. She was the one who wanted me to go to the Con.'

'You're as bull-headed as each other.' Amy sighed. 'I can't believe you're doing this just to spite Linsey.'

'It has nothing to do with spite,' Moss retorted. 'Haven't you heard of *integrity*?'

'Yes,' said Amy. 'But pragmatism makes the world go round. Be reasonable, Moss. Linsey has plenty of money. She's made a fortune since she started working for that bank of hers.'

Amy's objections still ringing in her ears, Moss looked at Finn defiantly. 'I was studying singing at the Melba Con. I dropped out a few months ago.'

'Didn't you like it?'

'I loved it. But I'd stopped talking to Linsey and she was supporting me, so you see, I couldn't go on. I've deferred. We'll see what happens.' *Oh God*, she thought, *I hope he doesn't think I'm here after money*. 'Grandma Kathy left me some money,' she added quickly. 'I've got enough to keep me going.'

It hadn't occurred to Finn that she might be after money. He generally believed the best of people; more often than not, he was right. But he was interested in Moss's refusal of Linsey's money.

'You must've felt quite strongly to stop speaking to her. I can see why you couldn't go on taking her money, though.'

'Can you? Everyone else says I'm crazy.'

'Perhaps. But your craziness might come from the not-speaking in the first place. I don't know anything about that, of course.' Finn spoke cautiously, wary of involvement. His agreement with her mothers had already been breached, and he didn't want the sort of entanglement that his intervention could provoke. He felt he was on shaky ground morally, perhaps even legally.

Anyone else would have asked why we weren't speaking, Moss thought. *Asked why I had to drop out of my course.* She could have continued without Linsey's money, working her way through university as so many students did. But in her anger and confusion over the circumstances of her conception, Moss punished herself as well as Linsey, excising from her life not only a loved mother but the music that brought them both so much pleasure.

Each slightly embarrassed by their revelations, Moss and Finn fussed over who would wash the mugs and empty the teapot.

'Can you go on with your story, Finn?' his daughter asked, almost plaintively, hoping to take her mind off her own painful thoughts. 'It must have been a very hard time for you.'

Finn wiped the sink with exaggerated care. 'I have to work

this afternoon and I'll be out between six and eight. Perhaps we can talk over dinner? I don't know what you'd like to eat . . .'

Moss had a healthy young appetite and had eaten nothing but bread and tea in the last twenty-four hours. Although she was not an enthusiastic cook, to avoid the prospect of more Vegemite on toast, she offered to prepare the evening meal. 'My treat,' she said firmly. 'I'll hunt about in the cupboard and buy what else I need. I think I saw some shops last night.'

'Yeah. Just around the corner from the bus stop where you got off. Or you could take the short-cut across the footy ground.' He gestured in the direction of the backyard. 'There should be some onions and spinach in the vegie garden if you need them.'

After a quick lunch, Finn disappeared down the hall to his room. Ever resourceful, Moss found some pasta and a bottle of bolognaise sauce in the cupboard and fetched some onions from the garden. This seemed to be a good basis for an easy meal. She put on her japara and took a shopping bag from behind the door. Instead of retracing last night's route, she set out across the footy ground. The ragged grass around the perimeter wet the hem of her jeans, but the day was sunny and she enjoyed the feeling of purpose. There were two small shelters just inside the fence and a low brick building with cyclone wire over the windows, above which a sign enigmatically proclaimed HOME OF THE OPPORTUNITY KNOCKERS. *Bizarre name for a football team*, she thought. She crossed a bridge over the creek, which flowed sluggishly after the night's rain. She could just make out the original sign, HALFWAY BRIDGE, smothered as it was under layers of graffiti.

Turning onto the main road, she looked down its length across the open landscape. A city girl, she could see no redeeming feature in its flat, unremitting yellowness. Apart from a few apologetic eucalypts, there was no green to define and control this amorphous space. Most of the houses bordering the road had sparse gardens that the rain had brought momentarily to life, but there was a mirage-like quality to the water that lay in puddles on fatally compacted soil. Only the geraniums seemed to do well in these conditions. Her Grandma Kathy had grown prim geraniums in pots, but these shrubs sprawled, wanton and leggy, like careless old whores grown tired of life.

In contrast, the little public gardens at the end of town (the OPPORTUNITY WAR MEMORIAL GARDENS, she read on the wrought-iron entrance gate) were pleasantly fresh and green. Moss looked in surprise at the well-tended lawn and garden beds. *They occupy enchanted space*, she thought. It was as though all the life and energy of the town were vested in this small oasis.

Moss noticed that most of the businesses in the main street provided a somewhat eclectic range of goods and services. There was a service station that also sold groceries (and offered electrical and lawnmower repairs), a small supermarket, a craft-cum-coffee shop, a newsagency-cum-post office/bank, a general store, and a rather fine old corner pub that boasted vacant accommodation. Across the road was a purveyor of fine antiques and bric-a-brac (also dry-cleaning). This had once been the Commonwealth Bank—the name was still etched deeply into the stone. Next door was Marisa's Boutique— ladies and children's discount fashions—a fish 'n' chip shop, a pharmacy and the Country Women's Association Op Shop (*Open Wednesdays*, the sign said. *Please leave only usable goods in the container. No electrical*). Despite this last plea, an old TV set had been dumped outside the shop, along with a rusty bike and a bulging green garbage bag. Peering at the window, Moss made out a faint gold outline advertising its former life as a barber shop and private men's club. Three other shops were boarded up, a forlorn testament to the slow dying of a country community.

With time on her hands, she wandered on past the shops to the Mechanics Institute (opened in 1891 by the Hon. Charles Sandilands, OBE). Now, she read on the fading noticeboard, it served as a meeting hall and, once a month, as a cinema. It would never again welcome young men, farmers' sons, doggedly seeking an education after a hard day's labour. Moss could almost see them, with their bullet heads and over-alls and grubby hands, sweating over their books with a faith in learning that was almost sublime; the great-grandfathers, perhaps, of today's urban lawyers and doctors and account-ants. At the far end of the street, on a little rise, stood a small stone Anglican church with modest gothic arches and yellow diamond-paned windows. It was there, she surmised, that many of those boys were christened and married. And bur-ied, too, most likely, under one of the crumbling headstones in the unpretentious little churchyard. Not all of them, of course. There were those whose graves were in Gallipoli or the Somme and whose names were engraved on the cenotaph in the gardens. The sign outside St Saviour's Church offered services for Anglicans at ten am on the first three Sundays of the month, Catholics at six thirty pm on the first and third Saturday nights, and a Uniting service at ten am on the last Sunday of the month. Moss grinned when she saw this. Even the churches saw the need to diversify.

She turned back and went into the supermarket. There was only one other customer, a woman, who smiled and said good afternoon, further offering the observation that it was nice to see a bit of rain. Moss nodded and moved on quickly. She wasn't quite ready to expose herself to the eyes of a small town. She loaded her trolley with mince, some salad vegetables, and parmesan in a plastic tub. There was a small delicatessen and bakery at the back of the store where she bought some fresh rolls.

'We don't have much call for fancy breads.' The saleswoman obviously disapproved of her request for rye. She relented a little when Moss asked for an apple-and-rhubarb pie and two vegetable pasties.

'Nice to see a bit of rain, isn't it?' Then: 'Come in on the bus, did you?'

'Yes. Good—the rain. Yes. The bus.' She hurried away to the checkout where a girl—SHARON, her nametag said—was painting her nails alternately black and green, studiously avoiding eye contact.

'Can you wait till this dries?'

'What? Yes. I guess I can.' Moss waited while the girl blew on her nails and flapped her fingers in the air.

'There. Finished. Nice to see a bit of rain, isn't it?'

Moss agreed once more that indeed it was, and after being wished a nice day, escaped back into the street. The only other pedestrian was a dog, an elderly kelpie, who trotted along behind her.

'Hello, boy. Nice to see a bit of rain, isn't it?'

The dog wagged its tail. It was a country dog. It couldn't have agreed more.

Meanwhile, Finn was having difficulty concentrating on his work. This hadn't happened for some time: his self-discipline was usually fierce. But today all he could see, all he could think about, was a girl lying grotesquely on the road where she'd been flung like an old coat. Random details from the chaos still lay in wait for him. He felt the sweat running down his back. Heard the strangely unsynchronised sirens. Smelt the heat rising from the bitumen. Grieved for the abandoned shoe. Most persistent of all, he saw a sheet and, encroaching on its whiteness, a red anemone, a monstrous, spreading bloom; life leaking away on a suburban street on an ordinary Tuesday night.

He took a folder from his desk drawer and turned it over in his hands. It contained some newspaper cuttings and a copy of the coroner's finding. Moss could read these. It would be easier for both of them. No-one had blamed him, but he knew that he wasn't fully in control that night. His alcohol test was just below the legal limit, and they couldn't test for drugs in those days, so he escaped the serious offence of culpable driving. The police had considered the lesser charge of dangerous driving causing death, but all the witnesses agreed that he couldn't have seen her in time to stop, even though there was some speculation (but no evidence) that he may have been speeding. He *was* speeding. He knew that. Not much over the limit, but enough to affect his braking time. He was also drug-affected, but no-one knew that either. In the end, he walked free. Shamefully free.

Finn looked again at the coroner's finding. Because the dead girl could not be identified, there had been a full inquest. There was evidence from the police officer in charge, the doctor who pronounced life extinct, a social worker, a street prostitute called Brenda, and several eye witnesses. There was no-one representing the dead girl's family. Her face was too badly injured for photographs to be of any use and, despite the best facial recognition techniques, no-one came forward to claim her. There was no-one to mourn, no-one to be outraged on her behalf.

The deceased was known as Amber-Lee but her surname is unknown. A local prostitute, Brenda Watson, was accompanying her at the time of the accident, Finn read. Although he could have recited it by heart.

'She called herself Amber-Lee,' Brenda had told the inquest. 'I don't think it was her real name—just a street name. She thought it sounded, you know, sexy. Like a film star or something.'

'I couldn't stop,' the truck driver had said, his face stricken. 'She just landed in front of me. There was nothing I could do.'

'I remember the name Amber-Lee. She came to the Ward Street Shelter once,' said the social worker. 'We knew she was on the game and probably underage, but we can't keep track of them all. We just don't have the resources.' She shrugged. 'We can only help those willing to be helped.'

All this had been translated into the dispassionate language of the coroner's office. Now its very blandness accused Finn anew.

There had been photographs. They were not in the folder, but were fatally imprinted on his memory. The cause of death was recorded as *catastrophic head injuries*. The post-mortem also found traces of old bruises and a partially healed broken rib. *There are needle tracks evident on her left arm*, the medical report continued. *She was injecting, probably heroin, although there is no evidence of this in the toxicology report. Her veins were still viable. There is evidence of early stage gonorrhoea. Her estimated age is between fourteen and sixteen.*

Michael cried as he gave evidence. But no-one asked if he'd been taking drugs so no-one ever knew. After the accident, his family and friends had drawn a circle around him, offering help and advice. His first reaction had been to accept his culpability and take whatever punishment was his due. On hearing this, his mother was distraught.

'Why on earth would you want to do that? It won't bring the girl back. You always react so *extravagantly* when something goes wrong. Vic, speak to him.'

His father leaned forward. 'Look, son. They said she just ran out in front of the car. It's a terrible thing, but how can you blame yourself for that? Let me get Stephen to advise you. He deals with cases like this all the time.'

Looking back now, Finn could see that his parents had always adroitly handled any problems that arose in his life. He was the long-awaited only child of older parents, and, grateful for their late blessing, they sheltered and indulged him. While another child might have become spoiled and selfish, Michael was loving, funny, popular and clever. Things rarely went wrong for him, but when they did, he relied on his parents to deal with them and secured their support by the deployment of tears, anger, charm—whatever he could see might work at the time. He'd carried this approach over to adulthood, when the generally smooth progress of his life had ensured that he needed it only rarely. So it was that when, at the age of thirty-eight, he was faced with something fundamental, he had no resources with which to deal with it. By the time Moss heard his story, he had carried his guilt for so long that it was grafted to his skin. It was part of who he was.

Is that why he chose to reveal his secret to Moss? he wondered. She was claiming him as a father and he felt he owed her the truth. If she chose to reject him, he would accept this rejection as delayed justice. He had always regretted allowing his mother to dissuade him from confessing. If he'd been punished at the time, maybe his life would be different now. He would have done his penance and been absolved. He shook his head wearily. Who knows? He had acted as he did, and there were consequences, one of which might be the loss of his newly found daughter. That would be no more than he deserved. Of course, on another level, one he preferred not to acknowledge, he was resisting entanglement. He had never wanted a child. He had made that quite clear to her mothers from the outset. It was too late to change now. He simply didn't have the emotional capacity to deal with the needs of an adult daughter.

He heard Moss return from her shopping expedition, but stayed in his room. At five to six, he left the house, telling her that he'd return at eight. He left the folder on the table and wrote her name on the cover with the ubiquitous magic marker. She watched him from the window and didn't pick up the folder until he was out of sight.

Moss didn't read everything. Some of the details were technical so she skipped to those sections that dealt with the story, the everyday tragedy of the girl they called Amber-Lee. She didn't even rate a newspaper headline. Two column inches in the *Age* reported that *a prostitute known only as Amber-Lee was hit by a car and run over by a truck in Pryor St, Churchill. Police are still trying to identify her. It is believed that Amber-Lee was not her real name. Anyone with information et cetera, et cetera . . .*

Moss tried to imagine what would lead a young girl to leave home for such a brutal life. *Who was she? What was her real name?* she wondered, in a manner uncharacteristic of either the casual Amy or the impatient Linsey. Her habit of introspection and the quality of empathy had stolen in with her father's genes.

The brief was prepared by Senior Constable Graham Patterson of Fitzroy police station. It began with a detailed report of the accident and witness statements and recorded that Michael's blood alcohol level was within the legal limit. What engrossed her, however, was the effort the senior constable had made to identify the girl. She didn't match any missing person's report, although there was some fruitless investigation regarding an Adelaide schoolgirl who'd disappeared earlier that year. Furthermore, Amber-Lee's head injuries precluded the use of dental records. Very little was gleaned from the interview with the prostitute Brenda. It was noted that she shared a flat with the deceased, knew her only as Amber-Lee, and that her attempts at facial imaging were 'unhelpful'. There were very few of Amber-Lee's belongings in the flat and some suspicion that Brenda had appropriated them. The usually helpful Prostitutes' Collective couldn't place the girl and suggested talking to the Ward Street Shelter, where they were told that a girl calling herself Amber-Lee had come in there one day, but left suddenly while she was waiting to be seen. The busy social worker had a very general sense of what she looked like, and the facial image from her description was nothing like the one produced by Brenda's.

Moss suddenly realised that the sun had gone down and the fire was burning low. She looked at her watch. It was after seven, and with a muttered *shit!* she jumped to her feet, stoked the fire and began to prepare the meal. At five to eight she heard the gate open and close, but the footsteps stopped short of the door. She pulled back the curtains. Was that Finn waiting in the shadows? Was he ashamed to face her? She opened the door and called to him in what she hoped was a reassuring tone, 'Come on in, Finn. I'm ready to dish up.'

Finn put a finger to his lips and remained standing in the garden for a few moments more. He peered at his watch a couple of times and then came in, taking off his coat and glancing quickly at the table where the folder had been. His eyes followed hers to the sideboard where it now lay.

'I read it,' she said. 'We can talk about it later, if you like, but let's have something to eat first.'

Finn went to wash his hands and returned to find a large

pot of pasta, with salad and bread, ready for serving. Moss would have liked a glass of wine but was reluctant to open the bottle she'd found in the cupboard. She poured them each a glass of water instead. Her father had good reason not to drink and she wasn't going to be the one to tempt him.

Finn sat down at the table and began to speak without pre-amble. 'I couldn't get her out of my head,' he said. 'It was her anonymity that got to me. She was somebody's daughter and her parents either didn't want to own her or simply didn't know where she was. In the end, she was buried without a name.' For the first time, he looked at his own daughter directly, appeal-ing to her to understand. 'It was as though she'd never existed, Moss. I could have coped if her family or even a good friend had been there for her. Even to curse me. *Especially* to curse me. Just think—a fifteen-year-old is buried and not one person there really cared.'

Moss longed to absolve him but knew she was impotent. He had taken the blame not only for the accident but for the girl's whole sorry life. She took his hand, which lay lifeless on the table.

'It's okay, Finn. It's okay.' Knowing it was far from okay. She was beginning to understand the emergence of Finn and why he had decided to leave Michael behind.

They finished their pasta in silence; heads bowed over their bowls, staring down at the roughly chopped vegetables, the pasta, the mince. Cutlery and glasses chinked softly, and at one stage Finn cleared his throat. Moss looked up expectantly, but he continued to ply his fork with grim tenacity.

Outside, a dog barked and a woman's voice called out,

'Come on, boy. Dinnertime.' A door slammed. A car drove past. The clock chimed the half-hour and ticked away another five minutes before Finn put down his glass and picked up the thread of his story.

'By the time I thought to offer to pay for her funeral,' he said, 'she'd already been buried. It happened within a fortnight. I went to the State Trustees, but they could only direct me to the gravesite.'

He saw it all again—the discarded chip packet at his feet, the rough yellow mound, the iron fence that drew a line between the living and the dead. He had picked up the chip packet and, for want of anything else to do with it, put it into his pocket. He should have brought flowers. He would always regret that. But he was a relatively young man, unfamiliar with mourning traditions, and he only thought of flowers when he saw them adorning other, luckier graves.

He absently picked up the mug Moss set down in front of him. Sensing his distress, she cleared the table and poured the tea in tactful silence.

'It was just a pile of dirt, Moss. Did you know that they bury the poor and the nameless in common graves? There she was, lying in an unmarked grave—with strangers. There was no name—just a number. At least they didn't put *Amber-Lee* on the grave. She deserved some dignity.' He stood up and began to pace the room, his tea slopping on the floor as he emphasised his point. 'Amber-Lee! It was such a silly name: a young girl's fantasy name.' He shook his head. 'You know what I wanted—*want*—most of all? To be able to put her real name on a headstone. It would have been an ordinary name. She was very ordinary, really. *Brown hair*, Brenda had said. *Average height and build. No distinguishing features.*' Finn recited the familiar litany. 'She was a Kerry, perhaps, or Maria or Susan. Maybe Linda or Margaret or Jackie. But not Amber-Lee. I know that for sure.'

'Do you know anything about the funeral?'

'No. I was still hiding myself away and no-one thought to tell me. The girl from the State Trustees' office told me that they sent a junior officer as a witness. A Father Leo from St Jude's Mission performed the service. There were three indigents buried that day. The service was ecumenical. I don't even know if she was a Christian. The priest told me that Senior Constable Patterson was there, in civvies. Apparently it was his day off, but he went anyway. Brenda didn't come. She was the only friend Amber-Lee had, but she didn't come.'

Perhaps Brenda feared a similarly lonely end, Moss thought. But she didn't say so. There was enough pain in this story already.

5

Finn and Saint Benedict

IN THE WEEKS PRIOR TO the inquest, Michael prayed that someone would come forward to claim the girl they called Amber-Lee. He was in a kind of fever of expectation and needed action to ward off the thoughts that jostled so urgently for his attention. He felt compelled to walk, and spent whole days roaming the streets around the area where the accident happened. He returned home each day exhausted but set off again the next morning. He searched the faces of passers-by in the vain hope of finding a clue to Amber-Lee's identity, and he finally took to accosting mortuary staff as they left at the end of their shift. *That couple who just came out—were they there to see her? Has there been any response to the latest photo fit? Were they sure they had checked for any distinguishing marks?* He lurked around the Fitzroy police station, offering suggestions to the officer in charge of the case. *Have you thought of questioning prostitutes other than Brenda? What about her clients? There must be a clue somewhere. Her clothes, maybe.*

'We've done all that,' Graham Patterson would reply wearily. 'We do know our job, Mr Clancy. We'll keep you informed,

I promise. Go home. There's nothing you can do here.'

Michael would go then, but return a day or two later and continue his harangue. 'Don't you see?' he implored of any officer willing to listen. 'It's not right to let it go. We can't just give up. We have to know her name.'

When the coroner's office took out a restraining order, Michael's father stepped in. 'You're not well, Michael. You need professional help. We'll ask Dr Donahue to give you a referral to a psychiatrist.'

But Michael knew that a psychiatrist was not what he needed. It was not his mind but his spirit that was sick. Empathy was one of the qualities that had made him so well liked. It was this that had enabled him to see Amy and Linsey's plight and act with humanity and integrity in their last desperate bid to conceive. But now empathy was his enemy.

He imagined the girl's family: perhaps kind and loving, waiting for a postcard or a phone call. Or were they evil and abusive? Did the girl run from them only to find a life of further abuse and evil? In his worst nightmare, he saw the small, broken body crammed into a box, her cries for recognition smothered by the weight of the indifferent earth. He would wake from this dream gagging and then lie on his back, staring at the ceiling, which became gradually defined as the pre-dawn light turned the room from black to smudgy grey.

He was now afraid to walk in case he was tempted to breach the restraining order, and he became increasingly claustrophobic in the miasma of anxiety and concern that surrounded him in his parents' house, to which he had been persuaded to return 'for his own good'.

'Just until you're feeling a bit better,' his mother promised. 'It's been a horrible experience. You need to rest.'

After two weeks of confinement he could take no more, and slipping away while his parents were out, he returned to his flat to pack a few clothes. Since the accident he had been unable to bring himself to drive his car, so he took a bus down to the coast.

'It's a Father Jerome, from the Benedictine monastery at Tunnawarra,' Michael's mother said that evening, her hand covering the receiver. 'He says that Michael turned up on their doorstep and asked for sanctuary.'

'God Almighty! Tell them we'll be down in a couple of hours to pick him up.' Already on his way out the door, Michael's father wheeled sharply. 'Did you say *sanctuary*? What on earth is the matter with him?'

'It seems that he doesn't want to come home. We can't force him, Vic. They said he could stay in their retreat house for a while.' She spoke into the phone again. 'He's very fragile at the moment, Father. Yes, I understand. Thank you. Call us any time—day or night.' She replaced the receiver and sat down heavily. 'He sounded very competent. And nice. Father Jerome, that is. He said he has a degree in clinical psychology, so that's one blessing. I told him about the accident. I thought he needed to know.'

'We can only hope it does Michael some good. At least he won't be hanging around the coroner's office. Who knows? Maybe he knew all along what he needed.' Seeing tears in his wife's eyes he put his arm around her. 'Don't worry, Paula. We'll go down and see him in a few days. Did the priest say when we could visit?'

'He suggested we give Michael some space for a week or two. He said when you hate yourself you can't believe that anyone else could love you . . . Vic, Michael thinks we secretly despise him for what happened.' She gave up the fight and began to cry in earnest. 'He says we can't help him. We've failed him, haven't we?'

Vic's shoulders sagged. 'Jesus Christ! What a mess.'

Michael had left with no clear plan. He had set out for the coast on a whim, because he loved the sea and hoped to find solace there. But as he waited at the bus station, the fever that had driven him for the last weeks, and which had finally impelled him to act, suddenly dissipated, leaving him nerveless and despondent. In the end, he boarded the bus because it required too much effort of will to turn back. Slouching in his seat, he stared at the passing countryside with little interest.

The bus stopped at a few coastal towns and villages but at each stop Michael sat frozen in his seat. They were passing through farmland now, with fields on one side and on the other, scrubby sand dunes with thick ti-tree obscuring the view of the ocean. The light was fading and the bus terminated at the next town; when it stopped to let out a passenger, Michael grabbed his bag and jumped out too. He had no idea where he was and stood, forlorn, as the bus disappeared around the bend.

His fellow passenger had turned down a side road, and Michael followed. The man had a bag. Perhaps he was going to a motel. After about five minutes, the man stopped to open a gate and then vanished down a gravel drive. The gate clanged shut behind him. Michael read the words worked into the wrought iron: OUR LADY OF SORROWS BENEDICTINE MONASTERY. AD MAJOREM DEI GLORIAM. He pressed the bell. By the time the porter reached the gate, he was hunched on the ground, dreadful sobs shaking his body.

The abbot, Father Jerome, was a tall, square-faced man with serious grey eyes and wispy salt-and-pepper hair. He took control with quiet authority. Michael was to eat, shower and then go to bed. They would talk in the morning. All he need tell them for now was a number where his family could be contacted. The priest went off to make the call, and Michael was attended by Father Boniface, a small elderly man with fluffy white hair and a sweet smile. He said very little, and Michael obediently ate the bread and soup and allowed himself to be silently led to one of several small cottages behind the main building.

'May God bless your sleep,' said Boniface and signed a cross on the younger man's forehead. He had to stand on tiptoe. 'Father Jerome will speak with you in the morning.'

Michael showered and then climbed into bed where, for the first time since the accident, he fell into a dreamless sleep, unaware that Father Jerome had asked one of the younger monks, Father Ambrose, to keep watch over him.

'I don't think he'll do anything foolish, Ambrose, but we'd best be sure.'

After breakfast the next morning, Michael met with Father Jerome again. Though his story was somewhat incoherent, the abbot listened without interrupting.

'So you see,' Michael concluded, 'this girl is dead without even one person to care. She had no opportunity to find a home or love, or even a real friend as far as I can see—no opportunity to redeem herself, because I took that away.' His voice rose in pitch. 'Because I was angry and drunk and drug-affected, a girl died without a name.'

The abbot nodded and they sat in silence for some time. Michael began to feel the need to fill the silence and started to speak, but Jerome held up his hand.

'Enough talk for today, Michael. I'd like you to rest a little more and then go to help Brother Kevin in the vegetable garden. It's just behind your cottage.' He stood up and walked with Michael to the door. 'We go to prayer now. Meet Kevin in the garden in about forty minutes. He'll tell you what to do. And you need to respect the fact that we have periods of silence here. Even at other times we speak quietly and only when necessary.'

Brother Kevin proved to be about Michael's own age, a nuggetty little man who might once have been a jockey. He handed Michael a hoe. 'Nice to have some help. Do the beds over there while I work on this.'

'This' was tying the beans onto a long trellis. The day was warm, and Michael sweated as they worked in silence until the chapel bell rang again.

'That's Sext. I'm off,' said Kevin. 'Take a break, if you like. Or you might like to wash up. Lunch is at one.'

Michael chose to work on. In the weeks when he had tried to walk out his fever, he had instinctively understood that physical activity relieves stress, but his mind still stubbornly churned over the same bitter thoughts. Here in the garden, though, his activity was purposeful and his thoughts less insistent. His body and mind were taken over by the rhythm of the hoe, and the silence, awkward at first, held some sort of promise that seemed to hover around the periphery of his consciousness. His palms quickly developed blisters, but he worked on despite the pain because he didn't know what else he could do. He had put himself solely in the hands of these monks and felt incapable of decision.

In the end, physical exhaustion forced him to stop. He'd eaten very little for weeks and his clothes hung loosely on his tall frame. He returned to his cottage, washed and changed, and followed the monks who were leaving chapel for the refectory. They ate without speaking while another monk read from *The Imitation of Christ* in a dusty monotone.

The outdoor activity had made him hungry, but Michael found that he could eat only half his modest portion. He felt guilty, like a child, and waited to be admonished, but his plate was collected without comment. As he left the table he was summoned once more to Father Jerome's office.

'How are your hands?' the abbot asked as they sat down. Michael showed his red, swollen palms. 'After this, go and see Father Timothy at the infirmary. Some of those blisters are broken and we don't want them to become infected.'

Michael didn't care, but he nodded.

The priest went on: 'I've spoken to your mother and told her you want to stay with us for a while. That *is* what you want, isn't it?'

Michael nodded again.

'We're happy for you to stay, but we need to set the ground rules.'

Michael wasn't going to argue. Rules were good. Rules meant you didn't have to make decisions. 'Firstly, Michael, you are free to go whenever you want, and we are also free to ask you to leave.' Michael's eyes widened in panic, and Jerome was quick to reassure him. 'Don't worry. We aren't going to do that for a while yet. But I must ask what you expect of us.'

Michael shook his head. 'I don't know. Absolution, maybe? Aren't priests supposed to have the power to forgive?'

'Would our forgiveness help?'

'No. At least, I don't think so. Not really.'

'Stay a while. Work with Brother Kevin. Pray if you can. And keep our rule of silence. At first you'll want to talk, to fill the silence, but if you pay attention, eventually the silence will fill you. That's all we can offer you. But it's a powerful thing.'

'Thank you, Father. I'd like to stay, if that's okay.'

Jerome became businesslike. 'I'm pleased. But we do have another problem: we already have a Michael in the monastery. It's not uncommon to choose a new name here. Do you have another name we can use for your stay?'

Michael thought for a moment. 'What about Finbar? That's my second name.'

'Finbar it is, then. Saint Finbar was Bishop of Cork, you know. But he spent most of his life as a monk. Off you go, Finbar, and let Father Timothy deal with those hands.'

Finn spent nearly four months at the monastery. The days unfolded quietly and rhythmically as the monks went about their liturgical tasks at the appointed hours. The days were measured in units of prayer: Matins, Lauds, Terce, Sext, None, Vespers, Compline.

In awe of Jerome, Finn came to love Kevin and Boniface. Boniface said very little, even at the times appointed for social intercourse, but his faded blue eyes looked out on the world, and on the damaged Finn, with a candour, a beneficence, a simple goodness that was innate. Finn wanted to be like Boniface more than anyone he had ever met.

Jerome was Finn's counsellor and Boniface his spiritual mentor, but Kevin was his friend. Kevin was different from the other monks. An irascible fellow, he spent much of his time trying to atone for his impatience. Jerome had given the garden to his keeping to help him find the tranquillity that so often eluded him, but it didn't always work.

'I don't know why they keep me here,' he would say ruefully, after another outburst directed at the recalcitrant tractor.

Finn would grin. 'Neither do I, old mate. Perhaps it's the vegies. Or maybe the wine.'

In the tradition of Saint Benedict, the monastery had a vineyard and produced its own boutique wines; Kevin also worked in the vineyard. On Sundays, the monks were allowed social conversation from lunchtime to Compline and could enjoy a glass of wine or beer with their meals. Finn was surprised to find himself listening more than talking.

'My name wasn't always Kevin, of course,' said the monk. 'I was baptised Matthew, but when I came here there was already a Matthew, so they told me to pick a saint. I wasn't too good on the old saints, but I said, *What about Kevin?* I didn't tell Father Jerome, but it was for Kevin Sheedy. You know, the footballer?

He wasn't the best player ever, but he was a determined bugger. A good role model for me. I haven't found it easy, being a monk.' He took a large gulp of beer. 'Good old Sheeds. I remember one game against Collingwood—we were three points down. There were seconds left on the clock. Well, Sheeds had been winded only minutes before, but he just snatches the ball out of the air and wham! Straight through the goalposts just as the siren goes.' Kevin's eyes shone with admiration. 'Lucky for me,' he added as an afterthought, 'it turned out there really was a Saint Kevin.'

'What made you come here?' Finn was puzzled. The man seemed to lack the spiritual dimension that was evident, to one degree or another, in all the other monks he had met.

'Funny you should ask. I'm an electrician by trade. Had my own little business and everything. I went to church but was never particularly religious. In some ways I came here kicking and screaming, but he got me in the end.'

'Father Jerome?'

'No—God.' Kevin was suddenly shy. 'I had a calling, you see, and in the end I knew I had to come.'

'I don't think I believe in God.'

'Doesn't matter, mate. As long as He believes in you.'

Finn's talks with Boniface were different, but imbued with the same strong faith. He spent an hour a day, four days a week, with the old man, usually sitting in the little summer-house in the front garden. Boniface spoke slowly, as though weighing the value of each word.

'God has already forgiven you,' he said once. 'Your task now is to learn to forgive yourself.'

'That's easier said than done.'

The monk remained silent.

'I mean, how can I do that? Can't you help me?'

'I wish I could, Finbar, but we all have to find redemption in our own way. Sit with me a while. The answer is in your heart and you will only hear the voice of your heart when all other thoughts are silent.'

Finn had never met anyone like Boniface and tried to define his unique qualities. Was he an ascetic? Not really. Asceticism suggested a remoteness, a severity, that was the antithesis of the genuine human warmth complementing the spirituality that lit Boniface from within. On that first night, he had humbly served Finn soup and made up his bed before bestowing a blessing. He could sit with Finn in a silence that was more powerful than words, but when he spoke, his message was simple and compassionate. The more time he spent with Boniface, the more Finn sensed that his humanity and spirituality were one.

He offered these thoughts to Kevin one day when they were working in the garden. 'Father Boniface is amazing. He hardly says anything when I meet with him, but I always come away—refreshed. What's his secret, do you think?'

Kevin leaned on his shovel. 'Boniface is unique,' he said. 'A saint, in his own way. He's managed to cut through all the palaver, all the crap, and see things with the eyes of faith. Look here.' Kevin indicated the garden. 'What do you see here, Finn?'

'A vegie patch.'

'Yes?'

'Beans, carrots, zucchini, tomatoes . . .'

'Yes?'

Finn was at a loss. 'An *organic* vegie patch?'

'All that. But do you know what Boniface sees here?'

Finn shook his head.

'He sees this garden as a little world with its insects, worms, plants, the earth itself—all part of God's creation. I'll never forget the first time we met. There he was, one of the most senior and learned priests in the Order and here was I, a nobody, with dirty hands and muddy boots, smelling of manure. Do you know what he said? *How blessed you are to be young and strong, Brother Kevin, doing the work of God in your garden. How wonderful to be an instrument of His creation.*' Kevin thrust his spade into the earth once more. 'What I'm trying to say, Finn, is that Boniface is the most Christ-like person I've ever met. Or am ever likely to meet.'

Finn looked at the garden again and continued to dig with a new reverence.

He had found some peace in his time at the monastery, but the silent reproach of Amber-Lee's ghost still haunted Finn. Although it happened less often, there were still nights when he awoke with a vision of a single shoe or a bloody sheet, or the taste of damp earth filling his mouth and nose.

'It's called post-traumatic stress disorder—PTSD,' Father Jerome had told him. 'You're having what are known as "flashbacks". It's hard to control their frequency, and the triggers are often quite unpredictable. PTSD is common among soldiers who've seen action. After the First World War they called it "shell-shock". No-one understood it then, but we're making some progress. If it continues, you may be able to learn to control it, but there's no cure as such.'

On the Feast of Saint Benedict, Finn went to the chapel for the first time. There had been no pressure to attend, but he felt that it was a mark of respect to honour the founder of the Order. It was also Open Day at the monastery, and his parents arrived after lunch. They were pleased to see him so much calmer. He was still thin and had become a little stooped from his work in the garden, but they saw there was a new, outdoors toughness in his body, and a healthy ruddiness in his cheeks.

'Time to come home?' enquired his mother hopefully.

Finn was evasive. He had a plan, and needed to discuss it with Father Jerome. 'I'll stay a while yet,' he replied. 'I have to help Kevin prepare the winter garden.'

'Whatever you think best, darling.' His mother was in her mid-seventies and the events of the last six months had sapped her strength. 'Just ring us when you're ready.'

His father clapped him awkwardly on the shoulder. 'Nice to see you so much better, son.'

Finn made an appointment to see Father Jerome the next day. He dressed carefully, and felt a churning in his gut as he entered the abbot's room.

Father Jerome put down his pen and looked up as Finn, red-faced and a little flustered, took his customary seat facing the painting of Saint Benedict that hung behind the abbot's desk.

'Good morning, Finbar.'

Finn had rehearsed the moment and finally decided that it was best to just say what he wanted without preamble. After briefly returning the greeting, he plunged in: 'Father Jerome, I'd like to become a Benedictine.' He beamed. 'Like you,' he added, unnecessarily.

Jerome sighed. He'd been afraid of this: Finbar's mother had warned him that her son was inclined to exaggerated gestures, so he proceeded warily. He didn't want the work of the last months undone. 'Now, why do you say that, my son?'

'Because I want to be like you. And Father Boniface. Or even Brother Kevin.'

'Why do you think *we're* here, Finbar?'

'Because . . . because, you know . . . like Kevin says, you've been called.'

'Have you been called, Finbar?'

'I think so—how can I tell?'

'You know, all right.' Jerome returned to the original question. 'You haven't really answered me, Finbar. Why do you think we're here? What is our *purpose*?'

'You help people like me?'

'Not as many as you might imagine.'

'You live a good life.'

'That's possible anywhere.'

'You work. Kevin has his garden. Timothy has his infirmary. Ambrose has his wine-making. Boniface has . . .' What did Boniface have? Finn felt he was on shifting ground. 'Well. Boniface is Boniface.'

'Boniface is a rarity—a truly holy man. The rest of us, Finbar, are trying. Our main work here is our relationship with God. You've seen the Latin inscription at the entrance to the chapel? *Orare est laborare, laborare est orare.* It means: *To pray is to work and to work is to pray.* Prayer is the centre of our lives. That's what it's all about. Prayer. Do you pray, Finbar? You rarely come to the chapel.'

Finn hung his head miserably. 'I'm not a believer, Father. You know that.'

Jerome smiled. 'Then there'd be many times during the day when you'd have real trouble being a Benedictine.' His voice sobered. 'Look, when you came here, your condition was acute; now you're in the chronic phase, and you have to learn to cope with life again. You won't recover yourself here, Finbar. This isn't a place to hide from life. We've done as much as we can. You're strong enough now. It's time you thought of leaving.'

Stricken, Finn returned to his cottage and looked around at the sparse furniture, his blue coffee mug, his few books, and the plain white bedspread visible through the open door of the bedroom. Out of the window, he could see a honeyeater perched on the bottlebrush and, in the near paddock, Kevin berating the hapless tractor. Walking away from the main cloister, Finn had felt angry and abandoned. *So that's it. They pick you up and throw you out like so much garbage.* Now, in this little place where he had lain each night with his brokenness, the anger turned to sadness. Not grief, he thought, surprised. Just a deep sadness and sense of loss.

Weariness suddenly turned his limbs to liquid, and he went into his bedroom to lie down. It seemed like hours before his head finally rested on the pillow and the viscous substance that was his body found the hollows and contours of his bed. Jerome didn't find him worthy. He turned onto his side and looked at the simple crucifix on the wall. He willed himself to believe. He prayed: *If you are there, make me believe.* But the plaster face, glazed with pain, was turned away. It was then that Finn accepted what he'd known in his heart all along. This was a monastery of Catholic monks whose lives were dedicated to serving a god he couldn't acknowledge. Father Jerome was right. It was time to go.

He left a few days later, again on a bus. Despite his professed love for the sea, he perversely turned inland, partly as a self-imposed penance and partly because he was attracted by a name attached to a tiny speck on the map. He had studied the towns along the bus route, looking for something small. Passing on the provincial city of Cradletown and the prominent town of Mystic, he found what he was seeking halfway between the two larger centres. Opportunity. That would be his destination.

Before he left, Kevin shook his hand.

'I'll miss you, old mate. Just like you to go off when there's work to be done.' He grinned crookedly. 'You look after yourself now, and don't forget all I taught you about vegies.'

Boniface traced a cross on Finn's forehead and murmured a blessing. 'You'll know what to do when the time is right, Finbar. Remember, the Silence isn't designed to let you brood. It's to give you space to listen. Look into your heart and listen, my friend. Go with God's blessing.'

Jerome walked him to the gate. 'Go in peace, Michael.'

'Thank you, Father. For everything. But from now on my name is Finbar.'

'Go in peace, Finbar.'

It was a long trip from the coast, and when Finn reached his destination and alighted from the bus it was mid-afternoon. He headed for the inevitable corner pub which was circled on both levels with a classic iron-lace verandah. He kept his eyes lowered, but was forced to nod to an old codger who was carefully negotiating the bar door. Finn felt his appraising gaze.

'Jes' steppin' out to check on old Blue here,' the man said, indicating a stringy cattle dog snoring peacefully in a patch of sunlight. 'Blue's me dog,' he added helpfully. 'I'm Clive— Cocky to me mates.' His face widened in a toothless grin.

'Nice to meet you, Cocky—Clive. I'm Finbar,' he said, as he bolted for safety through the door marked ACCOMMODATION.

The old man scratched his chest. 'See ya later, Finn.' By the time Cocky had swilled a few more beers, everyone spoke of the newcomer as Finn. It was a christening of sorts.

Finn had rung ahead and booked a room but it soon became obvious that booking was unnecessary.

The landlady said her name was Marlene. 'Don't get many strangers here,' she said as he filled in the required details. 'We get a few sales reps, of course . . .'

Finn chose to ignore the query in her voice and went up to his room, which was clean if sparsely furnished. Not so different from his little room at the monastery, when he came to think of it. His appointment with the real estate agent was not until five, so he had a quick shower and then went over to the window. In the hour he sat there he saw Cocky and his dog; two women, one with a shopping jeep; and a man who got out of a ute and unloaded some pipes. No more than half a dozen cars drove down the street in that time. When the school bus came in there was a little flurry of activity as three women arrived to collect the eight children who spilled out, one waving a painting, another clutching a drink bottle.

The signs were good, thought Finn. Opportunity appeared to be a very quiet town. All that remained was to find some permanent accommodation.

The agent had five vacancies. Three were too large for his needs and the fourth was in Main Street. The fifth, a forlorn little weatherboard cottage on the far side of the football ground, had only one neighbour.

'She's a funny old bird,' said the smartly dressed agent, indicating an elderly woman who, upon seeing them, tucked down her head and scuttled back into her house. 'You're lucky if she gives you the time of day.'

'I'll take the house,' said Finn. 'I want a long-term lease.'

6

Finn, Moss and Mrs Pargetter

ON THE SECOND MORNING OF Moss's stay, she and Finn were sitting down to breakfast. Relating the story of Amber-Lee's death had clearly been painful for him, and she wanted to return their conversation to something more general.

'How did you come to live here?' Moss asked.

Finn, happy enough to be diverted, responded with a much-abridged version of his life in the monastery. 'After the accident, I had a bit of a breakdown and some Benedictine monks took me in. Taught me a few things. That was ten years ago now. I still practise the Silence twice a day from six to eight, morning and evening. I try to avoid unnecessary conversation at other times. People used to be one of my strong points, but now . . . You know, it was lucky the bus was late the night you came. It usually gets in at seven fifteen.'

'What would you have done if I'd arrived on time?'

'I never make exceptions to the Silence. I wouldn't have answered the door. I was in that night because it was too wet to go outside, where I prefer to be.'

They both pondered this fortunate confluence of events.

'What do you do when you're not . . . being silent?' Moss asked.

'I work, and I try to do a little good here and there. I still haven't quite got the hang of that.'

'What kind of work do you do?'

'Bits and pieces. I do some hack work for the Bureau of Statistics and some interesting number-crunching for the Commission for the Future. Most of our communication is online. I have to go to Melbourne a couple of times a year for meetings, but I get back here as quickly as I can. It's a living, as they say. And there's my vegie patch, although the drought has pretty much buggered that up.'

'You wouldn't go back to your research?'

'You wouldn't go back to your singing?'

'Touché.'

Finn said he had to go out, and Moss decided to walk along the river.

'There's a path that goes about five kilometres,' he told her. 'Starts near the bridge.'

That night at dinner, Finn seemed distracted and not inclined to talk. Finally, he shifted in his seat and cleared his throat.

'How long do you plan to stay? Not that I want to get rid of you,' he assured her, remembering his panic when Jerome had asked a similar question.

'Not sure, really. I need some time to think things out. And—and I'd also like to get to know you better?' The upward inflection betrayed her uncertainty.

'I'd like you to stay a while.' Finn's tone also betrayed doubt.

'But we can't have you sleeping on the floor and I don't have a spare room so I . . . sort of took the, you know, *liberty* of speaking to old Mrs Pargetter. She lives next door, in the house with the blue verandah. She said you can stay with her.'

When he took the house, Finn was pleased that his elderly neighbour was a recluse. After a brief introduction, they had merely nodded politely whenever they happened to pass. One evening, a few weeks after he moved in, he answered a knock at the door to find her standing on his verandah, twisting her apron apologetically.

'Mr Clancy,' she began, 'I'm so sorry to disturb you, but my door is stuck and I can't close it properly. I won't sleep unless I can lock it, you see. Normally my nephew would . . .'

'Of course I'll help, Mrs Pargetter. Just let me get my tools.' Noting for the first time how frail she was, he took her arm as they went down his path and up to her house. 'Now, let's see what I can do.' He planed a little off the door and, disarmed by her old-fashioned courtesy, accepted the proffered cup of tea. As he left, he was surprised to hear himself promising to dig over her vegetable garden.

After that, Finn found it pleasant to do little jobs for her—taking her dog for a walk, pruning her roses, replacing a tap washer, changing a light bulb. In turn, she would call him in when she'd made scones or biscuits or a teacake. Once she presented him with a tea cosy. But she never asked personal questions, nor did she tell him anything of herself. They suited each other very nicely.

So for want of another solution, he turned to Mrs Pargetter for help with the problem of Moss's incursion into his life.

As he saw it, he had no choice. He didn't want to send her to the pub, so where else could she go? Besides, he often worried about his neighbour living alone. She was so frail. What if she had a fall or became ill? Here was a perfect solution—at least in the short term.

The old lady stared in dismay when Finn proposed that she take his daughter in for a few days. 'I didn't know you had a daughter, Finn. Not that it's any of my business,' she added hastily. 'I mean, a young girl! What would she want staying with an old woman like me?'

Despite his rationalisations, Finn already felt guilty for trying to pass his problem on to his elderly friend. He stepped back a pace. 'That's alright, Mrs Pargetter. I'm sorry I asked. I had no right to expect . . .'

Mrs Pargetter saw in Finn's face a montage of embarrassment, confusion and . . . something else. Something familiar. She swallowed hard. 'You've been good to me, Finn. I'd like to help. Just for a few days, you say? Bring her round tomorrow afternoon.' She said this rapidly, as though she had to get the words out before she regretted them. She even allowed Finn to leave without offering him a cup of tea. They were both aware that they had crossed some unspoken boundary.

'So,' Finn continued now, in the face of Moss's frown, 'you can move your things in tomorrow afternoon—if it's alright with you, of course. She's a nice old thing,' he added weakly. 'Knits tea cosies for the United Nations.' He indicated his own colourfully encased teapot. 'That's one of hers. She gives them as Christmas presents too.'

'Did you say United Nations?'

'Yup.'

'And it was *tea cosies*?'

'Yup again. There was some story involved, but I can't remember. She'll tell you. She could do with some company. Sometimes I wonder if she's a bit batty.'

Moss had been wondering the same thing, but sleeping on the floor had little appeal so when Finn said they would still have meals together, she agreed to move next door on a trial basis.

When Finn had gone, Lily Pargetter went up the stairs and stood looking at the closed door of her spare bedroom with something like fear in her eyes. She opened the room once a week to air and dust it, but this was different. If the girl came, then the room would be disturbed, unsettled. Things would be displaced. What would happen then to the sorrow she had folded and stored away there? Looking at Finn, standing irresolute on her doorstep, she had seen a sadness that echoed her own, and had let down her guard. She had been foolish to agree, but could always go next door and tell him she'd changed her mind. It was her house, after all. Her private domain. But what could she tell him? The truth was too painful, and a lie would drive him away. She didn't want that. She'd come to rely on his presence, his quiet companionship over scones and tea.

The door creaked a little as she opened it and switched on the light. Her fingers trailed over the wallpaper. She had decorated this room so long ago. A musty smell sent her hurrying to the window to let in some fresh air. She shook out the curtains. Perhaps the musty smell came from them. 'I have to do this,' she muttered. 'Merciful God, help me do this.'

Determined to concentrate on the task at hand, she applied herself in a housewifely manner, polishing the dressing-table, smoothing fresh linen on the bed, checking there were coat-hangers in the wardrobe. She switched on the little bedside lamp and was pleased to see its soft glow. The room remained curiously aloof, so she went out to the garden and cut some camellias. 'Thank goodness the drought hasn't got these yet,' she murmured to herself. She arranged the pale pink blooms in a blue-patterned vase and stepped back to admire them. This cleaning had taken on the elements of ritual, as though sweeping away the dust and polishing the surfaces would drive her sadness into the darkest corner. It still lingered in her heart—a small, hard knot of misery—but she called on her reserves of strength and refused to let it overwhelm her.

She was startled to hear the clock chime six and realised that she had achieved a victory of sorts: she could never have imagined spending so much time in that room. More than that, she was actually excited by the prospect of playing hostess for a few days. It was nice to feel needed.

The following day, Moss and Finn arrived just before three o'clock, Finn carrying a backpack and Moss a handbag and a basket of fruit. The old lady greeted them at the door, her hands in a flurry of flour.

'Come in. I've just put some scones in the oven. We can have a cuppa. Or would you rather see your room first? What am I thinking?' She smiled a welcome through unwieldy teeth. 'You must be Fern.'

'Moss, Mrs Pargetter. And thank you, I'd love a cup of tea.'

Mrs Pargetter pottered around the kitchen, insisting that

she wait on her guests. She was of medium height, her body melted into the shapelessness of old age. She carried the beginnings of a dowager's hump, a feature that was accentuated by her habit of holding her head down to one side whenever she spoke. Her grey hair was drawn back in an untidy bun, and what was once a wide and generous smile was marred by ill-fitting false teeth which she occasionally needed to slurp back into place. She found this manoeuvre quite embarrassing but managed to perform it with some delicacy, simultaneously sucking and patting at her mouth with a lace-edged handkerchief.

As Mrs Pargetter poured the tea, Moss commented on the Fair-Isle tea cosy.

'How pretty,' she said disingenuously. 'Dad has one just like it.'

The old lady smiled so broadly that her teeth wobbled dangerously and the handkerchief was hastily deployed. 'Thank you, dear. I've knitted three thousand and twelve over the past thirty-odd years. Jam? I'm afraid it's shop-bought. I used to make my own, but I'm getting on. Eighty-four next birthday.'

Moss helped herself to a scone and took a small spoonful of jam. She hesitated over the cream.

'Eat up. Young girls are all too thin nowadays. Men like something to hold on to.' Moss's eyes widened. 'Sorry, dear. I didn't mean to embarrass you. Your father's skinny, so it must be in the genes.'

Having encouraged Moss to tuck away a surprising number of scones, Mrs Pargetter then showed her to her room. It was large and airy, with a casement window and peeling wallpaper where little yellow teddy bears played on a blue background. A mahogany chest of drawers stood in one corner, and a battered wardrobe lurked in the other. The high, narrow bed wore a quilted silk bedspread the same colour as the teddy bears.

This room has been waiting, Moss thought suddenly. And for a moment she felt a heaviness of spirit. Mrs Pargetter seemed to sense it too and took Moss's hand.

'This room hasn't been used since . . . for some time. I'm entrusting it to you.'

Before Moss had time to think about the oddness of the last remark, the old lady began to bustle about, opening drawers and patting the bedspread.

'I picked you some camellias,' she said, touching the mass of soft pink blooms. 'As a sort of welcome. I'm afraid there's not much else in the garden at the moment.'

Moss smiled her thanks as Mrs Pargetter left her to her unpacking, which took very little time. Even when she had laid her things out, the room continued to brood. She sat on the bed and tried to analyse the feeling. There was no sense of threat or foreboding; rather it was something like—but not quite—nostalgia. Longing, maybe? Closer. Moss shook off the weight of her thoughts, chiding herself for being fanciful.

'All done,' she announced, coming back into the kitchen. 'It's a lovely room. Thank you, Mrs Pargetter.'

'It's Thursday. Let's have the Thursday pub roast,' said Finn as he left. 'My treat. I'll pick you up at eight.'

Moss watched at the door as her father fled down Mrs Pargetter's path and up his own, returning to the sanctuary of his house. She noted his haste and felt a wave of self-pity. *Another parent who doesn't want me.* Then: *He needs time*, she reminded herself sharply and, straightening her shoulders, she turned back to sit by the fire with Mrs Pargetter. The old lady was busy knitting a large purple square.

'That looks a bit big for a tea cosy.' Moss smiled.

'It's another jumper for your father,' she replied. 'That green one is getting very shabby. I'm glad you're here, dear. He doesn't look after himself very well, you know.'

Moss acknowledged this statement with a nod, and changed the subject. 'You've knitted over three thousand tea cosies, Mrs Pargetter? That's a lot of teapots.'

The old lady frowned. 'There are a lot of poor people in the world,' she admonished. 'I usually try for at least two a week. I have four weeks' holiday at Christmas, of course. All work and no play, as they say.'

'So how do they get to the . . . poor people?'

Mrs Pargetter sniffed. 'Well, first of all I sent some samples to World Volunteers and got a very terse reply, I can tell you. Apparently *they* could see no need for tea cosies. As though the poor had no right to a decent cup of tea.' Her breast, lumpy like an old pillow, heaved with indignation, and Moss shook her head at the World Volunteers' callous disregard for the poor. But Mrs Pargetter was a woman on a mission. 'I tried the African Aid Society. Their letter was nicer, but apparently they had enough tea cosies.' She stopped to count her stitches. 'It was then that I had a brilliant idea. Well, Errol has to take some credit.' She patted the dog, who woofed his agreement. 'It was so simple I could have cried. I sent a parcel of one dozen cosies to the quartermaster of the United Nations, New York City.' She spaced each word to emphasise her triumph. 'And I got a letter back from a Mr Lusala Ngilu, thanking me *personally* for my extreme kindness. That's what he said. I can show you the first letter. *Extreme kindness.*'

'That's wonderful, Mrs Pargetter. The UN has a quarter-master? In New York City?'

'Oh, yes. I get a lovely thank you each time. I can show you the letters. I have a box full of them. They're on official letterhead signed by Mr Lusala Ngilu, Quartermaster, United Nations. I get a card every Christmas as well.' She looked over her glasses. 'I know you young people like to make initials of everything. Your father thought he could get away with call-ing me "Mrs P.", but I soon put a stop to that. *It's just laziness*, I said. *My name is Lily Pargetter and you may call me Mrs Parget-ter.* So you see, dear, I must insist you show proper respect to the United Nations. If anyone asks what I do, tell them I work for the *United Nations.*'

The kelpie that had followed her home turned out to belong to Mrs Pargetter, and Moss offered to take him for a walk. He was named after Errol Flynn, and surprisingly, he bore no grudge. He loved Mrs Pargetter with all his doggy heart and they enjoyed many a good conversation about the old days. So far he tolerated Moss's presence in the house. She spoke softly and scratched his ears just the way he liked.

Thursday was obviously a busier day in town, and there were quite a few cars and utes angle-parked into the deep blue-stone gutter. A hum of voices came from the pub, and women stood talking under shop awnings. Most looked at Moss and Errol curiously, and a few nodded pleasantly. An old man in a faded flannel shirt lifted his hat. 'G'day, girlie,' he said, and gave her a gappy grin. She smiled back, wondering why she didn't mind being called 'girlie'. Her mothers had made it very clear that this was a demeaning form of address.

Moss and Errol returned home around five to find Mrs Pargetter already dressed for the pub meal, which she clearly looked on as quite an event. She had changed into a cable-knit jumper and a long cotton skirt. She wore pearl clip-on earrings and her bun was tidied into a black lace snood. The effect was spoilt by the shaky application of pink lipstick and pale blue eye shadow, but when Finn arrived an hour later, he gallantly kissed her hand and said she looked lovely. Moss, who had brought very little clothing with her, was going to wear jeans but in deference to the old lady's sense of what was proper changed into black trousers and a clean white shirt. Her taste in clothes mirrored Linsey's rather than Amy's. Neat, practical, classic—that had been Linsey's advice.

The pub's small dining room was crowded, and most of the patrons seemed to know Finn and Mrs Pargetter. Moss felt quite shy as she was introduced, and sensed Finn's similar discomfort in crowds. She was glad to be seated at a corner table with a glass of wine. Mrs Pargetter sipped a shandy, and Finn had a Coke. They were not left in peace for long. A large red face imposed itself and wheezed a greeting in a voice that sounded as though it were being forced out from somewhere high in the throat. The barrel chest, a perfect resonator, had no part to play.

'Heard you were here, Finn.' His diction was unexpectedly cultured. 'Needed to catch up with you about the project.' The speaker suddenly noticed that there were other people present.

'G'day, Aunt Lily.' Mrs Pargetter offered him a frosty *Good evening, George*, and returned to her shandy.

Finn introduced him to Moss, who felt her hand sinking unpleasantly into his soft, sweaty palm. She hastily withdrew her own. He was a strange-looking man, his small, quite handsome features all tightly corralled in the centre of his very large face, while tiny red capillaries traced complicated map lines on his cheeks. He was dressed in neat moleskins and an expensive-looking linen shirt.

Moss smiled politely. 'Pleased to meet you, Mr Sandilands.'

'Sandy, please. Everyone calls me Sandy.' Mrs Pargetter looked up sharply. 'Well, almost everyone.'

There was no room for Sandy to join them, so after making a time to meet with Finn the next day, he wandered off into the bar.

'What's this project?' Moss asked.

'You won't believe it,' Finn responded. He hardly believed it himself. 'You've heard of the Big Banana and the Big Pineapple?' She nodded. 'Well, Sandy is planning something similar for Opportunity.'

'What is it?'

'Actually, it's a Great Galah.'

'A Great Galah? What on earth gave him that idea?'

'His father was always calling him a great galah, apparently. Sandy seems to think it was a term of affection. He says it will not only honour his relationship with his father, Major Sandilands, DSO and Bar—I'm not joking, that's how he refers to his father: *Major Sandilands, DSO and Bar*—but he reckons that this galah thing'll bring in the crowds. You wouldn't know it, but he's the richest man in town. Worth squillions. He's willing to pay for the lot himself. He's very passionate about it.'

'He's barking mad,' pronounced Mrs Pargetter. 'And his father was a nasty bully of a man.' She drained her glass for emphasis.

'Drawing up the plans keeps him happy,' said Finn mildly. 'It keeps the demons at bay.'

7

Lily Baxter and Arthur Pargetter

WHEN MRS PARGETTER WAS LILY Baxter, she and her older sister, Rosie, were considered to be beauties, although it was generally agreed that Rosie, laughing and vivacious, was the more attractive. The girls were well-read and genteel, daughters of the schoolmaster, but it was still considered a great coup for eighteen-year-old Rosie when she married George Sandilands, the son and heir of a wealthy local grazier. Despite her supposed good fortune, the only peace Rosie Sandilands experienced in her thirty-eight years of marriage was the four years in which her husband was overseas becoming a major and winning medals. Rosie was always publicly addressed by her husband as *Rosalind*, and privately as *Woman*, in tones of exasperation, anger or contempt. He prided himself on using physical force only when he considered it to be absolutely necessary. Lily was the only one Rosie ever allowed to see the bruises.

Their son, George Junior, was known as Sandy. From an early age the boy learned that to show affection to his mother would only enrage his father. So he trembled in the suffocating dark beneath the bedclothes when he heard his mother cry, and cravenly sought his father's approval at every opportunity. This went some way to protecting him from the Major's anger, but not from his contempt. He was a bright enough lad, but not well coordinated, and his father's jeering voice could be heard at school sports days and football matches: *You great galah! Can't you do anything right?* The boy's attempts to read quietly, a pastime that he loved, called forth similar abuse. *Nancy boy*, his father called him, and in his misery Sandy ate the cakes and scones and sweets his mother pressed on him, the only way she could express her love and pity.

At nineteen, Lily was still not married and lived a quiet life, keeping house for her father and playing the organ at St Saviour's. She was a dreamy girl and looked forward to a future as a wife and mother. Her sister's early marriage had left her a little uneasy on this score, but her father, a widower for fifteen years, was in no hurry to marry off his second daughter. He was afraid of George and averted shamed eyes from any evidence of Rosie's unhappiness, privately vowing to protect his younger daughter from the same fate.

Lily was a talented musician and was often asked to play piano at various gatherings around the district. Because of this, she went to many dances but rarely danced, sitting con-scientiously at the piano with a straight back and firm wrists as she'd been taught. The women all agreed that she was a pretty girl but a bit too pleased with herself. The men granted that she was *a bit of all right*, but felt that she thought herself too good for them. *Why else*, they asked, *would she sit all snooty-like at the piano when she could be dancing? There are plenty more fish in the sea*, they told each other. *Don't have to chase Miss*

Up-Herself. Lily, meanwhile, would sit with her straight back and pretty face, wishing only to be swirling on the dance floor with some young man or giggling in the corner where the girls assembled like multi-coloured butterflies.

The ensemble she played with included old 'Trooper' Morgan on drums and Tony Capricci (Eyetie Tony) on the saxophone. Both men treated her with a kind of elderly gallantry, which she accepted with rueful gratitude.

The night she met Arthur she had slipped away from the piano for a cool drink, leaving Tony exuberantly calling for a 'Pride of Erin'. She was looking particularly attractive in a dress of butter-coloured lace, her long auburn hair framing her face.

'Is the pianist allowed to dance?'

She turned to see a small, dark-haired young man with soft puppy-dog eyes, and a nervous grin over which struggled a self-conscious pencil moustache. He was dressed in a navy-blue suit with an obviously new white shirt. His tie, she noticed, needed straightening, and his hair was just a little too long over his collar.

'I thought you needed looking after,' she would say on their honeymoon. 'That's the only reason I agreed to dance with you.'

'Not the only reason you agreed to marry me, I hope,' Arthur would retort. 'My good looks and charm must have had some effect.'

The truth was that his charm lay not in his looks, exactly, but in his shy smile. It had taken all his courage to approach her, but he managed to hold out his hand in invitation. Lily looked over at Tony. *Please?* her eyes said.

'Go ahead, *bella mia*. We can play without you.' Tony beamed.

Arthur was the new clerk at the Commonwealth Bank. *A job with prospects*, her father noted approvingly. Their courtship was brief. War loomed, and there was a kind of desperate gaiety and sense of urgency that fermented the social process. So, ten months after their first dance, they married at St Saviour's and honeymooned at Marysville, where they fumbled through their first sexual experience with enthusiasm and good humour, returning to Opportunity with smug little smiles.

Shortly afterwards, Arthur was promoted to a job in Melbourne. Lily was delighted as they began to furnish their little flat in Carlton, two rooms at the back of a sagging Federation house owned by a Mrs Moloney. Their landlady always appeared slightly harried, and her face and body were so angular that Arthur set himself a challenge to detect even the slightest of curves under her drab button-through housedresses. She didn't believe in becoming familiar with her tenants and always addressed the two young people as Mr and Mrs Pargetter. Lily was delighted to be addressed as Mrs Pargetter; she sometimes felt that she was still a girl, posing as a woman, and the 'Mrs' reassured her.

She loved to prepare Arthur's chops and vegies and always cooked a roast for lunch on Sundays. They made love (with increasing pleasure), stifling giggles at the thought of Mrs Moloney lying grim-faced in the next room. Eight months into the marriage, and three months into Lily's pregnancy, Arthur signed up.

'I can't let all the other blokes go, and sit here living the life of Riley.' He cupped her face in his hands. 'I have to look after my best girl and little Tiger here.' He patted her softly rounded stomach. 'Got to keep my family safe from the Japs.'

Lily clung to him fearfully. How could she bear to send him away? The past year had seen their love grow from attraction, and the love of being in love, to a deepening sense of each other's worth. His kindness, integrity and humour; her gentleness, optimism and generosity—all this hope, all this love, had fashioned a magic circle of two, which was miraculously soon to be three. They linked hands. 'No matter how many miles come between us,' Lily vowed, her face awash with tears, 'our circle will never be broken.'

After he left, she spent every day wrestling with her dread as she went about her household tasks and filled in the time knitting ever more fanciful layettes. She prayed to the God in whose church she had played the organ, in whose church she had made her vows. She told stories to the baby growing within her: stories about how they would greet Daddy on his return; stories about how they would picnic at the beach and the park, and take trips to the countryside. She painted mind-pictures of a young soldier, lean and tanned, holding them both in his arms. But an icy knot of fear remained, despite the long days of sunshine and blue skies as summer lingered deceitfully beyond its allotted time.

The telegram arrived six weeks before the baby was due. Arthur had been killed by a sniper somewhere in New Guinea and buried in the field. His effects included a dog-eared photo of their wedding and a lock of auburn hair in a hand-made wooden box. She liked to think that he'd made the box, although she knew that he wasn't clever with his hands. There was also a half-written letter.

How's my best girl? I hope you're looking after yourself and little Tiger.

We are—(Here a large block had been blacked out by the censors.)

I can hardly wait to see you both. I have a little wooden dooverlackie that the natives make for their children. It can be Tiger's first toy. I'll be home (censored) *to give it to him myself. Or it might be a her. Then I would have two best girls. I'll . . .*

The letter finished there. The toy was not with his other effects. She hoped he had it with him when he died.

When the shock wore off, Lily's sorrow bore down upon her physically and engulfed her mind in blackness. Mrs Moloney, who had experienced her own sorrows, tended her with gentleness and a delicate discretion which poor Lily barely noticed. Her father and sister came as soon as they heard the news; they feared for both her health and her sanity.

'Come home with me when the baby's born,' her father said. 'We'll manage. I can't be its father but I'll be a bloody good grandfather. Come on, love. Arthur would want you to. You know that.'

Lily stared out the window. She felt a strong affinity with the garden, which wore the overblown, enervated look that signalled the end of a long summer. It wasn't so long ago that green buds heralded new life. A life now depleted.

'Sorry. Did you say something?' She could hear her father's voice but was unable to comprehend his meaning.

Rosie picked up her nerveless hand. 'For the baby's sake, Lil.'

But the baby, entering the world at thirty-three weeks, was stillborn. In the throes of an agonising labour, Lily was given chloroform, and when she regained consciousness there was no evidence that her baby had ever existed. The nurses were firm. It was best to get on with life. But her milk flowed as she saw other babies at their mothers' breasts, and she felt a phantom presence where others saw only an absence.

Her father brought her home to Opportunity but became increasingly concerned as she sang lullabies and knitted little jackets. *For winter*, she said. *We must keep Baby warm in winter.* She had bought some teddy-bear wallpaper in Melbourne but had not had a chance to hang it in the flat. When her father came home to find the spare bedroom covered in teddy bears, he felt compelled to act.

Dr Grey had seen many grieving mothers. In those days children were still dying of diphtheria and measles. 'I know it's upsetting, Frank,' he said to her worried father. 'Most women get over it one way or another. Maybe *get over it* isn't accurate. They learn to live with it. I don't know much about psychiatry, but I'd say she's having a nervous breakdown. Give her a bit more time. Make sure she gets out and about, plays the piano—whatever will take her mind off it. I'm sure she'll come good in a month or two. Remember, she lost a husband and child within a week of each other. It's a hell of a thing. Time's the key, though. Time and patience.'

But Lily continued to knit, to sing lullabies and to walk the floor with her phantom child in the early hours of the morning.

'Sleepy-byes, sleepy-byes,' she would croon. 'The stars are shining in the skies. Come on, close your eyes—Mummy has to sleep too.' And then she'd lie exhausted on her bed, sleeping beyond noon.

She found the old family pram in the shed and took to walking up the street, stopping every now and then to adjust the covers or point out a birdie or a puppy dog.

'See the little birdie? He can fly. Mummy can't fly. Grandpa can't fly. Aunty Rosie can't fly. Only birdies.'

It was a small community, and those who saw her out walking pitied her, each in their own way.

Mad as a hatter, poor little bugger.

If only her mother was alive . . .

She was such a lovely girl. Pretty as a picture.

More and more, though, there were those who would say:

Why doesn't she snap out of it?

It's like she's determined to be unhappy. We've all lost someone.

They say some of her mother's family weren't right in the head.

Poor old Frank. He's getting too old to deal with this.

They all agreed on the last one.

Finally, Dr Grey referred Lily to a psychiatric hospital, where she spent the next twelve years in a twilight of drugs and therapy. Her rounded body became gaunt and she lost the bloom of her young womanhood. Quiet and compliant in most things, she continued to search for her child with a stubborn diligence that would brook no opposition. She shunned the company of the 'mad people', as she called them, and dreaded group therapy sessions. In order to distract her from her fruitless searching, and despite the fact that she was already an accomplished knitter, the occupational therapist taught her to knit tea cosies. It was here at Chalmers House that she learned to conform. It was here that she received the shock treatment that enabled her to function but cauterised her grief and left her, as the citizens of Opportunity agreed, just a little strange. It was here she lost Lily Pargetter.

Her father had visited her every Saturday and agreed, as people did then, to any treatment suggested by her doctors. Despite his frequent requests, they were always adamant that she was not ready to be discharged. He had some qualms when they suggested electroconvulsive therapy ('shock treatment,' they called it), but how can a schoolmaster argue medical matters with doctors? They seemed so sure it would work.

Frank died of heart failure before the course of treatment was finished, but before he died he made Rosie promise to bring Lily home. 'She needs to come home. We'll take care of her. This shock therapy is the last treatment we can agree to.'

At first the Major opposed the plan. 'I don't know why you'd want your barmy sister around. You'll be too busy with her to take proper care of the house.'

Then, when the psychiatrist confronted him with arrogance equal to his own, the Major's instincts—to win at all costs—kicked in. In those days it was much easier to be admitted to a mental institution than to be discharged, and for once the Major's bullying was put to good effect. In the end Lily was released, as if from prison.

'I've got a room ready at our place, Lil,' Rosie fussed as she tucked a rug around her sister's knees.

Lily pushed it off. 'For heaven's sake, Rosie. I'm not an invalid.'

She stayed with the Sandilands for a week and then insisted on returning to her father's house where, to supplement the small income her father had left her, she gave piano lessons on weekday afternoons from one till five. She aired the nursery once a week; the rest of the time its door remained closed.

She shopped each day, nodding to acquaintances in a furtive way as she hurried, basket over her arm, to buy her chop or lamb's fry or bacon. She sent homemade jam to St Saviour's fête committee and resumed her place at the organ, much to the relief of the congregation who, in latter years, had had to tolerate the doubtful harmonies of Annie Williams's daughter, Deanna. *It's the Christian thing to do*, they assured Annie, who was inclined to protest at Deanna's dismissal. Deanna herself was delighted. Playing the church organ had proved to be quite a handicap in her pursuit of the local boys.

Every Thursday, Lily and her sister would have morning tea in the café, known then, rather grandly, as the Regency Rooms. There they would talk quietly over tea and scones, always at the same corner table. These were the longest conversations Lily had with anyone at that time, and no-one else knew what they talked about. Angela Capricci sometimes tried to eavesdrop as she delivered their tea or wiped down an adjoining table, but she had nothing to report. 'They speak so softly,' she said. 'I can't catch a word they say.'

In June of 1957, Lily turned thirty-five and Rosie gave her a puppy for her birthday. 'He's the best of Jess's litter,' she said. 'He'll be company for you.'

The puppy whimpered in its basket, and Lily felt panic rising in her throat. He was so little. He'd need so much care. She wasn't sure she was equal to the task but, seeing the delight on her sister's face, her hand, on the way to a gesture of rejection, fell instead onto the puppy's paws. Surprised, she felt his warm tongue on the back of her hand.

Lily was engulfed by an unexpected wave of tenderness. She looked down at the little creature. Touched it tentatively. Stroked its softness. She was so lonely. Her bones ached with a longing that finally conquered her fear of inadequacy.

'Thank you, Rosie. I hope I can take proper care of him.'

'Why on earth couldn't you?' her sister replied with a confidence that didn't quite reach her eyes. 'He'll need a name, though. What will you call him?'

Lily didn't hesitate. 'Errol. For Errol Flynn.' And the puppy became the first of the Errols, of which her current dog was number six.

Rosie's doubts were understandable. Her sister had changed during her time at Chalmers House. While her behaviour after the death of her husband and child was extreme, something of the old Lily still lingered, distorted and damaged to be sure, but recognisable. Now, though, she seemed to have lost her spark, some important ingredient of her *Lily-ness*. She avoided social occasions and, when engaged in conversation, had a tendency to flight. Worse, she sometimes made a rude or inappropriate comment before escaping to the safety of her house. Conversations at the Regency Rooms had none of their old intimacy, and Rosie felt she had to carry the full burden. She would return home quite exhausted, submitting in silence to George's gibes about her barmy sister.

Rosie died in 1972 and was buried in the Sandilands family plot as *Rosalind, loving wife of Major George Sandilands, DSO and Bar*. Her son didn't even warrant a mention. Lily stood white-faced beside the grave as the Major, with self-conscious solemnity, threw the first clod onto the coffin. The faint thud reverberated through Lily's fragile brain, and her mouth filled with bile. Bleak and bitter, she spat viciously on the Major's polished shoes and spoke as she had never spoken to anyone before.

'She's free of you now, you bastard,' she said. 'I only wish you had gone first.'

Rosie's death left Lily with no-one to talk to, and that's when she began talking to her dog (Errol III, by this time). She could be heard by passers-by chatting away with a vivacity never witnessed in her conversations with people. All the Errols (with the exception of Errol II, who had poor concentration and limited empathy) were good listeners. They would cock their heads intelligently and look into her face with bright, sympathetic eyes. They would place a paw on her knee when she was sad, and whimper if the conversation flagged. They were perfect companions for an ageing lady who avoided the company of her own kind. Sandy kept up the supply of Errols, a small thing to do for his mother's sister, he thought.

It was Errol III, Lily swore, who gave her the idea of the tea cosies. As the number of music pupils dwindled, she had more time on her hands and decided, after discussing it with her dog, that she would do something good—undertake some grand endeavour for the betterment of mankind.

'I don't want to die having done nothing of note,' she said to the nodding Errol. 'The one useful thing I did at that place—' she couldn't bear to say its name—'the one useful thing I did was learn to knit tea cosies. And Errol, old boy, humanity shall benefit.' And so began her long association with the United Nations through the self-appointed quartermaster, Lusala Ngilu.

8

Mrs Pargetter and Lusala Ngilu

WHILE MRS PARGETTER AND ERROL III discussed the details, a young man, newly arrived in New York, was nervously presenting his credentials to a frowning official.

'Lusala Ngilu, University of Nairobi, Kenya,' he said. 'I'm here for the internship.' A diffident young man, with serious eyes and a slight facial tic, he had been chosen from his year at the University of Nairobi to work in the office of the United Nations. He wore one of the crisp white shirts his mother had lovingly starched and folded, and the silk tie his father had given him before he left. He looked at the other man's tie and wondered if his were not too colourful. The official's eyes strayed to Lusala's chest, and the young man almost apologised. *A present from my father*, he could have said with a smile that would show him to be a man of the world. Shamed to have even thought this, Lusala flushed. His father was a good man, worthy of respect.

After a brief orientation, he was sent to the mailroom, where, some weeks later, he opened the first consignment of tea cosies with Mrs Pargetter's letter.

23 Mitchell St
Opportunity
Victoria
Australia

Quartermaster
United Nations
New York
United States of America

Dear Sir,

Please find enclosed one dozen assorted tea cosies to be distributed amongst the world's poor as you or the Secretary General sees fit. It is my aim to send these every year around September. As I have no family to knit for, I expect to be able to send around one hundred in each parcel.

You may save some for yourself and your colleagues, although I imagine that you have all the necessary supplies. I would expect that no more than half a dozen, preferably from the next consignment, would be used in this manner.

Hoping this finds you well as it leaves me.

Yours faithfully,

Lily Pargetter (Mrs)

Nonplussed, Lusala took the parcel and letter to his boss, a dour little man in a black waistcoat.

'Excuse me, Mr Kennedy. Who is the quartermaster?' Lusala asked, handing him the letter and the parcel, which he had clumsily rewrapped. A knitted object fell onto the desk. Kennedy picked it up and stared at it.

'What on earth is this?'

'It's a tea cosy. You know, to keep teapots warm.'

'And why is it on my desk?'

At Lusala's request he read the letter.

'Some batty old dame. Throw them in the waste basket. Unless you need one.' He sniggered. 'I'm a coffee drinker myself.'

The young man obediently disposed of the parcel in the waste bin where it lay, exuding reproach. He retrieved a blue and yellow cosy for himself and felt slightly better. When Kennedy went to lunch, Lusala could stand it no longer and mounted a rescue, stuffing the bundle into his desk drawer, where it continued to brood for a week. Lusala was a business student, but he had imagination, and could clearly see an old lady knitting somewhere in a strange land. He saw her earnestly composing her letter, and imagined her smile as she dropped her parcel in the letterbox. He thought of his grandmother. And he stole some letterhead.

> *Dear Mrs Pargetter,*
>
> *Thank you for your extreme kindness in knitting tea cosies for the poor of the world. The Secretary General has asked me to thank you on his behalf. They are most welcome.*
>
> *Yours sincerely,*
> *Lusala Ngilu*
> *Quartermaster*
> *United Nations Organization*

Before his eighteen-month internship was over, Lusala wrote one more letter of thanks, folded it into a United

Nations Christmas card and then passed the baton to his successor, Ahmed Hussein, who passed it in turn to Cecile Piquet. As each new intern arrived, they would be briefed on the tea cosies.

'It's like a rite of passage—even a good luck ritual,' Andrew Nicholls told his successor, Chang Kyong-sil. 'Apparently it started way back when the current Kenyan Ambassador to the UN was a mail clerk. We always sign the letter Lusala Ngilu, Quartermaster. It's part of the continuity. This Mrs Pargetter must be about a hundred and eighty by now. Some of us even wonder if she's the same one who started it all.'

'What happens to the tea cosies?' Chang Kyong-sil was a practical young woman.

'That's the challenge. Apparently most of the first lot went to countries that drink tea, although some were distributed around the UN complex. The second "Lusala" sewed up the holes and sent them to a hill tribe in China for hats. They've been used to incubate eggs. And so on. My solution was to use them for the safe packing of medical supplies.'

Chang looked thoughtful. 'And no-one thinks this is strange?'

'Strange, yes. But comforting, somehow. It's a bit of old-fashioned kindness in a world where kindness is not valued nearly enough.'

Two months later, Chang wrote her letter and carefully signed the name Lusala Ngilu in a fair copy of the original. As she despatched the cosies, metamorphosed now into foot warmers, she felt a quiet sense of achievement. The following year, around the time Mrs Pargetter was making scones for Moss and Finn, Ana Sejka became the next Lusala, and listened with special interest to Chang's briefing.

'This Mrs Pargetter is Australian,' she murmured. 'I wonder where Opportunity is, exactly.'

9

Opportunity and Cradletown

OPPORTUNITY WEEKES WAS BORN ON the Californian gold-fields. His father, Jeremiah, was an itinerant preacher with smouldering eyes, a beard that rivalled Abraham's and a voice that could waken the dead. His mother, formerly Miss Clementine Witherspoon, was the eighth daughter of a Kansas crop farmer whom God had previously afflicted with seven plain daughters to marry off as best he could. The charming blonde Clementine was his only hope of a prosperous old age, and Farmer Witherspoon was understandably devastated when his lovely youngest daughter ran away at the age of seventeen to marry Jeremiah.

Perhaps it was the curse the farmer sent after them, or maybe it was his daughter's rebellious nature, but after Jeremiah's mesmeric eyes lost their power over her, Clementine ran away again, this time to join the eclectic band of young women in Miss Kitty's brothel. There she worked, watched and listened until she felt her education was sufficient to strike out on her own.

Before she left her husband she bore a child, whom Jeremiah insisted they name Opportunity, *in gratitude to God's gifts to all of us.* Jeremiah was of a faith that believed that once a person is 'saved', they become worthy not only of heavenly reward but also of worldly treasures. He could not make this point strongly enough to his congregation, and they obligingly cooperated with God's plan by contributing generously to his ministry. Jeremiah and Clementine both had a head for business.

When California became infected with news of gold in the faraway colony of Victoria, the preacher decided to take his son to a new land where the stain of his mother's occupation would never more blight his young life. Being of a dramatic disposition, he wrote to Clementine before he left, informing her that he was *removing his spotless lamb from the foul odour of his mother's scarlet sins.* There was also mention of the Whore of Babylon and the bold opinion that Jesus should never have stopped the mob from stoning the adulteress. He concluded: *I remain Your Obedient Servant, Jeremiah C. Weekes.* He felt a good deal better for this, and left for the colony with a light heart and a mission to convert the wicked and sustain the faithful who sought their fortune in the rich soil of the Victorian goldfields.

Young Opportunity was eleven by then, and not the appealing waif he once had been. Ungainly, his fast-growing limbs clumsy and graceless, he slouched and sulked while his father attempted to preach to men who, unlike his compatriots, could not or would not abandon themselves to the Spirit. If they came to his meetings at all, they came to stare stonily, to jeer or to laugh. Some would even pretend to feel the Spirit and stagger about gabbling in tongues, providing the small crowd with much merriment. Jeremiah hated these exhibitionists, but at least after such diversions a few people would good-naturedly make a small offering at collection time.

However, it was not enough to support him and his boy. They spent their days working on a small claim, and the evenings passed with Jeremiah teaching an increasingly resistant Opportunity his letters and numbers.

As more families and women came and businesses were established, the canvas town reached a critical mass, and serious building began. The streets of fine shops and dwellings, the ornate town hall and the several beautiful churches for which the town is now admired all owe their existence to the gold fever. The thriving settlement was named Cradletown in honour of the wooden cradle used by miners to separate the gold from the dross. When the Cradletown Methodist church was built, Jeremiah, weary of life on the goldfields, managed to secure the position of minister. Every Sunday his rich voice thundered wonderfully, exciting fear and trembling in the hearts of the wicked and thrilling misgivings in the hearts of the faithful.

Opportunity worked soberly as a sales assistant in McPherson's Drapery and Women's Apparel, his bony wrists protruding from white cuffs that in turn protruded from a blue pinstriped jacket. He sold linen handkerchiefs, lace collars and cuffs, jabots and shawls, gloves and hatpins. (Mrs McPherson herself sold the hats.) Drapery would seem to be a dull job for a young man, but it had its compensations, and his time passed pleasantly enough as young and not so young women came to buy their fripperies and flirt with him in a genteel sort of way.

Two days before his eighteenth birthday a stranger arrived at McPherson's, asking to speak to young Mister Weekes. The man had a sallow complexion and jowls like a bloodhound, but after hearing what he had to say, Opportunity could have hugged him. The stranger was a solicitor who had traced him to Cradletown all the way from San Francisco, where his mother had died of heart failure. She had left him—*after expenses, you understand*—the considerable sum of one thousand, three hundred and eleven US dollars, to be paid when he reached his majority.

For three years and two days, Opportunity chafed. On his twenty-first birthday, he resigned from McPherson's. He hadn't wasted this time, saving an additional sixty-seven pounds from his wages. Despite liberal advice to the contrary, Opportunity Weekes was ready to realise his dream.

About a hundred and fifty miles to the north of Cradletown was another goldfield town, Mystic, and bullockies, traders and disgruntled miners had worn a wide track between the two centres. Opportunity's plan was to build a hotel at Halfway Creek, providing accommodation and refreshments for the weary travellers. After a short battle with his conscience, he decided to also sell liquor. *Your mother's bad blood*, his father mourned. But the young man had his mother's business brain, and he set about building a handsome, two-storey pub with verandahs all round and a brass spittoon in the bar.

Opportunity focused on this vision as he rolled up his sleeves and worked beside the men who laboured to build his dream. He drove them hard but paid them well, and when it was finished, they were all justifiably proud of their handiwork. The hotel welcomed its first guest in 1885, and thus began a long period of prosperity for both Opportunity and the burgeoning township.

As his business flourished, Opportunity realised that he needed help, and he proposed to Harriet Westlake, a local farmer's daughter, as sturdy and loyal as she was plain. She accepted him, and the pub flourished as the reputation of Harriet's lamb roasts and plum puddings spread and Opportunity mellowed into an affable middle age.

The little town that grew around the Opportunity Hostelry was named for its founder. As he became a wealthy man, Opportunity's only sorrow was the loss of two baby girls, Faith and Hope, who had been named and christened by his father. A third daughter was born, with sad dark eyes, and having lost both faith and hope, Opportunity called her Dolour. *A popish name*, Jeremiah fumed as he immersed the child. *It means sorrow*, his son replied. *I won't tempt God again.*

But Dolour was the happiest and healthiest of children, with her mother's strong body and her father's deep, dark eyes. Over time, the area gradually transmuted into farmland, and at eighteen, Dolour married Charles Sandilands, son of a local farmer. When Opportunity died, Dolour and Charles sold the pub and established the Sandilands dynasty in a fine house on an expanded property.

The good citizens of Opportunity had suggested erecting a stained-glass window as a memorial to her father, but the practical Dolour said that the town was named for him and that should be enough. *What on earth would Father want with a window?* she said.

In its golden years, Opportunity boasted five hotels, several sly grog establishments and three brothels; by the time it began sending its young men to the trenches, however, it had become a very proper town with three churches and a school replacing four of the pubs.

Like many small towns, Opportunity was proud and somewhat insular, sniffing ever so slightly at the brashness of Mystic and the pomposity of Cradletown. The latter was always called 'Town' with an implied upper-case T. The former was simply referred to as 'That Place'. The good folk of Opportunity kept themselves to themselves, and generations were born and buried within the town's boundaries.

The nineteen sixties saw the beginning of its decline, when the young people, no longer content to be farmers, were lured to the cities to join the counter-culture. Some stayed; some returned; but change gathered pace in the eighties, when the economic rationalists began to seriously dismantle rural infrastructure. It was then that the busy farmers and traders of Opportunity looked up and saw that their town was dying. The bank, the farmers' co-op and McKenzie's bakery all closed within a year, with the loss of over forty jobs. Families moved to larger centres to find work so the school failed to maintain sufficient numbers. Even church services were rationed when the parish of St Saviour's was merged with St Matthew's in Mystic. By the mid nineties, Opportunity no longer lived up to its name.

Most of the farmers managed well enough during the eighties and early nineties, but now, after ten years of drought, a fatal lethargy held the town in thrall. It seeped out of the mud in the dying creek. It sent out tendrils that choked endeavour. It whispered in the ears of sleepers who thought themselves safe in bed. It loitered in the dust that hung in the air, or swirled ahead of the winds that swept unimpeded across a treeless landscape. You could see it in the eyes of your neighbours. You could taste it in your beer.

10

Sandy and the Great Galah

SANDY SANDILANDS WAS NEARLY SIXTY and he loved his home town. If asked what there was to love about Opportunity, he couldn't have given a rational reply. The blood of Opportunity Weekes still ran strong in the veins of this, the last of his heirs. It was his family's town, Sandy would say if pressed. What he would not say was that he felt responsible; that there was a sort of *noblesse oblige* arising from both his wealth and his heritage. That he was barely tolerated by his neighbours made no difference. The damaged child had become a stubborn man with a mission.

Rosie's son was christened George Francis for his father and maternal grandfather. There was the usual household confusion that occurs when father and son share names. 'Georgie' didn't work. It reminded the Major of the old nursery rhyme and the days when he was the target. *Georgie Porgie, puddin' and pie*, the boys chanted. *Kissed the girls and made them cry.* (*Well, that was prophetic*, Lily always thought. She remembered George Sandilands from primary school days.) Rosie was afraid to suggest 'Frank', so when his aunt commented on his red-gold curls, 'Sandy' seemed like a good option, echoing his surname as it did.

Sandy spent most of his childhood feeling fear and shame: fear of his father's violence, and shame that he failed to protect his mother. In later life he excused himself; after all, he was just a child—no physical match for the Major. He knew, but refused to acknowledge, that this was not the whole truth. For Sandy was not merely a passive spectator of his mother's abuse but was shamefully complicit. He was hers until he learned that discretion was the better part of valour, and as he grew older, he began to speak to her in the disparaging tone used by his father. He would snigger at the insults and caustic remarks that were his mother's lot, and while, unlike his father, he never resorted to physical violence, he was aware that he wounded her deeply.

At the same time, he was anguished by her pain, and longed to be able to protect her. He suppressed his love but penitentially ate the food she prepared, his lean young body growing rounder with each passing year. He accepted as due punishment his father's cruel jibes and the scorn of his schoolmates (Fatty Arbuckle, they called him). Mercifully, he was sent away to board for his senior schooling, after which he completed a commerce degree in Melbourne. For a while he was free, and even dreamed of a future in a merchant bank, but at his father's command he timidly returned home.

When his mother died, it was, shamefully, a burden lifted. When his father died a few years later, Sandy set about reinventing his childhood; in time he constructed a father endowed with a dry wit and a clever turn of phrase. *Fair enough, he could be impatient and hot-tempered*, Sandy would say, *but I was a bit of a scallywag and poor old Mum wasn't too bright. Dad would call me a galah if I did something crazy as boys do. It was like a nickname.* And the local sycophants would chuckle into their beer. But his father had been universally loathed as an arrogant bully. Old Minnie Porter remembered poor Rosie, white and tense at her husband's side.

'Major Bully-boy Sandilands. Drove his wife to her grave, God rest her soul. Thought he was too good for the rest of us. Mark my words, that youngster will turn out the same.'

So 'the youngster' inherited the general antipathy felt for his father, and his reverence for the Major only made things worse.

Sandy didn't have friends but socialised with three or four hangers-on. The dislike was mutual. He was, as Finn had told Moss, the richest man in the district. When his father died he sold most of the land, keeping only the house and a few acres on which he ran some cattle. Agriculture was booming then, so he realised considerable capital. While the other landholders sneered—*Hasn't got the guts to be a farmer*—Sandy began to study the stock market and invested in blue-chip shares as well as some speculative mining companies in Western Australia. He had pre-empted the mining boom by a few years and, while the farming community watched as drought wizened their land, Sandy was busy minimising tax on his share-trading profits.

He spent much of his time indoors, skilfully day trading online, and his large, white body contrasted sharply with the sinewy brownness of his neighbours. He held his beer glass with soft, clean hands, nails innocent of dirt, palms innocent of calluses. He was despised by the people of the district even as they drank his beer and accepted the cheques and the many trophies he donated to the various sporting and social clubs. The final straw came when he sold the farm. At least as a farmer he had some point of contact with his peers. But who ever heard of a day trader?

There's something shonky about making money that way, Merv Randall, the publican, would say to his customers. They all agreed. *Swanning around in those poncy shirts*, they said. *Look at his hands. Hasn't done a day's work in years*, they muttered. *The law'll catch up with him eventually*, they agreed, downing their beers in satisfaction at the thought.

As usual, it was Tom Ferguson, farmer and bush philosopher, who summed up the mood of the meeting. 'I'd rather do an honest day's work—mortgage, drought and all—than piss about on a computer all day. I don't care how much money he makes.'

A lonely man, Sandy wanted to be liked and admired, and not long before Moss's arrival in Opportunity, he devised his Great Plan.

He had gone to Finn for advice. By this time the enigmatic Finn was held somewhat in awe by the people of Opportunity. His arrival had caused a little flurry of excitement and curiosity, and it wasn't long before a small contingent of women arrived at his front door with baskets. He thanked them gravely for the scones, the sponge cake and the chicken casserole. He assured them that the eggs and chutney would be useful, and that he would indeed see them around. They left to report on his posh voice, his nice manners and his wonderful blue eyes. *So sad, his eyes. Sort of tragic, you know?* Their men snorted derisively, but allowed him to be a decent sort of bloke.

Unlike other newcomers to small towns, Finn made no effort to secure friendships or forge contacts. He went about, nodding pleasantly, resisting all efforts to pry. He didn't attend church, was not seen at the weekly film and, despite his enviable height, regretfully declined to play in the ruck for the Knockers. No, he didn't play cricket either, he told the local president, but would probably come to a few matches. This intransigence would have been fatal for any other new arrival, but Finn had such an abstracted air that the residents of Opportunity chose to treat him as a nice old man, although they could see he was probably only in his late thirties.

'Funny bloke,' Merv observed to his regulars. 'When I asked him about playing for the Knockers, I thought he'd jump at the chance. I know he's skinny, but he's even taller than young Bob Corless . . . *How about it?* I ask him. *We need another ruckman.* He just says, *Thanks very much for asking, but I don't play football.* Just like that. Polite as pie—but . . .' Merv shook his head. 'It's like he's—it's hard to put a finger on it . . . it's like . . .'

'Like he's an island,' Tom Ferguson offered.

'Exactly. You're dead right, Tom. An island.'

They approved of his concern for his neighbour, Mrs Pargetter, relieving them as it did from responsibility. But they were surprised and aggrieved when Finn befriended Sandy. How could that nice Finn take to Sandy Sandilands?

Finn didn't actually go out of his way to befriend him, of course, but Sandy was a dutiful nephew to his Aunt Lily, and so it was inevitable that he and Finn should eventually meet. When Finn first arrived, Sandy was away, so it was nearly two months before this happened. Finn was working on Mrs Pargetter's vegie patch when her nephew arrived with Errol VI.

'Dog. For Aunt Lily,' puffed Sandy. 'She'll call it Errol. Always does.' He thrust out his hand. 'George Sandilands. Call me Sandy. I'm her nephew,' he added unnecessarily. 'I come in every now and then to see how the old girl's doing. She talks to her dog, you know. Last one died a couple of months ago, while I was away. Time for a new one.' He looked at Finn expectantly.

'Good dog,' Finn said, stooping to pat the shaggy head. 'Nice to meet you, Errol.'

That's how Finn came to have a weekly cup of tea with Mrs Pargetter and her despised nephew. Sandy did most of the talking, but that was alright. The other two were good listeners, and Sandy somehow felt more valued in Finn's presence. There was no blame or scorn in the dark blue eyes that regarded him with such courteous attention. Finn hadn't known the Major, hadn't known Rosie, and Sandy could be more who he was, who he wanted to be, with Finn.

Finn, in turn, tolerated Sandy for his neighbour's sake but found the big man's garrulousness irksome. His morning teas with Mrs Pargetter had been quiet affairs. They discussed the weather, the garden, her knitting. There were many comfortable silences. Now here was her nephew, full of his own importance, dominating the conversation.

In fairness, Finn had to admit Sandy was good to his aunt. He would hover around her solicitously: *Do you want me to stoke up the fire, Aunt Lily? Can I get you something from the shops? I'll send Macca around to fix that switch.* While Mrs

Pargetter tended to be ungracious (*Stop fussing, Sandy*, she'd say irritably), Finn would notice the warring emotions that passed over her face when her nephew came in.

'He was such a pretty little boy—copper curls just like his mother,' she told Finn once. 'And the sweetest smile. When he went to boarding school we couldn't wait for the holidays. I'd make him a nice cream sponge. He loved passionfruit icing. *Aunt Lily*, he'd say, *I've been waiting all term for your passionfruit cream sponge.* He'd tuck away at least two slices,' she continued with satisfaction. 'He always had a good appetite—' She broke off abruptly. 'Well, that was then and this is now. Time does strange things to people.' She couldn't forgive him for his betrayal of Rosie, which she had watched with increasing dismay as the years passed.

Finn was returning with his newspaper one day when Sandy pulled up in his dusty BMW. Ambivalent about whether he wanted to impress or fit in, Sandy drove a luxury car but didn't clean it. Half the topsoil of the Opportunity district camouflaged its dark blue duco.

'Do you mind if we have a word, mate?'

Finn did mind but stepped aside for the other man, who was already bustling through the gate, brandishing a roll of paper.

'Tea? Coffee? I don't have any beer.'

'Not to worry. Tea'll do.' And Sandy cleared a space on the kitchen table to spread out the roll of paper, arranging a sugar bowl, an ashtray and two books to hold down the corners. 'There,' he said. 'What do you think? This is just a draft, of course.'

Finn squinted in bafflement at the sketches. 'Just a draft, then?'

'Yep. Once I get the concept right, I'll call in proper engineers and such. Just wanted to know what you thought.'

'Er, I'd need to know the detail. It's . . . still a concept, you say?'

Sandy finally took the hint. 'Sorry, mate. I'm getting ahead of myself. You know the Big Banana, the Big Pineapple, the Big Merino and so on? Well, this is the Great Galah. It'll be the making of the town. Tourists love that kind of stuff.'

Finn looked more closely at the sketches. Yes, there was no mistaking; it was a large, unwieldy-looking bird, its giant wings outspread. He struggled for a response. 'Any reason for a galah? Aren't they seen as a bit of a pest?'

'That's the beauty of it. This area is full of galahs. They drive the farmers crazy. What I'm doing is turning a negative into a positive.' He beamed. 'In the future, we're talking theme park. Big money. Serious money.'

Could Sandy be for real? Finn listened for irony and heard only enthusiasm. He needed to find a respectful but discouraging response. 'The town could certainly do with some help. But is this the way to go? The Big Banana and Pineapple are up north, with beaches and that sort of thing.' He brightened as a foolproof objection presented itself. 'I doubt that we'd get funding in a place like this.'

'Not a problem. It would be my gift to the town. A memorial to my father, Major Sandilands, DSO and Bar.' It was a cool day, but he mopped his forehead with a large handkerchief and went on: 'My family were pioneers of this district, you know. Been here since the gold rush. But now all the young people are leaving. We don't have many families left in town, and some of the farmers are close to broke.' He looked soberly at his friend. 'I don't want the town to die, Finn. It's my home.'

Moved in spite of himself, and racking his brains for something to say, Finn looked back at the sketch for inspiration. Steps led up into the belly region, where a door was labelled SOUVENIR SHOP. There was what appeared to be a corkscrew slide from head to tail, terminating in a swimming pool. Tables and umbrellas sprouted under one wing and there seemed to be a kind of lookout in the beak. The space under the second wing bore a question mark.

'Nothing under the second wing, then?' Finn was relieved to find something to say.

'Not yet. Maybe we could run a competition. You know, so locals can have some input.'

Finn imagined the kind of input locals would offer. He weighed his words carefully. 'A very interesting idea, Sandy. Challenging. Maybe a bit, you know, *innovative* for Opportunity? You might need to bide your time. Take things slowly.'

Since then Sandy had visited Finn several times to discuss revisions to his sketches. Finn knew he had to tell Sandy just how ridiculous his plan really was. *Next time*, he'd say to himself. *Next time I'll tell him straight.* And next time he'd look into Sandy's naively hopeful eyes and his courage would fail him. 'I just couldn't bring myself to crush the man's dream,' Finn explained to Moss as they returned from the pub with Mrs Pargetter. 'I suggested he keep it under wraps and we'd talk about it until the idea is fully fleshed out. I should've stopped things right there, that first day, but to be honest, I'm too much of a coward.'

'That boy has always been a bit soft in the head, if you ask me,' sniffed Mrs Pargetter. 'His father was right: he *is* a great galah.'

'He has his good points.' Finn thought of the dogs, the knitting wool that appeared regularly in Mrs Pargetter's letterbox, and the money left under the teapot after her nephew's visits. But he didn't say anything about those things. Not even to Moss.

The next day, Sandy spread his plans out once more on Finn's table. The frayed edges betrayed the many other unfoldings these plans had endured in the loneliness of Sandy's sprawling farmhouse.

'Can't you see, Finn? Tourism is the only way to save a town like ours. The Balfours are leaving next week. We're bleeding people, mate.'

Finn sighed. 'I like the quiet. That's why I came here. I'm sorry, but I just can't see tourist buses lined up in the footy ground car park.' He tried a comradely grin.

The footy ground was a sore point, and Sandy looked up sharply. 'Better tourist buses than to see the oval unused. Since the Knockers merged with the Mystic Wombats it's become a wasteland. I played cricket there in my young days. And footy. Only the Seconds, but I did my bit. I bet you didn't know that Dad won the Best and Fairest award three times? Even the trophy was named in honour of my grandfather, Nugget Sandilands. They reckon he won the 1912 grand final off his own boot.'

Finn tried to concentrate but was becoming annoyed at the incursions this man was making into his life. He shook his head in despair. The wretched plans were more elaborate than ever.

He suddenly tuned in to what Sandy was saying. 'The shire engineer? You've submitted the plans to the shire engineer?'

'Honestly, Finn. Sometimes I wonder if you listen to a word I say. Tomorrow. I'm meeting with him tomorrow, in Cradletown. He's had the plans for weeks.'

Finn felt the weight of responsibility begin to lift. The shire engineer could be the assassin.

'So you can come, then, Finn? I'll pick you up at ten thirty.' And he was gone before Finn could think of an excuse.

The shire engineer was an ambitious young man, totally devoid of imagination. His grave demeanour and careful grooming were evidence that he took both himself and his position very seriously indeed. He shook hands gravely, with just the right amount of pressure to assert his authority.

Pompous git, thought Finn as they were ushered into the office.

Smugly ensconced behind his large desk, the shire engineer sat back and steepled his fingers. 'So, Mr Sandilands. You want to build a tourist attraction.' He referred to his notes and frowned. 'A tourist attraction called, er, the Great Galah. And these,' he indicated the blueprints, 'are your plans.'

Sandy started to speak, but was silenced by a gesture. 'I'm afraid I cannot approve these plans, Mr Sandilands . . .'

Finn felt both pity and relief. Sandy would take it hard, but at least he wouldn't be humiliated.

The engineer continued: '... I cannot approve them until certain safety aspects are dealt with.'

Finn stared in disbelief. *What did he say?*

'I understand all that. This is just the concept stage,' Sandy said. 'Once I know the regulations, I'll have them drawn up by a proper engineer.'

'I will give your project every consideration,' said the smug young man. 'My job is to ensure all building and safety regulations are in place. Then I pass it on to the town planner and then to the business subcommittee ...'

'You mean, Mr Sandilands could invest in fully developed plans and have town planning or the business subcommittee knock it back?'

'That's the system, Mr ...'

Finn just stared at him and the young man was forced to refer again to his notes.

'That's the system, Mr Clancy. It has served us well until now.' He gathered his papers and stood up. 'Thank you for coming, Mr Sandilands; Mr Clancy. I look forward to the next stage of your project.'

Finn groaned inwardly. *Project! Now this crazy scheme was a project!*

Sandy babbled excitedly all the way home and Finn was required to say little. 'Bloody engineer,' he swore softly to himself more than once. 'Officious, smart-arsed engineer.'

Sandy stopped at one of Cradletown's bakeries and bought a cream sponge and several iced doughnuts.

'We'll celebrate with Aunt Lily and Moss,' he said, climbing back into the car. He grinned broadly. 'Plenty to celebrate, mate. I think we can safely say that we've passed stage one.'

Finn shook his head in disbelief. So now it was not only a project but had a stage one, implying God knows how many other stages. He had to disentangle himself somehow before it became public knowledge.

When Sandy burst in with the news, Moss was privately stunned but his aunt was sanguine.

'I must admit that I thought it was a silly notion at first, but if the shire engineer thinks it's a good idea . . .' The old lady trailed off vaguely. 'Well, it must be a good idea, mustn't it?'

Finn bit into his sponge slice and tried another tack. 'Your Memorial Park project's coming on nicely, Sandy,' he said. 'You need to be sure this other thing doesn't take your time from that.'

Moss remembered the green oasis and the cenotaph. 'What project's that, Sandy?'

'Well, when the lawns started to die and we weren't allowed to water, I brought in synthetic turf . . .'

'Synthetic turf?' Nothing was quite what it seemed.

Sandy shrugged. 'No other solution, as far as I could see. Some people objected, but once the lawns died off completely, the council gave the go-ahead. Helen Porter and the girls from the Country Women's have done some replanting of the gardens with drought-resistant shrubs. A couple of them use some of their waste water on the trees.'

'So there are some people who haven't given up, then?' said Moss.

'Really it's just me, Helen and one or two others. Everyone cares, but the job just seems too big, so a lot of them have given up trying. They're happy enough to survive, but I want more. I want us to *progress*.'

The other three looked at Sandy. A visionary without charisma. An eccentric with a passion. An obese, sweaty giant with a tiny voice and lonely eyes. *A little boy who was broken by his father*, thought Mrs Pargetter. *A kind man who keeps Errol alive and fills my letterbox with wool.* She patted his arm.

'Have another doughnut,' she offered. And he heard echoes of his mother, Rosie.

II

Jilly Baker and Amber-Lee

JILLY'S MOTHER, PATTY, HAD BEEN a wilful child, and with the onset of puberty she became uncontrollable. Her family were 'nice', as people say, and her parents spent many sleepless nights wondering if she'd been raped and pushed off the pier or had crashed on one of the motorbikes that revved impatiently outside the house as she applied another coat of mascara. They felt an odd relief, then, when they found out she was pregnant, at the age of seventeen, to a nineteen-year-old apprentice carpenter.

'This will slow her down,' her parents agreed. 'She's a bit wild, but a good girl, really. And he does have a steady job.'

His family were less pleased, but in a manner that harked back to another era, the young couple were married in Blackpool at St Stephen-on-the-Cliffs while the bride still had a waist. Patty was radiant in white, and her mother tearful in violet. Her sister, Ellen, was sceptical in cerise chiffon.

Jillian Maree was born seven months later, and the young parents were delighted to show off their pretty daughter. But despite her parents' optimism, Patty failed to settle down to motherhood. The wedding and the birth had only temporarily satisfied her need for attention and excitement, and domestic life in Blackpool left her irritable and discontented, her love for her baby being tenuous at best. Fortunately for the child she had a sweet little face, and Patty would play at dressing her, sometimes changing her clothes four or five times before she was satisfied. Her parents took comfort in the fact that at least she was giving her daughter some attention.

Her young husband would come home to find that his wife had bought an expensive new dress for their daughter and one for herself in a matching colour.

'We can't afford to spend that sort of money on clothes,' he would say, holding his wife's hand. 'When I finish my apprenticeship we'll be fine, but for now . . .'

Patty would pull her hand away. 'Well, I'm sorry if I want our daughter to look nice. Thank goodness one of us loves her.'

But Andy Baker did love his daughter. He had loved her from the moment he saw her wizened little newborn face; he loved the way she crawled to the door when she heard his key in the lock; he loved the way she giggled when he blew on her tummy. She was his little Jilly-muffin, and when he bent over her cot to kiss her goodnight he felt his chest tighten with love and fear.

Like Moss, Jilly's earliest memory was of the seaside. It was a mild summer day, and her parents took her for a paddle and ice-cream at Blackpool Pier. Her Aunty Ellen and family came with them. Jilly's cousin Meg brought her dog, a King Charles spaniel called Mr Pie, a puzzling name that seven-year-old Meg had insisted upon. They asked a passerby to take their photo; this would be the only memento that Jilly had of her childhood. There they were, holding ice-creams in various stages of consumption. Her mother pouted and posed in her denim shorts and halter-neck top. Aunty Ellen was holding baby Matthew, and Meg was grinning down at Mr Pie. Uncle Harry was scratching his ear, and her father, a dark-haired young man of twenty-four, was holding Jilly's hand. She remembered the strawberry ice-cream and the warmth of her father's body. She remembered how, later, he put her up on his shoulders and danced with her along the pier. She'd been afraid of the clown. He had a scary white face and false red smile.

No-one understood why Patty took Jilly with her when she left. Perhaps it was to spite Andy. Maybe, at the last minute, some maternal feeling prevailed. Nevertheless, she had Jilly with her when she disappeared with a New Zealand tourist called Brad.

Family relationships are complex, and it was almost with a sense of reprieve that her parents realised that Patty was now beyond their assistance. They felt a burden lift as they came to understand that they would no longer have to justify her actions or bear witness to the daily evidence of her selfishness. But they could not so easily reconcile themselves to the loss of Jilly. She had been a happy and affectionate little soul and they missed her dreadfully, mourning her as though she were dead.

Andy Baker had accepted some time ago that he no longer loved Patty. He didn't even like her much, and would have celebrated her desertion if it weren't for the fact that she took their daughter—his daughter—with her. He was nearly mad with grief. Coming home from work with the forlorn hope that she might have returned, he would pause at the front door and listen in vain for the sound of her little voice calling to him: *Is that you, Daddy? Here I are, Daddy.* And his arms ached to swing her up, and his face longed to feel her soft little cheek against his. He spent every spare penny trying to locate her.

He finally tracked them down to Sydney, where Patty and Jilly were living with a new man, Serg. Court orders were issued giving him access to his daughter, but Patty was always on the move and changed her name many times. The trail had gone cold by the time Patty—now calling herself Monique Tyler—and her daughter finally settled in Perth with Brian who, unlike Patty's other lovers, tried to be a father to Jilly.

Jilly had pined for her own father, of course, and Patty judged it wiser to tell her that he'd died. *In a car accident*, she had explained. *You mustn't be sad, though. You have Mummy and Brad* (then Craig, Harry, and so on).

Meanwhile, Andy had begun to drink. He would come home from work, pause at the door and then head for the fridge, gulping down a can of beer before heating up a pork pie or sending out for a pizza. Some nights, if he remembered, he'd bring home cod and chips. Whatever he ate, it was always washed down with a couple of cans of beer, and he'd drink another three or four before falling into his bed, never quite drunk enough. The house he'd been lovingly renovating fell into disrepair. His days were grey and his nights black. On Jilly's birthday each year, he'd get very drunk and cry. He always imagined her as she was when he had last seen her. For him, she was forever five years old.

Far away, in Perth, Jilly was beginning to dare to feel safe when, after nearly two years of relative security, she and her mother were alone again. It was usually Patty who ended relationships, but this time it was Brian who left.

'I'm sorry, Jilly,' he said. 'If I were your dad, I'd take you with me.'

'Yeah,' said fourteen-year-old Jilly. 'Whatever.' But she hugged him briefly and took the money he gave her.

'Don't waste it, Jilly. It's for an emergency,' he said. 'For God's sake don't let Patty know you have it.'

Jilly hid the money, of course. She had learned not to trust her mother.

After Brian left, life returned to normal: more parties, more men, and school shoes with holes. One day, shortly after her fifteenth birthday, Jilly came home from school to find a note on the kitchen table.

Dear Jilly

Im off to France with Dominik. Your old enough to look after yourself now and I need a life of my own Im only 33. The rents overdue but Ill send you some money when I'm setled. I left $10 to buy a pizza for your tea. I took your black jumper and red shirt. I'll need them til Dominik can by me some new clothe's.

Love

Patty

Since Jilly turned twelve she was no longer allowed to call Patty 'Mum'. They looked more like sisters, Patty thought. And she was right.

Children of such parents learn survival skills, and Jilly knew that once the authorities discovered she was living alone, she'd be put into foster care. Patty had always threatened her with a foster home as a priest might threaten his congregation with hell. She packed the few clothes she had left, stuffed her mother's note and pizza money into her pocket, and went to the shed where she'd hidden Brian's hundred dollars and a little box of mementos. When the school checked a couple of weeks later, it was assumed that the family had absconded to avoid the rent.

To conserve her money, Jilly decided to hitch to Melbourne. She thought it best to go to a larger city, where no-one knew her—where she could melt into the crowd.

Patty, meanwhile, had left France for Dominik's native Bucharest where, sitting behind a desk in a bright modern office, she stamped the papers of gullible Rumanian girls who wanted to work in London. The job paid well and she enjoyed herself for a time. Unfortunately, when she decided to move on, she met with a fatal and uninvestigated accident. She knew too much and Dominik took no risks.

'So what's your name then, love?' The truck driver leaned over and opened the door. He liked a bit of company.

Jilly was prepared. She had learnt caution from an expert. 'Amber-Lee,' she said without blinking. 'I'm going to Melbourne to see my cousin.'

'I'm going as far as Adelaide. We'll stop on the border for a bit of a kip.' He bought her coffee and a doughnut in Southern

Cross and an evening meal in Norseman. When he wasn't talking, he would sing along to a country and western CD, of which he had an endless supply.

Jilly wasn't surprised to find that when he pulled over for his 'kip', he slid his hands between her legs. As she approached puberty, her mother's boyfriends, with the exception of Brian, had all tried, more or less successfully, to have sex with her. This was one of the reasons that Patty felt it prudent to leave her behind. A nubile young daughter could get seriously in the way.

'You *are* sixteen?' the driver said as he pulled at her buttons and slid her bra straps down her arms. Her small breasts were white and strangely vulnerable. He paused and looked at her face, still and watchful in the shadows. He wasn't a bad man. For a moment, he felt something like remorse.

'You *are* sixteen?' he repeated, seeking reassurance.

'Just get on with it,' she said wearily. 'I'm tired.'

He took her then, brutally. And pushed her and her belongings out of the truck when he'd finished.

'You'll get another ride. A lot of trucks stop here.' Ashamed, he threw some crumpled notes out of the window after her. Jilly stooped and picked up the money, stuffing it hastily into her backpack. She sat on the embankment and, childlike, dug her fists into her eyes. A little shuddering sob escaped. She'd come to expect no better, but that didn't mean she enjoyed it. The first time had been a terrifying assault by a drunken and violent man. She was barely thirteen. She'd called for help but her mother had gone out to buy more booze. When she did come home, Patty had slapped her daughter's face. *Little slut*, she hissed. *Just keep your filthy eyes off of my boyfriends. And don't tell Brian*, she warned the sobbing child. *We don't want him to know his precious little Jilly is a whore.*

As trucks rumbled past, Jilly thought of Brian. Maybe she should have tried to find him. No, even Brian had let her down. Left her to Patty. There was no-one to care for her now but herself. With renewed determination, she took out the money the truck driver had given her and counted it. Fifty-five dollars. That was the first time Jilly had been paid for sex. She vowed to survive. No matter what it took. She stood up and waved down a passing truck.

Three days later, she was observing street prostitutes in Melbourne.

A car pulled into the kerb. 'How much for a blow job?'

She didn't know. 'Ten dollars?'

The car door swung open. 'Hop in, then.'

Brenda was a few years older than Jilly and wiser in the ways of the streets. She heard that the new girl was undercutting prices and took her aside for a word.

'You'll find yourself beaten up if you play that game,' she told Jilly, who was now calling herself Amber-Lee. 'I'll introduce you to my pimp. He takes a fair slice of the action but you can't work without a protector. You can stay with me for a while. I need some help with the rent.'

So Amber-Lee unpacked her belongings in the small alcove in Brenda's one-room flat and patted the lumpy bed. She hid her money in the lining of her coat and her box of mementos under the mattress. Among them was the photo of the day at Blackpool; looking at it, she wondered at how far she had come from the child in the photo.

She hated the work: the men, rough or kind, urgent or impotent, who used her body as though it were a thing. In the early weeks, however, something of Jilly remained. Perhaps there was another way.

She took herself to the Ward Street Shelter. A tall woman, with untidy hair and collar askew, asked her name.

'Amber-Lee,' she said.

The woman raised her eyebrows but didn't ask for a surname. She knew better. 'Okay, Amber-Lee. I'm Ilse.' She had a slight accent. 'I have to make a couple of phone calls and then we can talk. There's a café bar over there. Just help yourself.'

Jilly sat on the edge of the worn sofa, cupping her hands around the plastic mug. The room was shabby, and the three workers behind the desks all wore worried frowns. Ilse was talking earnestly into the phone, firing frequent glances in her direction. Panic rose in the girl's throat. Was the woman talking about her? Who was she talking to? What if they sent her to a foster home? When Ilse looked up again, Jilly had gone.

In the early days, Jilly had curled up under her thin blanket in Brenda's flat and made plans. She would do this work only until she had enough money for her fare home to England, a place that she had endowed with an almost mythical significance. She longed for her family, but she wouldn't go back until she was on her feet. She saw herself knocking on her grandparents' door, wearing long leather boots and a smart coat with a silk scarf. She felt the hugs and saw the smiles and tears. She sat once again in the kitchen, eating her grandmother's cake, the lost child returned. She even dared to wonder if her father was still alive. She had no illusions about her mother by now and suspected that she'd been lied to. She couldn't picture an ageing Andy. She still saw him as a young man who held her soft little paw in his big, rough carpenter's hands and ran with her, laughing, down the hill to the shops.

As the months went by, however, she saved very little. By the time she'd bought food and clothes, paid Brenda her share of the rent and given Vince the pimp his cut of the takings, there was very little left.

Amber-Lee worked the streets for eight months, and during this time, Jilly's voice and Jilly's tears became fainter. Her judgement was dulled as her sense of self continued to retreat. She had resisted for months, but her first experience of heroin provided the escape she craved. She worked harder but became more and more indebted to Vince, who was also her supplier. She'd earlier used a little of Brian's money for living expenses, but some delicacy of feeling at first forbad her from using it to buy drugs, even though she could no longer maintain the fiction that this little bundle of notes was the beginnings of her escape money.

Sitting on her bed one evening before work, she realised that delicacy of feeling was a luxury she could no longer afford. Regretfully, she took the money from her coat lining and put it in her little treasure box, ready to give to Vince for her supply. It was early in her addiction, and she still had some sense of decency. She understood that Brian's gift had been a sacrifice; he had little money left for himself after moving in with Patty. *Sorry, Brian.* She ran her hands through her hair, clutching fistfuls, tugging at the roots. *Sorry, Brian.* Fingers still knotted in her hair, she slumped and rested her elbows on her knees. *Fuck it, Brian. I've run out of choices.*

The photograph caught her eye, and she ran her fingers over its surface. *What were they all doing now, her parents, her aunt and uncle, her cousins? Mr Pie would probably be dead. Lucky Mr Pie.* She wiped her eyes with the back of her hand, snivelling a little in self-pity.

At that moment, Brenda came in. 'Wanna get a hamburger before we start?' She looked at the photo. 'What's that?'

'My family.'

'Who's the good-looking chick in the shorts?'

'My mother.'

'Funny-looking dog.'

'My cousin's dog, Mr Pie. Stupid name.' Jilly put the photo back in its box. 'What about that hamburger?'

They'd only walked a few paces along the footpath when Jilly (in that moment she was no longer Amber-Lee) caught a glimpse of a man on the other side of the road. He was about twenty-five, tall and dark. There was something about the way he held his shoulders. The way he walked. Where had she seen him before? It came to her all at once. It was the young man in the photo on the pier. *It was her father.* Filled with sudden, irrational hope, she ran towards him, right into the path of Finn's car.

12

Moss and Linsey

MOSS HAD BEEN STAYING WITH Mrs Pargetter for nearly two weeks now. Something of the town's lethargy had affected her too, and although she knew that one day soon she'd have to return to her life in Melbourne, she was reluctant to formulate any plans.

Her days took on a pattern. She would breakfast early with her elderly host and then call to Errol, who waited by the door for his walk. After a few laps of the oval, they'd head down to the creek, where the dog sniffed importantly every few steps, before looking back gravely for approval. Sometimes on these walks they'd see Finn, but Errol sensed that this was his quiet time and only wagged his tail briefly before moving on.

After her shower, Moss would set off for the shops. There was usually something to buy. Mrs Pargetter—and Finn, too, for that matter—had a 'just in time' approach to shopping. Moss made an effort to explore the town, but as she'd seen on her first day, the scope for exploration was limited. She knew a few residents by sight and nodded shyly if she passed them in the street. The old man who called her 'girlie' introduced himself as Cocky. He was usually sitting on the seat outside the pub, waiting for it to open.

She lunched with her father. Unused to company at meals, Finn often seemed at a loss for conversation. He didn't allude to Amber-Lee again, and as he had little small talk, Moss had to coax him to talk about himself.

She learned that he was an only child, that his mother was still alive and that he had enjoyed his years at university. He'd travelled around Europe while he was at Oxford; when she could draw them out of him, Moss found his travel stories entertaining. They were all light-hearted and impersonal: when he matriculated into Oxford, he told her, all the speeches were in Latin, except the exhortation not to light fires in the library.

'It went back to the days when students used to smuggle in candles so they could study after the sun went down. Electricity stopped all that, but the rule stayed. Things move a bit slowly at Oxford. Did I ever tell you about the time I passed the port the wrong way, just to see the reaction? You'd have thought I'd murdered the queen.' And he'd laugh quietly, his eyes crinkling at the corners. These were precious moments for Moss, but they were rare. She reconciled herself to the fact that Finn was naturally reserved, and as often as not, much of the meal was eaten in silence.

In the afternoons, Finn worked on his computer and Moss returned to Mrs Pargetter's. Here she'd read for a while, but sooner or later, her attention was drawn to the piano. Serene and regal, it stood in the corner of the front room, its polished beauty protected by a green felt cover. Moss would occasionally lift the lid and idly play a scale. It was a good instrument and had been kept in tune. Closing the lid, she would hum softly to herself for some time afterwards. Music had been the centre of her life, and the brutal incision she had made in anger had left a wound that refused to heal.

At these times, Mrs Pargetter would continue to knit without comment, but one evening she put down her needles and offered to play. 'I'm a bit rusty, but the knitting keeps my fingers supple and I still play at St Saviour's once a month.'

'I'd love to hear you, Mrs Pargetter. I'll turn the pages if you like.'

The old lady fussed with her sheet music. 'Let me see . . . I used to play dance music when I was young, but I always preferred hymns or the classics . . . Here, how about Chopin?' Mrs Pargetter played a few phrases *pianissimo* and then straightened her back. 'This is one of my favourites.'

She's a fine pianist even now, thought Moss as music filled the house. *I wonder what she was like when she was young?* Her performance ended, the elderly pianist inclined her head graciously.

'Bravo, Mrs Pargetter. That was wonderful.'

'Thank you, my dear,' she responded. 'Now it's your turn.'

'I'm not really a pianist, Mrs Pargetter.'

'But you are a singer, I believe. Let's see what we have here.' She ruffled through her music again. 'Ah. This one. You must know Schubert's *Ave Maria*.'

Moss began to protest; since leaving the Conservatorium, she had avoided music. She was afraid that once fully released, she would sing her own siren song, one that would tempt her into the future she'd renounced. She hovered on the edges of decision but couldn't help herself. She was drawn to the piano as Mrs Pargetter played the opening chords.

'It's so long since ... I need to warm up.' She did some breathing exercises and then ran through some scales, assisted by Mrs Pargetter. *I can still sing!* She sang her final scale and held the last note for the sheer joy of it, defying her unacknowledged fear that she might have lost her voice in this time of silence.

'Ready?' Mrs Pargetter played the opening chords of Schubert's haunting melody.

'Ave Maria, gratia plena ...' Moss began softly at first, her voice slowly swelling. '*Ora, ora pro nobis peccatoribus ...*' Pure silver sound vibrated the dust motes in Mrs Pargetter's stuffy front room, floated into the frosty night air and out into the streets of the tired little town. Helen Porter, walking her dog, felt a prickling along her spine. Cocky Benson, in a drunken stupor, brushed aside the tears that wet his corroded cheeks, and Sharon Simpson stopped painting her toenails and lifted her head to listen. Merv Randall, pausing as he wiped down the bar, briefly and wonderfully experienced the numinous. *You would of swore it was an angel singing*, he told his customers the next day.

The sound also drifted over the fence to where Finn was returning from his evening Silence. He sat down on the front porch and lit a cigarette, watching the small point of light as though it and the music were the only things left in the world. *Ora pro nobis peccatoribus*. Pray for us sinners. After the last note died away he remained motionless, looking out across the darkening oval.

Inside, both singer and accompanist looked gravely at each other in a moment of silence that neither was willing to break. Mrs Pargetter quietly closed the piano. There were tears in her eyes. When she finally spoke, her voice was unsteady.

'I had no idea . . . A gift from God himself, Moss. I had no idea . . .'

Moss gave the old woman an embarrassed hug and went outside where she found Finn, still sitting on his porch. She feigned a casual cheerfulness.

'Sorry, Finn. I lost track of time. Mrs Pargetter has made her famous Irish stew. She wants to share it with us.'

Finn stood up slowly and stretched his back. 'You can't waste a talent like that, Moss. You've got to go back.'

'Soon,' she murmured. 'Soon.' She was agitated but would not admit it, even to herself. She had been studiously avoiding a decision, and now the clamour of her reawakened ambitions rose to the surface of her consciousness. 'I'll think about it in the New Year,' she said.

But as it turned out, she had to return to the city much sooner than that.

The phone call came two days later.

'Hello, love, it's me. Is Michael with you?' Amy's voice sounded muffled.

'No. Why?'

'Are you alone, then?'

'No, I'm with Mrs Pargetter. We're having breakfast. Can I get Finn to call you back?'

'Yes—no, wait. I'm sorry. There's no way to make this easy, Miranda. I've just heard from Felicity. It's Linsey.' Moss sensed Amy's struggle for composure. The news came out in a rush. 'I'm so sorry, Moss. I have to tell you that Linsey—Linsey died last night, darling . . . I'm so sorry—she had cancer. It was so quick . . .'

Moss flinched painfully as the news hit her like a blow to the side of her skull. When she spoke, her voice was pleading. 'Mum! It's not true. It can't be. I didn't even know she was sick. Why didn't you tell me?' She had every right to be told. She was Linsey's only child.

'She didn't tell me either, Moss. It was ovarian cancer. She was only diagnosed three weeks ago but by then it was too advanced to do anything. You know what she's like. She didn't tell anyone, even then. She only told Felicity and Robert a few days ago. They got to London too late. They're organising a cremation over there—they'll bring her ashes back home . . .' Amy was speaking with a nervous rapidity. She stopped suddenly. 'Miranda—Moss. Are you still there?'

The phone had fallen from Moss's nerveless hand. She was gulping now, as though the air were suddenly depleted of oxygen. Mrs Pargetter picked up the phone and put it tentatively to her ear. She had gleaned the essence of the call, but wasn't sure if the caller was Amy or Linsey.

'Hello? Hello? Who's there? Moss is very upset. Can I help?'

'Is that Mrs Pargetter? This is Moss's mother, Amy. I've just given her some bad news: her mother Linsey died last night. Please, can you look after her until Michael gets back and then ask him to ring me?'

160

'Michael?'

'Yes—no—I think Moss said he calls himself Finn.'

Mrs Pargetter put down the phone and led the trembling Moss to the sofa where she held her close. 'It's alright to cry, dear. She *was* your mother.'

But the landscape of Moss's grief was bleak and arid. Mrs Pargetter heard the gate squeak, and gently disengaged herself. 'That'll be Finn, for morning tea. I'll let him in.'

Moss's dry-eyed grief worried Finn. He had an idea that women always cry at such moments, but Moss just sat with burning eyes, ceaselessly rubbing her temples. She hadn't spoken since she dropped the phone. Finn and Mrs Pargetter looked at each other. They both understood grief, and they both understood guilt. Finn patted his daughter tentatively on the shoulder. It was the first time he had ever touched her, and even in her grief, she was pathetically grateful. She reached up and placed her hand over his, holding him there for a few moments more.

Finn cleared his throat as an unfamiliar warmth stole over him. 'Talk to us, Moss. Tell us about Linsey.' But Moss remained silent.

'I'll make some tea,' decided Mrs Pargetter. 'Plenty of sugar, for shock.' That was what Mrs Moloney had said to her when the telegram arrived from the war office. *Sugar doesn't help at all*, she thought, but made the tea anyway.

As they silently sipped their tea, Sandy arrived, brandishing a manila folder. 'I've just been to . . .' he began, but the words died on his lips when he saw Moss's white face and met Mrs Pargetter's warning gaze. On hearing the news, he thrust the folder out of sight.

'Moss. I'm so sorry.' She gave him a little smile. Feeling helpless in the face of her grief, Sandy thought for a moment and then said diffidently, 'If you want to go back to your mother's, I'll drive you. We can't let you go on the bus.'

Finn looked at him with gratitude. 'We'd appreciate that, Sandy.'

Mrs Pargetter patted his large, soft hand. 'You're not a bad fellow, sometimes, George.'

Errol, meanwhile, had crept over to Moss, jumping stiffly onto the sofa beside her. He licked her hand and pressed his nose into her lap. He was the best of all the Errols. She stroked his head gently, and finally, when her tears began to flow, Errol whimpered a little in sympathy.

Finn felt responsible for Moss's welfare and insisted on coming to Melbourne with her and Sandy. It wasn't kindness alone that motivated him. There was also the fragile connection he had just made: a slender thread spun out of her grief and his pity. He found himself wanting to comfort and protect her. She was a child and she had lost her mother. Father Boniface would have offered spiritual solace, but all Finn could offer was his company on her journey. *Little enough*, he thought sadly.

Mrs Pargetter packed some muffins. 'Some for the road and some for your mother,' she said, handing Moss two plastic containers. She added a thermos of tea. She tended to forget that nowadays they were only two and a half hours from Melbourne, even on a bad traffic day.

Sandy drove in silence as Moss sat in the back with Finn, staring out at the dry yellow paddocks and the featureless winter sky. She failed to notice Finn's oblique glances and this time barely felt his hand as it moved tentatively to cover hers. While she understood the situation at the surface of her mind, Moss couldn't quite grasp the fact, the uncompromising finality, of Linsey's death. She couldn't imagine how all that energy and longing and striving for perfection had simply stopped. How all the unfinished business over which Linsey had surely fretted would be processed by other hands or remain unfinished forever.

'You okay?' Finn said finally. Moss nodded and continued to stare. 'Won't be long now. The exit's only a few minutes away,' he offered, feeling inadequate.

When Linsey left, all those years ago, she had assured Amy that she and Moss could stay in Aunt Shirley's house until Moss was of age. There was a careless generosity in Linsey's personal dealings that contrasted sharply with her hard-nosed practice as a banker. Consequently, Amy was still living in the family home even though their daughter had attained her majority several years before.

Moss felt the sickness of loss as the car pulled into the kerb and she saw the front door with its distinctive leadlight. Grief is not a constant state. It comes in waves, and at that moment Moss was engulfed, unable to speak or move. Linsey had loved her but she'd pushed her away. She had a flashback to that day at the beach; a little girl reaching out to Amy, leaving Linsey with her arms hanging ineffectually by her sides. It was what Moss had always done: blamed Linsey and exonerated Amy.

Music was their one shared pleasure. 'One day I'll hear you sing Mimi at the Sydney Opera House,' Linsey would say. 'And Violetta in Milan,' Moss would reply. 'Then Madame Butterfly at Covent Garden,' they would chorus gleefully.

Linsey was always planning, as though life could be moulded to her will. But even before the sweet young voice began to mature so wonderfully, she loved to hear her daughter sing. Her tense face would soften and her eyes shine. At those moments the dissonance between them abated; Moss realised only now that they'd been moving towards an acknowledgement of the love they'd always felt for each other but had expressed clumsily and only too rarely since her adolescence. And she, Moss, had chosen to sever the bond. After Amy's revelations regarding her conception, she had marched off to Linsey's apartment and, ignoring the bell, knocked peremptorily on the door.

Linsey smiled to see her daughter. 'Moss! What a nice surprise. Come in.'

Moss pushed past her mother and confronted her in the hallway. 'I won't be long,' she said coldly. 'I just want to tell you how I feel.'

Linsey was bewildered. 'Whatever's the matter? Has something happened to Amy?'

'Mum's fine. But she told me the truth. About how I was conceived. You *advertised* for a father for me. You chose a stranger. I suppose your friends weren't good enough? And as for taking your chances with a sperm bank . . .'

'Moss—Miranda, I don't understand. I wanted the best for you . . .'

'For *you*, you mean. I can see now why I was such a

disappointment. You wanted a genius, a beauty . . . You wanted a—a *paragon*, not a child.'

When she spoke, Linsey's voice was dry, but the struggle to control her emotions showed in her face. 'I made mistakes, Moss. Motherhood didn't come naturally to me like it did to Amy. And it's true, I did think that I could plan the perfect baby, but once I saw you, I finally understood. You *were* a perfect baby, just as you were. I wanted someone to love and care for, and . . .' She looked away. 'Someone who might love me.'

Moss almost gave in then, shaken by this evidence of her mother's vulnerability. Her impulse was to hug this woman who, though difficult in some ways, had nonetheless provided so much stability and certainty in her childhood. She moved forward slightly just as Linsey stepped back. And the moment for reconciliation was lost in that one uncertain gesture.

Stung by the apparent rebuff, Moss's anger returned. 'I just came to tell you that I won't be going on with my singing. That was your ambition, not mine.' She was beside herself now, shouting. 'I'm glad you left. You're a calculating bitch. You're not fit to be a mother.'

'Don't do this.' Linsey's voice fractured the air between them. 'Please don't do this.'

But Moss had turned and left with an air of grievance that later compounded her shame. She didn't look back, but she could see in her mind Linsey's stricken face, her eyes darkened with pain, and the delicate tremor in her cheek. Visualising that, Moss was almost exultant, and strode off to the lift with a fierce, triumphant little smile.

Linsey had watched Moss's retreating back and put out her hand as if to stop her. It was too late; Moss turned the corner and was out of sight, and Linsey's hand fell back to her side. She closed the door and went into her meticulously furnished sitting room where she sat down heavily. She picked up a cushion and held it to her, staring miserably at the wall. It wasn't so long ago, it seemed, that she had held Moss for the first time and experienced the surge of joy that changed her forever.

Such a fierce little baby, Linsey remembered. She would stiffen her body and scream if she didn't want to be held. In those early days, though, she was mostly happy for Linsey to hold her; happy to snuggle into her willing arms. Despite her tiredness, Linsey loved those early mornings when Amy slept and she had this bewitching little creature to herself. She would sometimes stand and watch her, smiling as the little nose wrinkled and twitched on the cusp of sleep and waking. To Linsey, moments like these were tiny, perfect stitches in the fabric of her life.

Was I too hard on her? Linsey wondered. Moss so often went to Amy when she was in trouble. Amy was the forest where Moss could explore and play freely, whereas Linsey created pathways, some of which led Moss to places she didn't care for, but others to hard-won goals of which she could be rightly proud.

She just needs time, Linsey thought. *Her music is too important to her.*

Then the sobering thought: *But how important am I?*

Amy had been watching for the car to arrive, and ran out to greet her daughter. They both cried then, holding each other and rocking in unconscious mimicry of their ancient fore-mothers' mourning rites. In another age, their stifled sobs would have been a full-throated keening. They would have rent their garments and covered their heads with ashes. The village women would have joined them in a circle of pain, sanctifying their grief. Now they stood, just the two of them, in a cold suburban street, drying their tears with crumpled tissues. This was probably enough for Amy. She had loved Linsey in her own way, but not enough to overcome their differences. She'd always carried her love lightly, and much of her present feeling was for Moss, who needed not only to mourn but to be shriven. She clutched her daughter and felt the shudders that reverberated deep in her own body.

'Shh. It's okay, sweetheart.' Murmuring words whose meaning was less important than their cadence. Lullaby words. Lullaby rhythm. 'It's okay. Shh. It's okay.'

Finn, meanwhile, stood holding Moss's bag, unsure of his place.

Sandy leaned out of the window. 'What do you want to do, Finn? I can come back later, if you like.'

Before Finn could reply, Amy turned towards them. 'Michael, it was kind of you to bring Moss home—both of you.' Her smile included Sandy. 'Would you like to come in for a coffee?'

'I've got a couple of things to do,' said Sandy, 'but thanks anyway.' He turned to Finn. 'You stay if you want. I can meet you back at the Coachman's Inn.'

'I won't impose,' Finn said. He looked at Moss. 'You two need some time to yourselves. I'll be by later.'

Amy held out her hand. 'Nice to see you again, Michael.'

Finn shook her hand but failed to meet her eye. 'Yes, you too. We'll be in Melbourne for a couple of days. I'll ring before we leave.' He put an unpractised arm around Moss's shoulder and pecked her cheek. 'You take care, now,' he said.

Moss sat at the kitchen table drinking coffee and, surprising herself, eating one of Mrs Pargetter's muffins. She scrabbled in her bag and drew out a woollen object.

'Mrs Pargetter sent this for you, Mum. It's a tea cosy.' She smiled faintly. 'One less for the United Nations.'

'That's kind of her,' Amy said, alternately squeezing and smoothing it with nervous hands. She had a difficult message to deliver. 'Moss, Felicity and Robert will be back tomorrow week. They're planning a memorial service for Linsey. They believe that she wanted you to sing.' She peered into her daughter's suddenly impassive face. 'You will sing, won't you?'

Moss's eyes betrayed her. 'I can't. I don't feel I can, after . . .'

Amy was uncharacteristically firm. 'I know that, but this is not about your feelings, Miranda.'

When they met the following week to plan the service, Felicity was even more blunt than usual. She loved her sister dearly and knew how much she longed for reconciliation with Moss. Now there was no hope. Linsey had died carrying the burden of that rejection. 'You hurt my sister more than you can know,' she told a weeping Moss. 'I can't say that I want you to come, either, but that's hardly the point. Linsey's last request was that you sing at her funeral. If you can't find it in your heart to do this one thing for her, then you're even more callous than I thought.'

So Moss sang. She chose 'Pie Jesu', not for religious consolation but because agnostic Linsey loved the music. She sang her grief and sent it soaring with the white balloons released by the other mourners. Finn stood among them and thought of the strange circumstances that connected him to the dead woman. He even smiled when he remembered her holding out the 'receptacle', as she called it, and her disapproving sniff as she handed him the magazines. He looked across the garden at his daughter and allowed himself to drown in her voice. She was so small and vulnerable. And brave. Yesterday she had been distraught, calling him in the middle of the night.

'Felicity and Amy are right, Finn. I'm so selfish. But how can I sing for Linsey now? I had every opportunity to let her back into my life and I blew it.' Her voice rose in pitch. 'She died thinking I hated her. Hated her! What sort of person does that make me?'

Finn felt a surge of panic. Here was the first test of his competence as a parent and he couldn't think of one reassuring thing to say. 'Moss, listen: you must sing . . .'

'I can't! My throat is so tight I can't sing a note. I can't do it!'

'You can,' said Finn helplessly. 'Moss, you can.'

Listening as the last notes of 'Pie Jesu' died away, Finn truly hoped that Linsey would rest in peace. She had been the driving force that produced this child whom, he now realised, he had come to care for very much indeed.

Linsey left a substantial estate. Felicity's children, Toby and Pippa, and Robert's son, Cal, all received generous bequests. She left smaller sums to the Red Cross and Médecins Sans Frontières, but the bulk of her estate, including the house, was left to *my goddaughter, Miranda Ophelia Sinclair*.

Felicity was outraged. 'That house belonged to our family,' she fumed to Robert. 'And she left it to that girl who's not even related.'

'Well, that's a moot point,' Robert replied. 'She always saw Miranda as her daughter, even after she and Amy split up.'

'And what thanks did she get? That girl broke her heart. There's nothing we can do about the will, but we're Linsey's next of kin, and I intend to make it clear where we stand on this.'

When his sister had one of her 'notions', Robert always found it easier to acquiesce.

And so it was that the brass plaque mounted over Linsey's ashes denied the motherhood that had been her greatest source of joy and pain: *Linsey Anne Brookes, died 2 August 2006. Loved and loving daughter of Meredith and John Brookes, loved and loving sister of Felicity and Robert. Returned to the universe.*

Moss had read the will in disbelief. The money, the shares, even the house were insignificant beside one stark fact: Linsey had referred to Moss as her 'goddaughter'.

'It's probably just a legal thing,' Amy said. 'She always thought of you as her daughter.'

But Moss wasn't interested in legalities. In her last will and testament her mother Linsey had repudiated their relationship. It was Moss's fault and now it was too late to make amends.

She felt the title *goddaughter* scorch her like a brand. Why hadn't Linsey adopted her? This question became a constant in her effort to deal with her bereavement. 'Isn't the fact that she left you the house enough?' Felicity retorted when asked.

Amy in turn was evasive. 'I don't know. We never really discussed it.' What remained unsaid was their knowledge that Moss had been the one who had wanted to hide the relationship. Averting their eyes, they both remembered the elaborate story Moss had concocted. How Amy and Linsey were sisters-in-law whose husbands had died in a fishing-boat accident. How they decided to live together for company and economy. They both remembered the first parents' night at Moss's new school.

'This is my mother,' Moss had said, indicating Amy. 'And this is my . . . aunt. Aunt Linsey.' And Linsey had smiled and shaken hands and made polite conversation, never once betraying her pain. Now Moss felt that this was the punishment she was due.

But, perversely, she was still hurt. She wanted answers, and decided to visit Robert. He'd been kind to her at the service, attempting to shield her from the worst of Felicity's venom and thanking her for the music. He had lived alone since his divorce. While he sounded surprised when Moss rang, he readily agreed to the meeting.

'Come about one,' he said. 'We'll have a bit of lunch.'

Moss arrived punctually and was greeted with a kiss on the cheek—a real one, where lips actually touch the face. Robert was the oldest of the three siblings; Moss estimated that he must be nearing sixty. His face had deep grooves from nose to chin, and his hair, thinning on top, left him with a greying tonsure. He was small like Linsey, and had the same large grey eyes, which looked mildly at Moss over his reading glasses.

'So, how are you, Miranda?'

'Moss, please, Uncle Rob.'

'Yes. Sorry, Moss. Come in here while I make us a sandwich.'

The kitchen/living room was neat and bare. There were no pictures on the walls or cushions on the sofa. A newspaper lay open on the table. Robert must have been reading when she arrived. *It looks temporary*, Moss thought. *Like a motel room.* Her uncle made sandwiches and tea with a minimum of fuss, the conversation easy and impersonal.

'Now,' he said, as they sat down. 'What can I do for you, love?'

Moss nibbled at her sandwich. 'I suppose you know that I had this silly fight with Linsey, and we weren't speaking when she died.' She corrected herself. 'No, that's not fair. *I* wasn't speaking to *her*. For all I know, she might have been waiting for me to come to my senses.'

Robert looked at Moss, whose eyes were lowered. *Poor little bugger.* 'As far as I understand,' he said, choosing his words carefully, 'you were upset about the, ah . . . *conditions* that brought about your birth. Would that be fair to say?'

Moss nodded without looking up.

'Well,' Robert continued, 'Linsey confided in me a bit. Probably more in Flissy, her being a woman and all, but I do know she wanted a child badly enough to go to all sorts of trouble to have one. I also know that she loved you from the moment you were born to the day she died.' He sipped his coffee. 'She was never an easy woman to get on with. I'm her brother and I know, believe me. She was a fierce little thing when we were kids. Used to insist that Mum cut her sandwiches a certain way—triangles, no crusts. Her schoolbag had to be packed in a certain order . . . That sort of thing. Even though I was a few years older, I was always a bit scared of her. But I'll tell you this, Mir—Moss. When she loved someone, it was the real deal. Nothing you could have done would have changed the fact that she loved you.'

'Then, if she wanted a child so much, why didn't she adopt me?' Moss had planned to ask composed and intelligent questions, and now here she was, whining like a child. She frowned, and lowered the pitch of her voice. 'I would have thought,' she said, gathering the shreds of her dignity, 'that adoption would have been *prudent* under the circumstances.'

'She did mention it at one point,' he said slowly. 'Her reasons for not going ahead were complicated. For a start, you already had a legal mother. The law in those days was a bit murky, and she was afraid you'd become a target of the tabloids if they dragged it through the courts. *Lesbian Couple in Child Adoption Bid.* You can imagine the sort of thing.' Moss acknowledged this with a slight inclination of her head. 'Then there was her relationship with Amy. She truly believed—against all the evidence, as far as I can see—that they'd be together *till death do us part*, if you know what I mean. She couldn't imagine her status changing. Flissy told me once that Linsey wanted to be your godmother so that she could have some public connection with you. She never believed in God, so why else would she have had you christened?'

Moss was still unconvinced. 'What if something had happened to Amy? Where would I have ended up? In care?'

'As far as I know, Amy provided for that in her will. She named Linsey as sole guardian. I don't think that was ever changed. Their separation was reasonably harmonious.' He grinned painfully. 'And I know what an inharmonious separation looks like. I'm telling you the truth, Moss.'

'I rejected her in the end, though, didn't I?' Even as she said it, Moss knew that rejection had taken place years before, at a school parents' night. 'Her loving me makes it even worse.'

'Young people do that sort of thing all the time. Don't let the fact that you had two mothers complicate what was no more nor less than a family row. Cal wouldn't speak to me for months after Trish and I broke up. I simply waited, then one night he rang and asked me out for a drink. Just like that. We get on fine now by agreeing not to discuss certain matters.'

'I didn't have the luxury of a healing time,' Moss responded, blinking hard. 'I said some pretty harsh things. And it's too late now to do anything about it.' *Having two mothers was an issue*, she thought bitterly. *I turned my mother into my aunt and expected her to still be there when I was ready.*

Robert continued as though she hadn't spoken. 'You know what she said to me? *Poor Miranda. I hope she returns to her music. It gives her so much pleasure.* Note she didn't say that it gave *her* pleasure—although it did. She was concerned for *you*. She was a mature adult, Moss, and you were barely out of your teens. I'm sure she knew in her heart that she only had to wait.'

'Thank you, Uncle Rob. I just wish that it hadn't taken her death to make me understand.'

Even though it clarified some issues, Moss's meeting with Robert did little to relieve her pain. She could accept that Linsey's decision regarding adoption was not a rejection. But there was an ambivalence inherent in that understanding. If she could continue to believe that Linsey had rejected her then her subsequent rejection of Linsey was to some degree justified. Now she'd been assured of Linsey's love, her own actions were even more open to censure. Not only had she denied her mother in public, but their last meeting was a source of pain for one and shame for the other. Moss's words had been cruel, and she would never have the opportunity to withdraw them. Even worse, each word had been calculated; she knew at the time the intensity of the pain they would engender.

'I used to hear them arguing sometimes. Or at least Linsey would argue,' she told Finn later that day. 'Afterwards Amy would simply go about her business, cold and polite, and there was Linsey, literally shrouded in misery. Eventually she'd apologise, just to see Amy smile at her again. I used to believe that Amy was the one person who could bring her undone. But I know now that I hurt her much more. She left because she couldn't keep hiding how much I was hurting her, and so she . . . so she wouldn't embarrass me.' There. She'd finally said the unsayable and looked at Finn, her eyes dark with misery.

Finn rubbed his chin. 'I don't know much about it, Moss, but it seems to me that the relationship between lovers is different from the parent–child situation. With a child, people seem to be able to forgive almost anything. It's part and parcel of loving them, I suppose.' He was struggling here. Guessing.

'In the end, people seem more able to forgive their children than their lovers.'

'You're probably right,' Moss replied, 'but it's much harder to forgive yourself.'

Finn nodded. He, of all people, understood the truth of that.

13

Moss and friends

IN THE FIVE WEEKS SINCE the memorial service Moss had done very little. She nursed her grief and churned over her last conversation with Linsey until her nerves were frayed and she snapped irritably at the mildest of Amy's comments. She could have been kinder to Linsey while still making her point, she mourned. She could have simply accepted the circumstances of her conception and kept a sense of proportion. She could have let Linsey stew for a while and then offered her forgiveness. But forgiveness for what? For being her mother? For loving her? Her head ached, and she either ate feverishly or picked at her food.

'For goodness' sake,' Amy said. 'You have to get out of the house. You can't brood like this forever.' This elicited a sharp retort and more tears.

'Why don't you see about re-enrolling in your course?' Amy said at last. 'It's certainly what Linsey would've wanted.'

So Moss made a desultory effort to re-enrol for the following year and was mildly flattered by Dr Cuicci's response to her enquiries.

'Talent like yours should not go to waste.' Dr Cuicci

frowned. 'But to succeed at the highest level you need more than talent. You also need discipline and an iron will. Do you have those qualities, Miranda?'

Moss didn't know. 'I'd like to think I did,' she said with painful honesty, 'but I need to sort out a couple of things before I can really commit.' She had no idea what these things were; she just felt unable to make a decision.

Emilia Cuicci sighed. *These young people with their dramas and busyness. I despair of them.* 'I will give you until the New Year to decide,' she told her student. 'Come to me by the first week in February. There are many other talents who wait for an opportunity like yours.'

Opportunity. The word now had a new layer of meaning. The little town beckoned and she was impelled to return. Her closest friends at the moment, she thought with surprise, were an old lady, a nutty visionary with sweaty hands, and her father, Finn, a man burdened with guilt. Perhaps she did have unfinished business there after all. She couldn't explain this feeling to herself, let alone Amy, and simply told her mother that she had a few loose ends to tie up.

Amy was ashamed to realise that she was happy to see her go. When Moss was in the house, undercurrents, ripples and whirlpools disturbed the calm waters of her life. Moss was a lot like Linsey.

'A good idea,' she said when Moss announced her impending return to Opportunity. 'You should call and warn them you're coming this time.'

So Moss rang Mrs Pargetter, who was delighted to hear the news. 'Moss is coming back, Errol, how about that?'

Errol's delight shone in his eyes, quivered in his tail. The old lady opened the door to the room with the stoic little teddy bears, confirming the absence that had returned to occupy its every dark corner. The pain of her long-ago loss had been held at bay in that room, imprisoned behind the white-painted door. When Moss had arrived, the old lady was inexplicably moved to allow living light to enter and felt, for the first time in years, a desolate little spirit begin to move timidly towards her. It had withdrawn with Moss's departure, leaving Mrs Pargetter to grieve afresh. She closed the door softly and sat for a while with Errol's head on her lap.

When Moss arrived on the evening bus, Finn was at the stop to greet her. It was his Silent time, she noted gratefully. She swung her backpack down to his waiting arms, and when she alighted, stood on tiptoe to give him a kiss on the cheek. He actually beamed, the down-drawn lines of his face relaxing, his expression suddenly youthful.

'Good trip?' he asked. 'At least the train was on time for this visit.' He fumbled with the straps of her backpack, trying to lengthen them to accommodate his broader shoulders. 'We missed you—*I* missed you,' he said diffidently, peering at the buckles as though they were marvels of innovation. 'Mrs Pargetter and Sandy are back at her place for a sort of, you know, welcome home.'

Errol met them at the gate and, in a surprising display of agility, capered joyfully around Moss, tongue lolling, tail wagging frenetically.

'Good boy. Good dog.' Moss knelt and rubbed his head and ears with both hands. 'Did you miss me too, Errol?' Leaving her in no doubt as to the answer, the dog led her to the front door where Mrs Pargetter greeted her with a kiss.

'I've got a nice lamb roast,' she said. 'Sandy brought the leg around specially.'

Sandy was hovering in the background like a self-conscious full moon. 'Nice to see you, Moss. Hope you like lamb.'

Moss hadn't forgotten the big man's kindness after Linsey's death. He'd been quiet and unobtrusive as he made her comfortable in the car, his face betraying real concern. He had sent her flowers and a handwritten card. *Losing a mother is a terrible thing*, he wrote in his large, square handwriting. No platitudes. No preaching. Just the truth. *Losing a mother is a terrible thing.*

Since then, Moss had begun to look at Sandy with new eyes. Forgetting her former distaste, she planted a kiss on his astonished cheek. 'I love lamb,' she responded. 'By the way, Sandy, I've never thanked you properly for driving me to Melbourne. I don't know what I would have done otherwise.'

'No worries, love,' Sandy replied gruffly.

The meal took on a festive tone, and the obsessive Sandy brought Moss up to date with his plans for the Great Galah. The blueprints were now with a design engineer, he told her. They'd have to make some adjustments to the slide for safety reasons, but, all in all, things were going along very nicely indeed. Mrs Pargetter seemed to take all this in her stride, but Finn squirmed in discomfort while Moss made polite murmurs, which were sufficiently encouraging for Sandy to raise one of his concerns.

'I do have a bit of a problem,' he said. 'And I'd be interested to know what you think, Moss.'

Finn gazed studiously at the curtains, ignoring his daughter's silent plea for help.

'The fact is,' confided Sandy, 'galahs are grey.' He waved his hand to ward off premature comment. 'I know they're pink as well. A very nice pink, when you think about it. But there's no getting away from it: there's just too much grey. Can you see where I'm going with this, Moss?'

'Um . . . grey. A problem with grey?'

'You've hit the nail on the head. What sort of tourist attraction is grey?'

'A grey one?'

'A grey one! Exactly. A boring, unattractive grey one. Now, can I make it yellow, or blue, or even all pink? Would it still be a galah?' He sat back, folding his arms. 'That's my question, Moss. My dilemma.'

Moss tried to sound judicious. 'I can't see a galah being any other colour, Sandy. You could maybe get away with a bit more pink than you'd find in nature . . . but not blue or yellow. If it's a galah, it has to be mostly grey.'

'That's what Aunt Lily and your father say too.' He looked momentarily hopeful. 'What about silver?' The other three shook their heads. 'Well, I'll keep working on it. You never know. Solutions can pop up out of the blue.'

'He's a strange bloke,' said Finn as Mrs Pargetter saw her nephew to the door. 'He's made a fortune on the stock market while other farmers are struggling to pay the mortgage. He looks after his aunt. He's done some fine things for Opportunity, but where on earth did he get this hare-brained scheme?'

Mrs Pargetter re-entered the room in time to hear Finn's

question. She held the curtains aside, watching Sandy's back as it retreated down the path. 'I may be wrong, but I believe there is more to it than meets the eye,' she said. 'The idea of a memorial to that brute of a father would be more than I could bear—except that it has to be a monumental failure. I'm happy to say that it'll make Major Bully-boy Sandilands a laughing stock.'

'But what about our Sandy? Won't he be a laughing stock too?' Moss was horrified. This nice old lady had a vindictive streak she hadn't guessed at.

'Poor George. He's not vicious like his father, but he is weak. He never stood up for his mother, even when he was old enough. I'm no psychologist, but I'd say that my nephew is killing two birds with one stone, if you'll pardon the pun. His Great Galah will not only punish his father—it will also punish him.' She went on as Moss and Finn looked at each other: 'I don't think he's really aware of this. Or maybe he is. Either way, it's for him to work his way through without interference.' And she sucked in her teeth in a very decisive manner.

After Finn left, Moss helped Mrs Pargetter clear the table and wash the dishes.

'I think I'll just start a new cosy—knit a few rows,' the old lady said when they were finished. 'You'll want to unpack, I suppose.' She picked up her needles and began to cast on the stitches . . . *Fourteen, sixteen, eighteen* . . . She looked up. Moss had vanished into her room. *Her room.* Mrs Pargetter felt a tension in her scalp.

As Moss set her case down on the bed, she felt a little exhalation, a sigh so small that it registered only on the periphery of her senses. At the same time, she became aware of an expectation, the waiting feeling she had experienced the first time she entered the room. It was all too subtle to grasp, and she simply stood for a moment before returning to her elderly friend, who was still counting her stitches.

'I seem to keep losing count,' she said crossly. 'Moss, can you check for me, please?'

Moss counted and found that there were almost twice as many stitches as were needed. She quietly unpicked the excess and rechecked the number before handing the knitting back. Mrs Pargetter making a mistake with her knitting? It was unheard of. Now that Moss came to think of it, the old lady had been distracted all night. Perhaps she was just tired.

'You look worn out, Mrs Pargetter. I certainly am.' Moss began the nighttime ritual of ensuring the fire was safe and setting the table for breakfast. To her relief, her companion took the hint. Folding away her knitting in an embroidered pillow slip, she headed for the bathroom, wishing Moss goodnight.

Moss, never a good sleeper, always read for an hour or two before settling for the night. She had just placed the bookmark when a movement at the door startled her. It was Mrs Pargetter, in a flannelette nightgown, a long grey plait hanging over one shoulder. She looked at Moss with hungry eyes.

'What is it, Mrs Pargetter?' She spoke softly, fearing to disturb the listening air.

The old lady bowed her head. 'They locked me away,' she said. 'They locked me away and I couldn't save my baby.

I brought it home. To this very room. But it just went away.'
Her eyes searched Moss's face. 'It comes back when you're here,
though. I can feel it.' She took a faltering step into the room.
'I need my baby, Moss.'

The two women sat together on the bed, and Moss took
the old lady's hands and held them between her own. They
were trembling, and cold to her touch.

'We'll just sit here for a bit, Mrs Pargetter. Until you're
ready. Then I'll make us a cup of tea.'

The room was cold, and the yellow bulb, swinging high
from the ceiling, cast more shadow than light. Moss glanced
around uneasily, sensing a faint susurration, a delicate splinter-
ing of the gelid air. The teddies froze, their eyes straining to
pierce the shadows.

The young woman looked at her companion and shivered.
Did she feel it too? But Mrs Pargetter gave no sign.

After several minutes, the old lady patted Moss's hands
and stood up. 'Take no notice of me, dear. I'm just a silly old
woman.' As Moss began to protest, she shook her head. 'Don't
worry about the tea. I'm really very tired.'

The young woman put her arm around the frail shoulders
and they walked together back to her room. Moss had to take
small, slow steps to keep pace as Mrs Pargetter's bare feet shuffled and whispered on the kitchen tiles.

She helped her into bed and pulled up the covers. 'Goodnight, Mrs Pargetter.'

'Goodnight, dear.'

In the light of day, Moss decided that the presence she had sensed in the room was the product of her overactive imagination. But she was worried about her elderly friend. She recounted the story to Finn as they took Errol for a walk. 'Do you know what happened to her, Finn? I'm terrified I'll say the wrong thing.'

Finn shook his head. 'I've heard bits and pieces but Sandy would be your best bet.'

Moss sought Sandy out that afternoon, finding him in the pub with two other men. They were all staring morosely into their beers, so Moss approached, confident that she wasn't interrupting anything important. 'Can you join me for a drink, Sandy? I need to ask you something.'

The other men leered at each other, and looked at Sandy with something like respect as Moss led him to a corner table.

'I was only a kid at the time,' he began in response to her question, 'but I used to hear Mum and Dad talking about it. Apparently she lost her husband in New Guinea and then their baby was stillborn. Anyway, she went a bit barmy, by all accounts, and she was in a mental hospital for years. Had shock treatment and everything. I was away at school then, but Mum used to take me to visit her in the holidays. Mum and Dad helped to get her out when Grandpa died.' He tossed down the last of his beer and wiped the froth from his upper lip. 'She was always nice to me. Made welcome-home cakes and took a bit of an interest. Dad used to say she should have stayed in the mental home, but I think she was just eccentric, not mad.' He paused. 'Dad could be a bit hard, sometimes,' he admitted. 'I can almost understand why Aunt Lily didn't like him.'

Moss sipped her drink. 'What you tell me makes it even worse. It's like she says: she'd locked things away, and now, for whatever reason, a door is opening. I wonder just how fragile her mental health is?'

Sandy's face was grave. 'I hadn't realised things were so bad.'

'Is there anything you can do, Sandy? You know her better than anyone.'

'Leave me to have a think,' he replied. 'Meanwhile we'll all keep an eye on her. And thanks for telling me, Moss.'

Once again, Moss felt humbled. This man had more depth than she had originally given him credit for.

14

Sandy and Rosie Sandilands

THE NEXT MORNING, SANDY SAT at his computer, swearing softly. He was sure he'd read the article in the last couple of years. He googled 'stillbirths'. He refined his search: 'stillbirths Melbourne'. There was a lot of medical information but no historical references. He tried again. 'Stillbirths, Melbourne, 1940–44.' This search turned up a little historical information, but not what he was seeking. He searched 'Melbourne Hospital for Women'. Plenty here, but no link to stillbirths. He tried 'Melbourne General Cemetery'. No information at all, beyond a map that marked out the multitude of reference points for gravesites. *Bugger!* He knew he'd read somewhere of a memorial service at the Melbourne General Cemetery for parents whose stillborn babies had been buried in unmarked graves.

He got up to find the chocolate biscuits he always kept as a bulwark against frustration, and stood looking out his window. He finished the first biscuit and reached for a second. The early spring sky, blue and cloudless, mocked the parched paddocks. He watched a flock of galahs crowding on the telephone wire, their sheet-metal screeches shredding the air. *Of course. Old technology!* He'd ring the cemetery. That was his best bet. He hurried to the phone.

'Yes,' a woman's voice responded. 'There are several neonatal sites scattered throughout the cemetery. They're looked after by the SANDS group.'

'SANDS?'

'Stillborn and Neonatal Death Support. I have their phone number.' She read it out to him and he wrote it on a post-it note. 'Now, do you have any information at all about this baby?'

'As far as I know, the baby was taken and buried without a name. Probably some time in 1941 or maybe '42. My mother tried to find out once, and the hospital told her that the babies were buried in common graves—no plaques or headstones or anything.'

'That's right. You might try the hospital again,' the woman said doubtfully, 'although I believe their record-keeping wasn't too brilliant at the time. There was a war on, remember.'

Sandy thanked her and hung up. He decided that his best course of action was to visit the cemetery. That might give him some information he could work on. He told Moss his plan and asked if she'd like to come. Bored and restless, she agreed.

'I could help you, and visit Linsey at the same time,' she said.

When he invited Finn, he was startled at the response. The other man's face rapidly registered shock and shame. Then confusion.

Finn's last visit had been to seek out Amber-Lee's grave, but the sight of the raw mound on the fringes of the cemetery had been more than he could bear. Not far away, elaborate tombstones and well-tended burial plots turned their backs on the graves of the poor and nameless. He had stood beside the mound and promised he'd be back, that he'd rescue her from this awful obscurity. But although he never forgot her, he hadn't kept his promise. And with this new opportunity, failed to do so again.

'I just can't,' he mumbled in distress. 'Maybe another time.'

Leaving the small car park that adjoined the main gates, Sandy and Moss went into the gothic-style bluestone building that housed the cemetery's administration. The young woman at reception was helpful, giving them a map on which she marked the various sites where the infant graves could be found.

'You'll find some commemorative plaques,' she said, 'but very few compared to the thousands buried there.'

As they were about to leave, Moss asked on impulse, 'Where are the public graves?'

'You won't find those any more. They used to be around the perimeter fence, here and here.' She circled the locations apologetically. 'There's no marker or anything. The plots have been reclaimed.'

Moss ignored Sandy's raised eyebrows and scanned the map with feigned concentration. She felt sick at heart to think of the total annihilation suffered by the inhabitants of those graves.

'Come on, love,' said Sandy. 'Let's do what we came here to do.'

The cemetery was bristling with tombstones, which grew

from the earth like rows of grey teeth, some carious and crooked with age, others straight and perfectly aligned. The graves came one upon another in tight formation, with their crosses and angels, their stars of David, their Chinese characters; some with photographs, some with plastic flowers, a few with fresh blooms. There were tall monuments crowned with kneeling angels, arms crossed and heads bowed. Other angels held a trumpet to their stone lips. Silent trumpets: it was not yet time to waken the dead.

They passed the Elvis memorial beside which sixty-year-olds in tight T-shirts and leather jackets posed for photographs. They passed the grand tombs of Melbourne's forefathers, and graves of the humble whose names were all but obliterated. They walked in silence until Sandy, who had the map, indicated that they should leave the main road and take a narrow path to the right. There were no signposts, and it was almost by chance that they came across the place they'd been seeking.

It was a small space under two peppercorn trees. There had possibly once been a lawn, but now a few lone weeds struggled in the hard soil. There was a wooden bench and four stones studded with brass plaques. The largest stone was inscribed with the words:

Never held. Never seen.
But never forgotten.
Cherished but not cradled.

The other plaques had names and dates and expressions of loss all the more poignant for their simplicity. *We had a home ready for you*, Moss read on one unadorned plaque. There were a few weathered toys, and two bunches of fresh flowers that had been placed there quite recently. As there were no dates after 1972, these fresh flowers were a testament to the longevity of grief. Moss could see the elderly mothers and fathers after forty, fifty years, still mourning their loss, visiting the baby they had never seen. Most of the plaques had no name, just dates: the birth day and death day of anonymous children. She sat down on the seat with Sandy and looked at the colourless sky, shivering as the cold wind moved through the trailing branches of the peppercorn trees.

'There's not much more we can do here,' said Sandy at last, heaving himself up with a sigh. Moss took some blooms from the flowers she had brought for Linsey and placed them gently beside the nearest memorial. Their warm yellow contrasted with the cold grey stone, creating a momentary illusion of sunlight.

They retraced their steps to the entrance and stopped at the row of walls where ashes were immured. Moss checked a piece of paper and found her way to Linsey's commemorative plaque. It was the first time she'd visited since the memorial service, and she read the inscription with dismay. In this last tribute to the life of her mother, she was not even mentioned. Felicity couldn't have chosen a better way to hurt her.

Moss arranged her flowers with numb fingers. *It's no more than I deserve*, she thought. *But I did love you, Mother Linsey. You have to understand that I just couldn't take the bullying.* She paused mid-thought as realisation dawned. *I guess you faced your share of bullies and bigots too. Maybe you understood more than I imagined.*

Moss glanced back at Sandy in mute apology for the delay. 'Take all the time you need, love,' he said.

Moss turned back to the wall. 'I'm glad I sang for you, Mother Linsey,' she whispered. 'If it weren't for you, I would never have found the discipline.' She paused. All at once, Felicity's words came back to her. Her exact words. *Linsey's last request was that you sing at her funeral.* At the time, Moss was still in shock and had not heeded the significance of these words. Linsey had *wanted* her to sing. Linsey had *known* she would sing. Had her mother sent her a message through Felicity? And if she had, did it mean that Linsey had forgiven her?

Moss spread her palm over the plaque. The cold metal resisted her touch.

'I'm sorry, Mother Linsey. I'm so sorry.'

'Come on, love,' said Sandy gruffly. 'It's okay.' But reminded of his mother's epitaph, he knew it wasn't okay at all.

Leaving the cemetery, they drove a short distance to a café, where they ordered coffee and sandwiches.

'I have the phone number of the organisation that set up the memorial,' Sandy told Moss. 'We don't know if the site we saw is where Aunt Lily's baby was buried or if it was one of the others. This group might be able to help us. There's no point in getting the poor old thing's hopes up.' In fact, Sandy had another source of information but chose not to tell Moss. It wasn't his secret to share.

As soon as he returned home, Sandy went to what had been his mother's sewing room. He stopped in the doorway and looked at the mess. Rosie had been fond of sewing, and when she died, her fabrics, cottons and notions had been bundled into two plastic garbage bags for donation to the charity shop. Neither Sandy nor his father had bothered to deliver them, and the bags now shared the space with boxes of magazines, old ledgers, books and sundry household items too good to throw out but not good enough to use. Rosie's sewing machine was still there. He remembered how happy she'd been to trade her old Singer treadle for an electric model. Now it sat there, its bland plastic cover casting a dumb reproach.

I should've given Mum's sewing machine away, Sandy thought. *She'd call this a wicked waste.*

But it was not the sewing machine that he'd come for. He went to the window seat and, sneezing violently, threw the dusty cushions onto the floor so that he could access the lid. He took a screwdriver from his pocket. The screws had rusted over the years, but they yielded one by one. He wheezed a little as he stood up and stretched his back. Even with good intentions, he felt reluctant to expose his mother's secrets.

Children living in a violent or conflicted household learn invisibility at a very early age. Sandy Sandilands was no exception, and he managed to move shadow-like through his childhood, avoiding any unnecessary contact with his parents. He must have been about eight when he first saw his mother opening this window seat and placing a book inside before screwing down the lid. He remembered his main feeling at the time was surprise to see that his mother could use a screwdriver. The Major liked to ensure that she was reliant upon him for everything. He sensed that this was a secret, and was guiltily glad to know that his father was out on the tractor. He slipped away, and thought no more about it until some years later when he came upon his mother writing at her small sewing table. She looked up with a start, protecting the book with her hands. There was fear in her eyes. She didn't need to speak; Sandy understood. 'Don't worry, Mum. I won't tell.' And he never did.

That was one of only three occasions when his mother had entrusted him with a secret. The second time occurred when he was about fourteen, and she was helping him to pack for the new school term. The Major, of course, was nowhere to be seen. *There's women's work and there's men's work*, he always said.

'Sandy,' his mother approached him timidly. 'I need to ask a favour.' His nod was neutral, but she continued. 'I'm afraid it means keeping a secret from your father.' Sandy's reading had recently taken on a racier tone. *Good Lord*, he thought, *was his mother going to confess to an affair?* He foolishly hoped she was. These romantic hopes were dashed when she gave him a letter to be sent to the Melbourne Hospital for Women, in which, she told him, she was making enquiries as to the possible whereabouts of Lily's baby's grave.

'Men don't understand these things,' Rosie said. 'I'm afraid your father might think I'm an interfering fool.' She looked steadily at her son. 'I've asked that the reply be sent care of you, at school. You can give it to me when you see me at half-term. Will you help me, Sandy? It's for Aunt Lily.'

Sandy was really afraid of his father by that time, and he visualised the consequences of participating in this deception. He wanted to say no, and that she was a fool to risk discovery.

What made her think she could trust him not to tell? But she did trust him, and after all the times he had implicitly or explicitly sided with his father, this was a rather wonderful foolishness. For once he felt worthwhile.

'Okay,' he said roughly. 'Give it here. I'll post it from the station. It's alright, I won't tell the old man.' But he pulled away as she kissed him.

The third time, just before her death, Rosie told him about the books in the window seat. 'My journals,' she whispered, still afraid. 'I had no-one to talk to, you see. Please destroy them for me.'

Again, 'Okay, Mum.' But his voice was kinder. 'I'll do the right thing, I promise.'

When the time came, though, Sandy couldn't bring himself to destroy the journals. They were all he had left of his mother's life, and he safeguarded them from all prying eyes, including his own. So they lay where she left them: under the cushions in the window seat. Biding their time until her son came, screw-driver in hand, to retrieve them.

Sandy hadn't made this decision lightly, and had set himself some ground rules. Firstly, he would only access the book or books from around the time the letter was sent to the hospital. Then he would scan the entries as quickly as possible, looking for keywords like *baby*, *Lily*, *hospital*, *letter*, *grave*—words that would point to the information he was seeking. In all other ways, he would respect his mother's privacy. He was only doing this to help Aunt Lily, he told his mother.

There were nearly thirty books in all, stacked in three neat piles; some were covered in black or green or blue cloth, others were no more than exercise books, but all were meticulously dated. Some were tied with ribbon. Sandy's hand hovered over these. They were the earlier ones, when Rosie was still a hopeful young girl. He picked up the top book and, despite his vow to the contrary, couldn't resist reading a little of his mother's early married life. The first book was marked 1936, and Sandy was surprised at the emotion he felt as he scanned the first page.

12 March. Arrived home today. Our honeymoon was wonderful but I can't wait to settle into real married life. Father and Lily met us at the station. Lily had prepared tea but George said we had to go straight home. I think they were a little disappointed, but George was understandably eager to bring me to our home. He's so practical. I asked if he was going to carry me over the threshold and he said that it was all women's nonsense. But he kissed me and called me his little duffer. I can't believe that I live in such a fine house. It needs a woman's touch, though.

13 March. George was gone when I woke but last night he was very masterful as we . . .

Sandy snapped the journal shut and mentally begged his mother's pardon. He felt he might be on safer ground in the war years and shuffled through the pile to find 1943.

12 May. George has returned to camp, and I feel such relief. It is a sin, I know, to feel so about one's husband. He has very little patience now with his little duffer. I feel he has lost all affection for me, and if it weren't for the conjugal act I fear he would barely tolerate me. Thank God I have been able to provide him with a son.

13 August. I went with Father to visit Lily today. My sister is so unhappy in that place. If ours were a different household I would bring her straight home and care for her here. Why must good men like Arthur die in this horrible war while George . . .

14 August. I am so ashamed of my entry for yesterday. George is an excellent provider and we want for nothing. I pray that he will return safely.

Be careful what you pray for, Sandy thought grimly. So it had taken only five short years for his father to reduce his new bride to the timid, apologetic ghost he remembered. He was sickened, but a dreadful fascination impelled him to continue. He picked up the next volume and opened it at random.

19 June. I couldn't go to church today. My back still aches from George's blows. He would have forced me to go with him but my cheek is bruised from where he pushed me down the steps. He's usually more careful. Now he blames me for bruising where it might show. I'm not able . . .

Sandy sat in the room that had been his mother's refuge and felt a terrible desolation. There, in his mother's handwriting, was the truth he had always denied. For the first time since his father's death, he looked, really looked, at his childhood. He saw his mother's pretty face become more ravaged, more haggard, as she strained to please her jeering, violent husband. He saw the warning in her eyes, felt the protective hands tighten on his small shoulders, tasted the treats she offered to sweeten the bitterness of their lives. Ashamed, he heard his youthful self speaking to her in his father's voice. He saw the bruises and the tears he'd chosen to ignore. Yes, he had been a frightened child at first, but as he grew older, he'd joined the oppressor. He could have found a job and taken his mother away, but he was too craven, and in the end too complicit, to challenge his father's power. And now, he realised, he was planning to build a memorial to the war hero who abused his own wife and all but stole her child.

Sandy had disciplined his memories for years, refusing to face the truth of his past. Occasionally dreams or rogue memories breached his defences, but he learned to put them aside, unaware of a slag heap of suppressed emotion that was becoming dangerously unwieldy. Now it collapsed, and he was horrified to see the slimy, eyeless creatures that lay hidden there.

Unable to continue reading, he went down to the kitchen and made a coffee laced with a generous portion of whisky. Then he sat on the sofa and had three more whiskies, neat this time. Finally, he went to bed with the bottle and fell into a drunken sleep.

The next day he awoke with a dry mouth and throbbing head, cursing the whisky, which always gave him a hangover, even when drunk in moderation. He made some strong coffee and went outside. The morning was crisp and clear, with some frost evident on the ground, on which there were pathetically few green shoots. The sky was cloudless: a hard, uncompromising blue. A flock of marauding galahs was attacking the old wooden shed by the home paddock. He thought of getting his shotgun—*I'll blow them to pink and grey pieces*—but he was too weary to move. Instead, he sat on the verandah and gazed out at the dry, flat terrain. *I* am *a great galah. You were right there, Dad. Maybe I should use the shotgun on myself. I'm just a great, useless galah.*

Staring out across the paddocks, he ignored the phone the first time it rang. *I'll tell you one thing, Dad: there'll be no Great Galah now. When I die, you'll be forgotten, you fucking bastard.* Anger energised him and when the phone rang again ten minutes later, he got up to answer it. It was Moss.

'Sandy,' she said. 'I've been thinking. I'd like to help Finn the way you're trying to help your Aunt Lily.'

Sandy was puzzled for a moment. He'd actually forgotten the reason he'd looked at the journals in the first place. *That'd be right. Too busy with my own problems.*

'Sandy? Are you there? I want to find out who Amber-Lee really is . . . Sandy?'

'Amber-Lee? Who's she?'

So Finn hadn't confided in anyone else. 'Just someone Finn knew once. She was buried at the City General,' she said vaguely. 'How are you going with Mrs Pargetter's baby?'

'Nothing yet,' he replied. 'I'll get back to you if I have any news.'

'The least I can do for Mum is to finish the job,' he muttered to himself as he hung up. 'I owe it to Aunt Lily too. I think she was the only person who really loved Mum.'

He returned to the sewing room and rummaged through the diaries to find the year he estimated the events took place. There it was: 1954. He opened it at random and then closed it again, taking it out to the kitchen where he made himself another coffee. After yesterday's revelations, he felt like a guilty child and didn't want to read it in his mother's room.

It was the beginning of the second term, he recalled, skimming the pages. They were packing football gear and his winter blazer. His eye caught an initial and he was unable to resist reading on.

9 May. I have entrusted the correspondence to S. He'll do the right thing, I know. He has a good heart, despite his father's influence. I must be patient and wait. I do miss my boy when he's at school, but it's safer there. G is becoming surlier by the day and this is such an unhappy house. I'm glad the bruises were gone by the time S got home for the holidays. He's so fond of his father. Perhaps in time he will see things more clearly. I was right to trust him. I'm sure I was right . . .

Such a little thing to ask . . . Sandy felt shame seep out through his pores where it lay, a clammy film on his skin. He read on.

10 June. S came home today for the long weekend. He has grown even taller in the last couple of months. Bought some linctus for his nasty cough. I'd like to know if they give him enough blankets at night but I daren't ask him. Sandy winced. *No letter from the hospital. Poor Lily . . .*

He moved on to the September break.

22 September. S home tomorrow. Have made cream sponge and some chocolate slices. G seems a bit mellower at the moment. I hope he stays that way while S is home.

23 September. S home. Taller than ever. He's put on even more weight. I'm sure he'll grow out of it. Neither his father nor I carry any weight. His school report was good. Nearly all As. He doesn't take after me, thank goodness. I never was a scholar. Not sure if S has a letter from the hospital. Will wait until G goes into town tomorrow.

24 September. The hospital has been no use at all. They say that the baby would have been buried in the Melbourne General Cemetery, but have no records of the birth. I was hoping we would at least know if it was a boy or a girl. Poor little mite may as well have never existed. I don't know what else I can do. Surely there are records somewhere? If only George were more sympathetic. He has a way of getting things done. But I daren't ask.

Sandy sighed and closed the diary. He felt immeasurably older. The temptation was to succumb to weariness and sleep for days, weeks, forever . . . it didn't matter. But having read her journal, Sandy knew that he owed it to his mother to carry through with his plan. Soft and flaccid on the outside, he had a small, hard core of courage, and he called upon it again now as he had when, as a frightened schoolboy, he agreed to post the letter.

If there were no records in 1954, it was unlikely that there'd be any now. Nevertheless, he fished in his wallet for the crumpled note on which he'd jotted down the phone number, and dialled the Stillborn and Neonatal Death Support group.

The volunteer introduced herself as Eva. 'Record-keeping was very poor in those days,' she affirmed. 'You say your mother tried to trace the baby through the hospital records?'

'Yes, but with no luck. You'd think there'd be something.'

'You have to remember that stillborn babies were not really regarded as children by the medical and legal authorities. They had no understanding of how a parent might grieve. We try to support these parents as best we can, but to be honest, it's very hard to locate babies born in the forties. You can usually only do it through the mother's medical records, but if you've already tried that . . .'

'What do you suggest, then?'

'You could take your aunt to one of the communal burial sites at the cemetery. They're scattered through the various denominations. Did she attend church at the time?'

'Church of England. She still plays the organ.'

'Well, perhaps if you took her to the Church of England area . . . She may find some comfort there. I'm sorry I haven't been much help. I can send you some information about our support groups, if you like.'

'Thank you. You've been a great help. Much appreciated.' Sandy replaced the receiver and wrote a generous cheque to the support group on behalf of his mother and aunt. He addressed the envelope, began to rise, then sank back into the chair, irresolute. Perhaps he was stirring up things that should be left to lie? There was very little to tell. Lily's baby boy, or girl, may or may not have been buried in the Melbourne General Cemetery, possibly in the Church of England site. Should he take this meagre offering to his aunt or just let her be? She was eighty-three and becoming frail. He felt unequal to the responsibility and decided to talk to Moss and Finn. They'd know what to do.

15

Moss and Amber-Lee

Moss's DECISION TO SEEK AMBER-LEE's identity was not wholly altruistic. Sandy's quest for his aunt's baby had been the catalyst, and the visit to the cemetery had moved her profoundly. She was truly saddened to think of the baby and the young woman, both buried without a name. She had also come to care for Finn and was disturbed to think of him growing old with his guilt and grief. But she had her own guilt and grief, and until she could return to the Conservatorium or some sort of employment, she knew that unfettered time would corrode her resolve. She was absurdly afraid of becoming an old lady who talked to her dog and knitted tea cosies for the United Nations. Or a person who spent hours a day in silence. She needed activity; she needed a challenge; and Amber-Lee's identity could provide both while Moss sought to help the parent who still needed her. It was too late to reconcile with Linsey, but Moss still longed for redemption.

She debated within herself whether she should tell Finn what she had planned. There was still a remoteness about him, and she often felt that he would have retreated from the world altogether had it not been for his friendship with Mrs Pargetter and her nephew. And now her own arrival too, of course. There was something suspect in his apparent solidity. She had moments of insight when she felt that his component particles were only held together by an effort of will. That one day he would simply give up and allow himself to disintegrate. She would have liked him to know she was planning to help him, but feared what would happen if she were unsuccessful.

So she set out for Melbourne alone. Before leaving, she had dug out the files, feeling like a thief but excusing herself on the grounds of the greater good. Finn was off on his evening Silence, so she had time to take notes. As well as the dates and places of the accident and subsequent inquest, she had the names of key contacts, such as the police officer in charge, the social worker, the doctor and the prostitute, Brenda Watson.

She caught the bus in time for the morning train, and as she watched the houses and trees fly past, she wondered at the wisdom of her undertaking. If no-one could identify the young woman at the time, what made her think she could do any better now, over ten years later? True, she had found her father, but he was a well-published academic; he'd made a name for himself (she smiled fleetingly at the irony). This girl had appeared as if from nowhere and left as anonymously as she had come.

Amy was holidaying with friends in Darwin, so Moss had the house to herself. She unpacked, opened a few windows, threw some clothes into the washing machine, and made herself a cup of tea, smiling as she replaced the hand-knitted tea cosy over the pot. She flicked through a three-day-old newspaper, took out her notebook, closed it again and went to check on the washing. It was only halfway through its cycle.

When Amy had finally agreed that she was old enough to stay alone in the house, Moss had revelled in the sense of freedom and ownership of her space. Now the house seemed vast, its outer walls retreating until she was a mere speck in the midst of the vastness. At that moment she understood Mrs Pargetter's sense of absence as a presence. Linsey, wherever she was, was not here.

Moss tried to dismiss these thoughts. *Mustn't become morbid*, she told herself sternly. *I need some company. Hamish*, she thought. *I wonder if Hamish is home?*

As she dialled his number, she had the grace to feel guilty. She always seemed to contact Hamish when she needed something. And he always responded. He was like a big brother, and she treated him with the careless affection characteristic of such a relationship.

Hamish was delighted to hear from her. 'We thought you'd dropped off the edge of the earth,' he said, then recollected himself. 'I mean, I'm so sorry to hear about Linsey. I would've come to the memorial service, but I didn't even know about it until I spoke to Magda. I was in Sydney at the time.'

'No need to apologise. Linsey hated a fuss. Now, what are you doing for dinner?'

'Beans on toast, I should think. Or perhaps pizza, if I can't be bothered cooking.'

'How about coming over here? We can order pizza and open a bottle of Amy's red.'

Hamish arrived promptly at seven with the pizzas, his grey

eyes smiling behind thick-lensed glasses. He stooped to kiss Moss's cheek as she took the pizza boxes.

'Come on through. We'll eat in the kitchen. It's cosier. The dining room's a bit grand for pizza.'

As they chatted amiably over pizza and wine, Hamish looked across at Moss and wondered where all this was going. They'd known each other since high school, where they'd both been involved in the annual musical productions. He grinned to himself as he remembered their performance in *Jesus Christ Superstar*. Moss had played Mary Magdalene, and he was cast as an unlikely Judas. They'd gone their separate ways at university, she to continue her music, and he to study landscape architecture, but they had remained friends.

I wonder why she asked me over? he thought. *It's usually me who makes contact.* He'd had a futile crush on her at school, but his temperament was phlegmatic, and when he received no encouragement, he moved on without rancour. An only child, he cheerfully took on the big brother role into which he was cast. Now, sitting in her kitchen eating pizza, he began to wonder, to hope that they might move on from 'just mates' to something more. He watched closely as Moss absently ran her fingers through her hair. She wasn't actually pretty, but her features were regular and those dark blue eyes—they got to him every time . . .

'Dessert,' she said, embarrassed by his appraising look.

He did a mock double-take when she brought out a home-made ginger fluff sponge. 'Don't tell me you made that. What happened to our vow to never make a recipe that had more than two steps? That looks like a six- or seven-stepper to me.'

Moss had to confess. 'An old lady I've been staying with—Mrs Pargetter—she made it for me. We can have it with our coffee.'

The sponge was a bit rich after the pizza, but Hamish wolfed down a second slice while Moss told him about Amber-Lee. She didn't tell him about her relationship to Finn, just that she was making some enquiries for a friend.

'The truth is,' she said, 'I don't know where to start. I thought we could, you know, toss around a few ideas.'

Hamish sighed. So she did just want his help with something. *The story of my life*, he thought ruefully, but he accepted it with good grace and put his mind to the problem at hand.

'As far as I can see, your best bet is to start with the police officer—what's his name?—Graham Patterson. You may have some problems with the privacy legislation, though. And he might have moved on by now. Almost certainly, when you think about it.'

'He was a senior constable at the Fitzroy police station. Finn, my friend, said he was quite nice. That's all I know.'

'Not much to go on. Tell you what. Mum's friend, Judy—her daughter's married to a copper—she might be able to help us. If we can't trace your man through Fitzroy police, I'll ask her.'

'Sorry to bother you with all this, Hamish.'

'No worries. Nothing like a mystery to put a bit of spice into life.' He leaned over and kissed her lightly on the cheek. 'Two heads are better than one, I always say.'

They finished their coffee, and Moss made some more. She enjoyed the uncomplicated company of someone her own age—someone she could laugh with. It was two am before Hamish left, promising to contact Judy's daughter if Moss had no luck at the Fitzroy police station.

She went there the next day. There was no Graham Patterson and no-one was telling her where to find him. 'They probably thought I was out to get him—that he'd arrested my lover or something,' she said plaintively to Hamish. 'Do I look like a gangster's moll?'

'Yep. It's that big handbag you carry. Could hide a concealed weapon.'

Judy's daughter proved to be a useful contact, however, and provided a phone number for Patterson—now a senior sergeant who was stationed at the large police complex in St Kilda Road. Moss rang him and arranged a meeting. The constable behind the desk was expecting them, and ushered them through a maze of corridors into the senior sergeant's office. Moss noticed the overflowing intray and guiltily thanked him for taking the time to see them.

'I remember the case quite well,' Graham Patterson told them. 'It was one of the first of its kind I'd dealt with. I'd seen plenty of road trauma and death, of course, but we'd always been able to identify the victim. I felt I'd failed her, you know?' He looked uncomfortable. 'Then there was your father. He wouldn't let it go. Used to come to the station all the time, asking if we'd found anything. Drove us mad, to be honest.'

Hamish looked up sharply. So this so-called friend was her father. Why hadn't she trusted him with that information? Surely he was entitled. He suddenly became aware that Moss was speaking again.

'He still hasn't let go,' said Moss. 'That's why we're here.' She was embarrassed to ask the next question. 'I'm not suggesting you didn't do all you could at the time, but . . .'

'But I did do all I could. We all did. Have you seen the coroner's finding? There was never any suggestion of negligence on our part.' Moss began to apologise again but he cut her off. 'The problem is, my investigation was hampered by the very fact that I was a police officer. I always felt that Brenda knew more than she let on at the time. But she didn't trust the police. For instance, when we searched her room, there were so few of Amber-Lee's belongings that we believe Brenda probably stole the rest.'

'Did you ask her about them?'

'Of course we did. She said that Amber-Lee was just a roommate: someone to share the rent. She had no idea what might have been missing. Brenda was a very aggressive witness, and she'd been beaten up badly by the time we spoke to her. I'm not even sure that I trust the description she gave us.'

'It all sounds hopeless,' said Moss. 'We haven't even started and we seem to have reached a dead end.'

'Not necessarily.' Patterson began writing on a pad and tore off the page. 'Here,' he said, giving it to Moss. 'This is the address of the Prostitutes' Collective. I've written a note to Georgia Lalor asking her to help you. You'll find her there most days. She's the only one I can think of who might be able to help.' He stood up and shook hands with them both. 'I always thought Brenda was the key. Funny—these things stick with you, even after all this time. I hope you find her.'

'We'll do our best,' said Hamish.

Waiting until they were back out on the street, he turned to Moss. 'Why didn't you tell me this was for your father? You used to tell me you didn't know who your father was.' His tone was aggrieved.

Moss took his arm. 'I'm really sorry, Hamish. It's not that I don't trust you. It's just that my father told me about Amber-Lee in confidence. In the end I had to tell Judy when she rang me for the details. They needed to know why I was interested in the case.' She searched his face. 'Okay now? We're still mates?'

'Alright. Still mates. But tell me, how did you find your father?'

Moss related the story of her search as they made their way to the Prostitutes' Collective, which was only a twenty-minute walk from the police station. They were so engrossed in their conversation that they almost walked past its unremarkable entrance. The Collective was housed in an old red-brick build-ing, and they entered through a single glass door which led to a large room furnished with several armchairs and a cluster of desks. Some young women were looking at a noticeboard, and another was feeding the photocopier.

Moss and Hamish looked at each other. It wasn't quite what they'd expected. An older woman, dressed stylishly in black, came over to where they were standing.

'Are you the reporters?' she said.

'What? No, we're here to see Georgia,' said Hamish.

'We have a letter of introduction,' Moss added.

'Georgia's in a meeting at the moment. Did you have an appointment?'

Moss was chastened by the woman's tone. 'Sorry. We didn't know we had to have one.'

The woman sighed. 'Who's the letter from? I might be able to fit you in later today.' Moss handed her the letter and she nodded. 'Graham Patterson. Yes.' She returned to her desk and referred to a diary. 'She can see you at three this afternoon.'

With nearly four hours to fill, Moss and Hamish decided to walk along the foreshore and have lunch at one of the bay-side restaurants. It was a clear spring day, with a hint of summer in the sun's rays. There were a few yachts bobbing on the water, sporting sails of red, yellow and sparkling white.

'When I was a kid,' Hamish told her, 'I always wanted to go to sea. I used to read books about explorers and pirates—anything about the sea—but my parents didn't even like the beach. We always went up to the mountains for our holidays. Anyway, one day my mate Ben's parents invited me out for a day's fishing on their boat. I was so excited, I couldn't sleep the night before. We'd been on the boat for less than twenty minutes when I started to throw up. It wasn't even rough. The sea was like a millpond. They were very nice about it, but I was so sick that they had to bring me back and ring my parents to collect me. I was mortified, and Ben couldn't wait to tell the story when we got back to school.'

Moss grinned. 'And that was the end of your seafaring ambitions?'

'No, I'd still like nothing more than to be able to sail the world. But I have to accept that it's never going to happen.' He looked at her earnestly. He didn't want to see her hurt. 'Some things that we want are just not possible. We can try to find Amber-Lee's identity, but there may be a point where we can't go any further. We have to be able to recognise that point when we reach it.'

'*If* we reach it.'

'Yes. If we reach it.'

At three o'clock they were back at the Collective for their meeting with Georgia. Patterson had told them a little about the organisation, which had been set up as a kind of union for prostitutes. It promoted safe sex and provided information to newcomers. There was a register of violent clients, and staff cooperated with the police to protect the safety of their members and, in some cases, the general public.

Georgia was a full-figured woman in her mid-forties, with rich chestnut hair caught in a clasp at the nape of her neck. She welcomed them in a pleasantly modulated voice and stood aside as they entered her office. They were surprised to find that it was like any other office—an untidy desk with a framed photo and a vase of daffodils, a phone, a computer and some shelves lined with dark blue folders. *Quality Procedures*, Moss was astonished to read on the spine of one folder. *What was I expecting?* she asked herself. *Crimson velvet curtains? Erotic artworks? Silk kimonos?*

'So Graham Patterson sent you to me. How is he?'

'He's well,' replied Moss, relinquishing her thought with a guilty start. 'Says to tell you hi.'

Georgia smiled. 'Now, how can I help you?'

Moss told her story as succinctly as she could, and Georgia listened without comment.

'. . . so if we could find Brenda,' Moss concluded, 'we might find the key to Amber-Lee.'

Georgia sat back in her chair. 'I remember the accident. I was working at the Kasbah at the time, but I knew some of the streetgirls. Didn't know this Amber-Lee, though. I knew Brenda a little. Just enough to pass the time of day. She was one of Vince's girls. He was a nasty piece of work.'

'Can you tell us anything about the accident?'

'Only that it happened and the police were trying to find out who the victim was. Brenda disappeared soon after.' She looked at them sharply. 'Look, I might know someone who can help, but I need to know I can trust you. What's in it for you?'

'It's just as I told you. I want to help my father to give Amber-Lee back her name, her identity. Honestly, I don't have any other motive.'

Georgia measured Moss with her eyes. She was usually a good judge of character, and this girl seemed sincere. So many street people died without a name and were buried without mourners. She'd been a streetworker herself in her younger days and was painfully aware of the fragility of identity in such a world. It was her sense of responsibility that had drawn her to work for the Collective, and in helping Moss discover Amber-Lee's real name, she was helping all the girls, in a way. *There but for the grace of God* . . . she thought grimly as she opened her desk drawer and took out a notepad.

'I'll have a word with Damara. I think she kept in touch with Brenda. Give me your number and I'll let you know if she'll speak to you. It might take a week or two.'

Thanking Georgia, they left, feeling elated. They hadn't reached that dead end yet. Moss returned to Opportunity to await developments, and Hamish went back to his studies. The interruption had been welcome. He needed to come up with an idea for a major project to support his thesis, but time was running out and ideas were elusive.

Finn was worried about Moss. She seemed so dejected, and her interest in her music had waned again. She was too young to drift into the lassitude that infected so many in Opportunity. She needed cheering up, but he was at a loss. What did young women enjoy nowadays? She didn't have a boyfriend; Mrs Pargetter had mentioned this a couple of times. The problem was that he didn't know any suitable young men. He'd have to come up with something else. *Women always like a nice dinner*, he thought. Some hopeful calculations indicated that it must be close to her birthday. A present too, then. Dinner and a present.

He was due to meet with the Commission for the Future next month, but, impatient to execute his plan, he brought the meeting forward and travelled down to Melbourne by bus and train.

Wandering aimlessly around the shops, he had a sudden inspiration. Jewellery. Women loved jewellery, didn't they? He slid diffidently into several jewellery stores and was finally captured by a well-dressed young man who looked doubtfully at his customer's dishevelled appearance.

'May I assist you, sir?'

'Yes. Yes. I'm looking for a gift. For a woman.'

'Our selection is very fine. Many items are hand-crafted.'

The assistant's tone implied that Finn couldn't possibly afford such merchandise.

Finn stood his ground. 'I was thinking of a pendant. You know—a thing on a chain. Gold. I want gold.'

Now there was a tinge of impatience underlying the studied politeness. 'All our gold is eighteen carat or more, sir.'

'Show me what you have. She's only twenty-four, so I don't want anything old-fashioned.'

The young man raised his eyebrows and Finn blushed. 'My daughter,' he snapped. 'Do you have anything to show me?'

Finn looked at the various lockets, heart-shaped, oval, with and without gems. There were tiny gold dolphins (*Very popular with young girls, sir*). Finn rather liked the pearl drops, but thought they might be a bit middle-aged. He felt helpless and wished he could ask a woman's opinion. Then he saw it. A gold filigree treble clef hanging from a finely wrought, tubular chain.

'That one. I'll have that one.'

The sales assistant sniffed. 'It's one of a kind, sir. Handcrafted. Very expensive.' He indicated the price tag.

'Gift wrap it, please,' Finn said. 'I've got a train to catch.'

Finn was pleased with his find and couldn't keep the smile from his face as the train sped through the familiar countryside. When he got home, he carefully unwrapped the parcel to look at the pendant again, then rewrapped it before clumsily retying the bow.

When Moss came in from walking Errol, her father was waiting at the door.

'Are you doing anything on Saturday night?'

Moss was surprised. When she was in Opportunity, she never did anything on Saturday night. 'No. Why?'

Finn hunched his shoulders and looked at her from under his eyebrows. 'I'd like to take you out to dinner. Somewhere nice. Chez Marie, in Cradletown.'

Moss was surprised and touched. 'Thank you, Finn. I'd love to come.'

She was unsure what to wear. Mrs Pargetter assured her that Chez Marie was indeed a very nice place. 'Very fashion-able. It's won the regional Fine Dining Medal five years in a row. It said so in the local paper. The couple who do that cook-ing show own it. You know the one—on Wednesdays: *Classic Chefs*.' When she heard this, Moss was glad that she'd brought a few more clothes back with her.

At the agreed time, Finn appeared, squirming self-consciously in a suit and tie. He looked at his daughter in her black scooped-neck dress. She was even wearing high heels.

'You look beautiful, Moss,' he said in genuine admiration. 'I've got a taxi waiting. Let's go.'

Finn ordered wine, and Moss was surprised to see that he tasted it and allowed the waiter to fill his glass.

'Special occasion, Moss. I'm not an alcoholic. I just choose not to drink most of the time. But with a good meal and good company . . .'

They touched glasses. The restaurant was in the old assay building, and the renovators had kept the mosaic floor tiles, the intricate timber panelling and Art Nouveau stained glass. A fire was burning in the grate and individual lamps cast a glow on fine glasses and silver.

Moss was impressed. 'What a wonderful place, Finn.' She was even more impressed by the ease with which her father ordered. Clearly, he'd been used to this at some time in his life.

Finn's response to his surroundings came from the subliminal impulse of memory. He didn't stop to think about how he should act, and his natural courtesy gave him a dignity that charmed his daughter. As they waited for their soup, he lifted his glass again.

'Well,' he said, 'happy birthday, Moss.'

'It's not . . .' Moss began.

'I know,' her father said gently. 'But I've missed so many; you'll have to allow me this one.'

Moss grinned to cover her emotion. 'As long as I don't have to age another year.'

Finn reddened and fished in his pocket. 'I've got a present. For your birthday.' He looked on apprehensively as Moss fumbled with the now awkwardly tied parcel. 'I hope you like it.'

Moss was embarrassed and took longer than necessary to unwrap the gift. Presents always made her feel uncomfortable, and a gift from the undemonstrative Finn would take them a step further in their relationship. She finally opened the box and took out the pendant, which caught the light of the table lamp. Her eyes widened. It was exquisite.

'Finn, you shouldn't have . . .' She saw the disappointment in his eyes. 'But it's wonderful. Beautiful. Truly, I love it.' She took off the silver chain she was wearing and clasped the pendant around her neck. 'There. What do you think?'

The old charm surfaced as Finn smiled at his daughter. 'You look like a princess,' he said.

As the meal progressed, Finn ventured a question about her plans. 'Did you catch up with your course supervisor?'

'I've got till February to decide,' Moss replied shortly.

'I'm sorry, Moss. I didn't mean to pry.'

Her eyes filled with tears. 'It's Linsey, Finn. I know I should continue for her sake as well as my own, but I feel so bad about the way I treated her and—I don't know . . . I went to the memorial wall and . . . She asked for me to sing, you know? That's a good sign, don't you think?' She looked at her father hopefully.

Finn was appalled to see her tears. This outing was supposed to cheer her up. He searched his mind for things to say: wise, compassionate things that would smooth the tension from her face and, most of all, stop her from crying. But he'd always been at a loss when women cried.

'I'm sure you'll get back to your singing,' he said, ignoring her last question. 'Let's talk about something more cheerful. You'll never guess what Sandy's been up to.'

Moss sighed and brushed her eyes. 'Don't tell me we're getting a giant cockatoo as well!'

16

Lily Pargetter and her baby

EAGER AS USUAL TO GET his plans underway, Sandy asked Moss and Finn to meet him at the pub for lunch. 'I don't want Aunt Lily to know for now,' he said. 'I've got some information, and I need to discuss where to go from here.'

'It's like this,' he said after they'd ordered their meal. 'There are identifiable places where babies were buried, but there's no record of Aunt Lily's baby anywhere. The woman from SANDS suggests taking her to the Church of England section of the cemetery. It might comfort her to see the burial place and the memorial—give her another focus. What do you think?'

'All I know is that she needs some sort of help,' said Moss. 'She's in pain, Sandy. She hides it well enough, but I've seen her with her defences down.'

Sandy sipped his beer thoughtfully, and they sat in silence while the pub noise rose and fell around them.

Finn finally spoke. 'So you don't know whether to tell Mrs Pargetter that the gravesites have been found, or whether to let it go.' Sandy nodded. 'Moss tells me that your aunt feels the baby's still in the house. She never said anything like that to me.'

'It only started happening again since Moss came back. Aunt Lily seems to think that Moss can bring the baby out of hiding.'

'It's become a bit distressing,' Moss admitted. 'Sometimes I find her standing in the doorway of the room. Other times I come back and find her sitting on the bed. When she sees me, she just says, *I'm looking for my baby*. Then she goes about her business as though nothing has happened.' She paused. 'The room does have a strange feeling . . .'

Sandy nodded. 'From what I overheard as a child, she brought an imaginary baby home with her from the hospital. Used to take it for walks, buy it clothes and everything. That's why they put her in Chalmers House. That was the mental institution just out of Cradletown. It was closed down in the seventies after a fire. Good thing too, from what you hear.'

Finn didn't feel qualified to comment on Mrs Pargetter's emotional state. 'You know your aunt best, Sandy,' he said. 'What's your gut feeling?'

'I don't know. Maybe if she can visit a gravesite, it will give her some peace of mind.'

Moss agreed. 'I read the plaques. It seemed to me that at least some of the pain the parents feel comes from not knowing. It's not time that brings relief in these cases—it's finally knowing where their babies lie.'

Finn stood up. This conversation was too close to home. 'It's not for us to decide,' he said abruptly. 'Everyone has a right to know . . . things. Sorry. Have to go and—and check some stats.' And before they could reply, he bolted.

Sandy wanted Moss to be present when he spoke to his aunt, but she declined. Firstly, she felt this was a family matter, and secondly, she was rattled by Mrs Pargetter's insistence on her own connection to the baby.

'I'll just complicate matters,' she said. 'This is something between you and your aunt.'

The next day, Moss returned to Melbourne and Sandy invited himself to his aunt's for lunch.

'Don't go to any trouble, Aunt Lily. I'll bring some ham and fresh rolls.'

The old lady sniffed. 'I can still feed my guests, George. I have some nice vegetable soup that I made with Moss. You can bring some rolls,' she conceded. 'We'll have them with the soup.'

Sandy, knowing his aunt's regular habits, turned up promptly at twelve thirty. 'I hate it when Moss goes,' she said petulantly after absentmindedly offering her cheek for a kiss. 'Errol doesn't like it either, do you, Errol?'

Errol woofed his wholehearted agreement.

They sat down to the soup, and Sandy, who had rehearsed the conversation in his mind, deployed his opening gambit. 'I took Moss to the cemetery the other day. She wanted to visit her mother Linsey.'

'Very strange arrangement, that one,' his aunt replied, juggling her teeth with the soup spoon. 'You didn't see that sort of thing in my day.'

Sandy was checked. She was supposed to say something about the comfort such a visit might bring. He'd have to prompt her. 'She said it helped—you know, in her grieving.'

But Mrs Pargetter was off on her own train of thought. 'I suppose they *existed* in my day. But we didn't know. Rosie hinted something about Abby Lawson and Stella McGuire once. I didn't know what she was talking about. Perhaps that was what she meant.' She shook her head in wonder at her own youthful innocence.

'We wandered around the cemetery a bit. It's an interesting place,' offered her persistent nephew, with a growing sense of desperation.

'I wonder if they call Moss's other mother a *widow*. Is there a special word for it, do you think?'

Sandy tried again. 'Listen, Aunt Lily. While we were walking around, we found a spot where they buried stillborn babies.'

His aunt looked at him steadily, her soup spoon frozen in midair. 'And why should that interest me?'

He looked at his aunt in disbelief. This wasn't at all the conversation he'd rehearsed. 'Well, I thought that, you know, you might like to—to visit your . . . baby.'

'My baby lives here, with me. I've just misplaced it.'

Sandy felt a throbbing in his temples and his hands began to sweat. The colour rose to the surface of his face, a fine network of capillaries revealing an ugly mottle.

He would remain forever ashamed of what he did next. He'd been tense leading up to the visit, and his planned conversation had gone awry as Mrs Pargetter prattled on about Linsey and Amy and Stella and God knows who else. Then she sat there, bold as brass, asking what it all had to do with her. He struggled for self-control and teetered on the edge until she calmly told him she had misplaced her child. It was then that he felt himself rushing headlong into the darkness that had fascinated and repelled him all his life. Stumbling to his feet, he grabbed her shoulders and shouted into her face: 'What's the matter with you, woman? Are you completely batty? What do you mean, *misplaced*?'

Appalled, he let his hands fall as she cowered away from him. *Cowered. From him.* He saw, in a moment, history repeating itself, and sank back into the chair as harsh sobs lacerated his throat. 'I'm sorry. I'm sorry. Aunt Lily, I'm so sorry. I'm not like him. Mum, I promise I'm not like him.'

His aunt twisted her hands in distress. 'George—I can't—oh dear, please stop crying . . . Rosie, Rosie, I don't know what to do . . .'

Errol had interposed himself between the two, snarling a warning to Sandy. 'Come here, Errol,' Mrs Pargetter murmured. 'It's alright now, old boy.' The dog put his paws in her lap, but continued to growl softly, keeping an eye on Sandy, still slumped in his chair.

As she stroked the old dog's head, her agitated heart gradually slowed and returned to its usual measured beat. Time dripped away in relentless drops that fell far back into the waters of her past and then swept her forward into a lonely future. Sandy. What would happen to him now? What would happen to her? Her vision blurred and her hands shook but she steeled herself. *I can do it, Rosie.* She cleared her throat.

'George . . . *Sandy*,' she said. 'Never, ever do that again. Rosie kept making excuses for your father, but the truth is he was a cruel and violent man. Cruel his whole life till the day he died. I—I don't know what to do. I can't . . . I'm too old. Oh, Sandy . . . what can we do?'

Sandy began to excuse himself, his usual reaction to feelings of guilt. 'I wanted to make you happy. To set your mind at rest. I wanted to do it for Mum's sake too. She worried about you all the time, you know.' Even as he spoke, he knew that there was no excuse. He had to accept that he was George Sandilands' son. A son who had inherited his father's brutality along with the family farm.

Mrs Pargetter's voice broke and her eyes pleaded with his. 'I'm speaking to *you* now—to *Rosie's* son. There's a lot of good in you, Sandy. I'll never call you George again. It's your father's name, not yours.' She articulated her next words distinctly, with pauses to emphasise her meaning. 'And you are not your father. You don't have to be. Do you hear me? You don't have to be.' She turned away. 'Dear Rosie,' she said. 'Such a gentle, loving soul.' Even after all these years, she missed Rosie more than she could say. Here was a chance to repay some of her sister's kindness. She would save Sandy. 'I'll come with you to the cemetery. It was kind of you to take the trouble.'

Her nephew looked up, his large face blurred and crumpled like wet cardboard.

'Go now,' she said. 'I'm very tired. I think I'll have a little nap.'

Sandy came over to give her his customary peck on the cheek but stopped, still deeply ashamed. He half raised his hand in farewell and went out, closing the door quietly behind him.

Lily Pargetter sat on in her chair. Sadness overwhelmed her. It was too deep for tears, so she continued to sit, stroking Errol's head until she was suddenly aware that night had fallen.

As he drove away from his aunt's house, Sandy looked with puzzled gravity at his soft white hands on the steering wheel. It was as though they had acted of their own volition. He recoiled again as the steering wheel became his aunt's stooped shoulders. It was lucky that he met no other drivers on the road home. He found himself unlocking his door without any further recollection of the journey.

He had to steel himself, but there he was the next day standing sheepishly on his aunt's doorstep, a lemon pie balanced in his hand. He knew that if he left it any longer, he would never have the courage to return to his aunt's house. The Major wouldn't have recognised this as courageous—there are no Distinguished Service Orders for acts of moral courage—but Mrs Pargetter realised what it must have cost him. She patted his arm.

'Now,' she said, 'let's have a cup of tea and you can tell me your plans for the visit to Melbourne.'

Gratefully, Sandy slipped into planning mode and suggested they stay in Melbourne overnight. 'That way it won't be too tiring. How would you like it if we went to a show as well?'

Mrs Pargetter smiled. 'That would be lovely. How about the opera?'

Sandy groaned inwardly. He was a country and western man.

'You don't get away scot-free, young man,' said his aunt, and never mentioned the ugly incident again.

Sandy took the car as far into the cemetery as he could, and then he and his aunt walked slowly down the narrow paths between the graves. She walked reluctantly, her head bowed, a straw hat shielding her papery skin from the sun. Sandy was pleased that the day was fine. He wanted everything to look as serene as possible, remembering the sullen sky and biting winds that assailed them when he and Moss had made their pilgrimage. Today the sky was benign, and despite the cool breeze there was a hint of warmth in the air. Nevertheless, the grey sentinels that stood over the graves were as bleak as ever. Sandy shuddered and was momentarily grateful for the family plots that awaited them both in St Saviour's little churchyard.

Mrs Pargetter stopped in front of one elaborate stone. '*In loving memory of Hannah Wilson, wife of John, mother of Matthew and Dora. 1895–1930. Rest in peace,*' she read. 'I wonder where John is? He wasn't buried beside her by the looks of things. Perhaps he married again and was buried with his second wife.' As though she'd heard Sandy's thoughts, she added: 'At least in Opportunity we all rest together.' She sat on the marble bed and patted it. 'Forgive me, Hannah Wilson. I need to sit a while. I can't get about as I used to.'

Happy to take a break himself, Sandy waited until she was rested, and they resumed their walk towards the straggling peppercorn trees.

'It's here,' Sandy said, indicating the seat. His aunt was

out of breath again and was pleased to be able to sit down. She sat with her eyes closed for a few minutes, touching her forehead and cheeks with a lace-edged handkerchief. Then she looked around her. The small clearing was surrounded by tombstones which stretched in ordered ranks as far as her eyes could see. In the middle distance, the two peppercorns strove unsuccessfully to provide a canopy over the memorial seat.

They're poor specimens, Mrs Pargetter thought, as she remembered the huge, gnarled trees of her childhood. She and Rosie had loved the peppercorn trees that grew beside the railway line. They used to collect the cocoons spun by the fat blue-green caterpillars that lived on the leaves, and then waited, usually in vain, for the emergence of the moth. They were wonderful trees to climb, too. The girls would sit dangling their legs over the branches and making veils with the trailing leaves, taking turns at being the bride.

By the time Lily was indeed a bride, the war had started and it became difficult to obtain suitable fabrics. So she wore a long veil of Limerick lace that her aunt, who had married a Catholic, was able to borrow from the nuns in Cradletown. She wore Rosie's wedding dress and her mother's pearl pendant. Her shoes were the only new thing she'd worn that day, but it didn't matter. She felt beautiful; she *was* beautiful because her Arthur never tired of telling her so. *So many years ago now.* Arthur had looked nervous and handsome in his striped suit and the paisley silk tie she'd given him as a wedding present. 'Gee,' he said when he opened the parcel. 'It's a ripper of a tie. I reckon I'll look like Errol Flynn in this.' He kissed her soundly and then produced his present for her, watching her open it with a look of sly anticipation. It was a pink satin dressing-gown with high-shouldered quilted sleeves and a wide sash. 'You've got such a tiny little waist,' he said. 'With your lovely red hair you'll look like Rita Hayworth.'

Mrs Pargetter could still remember her blushes. It was quite daring, shocking even, for a young man to buy what was tantamount to underwear for his sweetheart. She and Rosie giggled as they folded it into her case, still wrapped in the soft white tissue paper. After Arthur died, she had clutched the gown around her, rocking back and forth in her grief. It was a comfort of sorts, but no substitute for his arms.

She took it with her to the hospital when she went into premature labour. She wanted to wrap their child in something that was connected to its father.

'What a lovely gown,' the young nurse had said enviously as she helped Lily unpack. 'By the look of things, you'll be in the labour ward soon. I'll have this ready for you when you come back here.' And she hung it over the chair. That was the last Lily saw of the gown. When she came out of the anaesthetic, it was gone.

'I need it,' she told the duty sister. 'I need it to wrap my baby in.'

The sister looked down with pity as she injected her with morphine. 'Go to sleep now, Mrs Pargetter. You'll need your strength. Doctor will be in soon.'

'My baby. You haven't even told me if it's a boy or a girl. Please bring me my baby.' She clutched at the nurse's starched uniform.

'Sleep, now, dear. You aren't quite strong enough yet.'

She awoke a second time to find a short, balding man standing with her father and Rosie.

'I'm Dr Macgregor. How are we now, young lady? A bit sore, I imagine.'

'My baby. Where's my baby?'

'Your baby was very tiny. I'm afraid it didn't survive the birth.'

She looked at her father, and Rosie, who was crying. 'What does that mean? *Didn't survive the birth*. What does that mean?'

She came to know what it meant. It meant empty arms, milk overflowing from painful breasts, a sense of abandonment and feelings of shame and guilt. She'd not been strong enough to protect their child. *Look after little Tiger for me*. Those had been Arthur's last words to her and she'd failed him; failed their child.

She stirred in her seat and returned to the present, looking around her, bewildered. Then the memorial rocks swam into view, with their brass plaques and sad little messages. She felt very tired. 'Can you read them to me, please, Sandy?'

Sandy squatted uncomfortably, his large body obscuring the rocks from her sight. 'Let's see . . . There are some that only have names and dates. I'll just read the ones with inscriptions.'

'No. Read everything, please. It's only right to read everything.'

So Sandy began a litany of names and dates. '*Mary Simpson, 7 June 1971. Peter Ashley Moore, 15 September 1963. You are wrapped tightly in our hearts. Baby Sartori, 1 December 1954. We never forgot you, now we've found you at last* . . . Do you want me to go on?'

'Please, Sandy.' So much sadness in this place.

'*Alan Michael Thompson, 12 July 1961. Rosemary Jane Bartley.*' His voice was husky with emotion. '*The one day we had you is still precious . . . Nathan John . . .*' He finally stood up. 'That's all of them.' Only twenty minutes had passed but they had encompassed sixty years of sorrow.

So many, yet none of them hers. 'Thank you. Just let me be for a bit, will you, dear?'

Sandy walked away a little as Lily Pargetter bowed her head and said a prayer for all the lost babies and their grieving parents. Then she gathered her courage and looked for her child among the little souls that crowded her consciousness. She listened to the wind and opened her heart but found only silence.

'Sandy,' she said. Her tone was flat and passionless. 'My baby isn't here.' Sandy began to demur. 'It's not here,' she said simply. 'I know. I'm its mother.'

They laid the flowers they had brought and retraced their steps. Sandy was uneasy. He'd expected tears, but his aunt talked about the weather and the opera, even joking a little about some of the more elaborate monuments they passed. He responded cautiously, and later told Finn that she seemed almost indifferent. But at the opera that night, when Mimi died, she cried as though her heart would break.

They stayed in Melbourne for two more days, visiting the other three sites of infant burial. Each time, Sandy looked at her hopefully, but her response was the same: 'My baby isn't here.'

She was so sure that he came to believe her, and he had

to admit that he had failed. The old lady was quiet on the way home and Sandy put on a CD, *The World's Greatest Arias*, which he'd bought for her in Melbourne. She drifted off into an exhausted sleep, and he had to waken her when they arrived at her house.

'Sorry we weren't more successful, Aunt Lily,' he said, helping her up the steps. 'There probably are other sites. They just haven't been identified yet.'

'Oh, but it's confirmed what I knew all along, Sandy dear. Now I know for sure that my baby is still here with me in Opportunity.'

Gravely troubled, he settled her into her house and then left, promising to call in to see her the next day. He hesitated at the gate and then walked up Finn's path.

'So how did it go?'

'I think I've just made things worse,' Sandy replied. 'She's more convinced than ever that the baby is still with her.'

Lily Pargetter had to admit that she was getting old. The visit to the city had depleted her, and she spent the first few days after her return dozing by the fire with Errol. Her knitting lay on the sofa beside her while she sat and stared at the splayed fingers of her idle hands.

What had she expected of the visit to the cemetery? In truth, very little. She'd read of the memorial services in the newspaper, but could never bring herself to participate. Wherever her baby's body lay, its spirit had come home to Opportunity in her arms. She was now sure of that. At each site, she'd grieved for the bereaved and their lost children, but never once felt the presence of her own child.

Why did she go on this fruitless quest? she asked herself. In some part it was to acknowledge Sandy's goodness before he lost all belief in himself as a good person. *I think I've saved him, Rosie*, she told her dead sister as she sat by the fireside they'd shared as girls. Her other motive was deeper and more difficult to express. She had to satisfy herself that her baby was still with her. That it was still somewhere in the house, even though it hovered just at the periphery of her vision; just beyond the reach of her heart.

'Do you sense its presence, Errol?' she asked, stroking the old dog's head. 'They tried to burn away my memory, but memory survives in other places.' Her body still remembered the baby's weight as it grew inside her; it remembered the first stirrings, soft like a tiny fluttering bird; it remembered the growing strength of the little legs kicking. Her blood remembered its heartbeat, and her arms remembered its weight as she carried it home. She stroked the dog's greying coat.

'Errol, I brought my baby home and it lived right here with me until they took me to that terrible place.' Errol licked her hand and whimpered. 'I made a mistake, you see. I closed up the room, and it wasn't until Moss came to stay that I opened the door.' Her face seemed to melt in the firelight. 'Now I know that my baby has been hiding all these years. No wonder it hid from me. I closed my heart, Errol. Moss has a young, loving heart, just like mine was. My baby knows that.'

She looked down as the dog nuzzled her hand. 'You love me, old boy, don't you? But it's not enough any more. I need to find strength from somewhere to . . . to shine a light into that room and call my baby to me.' She was trembling now. 'I'm afraid, Errol. I'm afraid that when Moss goes, it will stay there in the shadows. Always out of reach.'

At the sound of Moss's name, Errol got up and padded over to her room. His mistress followed him and opened the door. The wind stirred the lace curtains, and the smell of furniture polish competed with the scent of freesias that floated through the open window. The dog whined and pressed against her as she stood in the doorway and willed her baby to appear. Her eyes strained at every shadow, challenged every shaft of light. She tried sliding her eyes sideways in a sudden movement that might capture a disappearing form. She stood until she was grey with fatigue and a bright spot of pain speared her temples. The teddies murmured their concern unheard, except by Errol, who growled softly. He remained at her side, stiff-legged, guarding her grief. That's where Moss found them when she returned home nearly an hour later.

'Are you okay, Mrs Pargetter?' she said gently as the old lady jumped, startled by her approach.

'Just thinking over the years,' she replied as Moss led her back to her chair by the fire. 'Do you know something, Moss? I was standing there, wanting to call to my baby, but then I realised why I couldn't. It has no name.'

17

Lusala Ngilu and Ana Sejka

ANA TOUCHED HER HAIR AND straightened her skirt as she stepped into the outer office. She presented her ID and waited for confirmation. The secretary checked her photo, swiped her card and looked up at her. 'Name?'

'Ana Sejka. I have an appointment with the ambassador at two thirty.'

The secretary indicated a chair. 'He's running a bit late, Ms Sejka. Please take a seat.'

Ana sat on the edge of her chair, hands clasped tightly in her lap. She was a neat-featured young woman, her heavy dark hair tied back with a silk scarf. Behind her glasses, her eyes were large and candid as she looked at, but did not see, a fine wood carving on the table beside her.

She'd been dreading this moment ever since she opened Mrs Pargetter's parcel. She'd opened the letter first and read the address with surprise. She and her family had arrived in Australia as refugees fleeing from Kosova in early 2000. They'd found a home in the country town of Shepparton, and it was there that Ana had finished school before continuing on to

Melbourne University where she had taken an honours degree in politics.

Opportunity. The confidence implied by the name appealed to her. She was sure she'd never heard of it; it was the sort of name you remember. A romantic at heart, Ana dressed Opportunity in clothes of her own designing, creating a mythical town where an ageless princess wove (this sounded better than knitted, she thought) fabrics with magical powers (again, better than tea cosies for her purpose). But despite her noble visions, Ana had failed where others before her had succeeded. Try as she might, she'd been unable to think of an original use for Mrs Pargetter's gift. And now here she was, waiting to meet Mr Lusala Ngilu, self-appointed quartermaster and long-time Kenyan Ambassador to the United Nations.

'The ambassador will see you now.' The secretary interrupted her thoughts, holding open the door of the inner office. 'Mr Ambassador, Ms Ana Sejka, student intern from Australia.'

Ana entered the room to be greeted by a short, thickset man who held out both hands in welcome. 'Come now,' he smiled. 'Let's have a cup of tea. Then we can have a little talk.'

Ana sat in the chair he indicated and was surprised to see that he was making his own tea.

'There,' he said, fitting a ragged tea cosy over the pot. 'We'll just wait for that to draw.'

He sat down opposite her and smiled again, a slightly lopsided smile that recalled the young Lusala Ngilu who had presented his credentials to the United Nations so many years ago. His large dark eyes shone, and Ana saw in them not only kindness but a determined optimism, a need to see gold among the dross. Embarrassed by such uncompromising faith, the young woman's eyes strayed to the teapot.

'I'm afraid my tea cosy has seen better days,' the ambassador said, his eyes following hers. 'I must be due for a new one. Do you have any left?'

Ana blushed. 'I'm afraid I have all of them left, Mr Ambassador. I . . . I'm afraid I haven't been able to think of an original use for them.' *It's not that I didn't try*, she thought, remembering her file searches, her discussions with colleagues, most of whom thought the enterprise peculiar to say the least. She'd even emailed home to her puzzled mother, who replied, *What is a tea cosy?* 'I'm sorry, Mr Ambassador. I've failed you.'

The ambassador poured the tea, asking only if she took milk or sugar. He sat back, and she noticed a small twitch in his cheek.

'I have to say,' he told her, 'that I'm impressed at the many uses our clever young interns have found for the tea cosies over the years.' Ana blushed again and started to speak. Lusala interrupted her, concerned that she'd taken his remark as a rebuke. 'No, no, I never thought that there should be a *new* use each time. I just wanted the young person to think about what it all means. What does it mean to you, Ms Ana Sejka?'

She sipped her tea, stalling for time, her mind blank. She had so wanted to impress this man who was widely respected at every level and across political divides in this complex organisation. She searched her heart before responding.

'It's respectful,' she finally said. 'We must use them properly out of respect for her—her *kindness*.'

Lusala smiled gently. 'I can see you're worthy of the task, young woman. Now,' he said. 'How many do you have?'

'Eighty-two.'

'What have you done with the others?'

'Nothing. That's all there were. This Mrs Pargetter may have lost count. Or she's slower than she was. She must be quite old by now.'

'She must have been younger than I first thought,' Lusala murmured, half to himself. 'But you're right. She'd be getting on by now.' He put down his cup. 'I've asked you here because I need you to do something for me.' He looked at Ana for confirmation and she nodded her head. 'Good. Firstly, I want you to distribute the tea cosies as I direct, and then . . . well, let's get the first task over with.'

So that was how Ana Sejka, Kosovar refugee from Shepparton, came to be standing at a soup kitchen in the Bronx, handing out tea cosies at the behest of the Kenyan Ambassador. She'd sewn the holes up to make beanie hats as he had instructed and then spent the best part of a week gathering her courage.

'You have to be mad,' her friends told her. 'Apart from anything else, it's dangerous.' When he couldn't dissuade her, Martin, an American IT adviser who worked on the floor below, announced that he would escort her.

'No strings,' he assured her when she demurred. 'Just helping a pal, a *mate*, as you Aussies say.'

At first they decided to stick to soup kitchens and emergency accommodation hostels. Neither of them felt up to scouring the parks and bridges at night. Lusala had been very specific regarding what she was to do. She was to approach a suitable person and politely offer the hat as a gift from Mrs Lily Pargetter from Australia. She had surprisingly few rebuffs. Her first recipient was an old man who accepted the gift with boozy gratitude. A man with wild eyes, dragging a useless leg, took another hat. *Australia*, he said. *They fought with us in 'Nam.* An old woman looked at the orange and red hat she was offered. *Rather have a blanket*, she said ungraciously, *but I might as well take it.*

After the first night, they realised that they'd approached only old people. The young homeless seemed more threatening, and Ana was too timid and Martin too prudent to approach them. They sensed an anger in many of them that was not so evident in the older people.

But Ana felt uncomfortable and couldn't sustain this discrimination. 'I'm sure the ambassador wants us to spread this right across the homeless community,' Ana said to a reluctant Martin, and the next night they gave hats to a shivering junkie, a youth proclaiming Judgement Day, and a young African-American woman pushing a baby and a wide-eyed toddler in an ancient pram.

It was a strange task, humbling the giver with the modesty of the gift, and enhancing the receiver as they accepted the odd-looking hats.

After two successful nights, Ana and Martin expanded their operation into the early morning, just after daybreak, leaving the small woollen bundles beside people sleeping rough. In order to fulfil Lusala's request they left a note pinned to each gift. There were some nasty incidents. Once, a junkie pulled a knife on them, and they were verbally abused several times, but they persisted until their task was almost complete.

'We've still got two left,' Martin reminded her when Ana proposed they head for home. 'Let's get rid of them first.'

'I keep one—that's what all the Lusalas do. It's supposed to be some sort of talisman,' she explained. 'And the ambassador asked me to save one for him.' She took out a cable-knit cosy of peacock blue with black borders. 'This one's just right for the ambassador, I think. I'm keeping the plain violet one.'

Martin put his hands on her shoulders and lightly kissed the tip of her nose. 'Thank you for letting me in on this, Ana. Maybe we could get together some time for a coffee?'

She smiled, her luminous eyes blinking behind her glasses. 'I'd like that.'

Summoned once again to the ambassador's office, Ana put the blue tea cosy into a gift bag and rode the elevator to the tenth floor where the secretary officiously checked the little parcel.

'It's a tea cosy,' Ana explained. 'For the ambassador.'

The secretary just rolled his eyes and handed it back. 'You're to go straight through,' he said.

'Ah.' Lusala smiled as she entered. 'Mission accomplished, I hope?'

'Yes, Mr Ambassador.'

'And that's my new tea cosy?'

'Yes, Mr Ambassador.'

He took it out of the bag. 'Very handsome. But I'll miss my old one. This is only the fourth I've had since I opened the original parcel.' He slid out a drawer and retrieved a carved wooden box. 'This is my first one,' he said, stroking the matted wool. 'I carry it with me everywhere. It keeps me grounded, you see. Reminds me of why we're here. Everyone in the UN is under constant threat of drowning in futile bureaucracy, and we have to make a conscious effort to keep our heads above all that political sludge. So our job, the job of all the keepers of the cosies over the years, is to foster simple decency.' He raised a quizzical eyebrow. 'Does that sound pompous?'

'No, Mr Ambassador. No. It sounds quite wonderful.' Ana felt tears pricking her eyes. He had lived so long, seen so much, and still managed to maintain his youthful idealism.

Lusala was speaking again as he offered her tea. He had remembered that she had milk, no sugar. 'Do you like my tie?' he asked inconsequentially, indicating its bright orange and yellow silk.

'Yes, Mr Ambassador. It's very nice.' Ana had ceased to be surprised in this office.

'My father gave me one like this when I first came to the UN. I was a bit embarrassed because I thought it might be too bright. But I always wear bright ties now. They cheer me up. My father was a wise man.'

'My father died in the Balkan war,' Ana said, surprising herself. 'They took him and my oldest brother and all the other men who were unable to hide. Then they shot them.' Her voice trembled and she fought for control. 'My mother managed to hide with the rest of us. Many of her friends were raped.'

Ana had never spoken of these events to anyone outside

her family. Through her teens, she had suffered terrible night-mares. They occurred less frequently now, but sometimes, without warning, the terror returned in a vision of a blood-spattered wall, of brains and viscera on the footpath, of the stench of urine in dark hiding places, or the sound of screams and pleas for mercy coming through the wall of their shallow refuge. Even in sunny Shepparton or in her cosy little New York apartment, the fear would return unbidden.

Lusala looked at her with a world of sorrow in his quiet eyes. 'My little friend. What can one say in the face of such pain?' And it smoothed her ragged thoughts to sit quietly in his presence.

'Thank you, Mr Ambassador,' she said after a time. 'I'm alright now.'

'Yes, my dear. I pray you'll find peace one day.' He stood up and became businesslike again. 'You're returning to Australia soon, I think?' he asked. 'Perhaps it's time to speak of the other request I have for you.'

'Anything at all, Mr Ambassador.'

Lusala smiled. 'I hope you won't regret saying that.'

'Me too,' said Ana, disarmed.

'The fact is,' he began, 'that I had intended to visit Australia myself some time this year. But my duties are set to become more onerous.'

Ana nodded. She'd heard the rumours. The position of Secretary General would soon be vacant and the ambassador was one of three serious contenders.

'That being the case, I would be most grateful if you were to seek out Mrs Lily Pargetter and give her a token of my esteem—of the United Nations' esteem. Do you know this town of Opportunity?'

Ana was eager to help. 'No, Mr Ambassador. But Victoria is not so large that I couldn't find her. It would be an honour to act on your behalf.'

'Very good. Very good.' Lusala turned to unlock a handsome oak armoire. He took out a parcel sealed with the UN seal. 'I hope this brings her pleasure. You must tell her it's from Lusala Ngilu, Quartermaster, on behalf of the Secretary General of the United Nations. And Ana . . .' It was the first time he had called her by her given name. 'I'd like you to call and tell me about her. Our Mrs Pargetter has been my mentor all these years.'

18

Moss, Brenda and Sir Donald Bradman

Two weeks after Moss and Hamish met with Georgia, she rang Moss with welcome news. 'Damara can help you, but you'll need to buy her time,' she said, and giving Moss the phone number, wished her luck. Moss could hardly wait for Georgia to finish. She hung up and called Damara straightaway.

'Damara? My name is Miranda Sinclair. Georgia has spoken to you about me?'

The voice on the other end was cautious. 'Yeah. I might be able to help, but it'll cost you. I'll need some money for expenses and loss of earnings.'

'Georgia told me that. How much for an hour of your time?'

'A hundred dollars. More if I've got the information you want. And you'll have to throw in a nice lunch.'

Moss asked Hamish to come along, and he was more than happy to desert his studies. 'Someone has to make sure you don't do anything rash,' he added. He wondered briefly how well she had thought through this quest. Nevertheless, he was pleased to see her when he picked her up from the station in his old Commodore.

'Let's get moving,' she said. Hamish drove in his usual careful manner while Moss fretted. 'You could have made that green light,' she said impatiently, more than once. 'You could overtake that truck.'

'Plenty of time,' Hamish responded curtly. 'You can always catch the tram if you don't like my driving.'

They arrived early at the small Greek restaurant that Damara had named, and looked curiously around at the other diners, in case she had already arrived.

'I told her I'd be wearing a black jumper with an emerald-green scarf.' Moss was rather enjoying the cloak-and-dagger aspect of their task. 'She'll be wearing a purple top.'

'And the password is "The bird of night roosts in the banana palm",' Hamish muttered from the side of his mouth.

Moss giggled. 'What an incredibly good guess! I . . . oh, this must be her.'

Damara sat down in the chair Hamish pulled out, and took off her sunglasses. Her dark brown eyes and olive skin indicated Mediterranean ancestry, and Moss and Hamish looked in awe at her pink mohawk, wondering why on earth she thought she'd needed to mention she'd be wearing a purple top. She met their astonished gaze with an ironic quirk of the eyebrow. She was clearly no fool.

'I met Brenda just after the accident,' she said, tucking into her calamari. 'We both worked for Vince. What a fucking bastard he was. He'd beaten Brenda up real bad and she couldn't work for weeks. Broke her jaw. I had to take her in. He nicked all her money and the other girl's too.'

'Amber-Lee's?'

'Yeah. He wanted Brenda to tell him where Amber-Lee hid her stash, but she swore she didn't know. She wasn't going to mess about with Vince, so she gave him a box from under the poor bitch's mattress and he found her money in it. But he just wouldn't believe there was no stash. So, as I said, he beat her up real bad.' Damara spoke dispassionately, as though she were describing a business transaction, spearing the calamari rings to make her point.

Hamish watched her with narrowed eyes. She was betrayed only by a slight tremor in the hand holding her glass.

'Did you keep in touch with Brenda?' Moss asked without much hope.

'Yeah, I did for a while. We went to Adelaide and worked together for nearly three years, then she met a bloke and they got married. He knew she was on the game, and he didn't want her mixing with her old friends, so we sort of lost touch. Last I heard she had a couple of kids.'

'Did she stay in Adelaide?' Hamish asked.

'Far as I know.'

'Do you have an address?'

'Nuh. Haven't seen her for ages.'

'What was her married name?' Moss asked.

Damara had already told them more than she'd meant to, and recollected herself in time. 'That sort of information doesn't come cheap.'

'How much?'

Her eyes narrowed. 'Five hundred.'

Hamish put a warning hand on Moss's knee. This was where he could be useful. 'One fifty. That's more than fair.'

'Three hundred.'

'Two fifty. Final offer,' said Hamish, preparing to stand up. 'Take it or leave it.'

Moss held her breath. She would have been happy to pay the five hundred.

'Okay. Two fifty.' Damara waited while Moss counted out five fifty-dollar bills. 'She married a man called Ivan Lefroy—don't ask me how to spell it.' Picking up the half-empty bottle of wine, she pushed back her chair, a warning in her dark eyes. 'I hope you're not going to give her any grief. We used to look out for each other.'

The other diners looked on with interest as she swaggered out of the restaurant. *What on earth are those two nice young people doing with someone like that? I'm sure I saw them give her money. Buying cocaine or ecstasy, maybe?* And the remainder of their meal was piquant with the sauce of speculation.

'Lefroy,' said Moss as they drove away. 'There can't be many Lefroys in Adelaide. How would you spell it?'

'L-e-f-r-o-y? Or it could be two words, L-e F-r-o-y.'

'Or "i" instead of "y". No, probably not.'

'She mightn't have changed her name. Or she could be divorced. What was her maiden name again?'

'Watson. There'd be a few more of those.'

As soon as they returned to Moss's house, they went online and searched the telephone directory.

'Adelaide has three Lefroys and one Le Froy,' said Moss. 'Let's see: there's one *I. Lefroy*. And a *B*. What do you think?'

'Write them all down,' said Hamish. 'And Moss, let's think this through before we go making the calls.' He could see her excitement at their success so far was in danger of propelling them into precipitate action. 'We don't want to scare her off.'

Moss nodded impatiently. Hamish was always so cautious. She was aware that she often acted impetuously, but surely here her impatience was understandable. Acutely conscious of the fact that she had left reconciliation with Linsey too late, she was desperate to settle the matter of Amber-Lee. She delicately scrolled her fingers around the little gold treble clef. So much thought had gone into her father's gift. Well, she decided, she wouldn't let him down.

Hamish helped her to plan what she would say. They decided to contact I. Lefroy first. He turned out to be an elderly man called Ian. He told them that he did have a younger cousin called Ivan who may have married a Brenda, but they'd lost touch years ago.

'There were rumours that she was a working girl.' He sniggered. 'Just like Ivan to do something like that. I heard he dumped her soon after they moved to Christies Beach. Not sure where he went. Took the kids, as far as I know. Anyway, my wife wouldn't have anything to do with them, so I didn't either. Suited me fine.'

'Let's hope "B" is for Brenda,' Hamish said as Moss dialled the next number.

The voice that answered was thick with smoke. 'Brenda here.' The woman gave a chesty cough.

Moss began her prepared spiel but Brenda cut her off. 'Yeah, Damara told me you might ring.'

So Damara had been in touch with Brenda all along, Moss thought crossly. 'Are you willing to talk to us?'

'Two hundred an hour,' she said promptly, clearly having been schooled by Damara. 'And a nice meal.' *Easiest money ever*, Brenda thought, reaching for the cigarette packet that was never far out of reach. She absentmindedly stroked her jaw. It still ached in a cold wind. She remembered the day she first saw the inexperienced Amber-Lee working the streets. Not a bad-looking kid. Very young, though. She looked like a schoolgirl in spite of the heavy makeup. Brenda still had a heart in those days, and she almost advised the girl to cut her losses and go to the Ward Street Shelter. But Vince had sent her to recruit this newcomer, so what could she do? The more girls Vince had, the less likely he was to pay her special attention. At least, that's what she'd thought then. She drew on her cigarette and mused on their separate fates. Sometimes she wondered whether Amber-Lee was better off where she was.

Moss ended the call after making a time and date to meet in Adelaide. 'Will you have time to come with me, Hamish?'

Hamish once again felt the burden of the responsibility he had taken on. Moss was becoming increasingly reliant on him. He could try to back out, plead study commitments. But when Moss had her heart set on something, he found her hard to resist. Besides, he rather liked the way she relied on him for advice. Companionship too, he hoped. He was confident that she enjoyed his company as much as he enjoyed hers. He shrugged his shoulders and accepted the inevitable. 'Okay, Moss. As long as it's no more than two or three days.'

'You're a star, Hamish. I don't know what I'd do without you.'

Hamish and Moss arrived in Adelaide two days later. 'I've booked us into the Grosvenor,' Moss said as they boarded the airport bus. 'We have adjoining rooms.'

Hamish felt a stab of rejection. He'd expected them to share a room. There was no particular reason for this expectation other than his wish that it were so. He and Moss had been getting on so well and he thought that this trip might be the catalyst that would move them to the next level. Still, he reminded himself, the rooms were adjoining . . .

After dinner, they stopped in the corridor outside Moss's door. *It's now or never*, thought Hamish as he leaned forward to kiss her lips. To his chagrin, he found himself offered her cheek.

'See you in the morning, Hamish,' she said, returning his kiss with a comradely peck. 'Remember we're meeting Brenda at twelve thirty.' She looked at him gratefully. 'You really are a mate, Hamish.'

Not quite in the sense I'd hoped, Hamish thought peevishly as he unlocked his door. A mate! It wasn't much fun being Mr Nice Guy. Did he have a sign on him saying, *Buddy/Mate/Pal*? A sign that only women could read? He glared at himself in the mirror, brushing his teeth with unusual vigour. Women always called on him when they needed something—a tap washer repaired, a partner for a special occasion, a shoulder to cry on after a break-up . . . He was everyone's ideal friend, and apparently nobody's ideal lover. He went to bed feeling very badly done by.

Brenda was a full head taller than Moss, with spiky red hair and a pale, pinched face. She was nervous and twitchy, her restless hands moving the pepper mill, the cutlery, her water glass; twisting her bracelet, smoothing her sleeves and folding and refolding her napkin until Hamish felt quite dizzy.

Moss came straight to the point. 'As you know, we need information, anything you know about a girl called Amber-Lee.'

'I told the police all I knew at the time,' replied Brenda, eyes narrowing. 'But I might have something you'd be interested in. What would you say to a photograph of Amber-Lee's family?'

Moss leaned forward, eyes gleaming. 'Go on.'

I hope Moss never plays poker, Hamish thought. He was in a more sanguine mood this morning.

The other woman saw she had the upper hand. 'I told Vince—he was her pimp—I told him where she hid her things, and he just tipped everything onto the bed. He took the money and left the other bits and pieces. He wanted her stash, but I didn't know where it was. He beat me up real bad, the fucking bastard. I'd of told him if I knew. Anyway, I don't know why, but when he left, I took the photo and stuffed it in my bra. That was just before the police arrived, so they didn't know anything about it.'

'Why didn't you give it to the police?' asked Moss.

'Why should I help them? Anyway, if I told them I had that, they would've thought I took her other stuff.'

'And did you?' Hamish felt the need to assert some authority.

'You a cop or something?' Brenda scowled. 'If you must know, all I got was a couple of fucking T-shirts and a poxy dress.'

'The photo,' Moss persisted. 'Do you still have the photo?'

'Yeah. As a matter of fact I do. Thought I might take it back some day or something. Then Damara said they might charge me—*withholding evidence* or *obstructing the course of justice*...' Her exaggerated vowels mocked all poncy lawyers.

'I'm pretty sure they wouldn't do that,' said Hamish.

'You a lawyer? I don't want to do anything till I'm sure I won't be charged. I'll deny it all. I'm not even sure I know where the fucking photo is now. It was a long time ago.' She sat back, gauging their reaction.

Moss chose not to believe her. That photo was still in Brenda's possession. She wanted to see it for herself and also wanted to ensure that it ended up in the hands of the police. Her aim, after all, was to discover the dead girl's identity. She had a sudden thought. 'What if I got you some legal advice? Would you hand it over then?'

Brenda couldn't believe her luck. 'Sure,' she said casually. 'But first we need to talk money. Information doesn't come cheap.'

As they made their way back to the hotel, Moss was almost dancing with excitement. 'We're so close,' she crowed, giving Hamish a hug. 'Let's find ourselves a lawyer.'

Hamish returned the hug, but his thoughts were troubled. He didn't trust Brenda one bit.

Moss's cousin Cal was a solicitor and recommended them to a Petra Gould. 'I'll give her a buzz and see if we can expedite matters,' he said.

Hamish had to return to Melbourne for a meeting with his supervisor, but Moss stayed on. She had arranged to pick

Brenda up in a taxi to ensure that she kept her appointment, and having some time to spare, wandered vaguely around the city. She was so desperate to keep occupied that she even went to the Bradman Museum, despite the fact that cricket had always been a mystery to her. Linsey had loved cricket. It was the only sport she had any interest in at all. *Such a precise sport*, she used to say. *It's so tactical.* 'Physical chess,' she'd called it. Moss looked at the photograph of the Invincibles, read about the infamous Bodyline series, and compared photographs of the dapper old gentleman Bradman had become with that of a fit young sportsman, signing a cricket bat for a fan.

There was an elegiac mood to the museum. Bradman and his teammates, most of them dead now, were remembered and honoured for the part they'd played in the nation's history. More than just sporting history, she learned; they gave Australians hope and pride during the long, hard Depression years.

But who would remember Linsey? When would her name be spoken for the last time? There would be no museum or newspaper cuttings or films to honour her life, yet she had lived honourably. In the midst of these thoughts, Moss began to see her situation with a clarity she had never before achieved. She had been focusing on herself, on her own pain and guilt. She must now focus on Linsey. She silently thanked the museum trustees. *I think I know what to do now.*

After Petra confirmed she'd met with Brenda, Moss returned to Melbourne where she was even more restless. Brenda had been reluctant to hand over the photograph immediately, saying she needed to give it to the police first. So Petra

Gould agreed to hold Moss's payment to Brenda until she was assured that Brenda had carried out her part of the bargain.

Moss was beginning to regret not staying in Adelaide but was somewhat distracted by her new project.

'Come over for a meal,' she begged Hamish. 'I'm going crazy waiting for Petra to call. We can talk about a new idea I have.'

Hamish groaned. 'Let's get idea one out of the way first. And Moss, I still don't trust that Brenda.'

In the event, Hamish's doubts were well-founded. Two days after Brenda met with the solicitor, Moss received a phone call. *It must be Petra*, she thought, snatching up her handbag and scrabbling eagerly for her phone.

'I'm ringing on behalf of Scott Macleod from *Across the Nation*, Channel 8,' purred the disembodied voice. 'We would like to interview you for a story about a young woman called Amber-Lee who was killed in a car accident. We believe we have a clue as to her identity, and our source has given us your name.'

Moss felt her body liquefy. She could barely stand up, let alone speak. 'I have no comment,' she said faintly.

'Well, could you tell us the whereabouts of a Mr Michael Finbar Clancy? We'd like to give him the opportunity to tell his side of the story.'

'No comment.' Moss was so distraught that she failed to hang up straightaway. What on earth had she done? Finn was such a private man, so fragile in his guilt. And she'd delivered him up to the press. Holding the phone at arm's length, she looked at it with revulsion. At that moment it seemed like a living thing, oozing black bile. With shaking fingers, she finally hung up. When the phone rang again seconds later, she flung it across the room, where it continued to ring every few minutes.

When Hamish arrived, he found her pacing the length of the carpet, grinding her heel into the floor with each turn. Her story came out in short, disconnected spurts; she actually tore at her hair, and he had to capture her hands and hold them still.

'Listen to me, Moss. *Listen.* You did what you thought was right. You were dealing with people who don't play by the rules. You expected them to act as you would in similar circumstances.' She tried to move away, but he continued to grip her hands. 'You must calm down. We have to warn your father. They'll find him easily enough. You did.'

Moss nodded dumbly and picked up the phone. She hoped it wasn't too late.

When he'd finally taken in the gist of Moss's frantic call, Finn stood frozen in the middle of the room. He had told his daughter his secret and she'd interfered, with appalling consequences. His mind was refusing to function and he struggled for something to say. Finally he croaked, 'Thank you for warning me,' and replaced the receiver, then simply stood, waiting for something to happen. He was almost indifferent as to what it might be, so long as it didn't require any action on his part. Then, dimly aware of a banging on his door, he moved towards it with something like relief. They were here. He might as well get it over with.

He opened the door to find Sandy, breathing stertorously in the night air.

'Finn! Grab a toothbrush and come to Aunt Lily's. Quickly.' Sandy pushed Finn into the bathroom and began packing a toilet bag. 'Socks and jocks,' he muttered, moving into the bedroom. 'A couple of T-shirts. Grab a jumper. Hurry up! Here—out the back way.'

Before he knew it, Finn was sitting in Mrs Pargetter's kitchen, where the old lady was twisting her apron in distress. 'Moss called,' she explained. 'She was worried about you. We all are.'

'We need to get you away,' added Sandy. 'What about your mother? Could you go there? Or to Moss's mother's place?'

Finn continued to stare in disbelief. His mind seemed to be several steps behind the conversation. 'You know about Amber-Lee?'

'Moss had to tell us, Finn,' replied Sandy. 'You're a mate and we're not going to let them find you.'

'Those wicked people, bringing it all up now. Well and good if they can find the girl's family, but why should you be dragged through the mill?' Mrs Pargetter's teeth clacked in indignation. 'We're here for you, Finn.'

Finn was moved by their loyalty, and squirmed with shame. Shame for his past and shame that he'd hidden it from such good and open people. *They offered me friendship*, he thought miserably, *and this is how I repaid them*. He couldn't bear to look them in the eye a moment longer. He wasn't the man they'd believed him to be, and it was best that he get away. He knew this, but somehow couldn't translate thought into action.

There was urgency in Sandy's voice. 'Finn, concentrate! We

have to get away before they come. I've got the car. Where can you go?'

'I know a place,' said Finn suddenly. 'Can you take me there, Sandy?'

Moss returned to Opportunity in time to watch the program with Mrs Pargetter and Sandy. Hamish had put up at the pub, and he joined them as they switched on the TV, good-naturedly fielding Mrs Pargetter's sly questions about Moss.

'We're just friends, Mrs Pargetter,' he said, to her evident disappointment, and settled down on the floor while the other three crowded onto the couch.

'Shh. It's starting,' said Moss.

'*Across the Nation*, with Scott Macleod.'

'Bastard,' muttered Sandy. 'Sorry, Aunt Lily.'

Scott Macleod's pleasant young face beamed from the screen. 'Good evening and welcome to *Across the Nation*. Tonight's stories include the plumber from hell and why diet pills don't work. But first, Lisa Morgan with another of our series of reports on unsolved mysteries of Melbourne. This time we bring you the tragic story of an unidentified young woman who died in a car accident just over ten years ago. Tonight we reveal a new clue to her identity, but we must ask once again: is this another example of police incompetence and cover-ups? Do our law enforcers show equal concern for all members of our society? Does an Oxford degree put you above the law? Lisa speaks to someone who was there when a young prostitute died on our streets.' The footage cut to a pretty blonde woman standing on a street corner.

'Thank you, Scott. Well, I'm standing within a few metres of where a young girl, known only as Amber-Lee, met her tragic end. It was here, on a warm night in March 1996, that Amber-Lee, a young prostitute, went for a hamburger with her friend, Brenda Watson. It was here that she ran out onto the road, when a car came around the corner and threw her into the path of an oncoming truck. Her true identity was never uncovered, but all these years later, Brenda Watson, now Brenda Lefroy, has come forward with a photograph that may well be the clue the police missed.' Cut to Brenda smirking at a square of paper. 'Brenda, tell us about the photo.'

'Well, I was, like, her friend, and when she died, I kept the photo as a sort of keepsake. It shows her family at the beach somewhere. England, I think. She reckoned she was English.' Cut to close-up of photo.

'Did she tell you about her family?'

'Not really. Only that the dog was called Mr Pie. She thought it was a stupid name for a dog.' For effect Brenda tossed back her hair, which had been cut and coloured especially for her TV appearance. (The appearance payment allowed her to splurge a little.)

Lisa affected a frown. 'So why didn't you give this to the police at the time? It may have helped them identify this poor girl.'

'I was beaten up by my pimp. He wanted her money. The photo was the only thing I could save. I was really out of it for a while, and by the time I was feeling better, I was too scared to go back to the police. I was, like, only young at the time.' Cut to a photo of a young Brenda, surely taken when she was still at school. (The current Brenda took on a tragic air. She thought it suited her.)

'Well, that's all we have, but maybe there is someone out there who recognises the photo, and we can help a family find closure. Back to you, Scott.' One lingering shot of the photograph, and then a cut to Scott in the studio.

'Thank you, Lisa, and thank you to Brenda for coming forward. In the interest of balance, we asked for an interview with the officer in charge of the case, without success. We've been given an official statement that the lead would be followed up once they have the photograph, which a courier is delivering as we speak.' (Pause to emphasise the program's integrity.) 'The question remains, however. Why wasn't this case investigated fully at the time? Why wasn't the car's driver charged? We have a filmed interview with a witness who says that the driver was speeding.'

Cut to an elderly man, blinking into the camera. 'He *was* going a bit fast, I suppose,' the man said doubtfully.

Scott oozed virtuous outrage. 'We wanted to allow the driver, former Oxford Fellow Michael Finbar Clancy of Opportunity, to answer these serious allegations, but he bolted before we could speak to him.' Cut to reporter and camera crew knocking on Finn's door. 'The neighbours were less than helpful.' Cut to Sandy pushing away the camera. 'Let's hope that if this photograph is recognised, the family will demand a full investigation.

'We'll return after the break with the rogue plumber who preys on the vulnerable.'

The producer was happy. 'Not a bad filler for a slow news week. We can milk it some more if the rellies turn up.'

⌒

'I can't believe it,' said Sandy. 'They managed to insinuate that Finn was to blame. I wish I'd beaten the shit out of them. Sorry, Aunt Lily.'

'*I* wish you'd beaten the shit out of them, if you'll pardon my French,' said the old lady grimly. 'They're vultures, that's what they are.'

Moss sat in appalled silence. She knew that Finn already blamed himself, although Channel 8 wouldn't know this. And poor Senior Sergeant Patterson. He'd simply tried to help her, and now they were accusing him of dereliction of duty. She'd made a complete mess of things and could think of no solution.

'Finn and I were getting along so well, and now he'll hate me,' she said miserably.

'Not true, Moss,' said Sandy. 'He knows you were just trying to help. He particularly asked us to look after you.'

'And so we shall,' confirmed Mrs Pargetter stoutly. 'We're all family, here in Opportunity.'

Hamish hugged Moss sympathetically. 'I have to go now. Take care,' he said. 'I'll give you a call tomorrow.'

The young man returned to the hotel. He couldn't help but smile at Mrs Pargetter's obvious interest in what she thought was a budding romance. She was wrong, but surprisingly that was okay. Despite his disappointment at the hotel in Adelaide, he realised that when he thought of Moss now it was with affection and concern, not passion. *We've been mates for too long to be lovers*, he decided with surprisingly little regret.

19

Sandy and Helen Porter

THOUGH DISTRACTED BY HIS ANXIETY for Finn, Sandy had a few problems of his own. On the day of the TV broadcast, a letter had arrived from the shire council.

At the time he perused it hastily, groaned aloud and threw it on the desk to be dealt with at a later date. But once Finn was safely settled with friends, he read it through again.

> *Dear Mr Sandilands,*
>
> *Your design for the 'Great Galah' will come before Council at our November meeting. The plans submitted by Constanopolous and Son have been approved in principle by the Office of the Shire Engineer and the Business Subcommittee.*
>
> *The Town Planning Department has called for submissions regarding your plans, and to date we have received four hundred and twenty-two responses, four hundred and fifteen of which are negative.*
>
> *We request that you meet with the Planning Committee on 7 November with your engineers and, may we suggest,*

*your lawyer, to address the issues the community has raised, a
detailed list of which has been attached.*
   Yours faithfully,
   Merriam Douglas
   Executive Officer, Planning Committee

Sandy's first thought was to talk to Finn, but he remembered that was impossible. How on earth did he get himself into this mess? Since Sandy read his mother's journals, the Great Galah, once his passion, had become an albatross. The mere thought of building a memorial to his father made him feel ill. He decided to write to the council to withdraw his plans in the hope that the fuss would die down.

This expectation proved to be optimistic. Preparing to write his letter, he booted up his computer only to find his inbox full of outraged emails castigating him for the folly of the Great Galah. The majority were from residents of the Cradletown district, accusing him of everything from environmental vandalism to money laundering. He was bemused to see that one H.T. Fairbanks of Burton-on-Waters, Oxfordshire, thought him a 'cloth-eared dolt', and that the Secretary of the Friends of the Galah was outraged at his money-grubbing exploitation of defenceless wildlife. But the one from Helen Porter hurt the most. *Sandy*, it said, *you can't possibly go on with this galah thing. I did warn you. We'll be a laughing stock.*

A lesser man would not have read them all, but Sandy did. Or almost did. He only had a dozen or so to go when he heard noises in his drive and looked out the window to see a small, determined group of his neighbours, armed with placards, marching up to his door.

They stopped short of the verandah and began their chant. '*What do we want? Dump the Galah. When do we want it? Now.*'

Unperturbed, the resident galahs continued to tear at the wooden shed while Sandy peered out from behind his blinds. The decision to abandon his project was suddenly replaced by anger. Who were these people to tell him what to do? Scratching around in the dirt all day, knee-deep in animal shit; losers, the lot of them. He was a Sandilands and, as such, worthy of respect. Deference, even. He'd show those tree-hugging do-gooders a thing or two. Striding into the hall, he was stopped short by the sight of his father in the hall mirror—the same livid purple, the same arrogant features, the same small, rage-filled eyes. He found himself shaking, whether in anger or fear he wasn't sure. Then his aunt's voice echoed in his head: *You are not your father, Sandy. Not your father.* No, he wasn't. He stood, breathing deeply, until the last of his anger was exorcised and the face in the mirror became his own benign full moon.

Meanwhile, two people detached themselves from the crowd outside and approached the door. They were obviously spokespersons for the group. Knocking loudly, they were startled at the sudden appearance of their quarry, who was, in fact, coming out to meet them.

'We are here,' said Tom Ferguson, regaining his composure with admirable speed, 'we are here to demand that you give up your plans for the building of the Great Galah.'

Sandy opened his mouth, but was firmly silenced as Freda D'Amico waved a bundle of papers at him. 'This is a petition to go to council. It has over five hundred signatures already and—' she glared at him darkly—'and I promise you, there—will—be—more!'

'Well, okay,' said Sandy.

'Okay what?' asked Tom.

'Okay, I won't build it.'

'You won't build it?'

'That's what you want, isn't it?'

The two leaders looked confused, then aggrieved. 'That's it?' said Tom.

'Yes. If there's nothing else . . . ?'

'Just a mo'.'

Tom and Freda returned to the waiting crowd, and the group conferred briefly. They all stood looking at each other, not sure what to do next. This was just Plan A. They had other, perfectly good plans ready to go—Plans B, C, D and, for some of the more radical among them, Plan E.

'We'll be off then, Sandy,' Ned Humphries finally called out. It was nearly milking time. They headed back to their utes and four-wheel drives feeling a little cheated. Freda left her sign, NO GREAT GALAH, as a reminder in case Sandy reneged. The resident galahs soon took care of that, and a few days later it read \c GI _/ I AI \ I. Still, as Freda maintained, it served its purpose.

Sandy chuckled as he wrote his letter to the council. 'That took the wind out of their sails,' he muttered. He hadn't enjoyed himself so much in years.

He was printing out the letter the next morning when there was a knock at the door. It was Helen Porter, her hastily pinned-up hair falling as usual in untidy tendrils. Sandy wasn't surprised to see Helen. They'd known each other since primary school, and her mother, Minnie, had been Rosie's close friend. Until Sandy went to boarding school, they used to play together while their mothers took a break in their busy farm lives to enjoy tea and scones on Minnie's verandah.

Helen's instincts had always been to protect Sandy. Her mother had referred to him as *that poor wee lad*, and Helen knew more about his family than he ever imagined. By the time Sandy had returned to Opportunity from university, Helen was married; she had been widowed now for fifteen years. She remained Sandy's friend despite the fact that he sometimes disappointed her, and she encouraged him in his better ideas, like the Memorial Park project. As he motioned her in the door, she looked at him with concern.

'Freda told me you've given up the Great Galah,' she said, taking off her anorak and peering into his face. 'Are you okay? You know I advised against it right from the start, but I guess you're feeling pretty disappointed.' She patted his arm and was surprised to see something like glee in his eyes.

As they shared a cup of tea, Sandy told her the story of the aborted protest.

'I can just imagine Tom huffing and puffing,' she chortled. 'And Freda—did she bring along that awful husband of hers?'

The conversation had moved on to more general matters when Sandy leaned forward. 'Helen,' he said. 'I need a replacement for the Great Galah. I still want to do something for

Opportunity.' He gave a small, deprecating gesture. 'I want it to be something for my mother, too. Something beautiful—I want to give her something beautiful.'

Helen nodded sympathetically. She had strong memories of the red-faced man with bullying shoulders and, beside him, the pale, pretty woman with defeated eyes. 'How can I help, Sandy?'

'I need an idea—and someone to talk it over with.' He grinned. 'My last idea had a few rough edges. I need someone like you—no, I need *you* to keep me on track.' His grin faded, replaced by an uncharacteristic humility. 'I don't have many friends here and you've always been so nice . . .'

Helen took his hand and wondered at his honesty. *Sandy's a strange mixture*, she thought. *But this could be worth doing.* 'We'll plan something wonderful for your mother and for Opportunity,' she said. 'What about you make me a sandwich and we'll begin right away.' Helen Porter was a practical woman.

20

Finn and Boniface

AD MAJOREM DEI GLORIAM. AFTER driving through the night with Sandy, Finn found himself standing once again at the wrought-iron gates of Our Lady of Sorrows monastery, this time seeking refuge from the press.

'Do you want me to wait?' Sandy had fussed and worried the whole way and was clearly reluctant to leave his charge standing at a locked gate.

Through his haze, Finn noted that technology had come to the monastery and there was now an intercom instead of a bell. 'It's okay, Sandy,' said Finn as he pressed the button. 'I have friends here.'

The porter's eerily disembodied voice came through the speaker. 'Brother Kevin here. How can I help you?'

'Kevin. It's Finn, mate. Please let me in. I need to come in.'

'Finn? Finn Clancy? Just a tick, mate.'

The gates slid open. Finn was sure that they had swung open on his first visit. He hastily shook hands with Sandy and almost ran into their embrace. 'I'll contact you in a couple of days,' he said. 'Tell Moss and Mrs Pargetter not to worry: I'll be safe here.'

Kevin came down the path to meet him and led him back to the porter's room. It was as clean and sparsely furnished as Finn remembered, and Kevin had changed little in the ten years since they last met. He began to relax. This place had been a constant in his memory, and some part of him had always dwelt behind these worn stone walls. He felt like a child returning home.

'You've got a new job,' observed Finn. 'Who's looking after the garden?'

'There aren't as many of us now,' Kevin replied. 'We all have to be—I think they call it multi-skilled.' He grinned and then looked at Finn soberly. 'You understand that I'll have to call Father Jerome.'

'Of course.'

Kevin left, and Finn sat on the wooden bench waiting for Jerome, who entered some ten minutes later and extended both hands in greeting. The years had not been kind to either of them, and they were both slightly shocked to see how the other had aged.

'Finn. It's good to see you,' the abbot said, raising his hand in blessing. 'I'm glad to be able to thank you personally for your generosity over the years. You're always in our prayers, you know.' He looked at the other man expectantly. 'So what brings you back to us?'

'It's a long story, Father, but the main reason I'm here is that the press found out my story and I can't face them. Not yet. It was all too sudden.'

Jerome, composed, as always, nodded as Finn went on. 'I know Moss—the person who tried to help—did what she thought was best, but I was dealing with things in my own way. I was happy—or at least contented—in Opportunity. Now I have the press scrabbling over my life. It's too much. I'll have to move on.'

'What do you want from us?'

'A few days. A few days to get my head together.'

'I've asked Kevin to make up your old cottage. You know the way. We'll talk this afternoon.'

'Thank you, Father Jerome. I can't tell you how grateful . . .'

Jerome raised his hand and shook his head, smiling faintly. 'Remember the virtue of silence,' he said. And ushered Finn out into the brightness of the new day.

Kevin had left sheets and towels on the bed and some teabags and milk on the bench. Finn smiled to think of the outrage the teabags would beget in Mrs Pargetter's tea-loving heart. He'd come to like the ritual of making tea in a pot, and he hoped that the three cosies he had in his bag would find homes on a real teapot. He was sure that Boniface, at least, wouldn't countenance teabags.

He showered and lay on top of the bed, willing sleep. Although he hadn't slept much the night before, his eyes remained wide open and gritty. Sighing, he got up and decided to take a walk in the grounds.

Matins was finished, and the monastery's workday had begun. He wandered over to the vegie patch, noticing the large water tanks that had been installed. He ran his hands over one smooth wall. Water was a problem all over the country.

There were a few weeds in the garden, and despite the fact that he was dressed in a good shirt and jeans, he knelt down and began to pull them out. He was so absorbed in the task that he didn't hear Kevin's approaching footsteps.

'Nice to have you back, Finn,' the monk said, and they worked in silence until the next bell called Kevin to prayer.

Finn sat back on his heels and looked at his hands. They were a good deal tougher than the first time he'd worked in this garden. He began to miss his own little vegie patch back in Opportunity, and the thought that he would have to start all over again somewhere else depressed him. He felt petulant and resentful. Hadn't he given up enough? How long would it be before his dues would be considered paid? But he wasn't thinking of leaving Opportunity because of the press. He knew that in a few days some new titillation would send them baying after another victim and all he needed to do was stick it out. What he couldn't bear to think about was the contempt in the eyes of his friends and neighbours now that his culpability had been exposed. He shook himself and reached for a dandelion. He liked the satisfaction of pulling out the long taproots. But he stopped mid-motion, and his hand fell onto his knee. He was so weary; too weary to bother. Stretching his back, he stood up and returned to his cottage where he fell into a troubled sleep.

He awoke in time for lunch and ate in silence as the reader intoned the Acts of the Apostles. *They certainly don't try to entertain*, Finn thought as he fought off the soporific effects of the droning voice. He looked around the table. All but two of the faces were familiar, but there were several missing. Where was Boniface? Not seeing him in his usual place, Finn looked around with increasing concern. Perhaps he was working in the kitchen today? Kevin said that they all needed to multi-task, but surely a man of that age wouldn't be made to peel potatoes? Perhaps he was . . . Finn wouldn't allow himself to finish this thought and tried to speak to Father Timothy, who frowned and shook his head. *The Rule demands silence*, his look said, and Finn lowered his eyes to his soup.

'Where's Boniface?' he asked as he caught up with Kevin in the cloisters.

'He's not well, Finn. He's nearly ninety, you know. You really need to speak to Father Jerome.'

So when Finn met with Jerome later that day, his first question was about Boniface.

'He's not himself, Finbar,' Jerome replied, his eyes sombre.

'Is he sick? Can I see him?' Finn's dread was manifested in the fast beating of his heart, the nausea that gripped his gut.

'He's not himself,' Jerome repeated. 'I can take you to him now, but be warned: he probably won't know you.'

The abbot led Finn to the infirmary. Pallid sunlight filtered through the curtains to reveal an old man lying between snowy sheets. A nimbus of silver hair framed his face, where a scaffold of bones betrayed his mortality. He lay still, his milky blue eyes open but confused.

'Is that John?' he quavered. 'I've lost John.'

Finn was puzzled. 'Who's John?'

'*He* is,' replied Jerome, stroking the frail old hand. 'When he came here nearly seventy years ago, he was John. He's been Boniface all these years, but now . . .' The abbot shrugged helplessly. 'He still prays. I pray with him when I can.' Hiding his emotion in busyness, Jerome straightened the sheet around the old priest's chin. 'He was an eminent theologian, you know.'

Finn expressed surprise.

'An *eminent* theologian,' the priest reiterated. 'His book *On the Humanity of Christ* is still used in theology courses. He was Abbot before me. I remember when I came here to take his place: he was so happy, Finbar—his face was truly alight with joy. He hated being Abbot, although he carried out his duties conscientiously, as you might imagine. He carried them humbly, as God's burden. *His burden is sweet and His yoke is light*—that was what Boniface used to say.'

Jerome murmured a blessing and turned to go. 'Finbar, Boniface was blessed with a fine intellect, but all he really wanted was a life of prayer. Less prestige, maybe, but a powerful example to us all.'

'Do you mind if I stay with him for a while?' Finn asked.

'Of course. We can talk tonight.'

Finn looked down in pity as Boniface clawed at the sheets, calling again and again, 'John? Is that you, John?'

'It's Finn, Father Boniface—Finbar Clancy. I guess you don't remember me,' he said wistfully. 'You were my spiritual mentor many years ago. I worked with Kevin in the garden. Remember? I killed a girl with my car. You told me I'd find answers.' Finn was floundering, trying to elicit some recognition of their former relationship. He sighed, and held the fragile old hand. It felt light and insubstantial, with fine, brittle bones bundled under tissue-paper skin. The hand was bruised, and he held it gently, fearing that further purple blooms would grow under the slightest pressure.

Boniface looked at Finn. 'You're not John. You're too tall,' he accused. 'I have to find John before I go.' He became confiding. 'I think they've sent him to Rome. Can you check for me? They won't tell me anything,' he said, now aggrieved.

Finn was at a loss. 'Let's say a prayer,' he suggested in desperation. 'Hail Mary . . .' A rosary was on the bedside table and he twined it around the old man's fingers.

Boniface closed his eyes, and his face relaxed as he recited the familiar words. 'Hail Mary, full of grace. The Lord is with thee . . .'

Finn stayed until, soothed by prayer, his old friend drifted off to sleep.

'He has lucid moments,' Jerome told Finn as they walked through the cloisters that evening. 'But you can never predict them.' He studied Finn's face. 'I'm not sure what we can do for you, though, Finbar. You're welcome to stay for a few days, but you may be putting off the inevitable.'

Finn shook his head. 'I feel safe here. I ran away, I guess. Just like last time.'

'Not *just* like last time,' Jerome responded thoughtfully. 'I can sense that you're stronger now. How do you account for that?'

'I'm not sure. I do keep the Silence after my own fashion. That helps.' His eyes slid away. 'I also found my daughter— actually, she found me.'

'Daughter? You've never mentioned a daughter.'

Finn smiled wryly. 'It's a long story, Father. She turned up on my doorstep a few months ago.' He chose his next words carefully. 'I'm not sure I'm . . . father material, but she—she's a good person.'

Jerome nodded. 'You're lucky to have found family, Finn. It must make your life less lonely.'

'Yes. I guess it does. And I do have a couple of friends in Opportunity.' *Good friends*, he thought, surprised. 'They sort of fill out my life a bit.'

'What do you expect your friends might do now they know all about your past?'

'I don't know.'

'Will they turn their backs on you?'

Finn remembered the concerned faces as he stood paralysed in Mrs Pargetter's front room. 'No,' he said finally. 'No. They wouldn't do that.'

'So why did you leave?'

'I don't feel worthy of love or friendship. I don't want to taint them with my troubles.'

Jerome stopped and turned to him, signalling the end of the conversation. 'I'd like you to go away and think about what you just said, Finbar. We'll talk again tomorrow.'

'Do you mind if I sit in the chapel for a while?'

'You're always welcome in God's house.'

Finn made his way to the chapel and paused to savour the quiet interior. Two monks were kneeling in prayer, and another was sweeping the aisle, his broom whispering rhythmically on the polished floor. Coloured light filtered through the arched windows and gathered in pools on the marble steps of the altar. Carved wooden figures looked out at the worshippers: Saint Benedict on one side, holding his book and crozier, the Virgin Mother on the other, holding the Christ child.

Slipping into a pew, Finn sat, head bowed, hands dangling

between his knees. He needed to think things through. He knew that his friends would stand by him. They had already demonstrated that. He had told Jerome that he felt unworthy of love. Was he being disingenuous? He was loved. He hadn't really thought about it before, but he *was* loved. His daughter had loved him enough to try to help him come to terms with his past. That it had gone disastrously wrong was not her fault. Mrs Pargetter and Sandy were fiercely loyal friends. More than that, he knew they loved him. They all shared a circle of dependence and support; each of them a little broken, but brave. Not fearless, he thought, but brave.

So why would he want to fend for himself? Why would he want to leave his friends to fend for themselves? Finn knew that he'd become a loner. The charming, sociable Michael had been left far behind, and the Finn he'd become was insular and obsessive. When he looked honestly into his heart, he saw that his greatest fear was of commitment. He saw now, with sudden clarity, that he was not just running from the press and from his own shame; he was running from the obligations of love and friendship.

These thoughts led back to his parents, who also loved him. After the accident, he had refused their love and all but disappeared from their lives, returning only for rare visits, when he sat at the dinner table chafing to be gone. His father had died three years ago, and his mother was in a retirement village now, frail but still alert. How long would it be before she, like Boniface, failed to recognise him? He looked up at the statues and then lowered his eyes. Was there accusation on the face of Mary, patron of mothers? He felt like a guilty child as his eyes slid back to the carved face. No accusation there. Just sorrow. Our Lady of Sorrows.

He was suddenly aware that the monks were filing in for Vespers. Keeping his eyes averted, he slipped out the side door and made his way to the infirmary. He stopped short when he saw Kevin reading the evening prayers at the old man's bedside. Boniface was smiling and nodding, his troubled mind clearly soothed by the long, familiar cadences. Kevin's voice was low, his eyes alight with faith. Finn lingered and saw Kevin rise from his knees and, like a parent, tuck in the bedclothes and gently kiss the now sleeping face. Afraid of being seen, Finn turned and walked swiftly back to his cottage. He had intruded upon a private moment, but rather than embarrassment, all he could feel was humility.

He put on the kettle and made some tea, moving aside the tea cosies that still lay on the bench. Tomorrow was Sunday, and conversation was allowed—a good time to give the tea cosies to their intended recipients.

Finn gave one each to Jerome and Kevin at breakfast the next morning. They accepted their gifts with pleasure and listened with genuine interest as Finn told Mrs Pargetter's story.

'We'll pray that she finds peace,' Jerome said.

'We'll pray that she finds her child,' Kevin promised.

Finn was once again touched by the kindness of these men. It would be so easy to again immerse himself in the tranquil rhythm of their days. In reality, he had to be resolute. Without belief, he'd be living a lie. 'I think it's time to go back,' he said to Jerome. 'I'll take the bus tomorrow. I can't say how grateful I am for all you've done.' He hesitated. 'Can I ask one more thing of you? Can I see Boniface again before I go?'

'You can keep watch a while this evening,' said Jerome. 'He's dying, Finn, and will soon see Our Blessed Lord face to face.'

Finn spent the rest of the day in the garden with Kevin, but his thoughts were of Boniface. After the last Office of the day, Jerome indicated that the time had come, and Finn almost ran through the cloisters to the infirmary. He nodded to the monk who was sitting by the bed, and slipped into the chair he vacated. Boniface was sleeping, his breathing shallow and harsh. Taking his hand, Finn looked down at the dying man's face.

'I've decided to go back, Father Boniface,' he whispered. 'You told me once that I would know what to do when the time came. I don't know. It might be now ... Could it be now?' He searched the old face for answers, but it remained shut. 'I'll go back, but then what? I still want forgiveness. I wish I had your faith—redemption is easier with faith. But people like me ... we have to make reparation in whatever way we can. The Holy Spirit ... he doesn't speak to people like me.'

Boniface stirred and opened his eyes. 'Finbar,' he said. 'Could you open the curtains, please?'

Startled, Finn did as he was asked and looked out at the sharp sickle that sliced the clear night sky. The stars, framed by the window, pierced the surrounding blackness with cold needles of light.

'There'll be a frost tomorrow; the sky is so clear,' remarked Boniface in a conversational tone.

He has lucid moments, remembered Finn, and swiftly crossed the room to sit beside the old man. 'Father Boniface. It's me—Finbar Clancy. I . . .'

'Silence allows us to look into our hearts,' murmured Boniface, as though they were continuing a conversation begun only a minute before. But Finn was acutely aware that this was a conversation started over ten years ago.

The monk continued. 'If your heart is open, silence leaves space for the voice of God.' The old priest's voice was faint and his breathing laboured. 'Look into your heart, Finn. That's all the help I can offer.'

'It's not easy, Father Boniface. I'm not sure I know how.'

'Your Silence. How do you spend your Silence?'

'I fear I may have squandered my Silence, Father.'

'Squandered?'

'I used the time to relive my guilt.'

'Wiser to seek beyond your guilt. Listen to your heart.'

Finn nodded slowly. 'I spent so many years not listening, Father. But in this last year, I believe I have listened—just a little.'

'Then follow your wisdom. You mustn't allow your past to consume you, Finbar. That's a sin. It's a good heart, Finbar. A good heart.' His eyes, which seconds before had looked at Finn with intelligence and compassion, slid away to the window and the moment was gone.

'Did they tell you where John is?' he asked again, plucking fretfully at the sheet. 'He should be here by now.'

'You'll see him soon,' said Finn, and held the frail hand until Boniface fell once again into a shallow sleep. Finn took the tea cosy from his pocket and placed the cold hands inside. Boniface stirred but didn't waken.

'A gift from a good old lady.'

As the soft wool warmed his hands, the old man's body visibly relaxed. Finn was not to know, but the Kenyan Ambassador himself could not have thought of a better use for Mrs Pargetter's gift.

21

Jilly Baker and Mr Pie

SENIOR SERGEANT GRAHAM PATTERSON WAS annoyed, uncharacteristically slamming his office door behind him as he left at the end of his shift. The commissioner hated bad publicity, and here he was, accused of missing vital evidence in a case in which he knew he'd followed every lead and obeyed every protocol. The file had been sent upstairs and now the system was going into damage control. Patterson was mortified to be second-guessed by his fellow officers. However, beyond his mortification, he felt some excitement. Amber-Lee's death had been the first case of its type he'd investigated as the officer in charge. He'd given the girl—Fern, was it? No, Moss. He'd given Moss as much help as he could because he wanted the case closed, and this new piece of evidence could well provide the key. So he was waiting impatiently for Forensics to report on their findings. Meanwhile he had to deal with the fall-out from the press.

As he pulled out of the car park, he turned on the radio. The deputy commissioner would be interviewed in a few minutes. She was the consummate political animal, and Senior Sergeant Patterson had no great hopes of support from that direction.

He listened grimly as the interviewer began. 'Good morning, Deputy Commissioner. You're a busy person so we'll cut to the chase. I presume you're aware of the new evidence in the case of the accident victim known as Amber-Lee. What action are you taking now the photograph has come to light?'

'Good morning, Peter. I'm sure your listeners will be pleased to know that Forensics is working on the photograph now in an attempt to identify when and where it was taken. You must remember, though, we only have Brenda Lefroy's word that it did belong to Amber-Lee and that it was, in fact, a photo of her family.'

'Of course, time will tell. But what about Graham Patterson, the officer in charge of the case—has he been reprimanded?'

'Hold on, Peter. We're looking at the files and in due course we'll make a decision regarding the thoroughness of the original investigation. Senior Sergeant Patterson is a respected officer and must be given the benefit of the doubt until we learn otherwise.'

Graham Patterson was surprised by but grateful for this qualified support, and as the interview moved on to budget allocation for new police vehicles he switched over to a music station. He was heading for home, but on a sudden whim he pulled into the car park of the forensics laboratory. He went to reception, showed his ID, and followed directions to Lab 4 where he found his friend, Clara Thomasetti, hard at work.

'The photo?' she said. 'That was easy. I've already sent out the report. You know how they're hurried through when the press get their teeth into a story.'

'So what did you find?'

'It was common photographic paper for the time. Used all over by Kodak. The photo was developed around '83, '84, we reckon, which would fit with her estimated age. So would the clothes and hairstyles, according to our expert.' She looked at him with sympathy. 'Anyway, how are you? It must be a tough time right now.'

He shrugged. 'Comes with the territory. I heard the deputy commissioner on the radio. She was okay. But to be honest, I'm just interested in what else you found out from the photo.'

'There are two young girls in the photo. That Brenda person didn't know which one was Amber-Lee, but one of them is looking at the dog as though she owns it. Only a guess, but I reckon the other one's our girl. She told Brenda that the dog was her cousin's, remember?'

'Yes, Mr Pie. Brenda said she thought the snapshot was taken somewhere in England . . .'

'Easy, that one. Blackpool Pier. She either lived nearby or was there on holiday.'

'If only I'd had that photo ten years ago.'

Clara squeezed his arm. 'If Brenda didn't want to give it to you, what could you have done?'

'I could've leaned on her more, maybe. But she was a terrible mess after the beating. Not very professional, but I felt sorry for her.'

'You did what you could with what you had. The word is they're handing this new investigation back to you. Someone up there likes you, mate.' She stood up and gestured at the bench in front of her. 'I'd better get back to work. We'll have to catch up for a drink. It's been too long.'

Graham thanked her and left. If only it were true that he was to be given a fresh opportunity with this case . . . He found himself humming as he backed out of the car park, negotiating the peak-hour traffic with a lighter heart.

A few nights later, he received a phone call from Blackpool, England.

'Hello,' said a woman's voice. 'Are you the person I have to speak to about a girl who was killed in a car accident? Amber-Lee? There was a photo shown on TV here yesterday. I've got one just the same.'

Finn boarded the bus and sat gazing out the window at the ti-tree that hid the sea from view. Its dull grey-green was soothing in a way; he'd left the monastery knowing that it was the last time he'd see Father Boniface, and the colour matched his sombre mood. He pushed away thoughts of what might be waiting for him in Opportunity, and concentrated on the countryside and small towns as they flashed by. He realised that he could have ended up in any one of these towns: Sickle Bay, Seal Point where the surfers hung out, or, as the bus turned inland, Tarneesh, Currawong or even Mystic. But he'd chosen Opportunity, for better or for worse. Recalling his house, the sleepy main street, the old pub, and his friends, Mrs Pargetter and Sandy, he was inclined to think it was for the better. Would Moss have found him in another town? Probably, but he liked to think of the town's name as a talisman. He'd chosen it for its name; he liked to think that names have power, and whatever had befallen Opportunity in recent years, it was still battling along somehow. The motion of the bus and the monotony of the countryside finally sent him into a half-slumber, and his mind rambled through forests of ti-tree until he finally fell into a dreamless sleep.

He awoke to see that the road unspooling before them had darkened and the shadows lengthened. As the bus sped on, the sun's last rays randomly painted the embankment with a brief fiery palette, and the new gum tips glowed red in the slanting light. Leaning into the window, Finn felt a sense of place, of homecoming.

They were approaching Mystic, and Finn observed that the Lions and Rotary clubs were happy to welcome him to a town with a population of 3500. Most of the passengers alighted here. Finn shrank back in his seat as Helen Porter clambered untidily onto the bus, carrying two overflowing shopping bags. *Don't let her see me*, Finn prayed, but she looked up and smiled as she approached, and he was forced to assist her to stow her bags. *Why didn't I bring a book or a newspaper?* he thought as she settled beside him and commented on the weather.

He answered in a monosyllable, and she looked at him sharply. 'Are you okay? We heard you left town.'

'Embarrassed—TV show,' Finn mumbled.

'That may be, but you had us all worried. No-one takes that program seriously. Well, some do,' she added dryly, 'but they don't have a very long concentration span.'

Finn nodded his gratitude, and Helen tactfully took out a magazine, allowing him to once again follow his own thoughts. As the bus approached Opportunity, he retrieved Helen's bags and carried them the short distance to her house.

'Thanks, Finn.' She grasped his arm. 'Look, the gossip will flare up for a bit now you're back, but ride it out. This is your home.'

As he turned the corner into his street, he saw that Sandy's car was parked outside his aunt's place. He hoped Moss was there too. It was better to get it over all at once. Steeling himself, he knocked on the door to be greeted by Errol's bark and the sound of his paws skittering down the passageway. The door opened, and in a moment he found himself swept inside and seated in the familiar kitchen. Moss was there, looking apprehensive.

'Finn, I'm so sorry,' she wailed, flinging herself at him.

He was startled by the intensity of her emotion and patted her ineffectually, murmuring, 'It's okay, Moss. It's okay.' She continued to sob until, holding her at arm's length, he gripped her shoulders and looked straight into her eyes. 'Listen. It really *is* okay. In one way, it's a weight off my mind and—who knows?—it might lead us to Amber-Lee's family.'

Sandy couldn't contain himself. 'It has, Finn,' he chortled. 'Moss has heard from the police. A woman contacted them from England. She's the other girl in the photo. She had a dog called Mr Pie. Remember? That's what Brenda told the TV people: that Amber-Lee said Mr Pie was a stupid name for a dog.'

22

Blackpool and Opportunity

MEG TURNER WAS NOT SURE what to pack. She would need something smart for the TV interview and had already spent some of her expected payment on a stylish new suit. She was a shrewd woman, and had negotiated herself a rather good package, which included accommodation, return airfares to Melbourne for two, plus a sum that would cover a nice little holiday on the Great Barrier Reef. All she had to do was take part in an interview regarding her missing cousin. She'd seen the photograph on the local news along with an appeal for anyone in the Blackpool area who might know its origins to come forward. The woman she'd contacted passed her details on to the producer of *Across the Nation*, who signed her up immediately, expressing the hope that the interview would be sufficiently emotional. *So the viewers can understand the depths of your loss*, the producer explained. Meg also agreed to cooperate with the police investigation.

Folding her T-shirts and pants, she wondered how much she should tell. She'd never really missed Jilly. They were four years apart in age so they were never friends. She was quite a nice little kid, as Meg recalled. A bit shy, but biddable. To be honest, she could barely remember what her cousin looked like. She did remember the kafuffle when Patty ran away. Her own mother, Ellen, had pursed her lips and said, *I expected as much of that sister of mine*, but the grandparents never ceased to mourn the loss of their granddaughter. When he failed to get his daughter back, Jilly's father went crazy and took to the drink. He somehow managed to work during the day, but according to the whispered conversations Meg overheard, he would return home each evening to drink alone. Sometimes he would come to her house, crying. Meg had hated that. Adults weren't supposed to cry.

'I feel sorry for him,' Meg's mother would say, 'but he should pull himself together. Even if they do find her, they'll say he's not a fit parent if he keeps carrying on like that.'

Meg paused as she held up her new swimmers and posed in front of the mirror. Very nice. Just the thing for a tropical holiday. It was all amazingly lucky. Still, her cousin owed her something. Her grandparents did nothing but talk about Jilly till the day they died: where she might be, what she might be doing, what she would look like at this age or that. By contrast, they treated Meg and her brother with an abstracted sort of kindness, and as children they always felt that they were poor substitutes for the missing Jilly. Meg felt some satisfaction in the knowledge that her cousin had been working the streets. What would Grandpa and Grandma have thought of *that*?

Pressing hard on the lid of her case, she closed the zip and picked up the photo. It belonged in the hand luggage, she'd decided. She couldn't afford to lose the evidence.

Poor old Uncle Andy, she thought suddenly, looking at the fresh young face smiling at his daughter. *It broke his heart. Maybe it's just as well he's not here to find out what happened to her.* Despite the fact that there was no firm evidence as yet, Meg was sure that this Amber-Lee really was her cousin Jilly. Ellen agreed. She wasn't in the least surprised that Patty's daughter came to a sorry end.

Ellen saw them off at Heathrow and reminded Meg that the family honour was in her hands. 'Aunty Patty may have been a tart,' she reminded her, 'but you don't have to broadcast that to the world.'

As it turned out, Meg did rather well. She managed to paint a picture of a family bereft when a headstrong (but not wicked) young woman took her daughter and ran away with her lover.

'We all missed them so much,' she told a nodding Lisa Morgan. 'Jilly's father died of a broken heart, and my grandparents never really got over it.' She looked into the camera as she'd been instructed. 'And now that we know, it's too late.' A discreetly applied tissue added to the effect.

The studio scene faded out to a shot of Meg placing flowers on the corner where her cousin died. She looked quite forlorn, standing there with her head bowed.

'Cut,' said the producer. 'Good value for money, I think.' She turned to her assistant. 'We can get some more out of this one. How about this for an idea? Let's try to arrange a meeting between the cousin and the bloke who killed her. That ought to keep the punters happy.'

Unaware of this plan, and having fulfilled her obligation with the interview, Meg was ready to cooperate with Senior Sergeant Patterson. She showed him her copy of the photograph and formally identified her cousin and family.

Graham Patterson was cautious. 'Our problem is that we only have Brenda's word that Amber-Lee said it was a photo of her family. She was paid by the TV station, you know. It makes her testimony a bit suspect.' Meg had the grace to blush but the policeman went on, oblivious. 'We'd like to do a DNA test. Do you have a problem with that?'

'Apparently the more distantly you're related, the less accurate they can be,' Meg told her mother later on the phone to England. 'They'd like you to do one too, if that's okay. Something to do with mitro-something-or-other DNA. The copper tried to explain—it's something to do with the mother's line— but I don't really understand. Doesn't matter. Anyway, they'll get the local police to take your sample and compare by computer.'

The results were inconclusive. The DNA was not such a close match that identity was beyond reasonable doubt, but a relationship was considered to be 'likely'. The existence of the matching photo strengthened the conclusion that the victim was Jilly Baker, but there was still no guarantee that Brenda was telling the truth regarding its origins.

'On balance, I'd say that the victim was your cousin,' Graham Patterson told Meg. 'But the evidence isn't absolutely conclusive. She had no siblings and her father is dead. If her mother planned on coming forward, she would have by now, you'd think. The case has had max publicity. This is probably as far as we can go.'

'What do you mean by that?' Meg asked.

'Just that the records will still show her as unidentified. The new evidence will be put on her file and referenced as a "probable" ID.'

'Oh well, there's nothing more we can do then,' she said, shrugging her shoulders. 'Best be off. We only have another two days to see Melbourne.'

Meg's off-hand response to this news didn't surprise him. He'd sensed her lack of empathy in the earlier interviews.

Returning to her hotel, Meg was met by her husband who told her that the TV people had been trying to contact her again. They wanted her to meet the man who'd killed her cousin.

'How much did they offer this time?' With this, she even shocked herself. She hadn't been fully aware of the depths of her venality.

In Opportunity, Finn and his friends had watched Meg's interview. While the others discussed the possible ramifications, Finn slipped out of the house and walked down to the old Halfway Creek footbridge. He often spent his Silence sitting by the bridge or leaning against its railings. Tonight he sat on the smooth rock just under the bridge. In better times, this seat would be under water, but the stream had shrunk away from its banks, exposing not only rocks but also rubbish from downstream, which had been stranded at the two-mile bend. There was a muddy, slightly rotten smell, but Finn didn't notice. He was only aware of his heart pounding in his chest, and a faint, sweaty nausea. He had to think this one through. So now he knew her name: Jilly Baker. Of all the possible names, he hadn't thought of Jilly, but it sounded right, now that he knew it. The next question was: what was he to do with the knowledge?

Finn had always thought that knowing the dead girl's real name would be enough. It would establish her as an individual, with a family, and a history beyond those few terrible months on the streets. But now that her cousin was here in Melbourne, he needed to speak with her, to say how sorry he was, to seek forgiveness. He feared this as much as he wanted it. Why should she forgive him? He'd killed the woman's cousin, caused so much heartache . . . Logic told him that the family may never have found Jilly anyway; that her mother had severed all ties; that she was hardly in a position to return home. He wanted to focus on that, but a small worm ate through the logic and whispered that while ever life persisted, there was always hope of reprieve. And he had taken that possibility away from Jilly Baker. He saw its application to her quite clearly, but it never occurred to him to apply it to his own case. He still felt beyond redemption.

He'd have to meet the cousin, he decided. He'd get Moss to ring Graham Patterson to see if it could be arranged.

Unaware that *Across the Nation* had pre-empted his decision, Finn returned to Mrs Pargetter's and told them he wanted to meet with Jilly's cousin Meg.

The others looked doubtful. 'Are you sure, Finn?' his daughter asked.

Finn would brook no argument. 'Absolutely.'

Senior Sergeant Patterson wasn't so sure. He'd detected a hardness and cupidity in Meg and wondered how this would affect the fragile Finn. There was also the trouble caused last time he'd helped out. After Moss's call, he doodled on his pad for a few moments before shrugging and picking up the phone. He liked closure, and this case still had loose ends.

'Senior Sergeant Patterson,' he told Meg's husband. 'Can I speak with Mrs Turner, please?'

'I'm sorry, Senior Sergeant, she's out. Left a couple of hours ago with the TV people. They're taking her to see the man who killed her cousin. Do you want to leave a—? Hello? Hello? Are you there?'

Graham Patterson tried to ring Moss but the line was busy. He shook his head. Things would just have to take their course.

The TV crew took Finn by surprise. They arrived at his front door without fanfare, and with an increasingly reluctant Meg in tow. Finn was working on his statistics when the loud knock shattered his concentration. He had always found the lovely precision of maths a haven in the midst of turmoil, and resented any interruption.

'Coming,' he grumbled. He wasn't expecting anyone.

He opened the door to see a plump, well-dressed woman, flanked by a younger woman and two young men, one of whom was wielding a fuzzy grey phallus.

'Michael Clancy,' announced the younger woman. 'This is Meg Turner, cousin of the woman you killed.'

Meg and Finn stared at one another. 'I've been wanting to meet you,' Meg said uncertainly. 'My cousin . . .' She trailed off and started again. 'Jilly, my cousin . . .'

Finn continued to stare as the microphone was thrust into his face.

'This woman has come all the way from the UK to seek news of her cousin. What do you have to say to her, Mr Clancy?' The reporter was experienced enough to see that Meg might not provide all the drama required.

Finn blinked and swallowed before attempting to collect his thoughts. 'I say to her—' he stalled for time. 'I say to her—would she like to come in and talk? Not you,' he added as the crew pushed forward. Meg hesitated and stepped through the door, which Finn closed firmly behind her.

'We'll return you to the studio,' said the reporter, 'and wait here to see what develops.' She turned to her colleagues. 'Let's hope something happens. What a godforsaken place to be stuck in. See if you can round up some coffee, Steve.'

Meanwhile, Finn was pouring tea with unsteady hands. He had wanted time to prepare before talking to this woman, but here she was, sitting in his kitchen, before he was anywhere near ready.

'Milk? Sugar?' His old diffidence swept over him and he couldn't think of anything else to say.

Meg nodded and looked down at her freshly manicured hands. *How long should I stay here?* she wondered, surreptitiously checking her watch.

'So you're from Blackpool?' Finn finally said, feeling foolish.

'Yes. Blackpool.'

'I've never been to Blackpool.'

'No.'

'Been to Oxford, London and, you know, other places. But not Blackpool.'

'No.'

'Never made the time. Sorry now.'

'Yes.'

'Nice place, Blackpool?'

'It's alright.'

They sat a while longer in silence, while outside the TV crew grimaced over the instant coffee purchased from the fish 'n' chip shop.

'What was she like?' Finn finally asked.

'She?'

'Jilly. Your cousin.'

'A nice enough little kid. I was four years older. Not really a friend.'

'What about her mother?'

Meg was tired of it all and decided to tell the truth. She wasn't on TV now. 'Look, her mother was hopeless, from what I hear. My mum always said she wouldn't stick. They were sisters, but I don't think they were that close.'

'And her father? You said he was dead?'

'Yes. He died of some liver disease. He took to the drink after they left.'

'What was he like?'

'A good bloke, really. Always nice to me and my brother. He wasn't a violent drunk or anything like that. He just got sad. Looked a lot older than his age. He sort of collapsed in on himself, if you know what I mean.'

'When did he die?'

'A few years ago now. Let's see, my youngest had just started school . . . Yes, about four years ago.'

'And he never saw Jilly again.'

'No. He never did.'

Finn absentmindedly topped up their teacups. When he spoke, his voice was low. 'I wanted to find out who she was. I always have. I know what the coroner said, but I have to tell you, I was responsible for her death.' He leaned forward to emphasise his argument. 'Who knows? She might have got home to see her father, somehow. I cut her off from that possibility.' He looked at her, his features hard with misery. 'You must hate me, now that you know.'

Meg shook her head. 'Why should I hate you? My cousin ran out in front of your car. She died. That's it.'

'I expected you to be angry. To be grieving.'

'Look, I was eight when she left. She was really nothing to me. I just came out because the TV people offered to pay. That's why I came in with you just now. They wanted me to abuse you and cry but I can't. I'm not a bloody actress.'

Finn was shattered. He'd been about to say how sorry he was, how he wanted to make up for the harm he'd done. It would have been better if she had abused him. He would still say sorry, but he knew in his heart that she couldn't offer the absolution he craved. It could only come from someone who cared for Jilly Baker. With her father dead, there was no-one alive who could restore Finn to a state of grace. He knew her name, but redemption was still beyond his grasp.

'I'm sorry, anyway.'

'Yeah. Well, it was a long time ago . . .'

Meg left the house and faced the camera. 'I'm too emotional to speak for long,' she said. 'I just want to say that Jilly will always be in my heart. Now that I've seen where she died, and spoken to the driver, I'm content.' (*I'm getting better at this*, she thought as she paused on the steps.) 'And now,' she dabbed her eyes, 'if you don't mind, I need some time to myself.'

Which she took at the Seahorse Hotel, Palm Beach, on the far north coast. The swimmers she'd brought from home made her look hippy so she bought new ones. The new ones looked much better.

When the film crew were finished and had adjourned to the pub, Sandy, encouraged by his aunt, called out at Finn's back door.

'Finn, it's Sandy. Can I come in, mate?' He pushed at the door, fully expecting it to be open as usual. The door stayed stubbornly shut. *Of course!* Sandy realised. *He'd want to keep out the TV crew.* He tried again. 'It's me, mate. The door's locked.'

'Go away.'

'Just checking how you are. You are okay?'

'Yes.'

'Sure?'

'Go away, Sandy.'

Sandy returned to his aunt's house. 'He won't let me in, Aunt Lily. He sounded sort of down. I'm worried. Should we leave him alone?' Disquieted, they looked at each other. They'd both experienced depression and knew the thoughts that arose in times of darkness.

'I'll go back,' said Sandy in response to Mrs Pargetter's unspoken command, and he headed up the path again, to the front door this time, feeling for the key hidden under the loose verandah board. This decisive action surprised him. The incident with Aunt Lily, his mother's journals and the Great Galah protest had served to slough off the fears that had encased him, and from this unpromising chrysalis there emerged a man that even he was beginning to respect.

'I'm coming in, Finn,' he announced as he turned the key in the lock. 'We need to talk.'

Finn was slumped in the armchair by the fire. He didn't move or speak as Sandy came in, switched on the light and sat down in the chair opposite.

'Talk to me, Finn,' said Sandy, looking at him steadily. 'Talk to me. I'm your mate.'

Finn stared at the wall and drew hard on his cigarette. All he'd ever asked was to be left alone, and now it seemed he'd acquired the obligations of a friendship he'd never sought from a man whose ambition it was to build a giant galah. He didn't want to talk; he wasn't even sure he could articulate his pain. He continued to stare resentfully at a point somewhere above Sandy's head.

With new-found wisdom, the usually garrulous Sandy sat challenging Finn's silence with his own. Finn was more practised, but with enormous self-control his visitor remained determinedly mute, waiting him out.

'She didn't care about her cousin, you know,' Finn said finally. 'It was all about the money. Even the police won't absolutely confirm her identity.'

'Are *you* convinced she was Jilly Baker?'

'Of course. That's obvious to any idiot.'

'So what's the problem? Isn't that what you wanted?'

Finn shook his head in irritation. 'Yes, of course I did. But I also wanted her to have a caring family. People to mourn her.'

'That's not going to happen, Finn.' Sandy's voice was firm. 'You'll just have to accept that and get on with your life.'

Finn fought to contain his anger. He stood up and looked down at the seated man. 'You're presuming on our friendship, Sandy. I want you to get out of my house. Now.'

'I'll go. But before I do, think about this. You have a daughter who cares for you and an old lady who relies on you.' Sandy stood up and indicated his own broad chest. 'You have someone who's willing to risk losing his only friend to tell him the truth.' He took a deep breath. 'It's time to move on, Finn. I know what it's like to be stuck in the past. You have what you say you've always wanted. Be grateful. All the rest is just self-indulgence.' With some dignity, Sandy turned and opened the door. 'I'll see myself out.' Heading down the path, he heard the decisive click of the lock behind him.

'I don't think he's in any immediate danger, Aunt Lily,' Sandy reported. 'We'll keep an eye on him. I'll give Moss a call.'

Finn, meanwhile, had returned to his chair, shocked at Sandy's outburst. *Self-indulgent*. That was so undeserved. Was it self-indulgent to care about the fate of another human being? Was it self-indulgent to accept blame where blame was due? Sandy may have had his own epiphany, but he, Finn, would always be bound by the past. No-one could say he hadn't tried to lay Jilly Baker to rest.

He stopped himself there as an unpleasant truth presented itself. He *had* tried to do so for the first few weeks after the accident but then he'd just given up. It was Moss who'd tried to uncover the truth. Even the TV people had tried, whatever their motives were. He, Finn, had given up. Through this fog of self-loathing, the memory of an old man's voice echoed in his head. Boniface had never given up on him.

Look into your heart, Finn. That's all the help I can offer.
It's not easy, Father Boniface. I'm not sure I know how.
Your Silence. How do you spend your Silence?
I fear I may have squandered my Silence, Father.
Squandered?
I used the time to relive my guilt.
Wiser to seek beyond your guilt. Listen to your heart.

The old priest's voice faded, and Finn stirred the fire. Sandy's words had shaken him, and he needed time to work things through. Ashamed of his outburst, he picked up the phone.

'You've given me a few things to think about, mate,' he told the relieved Sandy. 'I'm going to go bush for a couple of days. No, I need to be alone, but I'll be okay. Tell Moss and Mrs Pargetter I'll see them when I get back. I'll get a few things together in the morning and hike along to the Two Speck—you know, the usual camping spot—near old Jim's.'

'Okay, Finn.' Sandy kept his voice neutral. 'Don't do anything I wouldn't do, mate.' He hung up the phone and turned to Mrs Pargetter. 'Finn's going bush for a couple of days. Do him good. As a matter of fact, I need a couple of days away myself. I'll ask Nessie Ferguson to look in on you until Moss comes up for the weekend.'

The old lady clicked her teeth in annoyance. 'I've managed alone for most of my eighty-three years, Sandy. I don't need a babysitter now. Anyway,' she added, 'what's wrong with asking Helen? Nessie Ferguson is a nosey parker.'

'Helen's going to be busy,' he said, and disappeared out the door before she could protest any further.

23

Ana and Mrs Pargetter

IN A NEAT LITTLE HOUSE just outside the country town of Shepparton, Rozafa Sejka leaned across the bed and opened the window. The weather was milder, she noticed; spring was her favourite season. When she'd first arrived, she thought the flowering of the wattle was the first harbinger of spring, but now she knew better and looked instead for blossoms on the fruit trees and the green spears of daffodils she had planted in her third year—the year she began to feel she belonged here. She and her daughters had come to this country town as refugees in late 2000. Their tragedy had almost overwhelmed her, and if it hadn't been for Ana and Zamira, Rozafa would have given up long before they reached the relative safety of the refugee camp. Instead, she battled fear, hunger and fatigue to bring her daughters to this safe corner of the world.

Ana had always been so clever. At school in Kosova she'd topped her class, and Rozafa and her husband had hoped that one day she'd go to the university in Prishtina. 'Ah, Jetmir,' Rozafa murmured. 'She did go to university—in Melbourne, a place we had never heard of. You would be so proud of your Ana.'

Rozafa roused herself from her reverie and continued to prepare Ana's room. She had bought new yellow sheets and a doona cover in shades of sea-green. She ran her hand over the cover and frowned. What if Ana found this old-fashioned or ugly? What sort of furnishings was she used to now that she'd lived in New York?

'Zamira,' she called, and her younger daughter came running into the room, landing on the bed with a thump. 'Miri! I've just made the bed for your sister.' Rozafa shooed the young girl away, but she was smiling. 'Come and help me,' she said. 'I'm going to prepare the *meze* for Ana's welcome home feast.'

Twelve-year-old Zamira helped with more enthusiasm than skill, picking at the olives and pickled cucumbers as her mother attempted to arrange them on the plate.

'Slice the cheese for me, wicked girl,' her mother said, smiling in spite of herself. 'And leave some food for your sister.'

'I can hardly wait to see Ana,' sang Zamira, dodging her mother's wooden spoon. 'She said she had a present for me.'

'Greedy child.' Rozafa's reproof was mild. It was the Australian way to hide emotions but she understood the fierce bond between her daughters. They'd been through hell together, after all.

It was a long wait at airport customs, but eventually Ana rushed out to hug her Uncle Visar and looked around expectantly for her mother and sister.

'I've had to come straight from a job,' Visar explained, noting her disappointment. 'Rozafa and Miri are waiting at home.'

As the truck approached Shepparton, Ana heard the faint call to evening prayer. She wasn't religious, but the sound stirred her heart and echoed deep in her cultural memory.

'Do you want to stop to pray, Dai Visar?' she asked her uncle.

'We're nearly there, *xhan*,' Visar said. 'Allah will forgive a little tardiness.' He stopped outside her house, and Ana's eyes filled with tears as her mother and sister ran to the car from the verandah where they'd been waiting. They hugged and hugged again, finally moving Ana and her luggage into the house, where Visar discreetly left them to themselves.

As Miri clung to her arm, Ana felt her tiredness melt away. She loved her life in New York, but right here in Shepparton were the two people she cared about most. After her sister reluctantly went to bed, Ana and her mother sat sipping bitter black coffee and a little *raki*, talking well into the night.

When Ana recounted the strange story of Lusala Ngilu, Mrs Pargetter and the tea cosies, Rozafa shook her head. 'Such a story! And the lady comes from here, in Australia?'

Ana had already quizzed her Uncle Visar, whose one-man truck-driving business took him all over the state. 'It's only a few hours away by road. I'm sorry, Mama, but I'm going to have to deliver the gift from the ambassador as soon as possible. Dai Visar is going up that way in a few days. I hope you don't mind. I'll only be away for a night, two at the most.'

Rozafa, who'd been looking forward to this time with her daughter for months, did mind, but said nothing. She was proud that the ambassador had trusted her Ana with his gift. 'I've seen that man on the television,' she said. 'They say he may soon be chief of the whole United Nations.'

'He's a good man, Mama. I hope they're right.'

Visar loaded his truck and drove around to his sister's house. He'd had some problems with a late delivery and it was after one when he and Ana were finally ready to set off.

'I've booked us in at the Opportunity Hotel,' he told his niece. 'I don't think you should call on the old lady so late.' He turned to Rozafa. 'Don't worry, Rozafa, I'll take care of your baby.'

Ana smiled. She had lived alone in New York for eighteen months, and yet her mother and uncle were fussing about a couple of days in a country town. However, unlike many young women of her age, she was grateful for their concern. Her family was so small now, and all the more precious.

Visar's plan was to stay overnight in Opportunity and continue north with his load the next day, returning to collect his niece two days later. They arrived at the old-fashioned pub just in time to unpack and go down to dinner.

'Dining room closes at seven thirty,' said Marlene, who acted as receptionist, barmaid, and even waitress on slow nights. 'Your room key opens the bathroom—down the hall to the right. Toilet's next to the bathroom.'

There were three other diners. They were all engrossed in conversation, and Ana was too shy to interrupt to ask if any of them knew Mrs Pargetter. Marlene was too busy to stop; tonight she was also in charge of cooking, as the regular cook had asked for the night off. Despite her curiosity, Ana had to wait until morning.

As she and her uncle left the dining room, Marlene called out after them: 'There's only one other overnight guest and he's gone out, so now's a good time to use the bathroom.'

Ana said goodnight to Visar, who decided to watch the TV

in the bar. She was pleased to find that her room was clean, but noted that the sheets and towels were worn. She padded down the hall to have a shower and, returning to her room, climbed into bed. There was no television so she read a little then slept surprisingly soundly until, at five thirty, she heard her uncle leave the room next door. He'd mentioned an early start. Breakfast was from seven till eight, so Ana snuggled down and tried unsuccessfully to get back to sleep. At twenty to seven she got up and headed for the bathroom, surprised and embarrassed when a young man opened the door from the inside just as she was about to insert her key. They fumbled apologies and she slipped into the bathroom, clutching her robe to her throat. When she went down to breakfast, she saw that the young man was the only other diner.

'Might as well sit you two together,' the busy Marlene said. 'Saves washing the tablecloths.'

'Hello.' The young man smiled. 'I'm Hamish.'

'Ana,' she replied. 'I hope you don't mind . . .' He had a nice smile.

'My pleasure. I was lonely anyway and I wouldn't dare defy Marlene.'

Marlene brought coffee and Hamish looked at the newcomer over the rim of his cup. 'Can I ask what brings you to Opportunity? I'm not a local myself. I'm a landscaping student. I'm spending a few days here to work on . . . a project.'

'It's an interesting town,' she said politely. 'I'm not a local either. I'm from Shepparton.'

He'd been listening carefully, but couldn't quite pick her accent. 'And before that?'

'Kosova,' she said briefly. 'But I've just come back from New York.' Anything to deflect questions about Kosova. 'Actually, I've come to see someone. I was going to ask if you knew them, but if you're not a local . . .'

'I know a few people. Who are you looking for?'

'A Mrs Pargetter. I have a package for her.'

Hamish did his double-take. 'Talk about coincidence! A friend of mine stays with Mrs Pargetter when she's in town. I can take you there after breakfast, if you like.'

Ana smiled her thanks, and they shared a grimace as they started on the lumpy porridge. 'I'd like to let her know I'm coming first,' Ana explained. 'It's a rather important package.'

'I can call her for you,' Hamish offered. 'Can I ask why you're delivering by hand? It's a long way from New York.'

Ana felt the need to impress this helpful young man. 'It's from the United Nations,' she said, then coloured. She thought she sounded a bit pretentious. 'I mean, I happened to be coming home and the ambassador asked me . . .' She trailed off. 'I should wait until I see Mrs Pargetter herself.'

Hamish looked at her quizzically but didn't enquire further. They spent the rest of the mealtime chatting pleasantly and were suddenly guiltily aware of Marlene hovering like a mascara'd vulture, ready to clear the table so she could move on to service the rooms.

Hamish rang Mrs Pargetter and told her he was bringing someone to meet her.

'Come around eleven,' the old lady said. 'We can have some morning tea.'

Hamish reported this to Ana. He was enjoying her company and wasn't ready to lose it just yet. 'If you like, we'll leave a bit early so I can show you around the town,' he suggested with a proprietorial air. 'New York it ain't, but it's nice enough, as these places go.'

'I come from Shepparton,' Ana replied, smiling. 'That's not exactly New York either.'

They set off down the main street, Hamish carrying Lusala's package. 'It's quite heavy. What is it?'

Ana had to confess that she didn't know, but she told him the story of Lusala Ngilu and the tea cosies.

'Moss told me about the tea cosies,' he said. 'In fact, Mrs Pargetter is knitting one for me at the moment. Apparently it's a sign that I'm approved of.'

'Moss?'

'A girl I went to school with. We've been working on something together.' Hamish was being evasive. He wasn't sure how he wanted to identify Moss to this interesting new acquaintance. 'She's not a girlfriend or anything,' he added, wishing he hadn't as he saw Ana's embarrassed smile.

'The gardens look nice and green,' she said, randomly.

'Astroturf,' explained Hamish. 'Thanks to Mrs Pargetter's nephew. A strange sort of bloke.' At the thought of Sandy, he stopped. 'Look, I know it's an awful cheek but if the parcel is some sort of presentation, I'm sure there are people who'd like to be there. Mrs Pargetter is a much-loved lady. Would you mind very much if we take it back to the hotel until we see who's around at the moment?'

Ana would have preferred to return to her family but

couldn't help wondering what Lusala would have done. 'You know her best. Whatever you think.'

So Hamish returned to the hotel with the parcel, asking Marlene to put it in the safe.

Mrs Pargetter had been watching for them and opened the door before they knocked. She was a bit flustered to see Hamish with a young woman, and looked at him severely.

'Come in. I'm not expecting Moss until the weekend. We're going to practise her new song. Moss sings beautifully,' she added for Ana's benefit.

Hamish made the introductions, and Ana sat down shyly on the proffered seat. Without her parcel, she felt something of an intruder.

'Thank you for seeing me, Mrs Pargetter,' she began. 'I've just come back from New York. I've been working for the United Nations.'

'What a coincidence.' The old lady clicked her teeth in amazement. 'I work for the United Nations too. From here, you understand. I couldn't go all the way to New York. There's Errol to consider. And far too much crime, from what I've seen on television. How long have you been working for them, dear?'

'About eighteen months. I was on a student internship.'

Mrs Pargetter gave a smug little smile. 'I've worked for them since before you were born. But don't worry,' she added kindly. 'We all do our bit in our own way.'

Ana nodded, not quite sure where to go next.

'Ana knows the quartermaster, Mrs Pargetter,' Hamish volunteered, eyeing off the pumpkin scones.

The old lady looked at her guest with new respect. 'You know Mr Lusala Ngilu?' she asked. 'Tell me, what's he like?'

Ana was happy to oblige. 'He's not tall, but he's . . . a person of *stature*.'

Mrs Pargetter nodded, her own judgement confirmed. 'Stature. Precisely. Go on.'

'He's very well respected and good at his job.'

'I'm sure. Very thorough, I imagine.'

'True. And he's considered a man of great foresight . . .'

'Exactly. He was the only one to have enough foresight to snap up the tea cosies. Not everyone saw their potential, but Mr Ngilu—he knew right away.'

'He did, Mrs Pargetter, and he wants you to know that every one of them has been used for a good purpose.'

The old lady was puzzled. 'What an odd thing to say. Of course they would be.' She stood up. 'Now the kettle's boiling. Let's have some tea and scones.'

While they drank their tea, Ana talked some more about New York, and Hamish managed to glean from Mrs Pargetter that Sandy would be back soon. Spurred by his new confidence, Sandy had offered to cook a traditional Christmas lunch for them all out on his property. The only problem, the old lady explained, was Finn.

'Sandy said he was going bush, but we're not sure how long he'll be gone. You can never tell with Finn. Mostly it's only a few days, but I've known him to be gone for as long as a month. Still, you'd think he'd be home for Christmas.'

When her visitors left, Mrs Pargetter went straight to the phone. 'Make sure you come up as soon as you can, Moss, dear,' she warned. 'Your Hamish has been here with a young woman. She seems like a nice enough girl, but you never know.'

'He's not *my* Hamish,' Moss protested, but she was intrigued. 'Who is she, Mrs Pargetter?'

'An envoy, as we call them in the United Nations.' The old lady lowered her voice. 'Perhaps we shouldn't talk too much over the phone. You never know.' She had recently become quite fond of spy novels and knew all about surveillance.

24

Finn alone

THE TWO SPECK WAS ABOUT thirty kilometres downstream from Opportunity. Here, just before a sweeping bend, the stream broadened and ran noisily over pebbles and coarse sand. Finn had found this camping spot years ago and came here when even his limited social life in Opportunity became too much. Sheltered and isolated, the place seemed ideal, but on his first visit he soon became aware that he had a neighbour. Jim was an old prospector who lived in a lean-to that teetered above the steep embankment. Resenting Finn's intrusion, Jim lurked malevolently in the bush for several days but was finally driven into the open by the smell of Finn's tobacco. 'Spare a smoke, mate?'

Finn obliged and they sat in silence, watching the twin spirals of smoke fade into the blue haze of the eucalypts.

'Ta, mate,' said Jim before returning to his lean-to.

Thereafter Jim and Finn understood each other, and on Finn's irregular visits they spent many an hour in affable silence, squatting on their heels beside the campfire, drinking billy tea or smoking roll-your-owns. Sometimes, quite out of the blue,

Jim would have a 'bit of a yarn', as he called it. His voice was creaky with disuse.

'Know why they call it the Two Speck?' he asked Finn once. 'Because they reckon that's all they found when they panned here—but me grandad used to say they found more than they let on.' He touched the side of his nose and nodded towards the river. 'Either that or the gold's still here. If it is still here, I'll find it, my bloody oath I will.'

Jim used to pan for gold along the creekbed, and the few specks he found he stored in a little jar of river water hidden under his stretcher bed. He was a philosophical old bloke, Finn remembered now with affection. *I'd stay here on the Two Speck even if they found Lasseter's lost bloody reef*, he'd say. *The bush'll do me any day.* Finn had felt a kinship with this reclusive old man; they both respected silence and gave each other space, but there was a companionable element to their encounters.

We could've started a monastery of our own, Finn thought. *The Bush Brothers.* He grinned. No, that sounded like a country and western band.

The shack was empty now and had deteriorated since Finn was here last. Jim had been dead a few weeks before he was found, and, while outrage was expressed in the local paper, Finn was glad. His old friend had escaped the hospital death he dreaded. *They roof over the stars, Finn, and you can't smell the bush.* All the old man had wanted was to live and die on his beloved Two Speck.

Finn put down his pack and looked around. There'd been a time when he'd have taken a sudden flood into account, but the

Two Speck flowed sluggishly now. A faint but ominous cloudiness defiled the formerly clear water.

I'm glad old Jim didn't live to see this, Finn thought as he pitched his tent. He made a campfire the way the old man had taught him, and emptied a can of baked beans into the pot, stirring them desultorily with a stick. The sharp scent of eucalypt mingled with the smoke, and furtive little shuffling noises betrayed the first stirrings of nocturnal bush creatures.

Finn had walked the thirty kilometres from Opportunity, stopping two nights to camp and re-provision on the way. Walking usually helped him think, but this time he resolutely refused to face his situation until he'd reached his destination. Now that he was here, he procrastinated once again. *Maybe I'll eat first*, he decided. He ate his beans with some bread that he'd toasted—burned—over the fire. He rummaged in his pack for his enamel mug. *A cup of tea and then I'll think.* But despite his good intentions, his mind stubbornly refused to cooperate. The short twilight retreated before the encroaching bush night and though the campfire warmed his front, a chill was settling over his back. *Time for the sleeping bag*, he told himself. *Better to think in the morning when I'm fresh.*

He was awakened just after dawn by the chorus of birds and the secret, rustling life of the trees. The fire was down to a few smouldering coals, so he stoked it up and soon bacon was sizzling, filling the air with its strong salty aroma. *Bacon and eggs. Nothing better for a bush breakfast.* He'd finish his breakfast and then he'd think.

Mopping up the last of his egg, Finn sipped at the scalding billy tea and attempted to apply logic to his undisciplined emotions. He understood that he'd reached a milestone in the discovery of Amber-Lee's real identity, but from now on there were no signposts to direct him. Amber-Lee's shadow had walked beside him in lock step for over ten years, directing his life and his sense of himself. Now that she had transmuted into Jilly Baker, the idea of Amber-Lee was drifting from him. He had the practical means to commemorate her life and death, perhaps with some sort of charitable donation, but what he had cherished as a great tragedy had become human-sized, even banal. Without Amber-Lee and the life they'd shared, he felt disorientated. He needed a compass or, better still, a map. This could be the end of the road. On the other hand, it could be the beginning of a new one. How do you know such things?

The memory of a voice prompted him. *I can sense that you're stronger now. How do you account for that?* Father Jerome was right. He *was* stronger now, and looking back, he could see that his strength had begun to return even before he met Amber-Lee's cousin, before he'd heard the name Jilly Baker. He'd felt the beginnings of its tentative re-emergence the night Moss told him that her mother was Amy Sinclair; the night he met his daughter for the first time. In retrospect he was amazed that he'd let her in—a strange young woman, coat streaming with water, hair plastered around her tense, white face. He smiled now as he remembered his caution, his blathering on about names. They'd both seemed a little mad that night. *Like father, like daughter*, he thought and was pleased to apply the old cliché to himself. Poor Moss: she'd needed his support when Linsey died, and while he demonstrated his concern in all sorts of practical ways, his emotional commitment had been nig-gardly at best. He had to admit that he'd avoided confidences when Moss clearly needed someone to talk to. It wasn't that he didn't want to help; just that he felt singularly unqualified to advise anyone about—well, anything, really.

He stood up and stretched his back, then went down to the river to splash water on his face, which was stung to numbness as its iciness pierced the residual warmth left by the fire. He was getting soft, he thought, and imagined old Jim scoffing at his startled recoil from the cold. He dried his face on a small towel. A good walk would get the blood flowing.

Taking the goat-track by the river, he walked briskly for a while and then slowed down as he returned reluctantly to his earlier train of thought. There was Moss, of course, but also Sandy and his aunt. They were another reason for his renewed strength. He needed to understand how his friendship with Sandy and Mrs Pargetter had come about. Was it simply the attraction of similarly lost souls? In part, it was. They were all damaged in some way. But beyond that was the simple warmth and fellowship that characterised ordinary friendships, like the one he'd shared with Phil in the old days. He, Moss, Sandy, Mrs Pargetter—their reliance upon each other had strength-ened them all.

He returned to the core question. For ten years now he'd lived with his self-imposed obligation to Amber-Lee, whom he now knew to be Jilly Baker. Knowing was supposed to be enough.

You have what you say you've always wanted, Sandy had said. *Be grateful. All the rest is just self-indulgence.*

Where had Sandy found this new dignity and authority? He'd always been so diffident, so dependent. Good-hearted, yes, but something of a buffoon. Sandy had always looked up to Finn, yet in the end he had been willing and able to judge him. *Perhaps that was because he knew the depths of my culpability*, decided Finn, his thoughts once again turning inwards. He pulled himself up sharply. No; this wasn't about him at all. It was about Sandy. Sandy had grown in the past few months, and the man he really was had found the voice and the courage to reprimand his friend.

Finn had a daughter, a home, friends. He no longer really knew Michael Clancy and couldn't have picked up his old life even if he'd wanted to. The only remnant of the Michael he had been was his daughter, conceived so thoughtlessly—no, so *unthinkingly*—to fund his social life. Looking back on that time, Finn was grateful that he'd given generously in the end. If Moss wasn't conceived in love, at least she was conceived in kindness.

What more did he want of life? Why was he so reluctant to let go of the corrosive remorse he'd nurtured over the years? It had seen him retreat from the world and from all his former attachments, living a monkish existence in a forgotten country town. But life has a way of continuing. He'd formed new attachments. Not because he sought them, but because he lived in a real place with real people, all of whom demanded time and respect. He could live a hermit's life like Jim, a contemplative life like the Benedictines, or he could live, an imperfect man in an imperfect world.

Back at his camp now he squatted on his heels in front of the fire. He pushed a twig into the coals and touched the spark to his cigarette. *This is who I am*, he thought. *This is who I can be.*

Finn had sloughed off his old skin, but the new skin was still raw and tender. He didn't feel ready to return to Opportunity. This reborn Finn was not a return to the old Michael. Michael Clancy was a person Finn looked back on as he might a naive younger brother or a feckless but charming friend: with affection and a little regret.

The old Finn, trapped in his self-imposed penance, was still too recent, too ingrained to be discarded lightly, and remained as a shadow of the possible future. The new Finn needed time to grow into his skin.

He decided then to linger a while by the Two Speck, walking the five kilometres to Tungally pub each day for a meal. There he could mix a bit with the locals or the passing truckies who stopped for lunch on their way to or from Melbourne. Strangers wouldn't ask difficult questions; even if they did, he owed them no answer.

For two weeks he was a familiar sight at the bar, eating his counter lunch or drinking his Coke. Once or twice, a truckie stopped to give him a lift, but mostly he was content to walk. The locals were curious, but the first conversations he had were the general conversations of strangers passing the time.

G'day, mate. Where you from, then?

Camping on the Two Speck, eh?

What about the Magpies? Can they win without Johnson?

No bloody rain in sight, eh?

Fuckin' politicians haven't got a clue, mate.

You don't have a beer, then?

Later, the conversations became more specific and personal.

Me daughter's gone to Melbourne for work. Nothin' for her here, mate. You got kids?

So what do you do for a crust? Maths, eh? Wasn't much good at maths meself. Me son's an accountant, but. Since he moved to town we don't see the grandkiddies much.

I can last one more season, I reckon. Poor old Dad'll turn in his grave if we're forced to sell.

I applied for a country school. I love it here, but we're running out of kids. It'll close in two years if we don't get more families.

You don't fancy pulling on the boots, do you? No, we've got older blokes than you in the team, I reckon.

Finn listened to them all; all the concerns of ordinary lives, all the same, yet all unique. He offered something of himself in return.

I moved from Melbourne to Opportunity about ten years ago.

Yeah, I like the country life.

No, never played for the Knockers.

A daughter. She comes and stays with me sometimes.

No. No grandkids.

He wasn't so different. Soon, he told himself. Soon he would return.

One morning he woke up and knew it was time. Methodically, he began to gather his things, taking care to collect his rubbish in a plastic bag, which he stowed in his backpack. Finally, he doused the fire with river water and smothered it with earth. With one last look at Jim's disintegrating shack, he swung the pack lightly over his shoulder and set off down-river, back to Opportunity. He suddenly wanted, more than anything, to be home for Christmas.

25

Sandy and Rosie; Moss and Linsey

WHILE FINN CAMPED OUT ON the Two Speck, Sandy had been very busy. He spent nearly three weeks in Melbourne, visiting printers and art suppliers, poring over manuscripts, testing the quality of the softest leather. He learned about gold leaf, and explored the mysteries of the labyrinth. The Great Galah faded to nothing. Sandy Sandilands had a new plan, and this time it was shared. He and Helen had talked long into the night about a suitable new project to replace the Great Galah.

'What we need is something that not only honours Mum's memory, but which Opportunity can be proud of.' These were the simple specifications they had discussed over pasta and a bottle of cab sav in Sandy's kitchen. The discussion was animated. Helen had even risked teasing Sandy a little about the Great Galah and was pleased to see that he was able to laugh along with her. *Something has happened to Sandy*, she thought, looking at his affable grin. Even his body seemed more solid; the soft, sprawling flesh gathered in and disciplined as he sat with his shoulders back and his chin high.

So Sandy went to Melbourne and Helen stayed in Opportunity. There was a lot of work to be done. Before he left Melbourne, Sandy collected an order from the workshop of a master craftsman.

'It's first rate,' Sandy said simply. 'I hadn't imagined anything so . . . fine.'

'Thank you for the opportunity, Mr Sandilands,' the man replied. 'I have to say, it's the best thing I've ever done.' He touched the leather in a final tribute and reluctantly began to wrap it. 'I really hate to let it go.' Sandy looked alarmed, but the other man shook his head. 'Don't worry, mate. I can't afford to keep it.'

As he drove home, Sandy also felt the need to touch the parcel several times. Having no artistic talent himself, he was in awe of the beauty that flowered under other, more skilful hands.

Meanwhile, Hamish booked into the Opportunity Hotel again and began his work on the project. He had been slumped in front of his computer when Sandy rang, and had listened with increasing interest to the big man's proposal.

'So, if you'd like to go and work with Helen, I'll catch up with you in a couple of weeks. Could you have something ready for me to look at by, say, the second week of December? And a ball-park quote?'

Hamish was only too happy to comply. Here was the major project he'd been seeking—and he was going to be paid! He began to pack, gleefully throwing an assortment of clothes and textbooks into his backpack. Then he stopped. Sandy was gambling a large amount of money, not to mention his reputation, on the skills of an inexperienced student. Hamish prided himself on his integrity. He couldn't let Sandy run away with another idea that might come to grief, so he picked up the phone. 'Sandy,' he said. 'I know how important this is to you, but you have to remember, I'm still just a student. You need someone with qualifications. Someone who's done this kind of thing before.'

Sandy was firm. 'No, Hamish. What I need is someone with passion and a fresh vision. Someone who knows Opportunity. I think you fit the bill nicely.'

There was much discussion at the bar and the supermarket about what Helen Porter and that young Hamish were doing as they wandered around town, heads bent over notebooks, taking photographs and measuring all manner of things (they even had a theodolite). They spent a lot of time at Helen's too, it was noted.

Tom Ferguson didn't trust Sandy one bit. 'If it's that galah thing again, by the living Harry I'll . . .' He stopped. He couldn't think of a punishment horrible enough.

Cocky chuckled into his beer. 'You tell 'im, Tom.'

'Marl reckons Helen's sweet on him,' Merv offered.

'Helen sweet on that young bloke? Give us a break, Merv. She's twice his age and not exactly an oil painting.' Milo D'Amico, sensing he'd gone too far, back-pedalled as fast as he could. 'Don't get me wrong. Helen's a lovely woman. Salt of the earth—it's just the age difference . . .'

Those who opted for sexual intrigue were disappointed to see that Hamish spent each night at the pub, and it wasn't until

Ana reappeared a few days before Christmas that Marlene felt she had a legitimate romance to announce.

Ana had come back for Sandy's Christmas lunch as that seemed to be the best time to make the presentation to Mrs Pargetter. Public transport would have been difficult from Shepparton, so she came back on her uncle's last run before Christmas.

Though he was busy drawing up plans, Hamish made time for Ana. They had breakfast and dinner together, and one day took a picnic lunch to the old rail bridge that spanned the nearby gorge known as Harriet's Leap.

That day Hamish's mood was buoyant. He'd become something of an expert in the town's history and was pleased to share it with Ana. 'Apparently Harriet was the wife of the town's founder, Opportunity Weekes,' he told his attentive companion. 'But there's no record of her ever having leapt or even threatened to leap into the gorge. From all accounts she was a practical woman.'

'Maybe she encouraged others to leap,' Ana suggested, unwrapping the sandwiches that Marlene had grudgingly slapped together.

'Or maybe her neighbours hoped that she'd leap.'

'Yes, they hoped she'd take the hint.' Hamish waved his cheese and pickle sandwich for emphasis.

Ana giggled, a little ashamed. 'Poor woman. She was probably loved by all who knew her. The name may not refer to her at all.'

Once they'd finished eating, they packed up their picnic and walked down the steep path into the shallow gorge, Hamish holding Ana's hand as she slid on the loose scree.

'Hardly worth the effort,' he puffed as they reached the bottom and took in the spindly shrubs and scattered refuse. He looked up at the rail bridge. The angle was interesting and he took a few photographs before turning again to his companion.

She had nice eyes, he thought, and her slender body looked good in her neat jeans and red top. She wore little makeup, and her warm olive skin was smooth over her cheekbones. He took her hands and kissed her gently, then more passionately as she responded.

As he became more urgent, she pulled away. 'Enough for now,' she said, smiling up at him. 'Let's take it slowly.'

'Of course.' Hamish took her hand again. 'I hope you'll let me get to know you better, Ana.'

'Me too, Hamish,' she said shyly, and he felt a sudden lurch of joy at the sound of his name on her lips.

After Finn left to go bush, Moss had returned to Amy's house. Arriving in the late afternoon, she threw her backpack on her bed and opened a bottle of wine. Holding bottle and glass in one hand and a bowl of nuts in the other, she went out and sat on the long verandah that faced the rose garden. The low rays of the summer sun cast a benign glow over the roses, which were in an early second bloom. They were particularly fine that year, and Moss grinned as she remembered Linsey's stories about Flash Jack and the unfortunate Aunt Shirley. If it weren't for those Marrakech oysters, she might not be looking over this beautiful garden. It had always been a place where she could sit and think things through.

While the TV fiasco had been painful and chastening, the revelation Moss had experienced in the Bradman Museum had revitalised her. She knew what to do now. She was resolute. Not *pig-headed* (a term that Amy often used to describe her) but resolute. Since Linsey's death (in truth, since the ugly incident at Linsey's apartment), Moss had been restless. Dropping out of her course left her with little to do, and her search for her father filled a number of functions, one of which was to give herself focus. But instead of stopping once she had found Finn, she couldn't leave well enough alone. She had to try to organise his life. *I mightn't have your genes, Mother Linsey*, she thought ruefully. *But I picked up something along the way.*

What would Linsey tell her to do? Want her to do now? That was too easy. It was what she, Moss, wanted to do; that is, continue with her singing. She hummed a little scale in a minor key. It tasted smooth, like chocolate. She ran through some more scales—*la, la, la, la la, la, la, laaaa*. She stood up and sang to the roses, sensing the music vibrate along their treacherous stems to the waiting ear of the petals.

Moss giggled self-consciously. *I've only had one glass of wine. I can't be drunk.* But she was intoxicated—by the precarious light that bridged day and night; by the sound of her own voice and the taste of her music; by the knowledge that she was now ready to move on with her life. If her time in Opportunity had taught her anything, it was that regret is too great a burden.

'One more project,' she promised the roses. 'One more project for my mother, then it's back to the Con.'

Over the next few days, Moss met with the family solicitor and the bursar of the Melba Conservatorium. They were confident Moss's plan could be put in place for the end of the next academic year.

When she arrived in Opportunity a week before Christmas, she was disappointed to find that neither Finn nor Sandy had returned. She had to tell someone her plans, so she confided in Mrs Pargetter.

'It will be called the Linsey Brookes Memorial Scholarship and will go to advancing the career of a young Melba graduate.'

The old lady seized Moss's hands. 'What a lovely thought,' she said. 'It's the very thing.'

Moss went to bed feeling better than she had for longer than she could remember. If she could be sure that Finn had forgiven her, she would be truly content. She looked with affection at the teddies on the wall and settled her pillow with a little sigh. A soft, moth-wing whisper echoed from the shadows.

'Goodnight, little one,' Moss said, and fell into a dreamless sleep.

26

Gifts and givers

CHRISTMAS EVE WAS HOT AND oppressive. The citizens of Opportunity were becalmed on a sea of heat. Little rivulets of sweat ran down their foreheads and prickled their underarms, and their eyes were dazzled by the specks of mica that danced crazily on the ground.

'It must be over a hundred in the old.' Merv set a cold beer down in front of Cocky and flapped his shirt.

'Won't touch the sides, mate,' said the old man, swigging the beer in two gulps before rubbing the glass on his sweaty singlet. 'I'm still comin' for Chrissie dinner, aren't I? Marl's still cookin' in the heat?'

'She's out there stuffing the turkey right now. A bloody marvel, Marl.'

Cocky grunted his agreement as he gestured for another beer. 'An' one for me mate,' he said as Tom came in, wiping his forehead.

'Nah. My shout,' said Tom, as Cocky well knew he would. 'Merry Christmas, mate.'

'Anyone seen Finn?' Helen poked her head around the bar

door. At the chorus of nos she disappeared again. 'Enjoy your Christmas,' she called over her shoulder.

'I have to go,' she told Hamish, who was waiting outside. 'I'm giving Sandy a hand. See you tomorrow.'

Hamish had offered to drive the others out to Sandy's property the next day. Finn had still failed to return from the Two Speck, and Moss and Mrs Pargetter were becoming uneasy.

'It's nearly three weeks since we've seen him,' Moss worried.

'Sandy was confident that he'd be alright,' the old lady said with more conviction than she felt. 'He must be enjoying his camping.'

As Finn hadn't returned by the time they were leaving, they left a note on his door. Moss was disappointed that he would miss the presentation, but Mrs Pargetter was oblivious to her place of honour.

She and Moss were surprised to see Helen's car parked in Sandy's drive. 'She's helping with the cooking,' Sandy explained.

They were settling into their chairs in the living room when Moss saw Bill Green's cab crunching up the gravel drive to disgorge a dishevelled Finn.

'Am I too late?' Finn puffed as he rushed in the door. 'When I saw the note, I didn't even stop to shower.'

Moss hugged him, wrinkling her nose. 'I can tell. No, you're not too late. We've only just arrived.' She gave him an extra squeeze. 'I'm glad you could make it. It's our first Christmas.'

Finn kissed the top of her head. 'But not the last,' he promised. At Sandy's invitation, Finn went off to the shower, and returned wearing his own grubby jeans and a large white shirt that flapped around his lean body.

Moss indicated the Christmas tree, draped with lights and tinsel. An angel wobbled precariously at its tip. 'Beautiful tree, Sandy.'

'Yeah.' He looked pleased. 'Helen helped me. Dad and I didn't bother much after Mum died.'

'I'll do the drinks,' Hamish offered.

'Leave the wine,' Sandy said. 'This calls for champagne.' The champagne had been on ice to toast Sandy's announcement, but changing his mind, he popped the cork with a flourish and Hamish filled the glasses.

While Sandy took round the drinks tray, Hamish went over to Ana. 'As soon as everyone has a drink, you can start.'

Sandy gestured for her to come forward. 'As you all know, young Ana here worked in New York for the United Nations.'

Finn didn't know, and looked at her curiously. For one so young, she carried herself with a certain dignity.

'Ana, you have something to say, I believe,' Sandy said.

Ana stepped forward, a bright spot of embarrassment on each cheek. She'd prepared a speech that she hoped was worthy of both donor and recipient. 'Many years ago,' she began, 'a parcel of tea cosies arrived at the UN headquarters . . .' (Mrs Pargetter sniffed and muttered, 'United Nations, girl. United Nations.') 'The parcel was opened by a Mr Lusala Ngilu, from Kenya,' she continued, 'and it was the beginning of a wonderful tradition that has lasted to this day. Mrs Pargetter has served the United Nations for thirty-five years, as has Mr Ngilu, and before he leaves his current position, he wishes to honour the work done by Mrs Pargetter for so many years.'

She paused, and Hamish handed her a box, patting her arm

affectionately. Mrs Pargetter looked bemused, blinking rapidly behind her glasses and sucking in her teeth nervously.

'It's my great pleasure,' Ana said, 'to present this award to Mrs Lily Pargetter, on behalf of Ambassador Ngilu and the United Nations.' She walked over to where the old lady was sitting and offered her the box.

'I must stand to accept this honour,' Lily Pargetter said. 'Finn, help me up.'

Ana presented the old lady with the box, shaking her hand before kissing her on the cheek. 'You've been an inspiration to more people than you can imagine, Mrs Pargetter, me included.'

Lily Pargetter's hands shook as she sat down and attempted to prise away the seal. Moss knelt down to help her, as the others crowded round with their congratulations. The seal was broken, and the box opened to reveal straw packing. Cradled in the straw, shining softly in the lamplight, was a silver teapot.

'There's something engraved on the front,' said Sandy. 'What does it say?'

Overcome, Mrs Pargetter thrust the teapot into Moss's hands. 'Read it for me, will you please, dear? It's very small—I can't quite make it out.'

Moss stood up and read: '*To Lily Pargetter, friend of the United Nations and mentor of a grateful Lusala Ngilu.*' The little group looked at each other. 'Wait. There's more. There's the emblem with the olive branches and more words. *Reaffirming faith in the dignity and worth of the human person.*'

'That's from the Preamble to the Charter,' said Ana, and they all fell silent.

Lily Pargetter's eyes began to fill. 'I'm not up to a speech,' she murmured. 'Just . . . thank you, dear. And thank the quartermaster from the bottom of my heart.'

'A toast,' said Sandy. 'To Aunt Lily and the United Nations.'

Mrs Pargetter raised her glass. 'And to Quartermaster Ngilu and all of you here.'

'Could be in for some rain,' observed Hamish as they sat down. The window looked out on indigo clouds, which had been massing on the horizon all day. Uneasy thunder slunk through the distant cloud-mountains, but overhead the sky was brushed with a lucent grey. There was an evanescent quality to the light that drained some colours, while others stood out in sharp relief.

'It'll be a while yet,' said Sandy. 'That's if it comes at all. Drought clouds are a bit like mirages. They look like the real thing, but . . .' He picked up his father's old carving knife and, beaming in an avuncular way, began to carve the turkey while Helen, slightly flustered, passed around the vegetables.

'There are two gravy boats,' she fussed. 'Bother! I left one in the kitchen.' She bustled out to get it, tucking her hair behind her ears.

'Whatever's the matter with Helen?' Mrs Pargetter asked. 'She's usually cool as a cucumber. Must be the heat,' she murmured, dabbing at the perspiration on her upper lip. She was wearing a new white cotton blouse with a lace inset. She hoped it wouldn't end up all stained under the arms. Not very ladylike.

The others nodded. The air was oppressive and the

barometer on the wall in Sandy's study signalled change to an empty room. There was a feeling of controlled anticipation among the diners, who did their best to engage in light conversation. A little inhibited by Ana's presence, Sandy's old friends were careful to keep the discussion to generalities, courteously including her as much as possible.

Finn looked quizzically at Hamish and Ana, but made no comment. He'd never been as convinced as Mrs Pargetter about the existence of a romance between Hamish and Moss, and he continued to eat in silence. His attention was drawn to Helen, who was talking to their host in a low voice. Finn had come to consider Sandy a confirmed bachelor like himself, and was put out by the sudden thought that Helen and Sandy might be a couple. He confided his suspicions to Moss in a whisper. 'What do you think?'

'Hard to tell,' she replied. 'From what I hear, they've certainly been spending a lot of time together lately.'

It wasn't until tea and coffee were served that Sandy finally stood up and called for silence. Finn supplemented his host's ineffectual voice by tapping on a glass.

'Thank you all for coming,' Sandy began. 'And thank you once again to Ana for her presentation. I called you all together originally to make an announcement.' He paused for effect. 'I want you to know that I've purchased the site of the Opportunity footy ground.'

Finn, Moss and Mrs Pargetter looked at each other in horror. They'd all thought the bizarre project had been put to rest, but once again the shadow of a gigantic galah was flapping across their landscape.

Mrs Pargetter was the first to gather her wits. 'You promised, Sandy. You promised and . . .'

Sandy looked puzzled. 'I promised what? Oh, you mean the Great Galah. No.' He laughed, a full-bodied, confident laugh. 'No. That's not what it's for. This idea is quite new, and with the help of Helen and Hamish here, we can make it a reality. It will be my gift to you, my special friends, and a gift to Opportunity. Come back into the lounge. Leave your coffee. I've got something to show you and I don't want anything spilt on it.' He strode away and the others followed, gathering around a card table he'd placed in the middle of the sitting room. One of Rosie's hand-crocheted tablecloths lay over a rectangular object which glowed red through the patterns in the lace.

Once they were all assembled, Sandy looked around, ensuring that he had everyone's full attention. Hands trembling, he removed the cloth as a father might remove a coverlet from a sleeping child, and stepped back, as if to savour the admiration of those encircling the cradle. On the table lay a book, bound in leather the colour of red wine. Fine gold lettering flowed across the soft kid cover.

'It's gold leaf,' Sandy told them. 'And the clasp is twenty-four-carat gold.'

Mrs Pargetter recognised the clasp. 'It's Rosie's brooch,' she said. 'Our mother's filigree brooch.'

'I hope you approve of me using it, Aunt Lily,' Sandy said. 'I'm sure you will, when I tell you about it.'

'*Book of Remembrance*,' read Moss. 'What does it mean, Sandy?'

Sandy opened the book, revealing pages of handmade silk

paper. 'If you'll all sit down, I'll explain.' He waited for them all to be seated.

'Aunt Lily, Finn, Moss—we're all haunted, in one way or another, by spirits who need a resting place. This book is a place where we can honour the occupants of unmarked graves, name the nameless dead and acknowledge those to whom we owe reparation.' The big man delivered this carefully prepared speech with a peculiar grace, then all at once collapsed into the diffident Sandy they all knew. 'Well, um, if you agree, you write the name in the book. Basically, it's where we can reclaim them, and ourselves, by letting them go.' His hands hovered over the book. 'I hope you understand . . .'

'It's wonderful, Sandy,' said Moss, kissing his cheek, and the others murmured assent.

Encouraged, Sandy continued: 'After I thought of this, I realised we'd need a place of safekeeping for the book, and that's where Helen and Hamish come in. Hamish has brought some preliminary plans. I'd like to open this to the whole community. That's why I bought the footy ground.' He turned to Hamish who had opened a laptop computer and was directing a Powerpoint presentation to the opposite wall. 'Hamish? Can you take over now?'

Hamish clicked the mouse. 'This,' he began, 'is the footy ground as it is now.' They all looked at the familiar oval—the ramshackle club rooms covered in graffiti, the tired cyclone fence, the litter-strewn playing field with its patchwork of dried grass and flourishing weeds.

He clicked again. 'And this is how it will be.' Projected on the wall was a virtual garden, a shallow bowl shape, landscaped with acacias, banksias and ironbarks; tussock grasses, wallaby grasses and small-leafed clematis; river bottlebrush, speedwell and sweet bursaria. Helen named each one as Hamish clicked to close-ups.

'All drought-resistant,' said Sandy. 'All native to the area. We have Helen to thank for that.'

Hamish clicked again. 'As you can see in this close-up, there will be a central labyrinth leading to a rotunda. So people can sit out of the weather.' He clicked again to show a small building with a balcony of finely wrought iron lace and lead-light windows.

'I've managed to source the lace from a demolition site in Fitzroy,' Hamish explained. 'It's the real deal—genuine Victorian craftsmanship. The windows are going to be made by Tom Ferguson's nephew from Mystic. He's quite a well-known artist in his field.'

'We'll keep the book in a case in the rotunda,' added Sandy. He turned to Helen. 'Tell them about the labyrinth.'

Hamish clicked again and Helen stood up to explain the labyrinthine symbol of birth and death. 'Some say our spirits enter and leave this world through the same door,' she said. 'There are many false paths, but only one leads to the centre. Our path will be made of pebbles and stones, and we will lay a special one for each of the dead whose name is inscribed in the book. The stone should be chosen by a loved one or a keeper of the memory.' The image on the wall was now a model of the completed path. 'As you can see, the path will not be uniform, as each stone represents someone unique.' She paused. 'This labyrinth won't be a maze. The goal is always visible.'

Sandy's face was strained and eager. 'So—what do you think?'

Finn took his friend's hand. 'Sandy, I think I can speak for us all when I say that we're privileged to be part of this.' He gestured to the others, and one by one, they came forward to congratulate the modestly smiling Sandy.

The big man reddened and then became bustling and practical. 'First, the book. I've got a special, soft-tipped pen. We'll leave the book here so we can give the writer some privacy. Aunt Lily, would you like to start?'

The old woman's face crumpled, and tears rolled down her cheeks. 'I can write *Arthur*, but my baby has no name. What can I write in the book when my baby has no name?'

'Sit here, Aunt Lily.' Sandy's voice was gentle as he pulled a chair up to the table. 'Take your time. We can leave a space for your baby, until you've thought it through.'

As the sky outside darkened, the light hanging high from the ceiling failed to penetrate the shadows, and Mrs Pargetter peered myopically at the book. Sandy, always alert to his aunt's needs, switched on the lamp, and left quietly with the others.

Lily's page

Lily Pargetter sat looking at the creamy parchment as its silk webs reflected the glow of the lamp. She placed her palm on the page and looked in wonder at her hand. The slim white fingers of her youth were now swollen, the joints gnarled like old tree branches. Ugly brown spots speckled the back of this alien hand, competing with the purple bruises that now appeared so frequently. That hand, smooth and white, had once caressed Arthur's hard, brown body, and the worn circle of gold that cut into her swollen finger had once been a broad wedding band that she'd vowed never to remove.

Arthur John Pargetter, she wrote in her best copperplate. *1921–1942.* She used to write so well. She'd even won prizes at the local agricultural show. Now a light, spidery track faltered across the page. *An old woman's writing*, she sighed to herself. *It's the best I can do, Arthur.*

She put down the pen and then picked it up again. *Baby Pargetter*? Should she simply write *Baby Pargetter*? It didn't seem right. If she was going to do this, it had to be right. She thought back to the plaques in the cemetery. Perhaps something from there . . . But both memory and imagination failed her. *Help me, Arthur.*

A smiling young man, handsome in his khaki uniform, was patting the tiny mound of her belly. He kissed her and suddenly she knew.

Tiger Pargetter, she wrote, *born and died 23 November 1942. Loved child of Lily and Arthur. I've found you at last. Both in God's care.*

She sat with the book for a long time, then slowly walked back to the dining room. 'Thank you, Sandy,' she murmured. 'Rosie would be proud.'

Finn's page

Finn had made his peace by the river but still felt he needed to use the book to formally redress the wrong he'd done. He took out the photo Graham Patterson had copied for him. Jilly's eyes were full of mischief, and Finn could see that her father was attempting to hold her still for the photo. He was sure that as soon as her father had taken his hands from her shoulders, she would have been off along the pier, laughing and chasing the seagulls. *I'm so sorry, mate*, he said to the long-ago young man. He couldn't bring her back, but his tightly twisted guilt had unravelled and he was left with something softer and more flexible. Sorrow was more forgiving than guilt. It allowed tears to flow.

Jillian Maree Baker, Finn wrote. 1981–1996. *Daughter of Andrew Baker.*

Finn thought gratefully of Moss. He would never have defaced this book with the name Amber-Lee.

Moss's page

Moss took her place at the table and picked up the pen. What would Linsey have thought of all this? For all her sharp edges and volatility, Linsey's centre was delicate and subtle, and this was something very few understood. When she sang for her mothers, Moss remembered, it was Linsey who felt the music most deeply.

Linsey Anne Brookes, Moss wrote. 1952–2006. *Mother of Miranda Ophelia Sinclair.*

'It's a bit late, Mother Linsey,' Moss said. 'But I'm claiming you here—and there's nothing Aunt Felicity can do about it.'

Ana's page

When Moss returned to the others, Ana stood up. 'Sandy has kindly allowed me to write in the book. I lost my father and brother in Kosova,' she explained. 'Their bodies were dishonoured and buried in a mass grave. It will give me and my family great joy to honour them here, in a place so close to us.

'Baba,' she said, as she prepared to write. 'And Edvin. You lie in our beloved Kosova, but you are here, too, in our hearts.'

Jetmir Sejka, she wrote. 1954–2000.
Edvin Sejka, 1983–2000.

Sandy's page

Sandy slipped away upon Ana's return. He had originally planned this book for his mother, but his new understanding enabled him to think beyond his own needs.

'I think I got it right this time, Mum,' he said. 'It's way too late to make your life easier, like I should have, but if you're looking down on us, I hope you approve. The way I supported Dad was shameful, and I wish you weren't lying together now.'

Rosie Maud Baxter, Sandy wrote. 1922–1974. *Mother of Sandy, sister of Lily.*
Rest in Peace.

'You're safe now, Mum.'

And with the stroke of a pen, he repudiated his mother's unhappy marriage.

Ana's uncle was picking her up at seven o'clock, so she and Hamish had to leave Sandy's place by five thirty. Mrs Pargetter was looking weary, and they offered her a lift. The others stayed to help Sandy tidy up, and Helen agreed to drop Moss and Finn off on her way home.

Sandy stepped outside and cocked his head. The birds were twittering their agitation. He looked up at the sky and came back inside. 'You'd better get going,' he urged his guests. 'It looks as though that storm is finally on its way.'

'We'll stay, Sandy,' said Moss. 'It won't take very long to clean up, and it's only a twenty-minute drive.'

The pearly grey sky had been gradually darkening, and it was now uncompromising basalt; a hard blue-black vault that sucked in the light. The thunder no longer growled in the distance, but tumbled and crashed through the cloud wall in the wake of vivid white lightning.

No rain yet. Mrs Pargetter looked out of the car window, hoping it would rain, but not until she was safe inside. She clutched the box holding her teapot. She'd display it on the piano. She couldn't possibly use it. It was a sign that her years hadn't been wasted. She jumped as a new crash of thunder shattered the sky. The air was unbearably oppressive.

'Here it comes,' said Hamish as heavy drops starred the windscreen. 'Thank goodness we're nearly there.'

Sandy had given them an umbrella, so Hamish was able to usher the old lady inside with some protection, although both their shoes were squelching as they stepped into the hall.

'Are you sure you'll be okay, Mrs Pargetter?' Hamish asked as he turned to leave.

'Of course, dear. I've seen rain before.' Mrs Pargetter wanted him gone. He was a nice enough lad, but she had things to do.

Hamish ran back to the car, and the old lady took off her wet shoes. Errol padded up the passage to greet her, his old head nuzzling her hand. She ruffled his ears.

'We're both getting on, Errol,' she reflected ruefully as the dog, whimpering a little, returned to his basket. She should mop up the puddle in the hall but she was just too tired. She took off her jacket and switched on the lamp. The pink shade spread a cosy mantle of light, but suddenly she felt a chill and turned on the electric heater. What next? She had something else to do. The teapot. She took it out of the box and put on her reading glasses. *To Lily Pargetter, friend of the United Nations* . . . It was nice to have her work recognised. She put the teapot carefully on the table and went over to the piano, removing and folding the green cover. What now? She opened her linen press and took out a box. As she opened it, the faint fragrance of lavender rose from the tissue-paper lining. How long ago had she filled this box with scraps of embroidery and crochet—handiwork of her mother and grandmother, of Rosie and her own young self? She hadn't used these items for years now, but each year she replaced the dried lavender with the new crop from her garden. She sifted through the contents. There it was—the doily she'd crocheted for her hope chest. So much hope, turning thread into lace. She smoothed the filigreed fragment onto the piano and placed the teapot in the middle. All those tea cosies . . . and she was behind schedule with next year's quota.

She crossed the room, picking her way around furniture that suddenly seemed like obstacles. She was patient. Another few minutes wouldn't matter. Each step was an effort. Such a day. And she was going on eighty-four. No wonder she was tired. She thought longingly of her warm bed and hot water bottle. But there was one more thing to do before the day's business was over. She had left this most important thing till last.

Lily Pargetter opened the door to the nursery. Errol climbed from his basket and stood sentinel behind her. The teddy bears huddled together on the wallpaper as she slipped into the room. They looked at her with anxious, boot-button eyes.

'I'm here, Tiger,' she whispered, holding out her hand. 'I'm here, little Tiger.'

She felt the touch of a soft palm as tiny fingers curled around hers.

Rain lashed the window and drummed a frenetic beat on the tin roof. The whole world was awash. But it was alright. She could sleep now.

Epilogue

OVER TWO YEARS HAVE PASSED since the Christmas gathering at Sandy's house. Grey cloudfields stretch to the horizon, washing the rooftops and gardens of Opportunity with intermittent rain. There is an ice-cream van, a hot-doughnut vendor, balloon sellers and coffee tents. The Country Women's Association is serving Devonshire teas, and the district scouts have organised a sausage sizzle. Coloured umbrellas mushroom among the burgeoning throng who, despite the showers, are all cheerfully determined to enjoy the carnival atmosphere. After all, it's their day.

Sandy, tree-solid, looks around. He's at ease with himself. His roots grow deep and wide in the soil of Opportunity. He is standing by the rotunda where he had planted *Arthropodium strictum*, a fine-stalked purple lily, and *Boronia serrulata*, the native rose. He sees with satisfaction that they appear to be flourishing.

Helen is talking to Rozafa, who belongs to a shawl-knitting group in Shepparton. It was she who had given Helen the idea.

'We had eleven people at the initial meeting,' Helen

tells her. 'We have about twenty now. We've sort of adopted Afghanistan and most of them go there.'

'The old lady—she would be happy, I think?'

'I'm sure she would.'

Ana comes to fetch her mother, and Helen moves on. Sandy looks up and smiles as she approaches with a young family in tow.

'You remember Paul, Tom and Nessie's son? And this is his wife Cate and their children, Charlotte and Julian.'

Paul offers his hand. 'It's a pleasure to meet you again, Mr Sandilands—Sandy. Dad's kept us posted on the working bees. I believe even old Cocky pitched in to help.'

Sandy grins. 'Might have been the free beer Merv put on— but seriously, everyone did their bit and I have to admit that Cocky earned that beer.'

Freda D'Amico joins them and gestures towards the gardens. 'Beats a great galah, eh, Sandy?' She gives him a playful nudge.

'New plan, Freda. I'm building one just opposite your home paddock.'

'Beware the protestors, my friend.' She waves to an elderly woman who is flustering about in a floral apron. 'Okay, Liz. Coming.' She turns back to Sandy and Helen. 'Got to go. Have to deliver these scones to the tea girls.'

Tom Ferguson and Ned Humphries want to discuss business. 'Hey, Sandy. When do you reckon the council will approve the river walk?' This was a plan to extend the garden along the river to join up with the Memorial Gardens.

'Not yet,' Sandy replies. 'But I'd say it's in the bag.'

Sandy walks hand in hand with Helen, accepting backslaps and handshakes from friends and neighbours. They stop by a corner garden bed, planted with fine-leaf tussock-grass, bluebells, everlasting daisies and a shrub that Sandy can't identify. Sharon Simpson is there with a group of children.

'It's a sweet bursaria,' Sharon tells him, pleased and officious. 'Has these white flowers in summer and then red seed pods.'

Her mum had bullied her into coming to one of the Sunday working bees. Sharon had been standing around, feeling awkward, and fearful for her new acrylic nails, when Moss, in overalls and gloves, had grabbed her.

'You want to help? Look after the kids. They're driving us crazy.' In this way, the Children's Corner was born, and Sharon lost three expensive nails. It wasn't part of the original plan, but Hamish was pleased. As he said, it was Opportunity's garden, not his.

The night before, there had been a candlelight gathering of the first people of the book. Each of them had walked the labyrinth and placed their stone on the curving pathway.

Finn had found Jilly's stone on Blackpool Beach when he returned to England for a maths conference. He laid it on the path with care. He wasn't doing it for himself; he did it for her father, Andy Baker. 'He'd want this for you, Jilly,' Finn said as he patted the pebble into place.

Moss is to sing at the opening, but she came a day early and stooped to lay a sharp piece of glittering quartz with a vein of gold at its centre. 'Just like you, Mother Linsey.' She smiled.

Hamish drove Ana up with her mother and sister, Uncle Visar following to take Rozafa and Miri home. They brought two stones from their garden in Shepparton. That way, their beloved Jetmir and Edvin could share in their new home in this land so far from their common grave in Kosova.

Sandy placed five stones. Foreseeing this day, he'd gone down to the river even before the plans were approved, and spent hours sifting among the pebbles on the riverbed. He wanted each one to embody the person it represented, and he chose with care. For Rosie, he selected a smooth flat pebble, its creamy white surface shot with a roseate vein. He laid his mother to rest with gentle hands.

He thought sadly of his Aunt Lily, wishing that she could have been here for this final act of homage on behalf of her own dead.

'One for you, little Tiger,' he said, laying a small white stone, perfectly round, with a soft luminescence. For Arthur, he had found an odd-shaped stone the colour of military khaki. 'I never knew you, mate, but I know Aunt Lily loved you, so here you go.'

In the end, Sandy couldn't bear to exclude Lily from this family of stones. Technically, she didn't fit the criteria for a place in the labyrinth. She lay in peace, under a headstone bearing her name, in the family plot at St Saviour's.

'I can break the rules for you, Aunt Lily. You and Arthur and little Tiger. You were apart for too long. You can all lie together now.' Lily Pargetter's stone was curiously banded in yellows, browns and greys. 'Just like a tea cosy.' Sandy grinned affectionately as he placed it next to the others.

He reached into his pocket and took out a rough blue-grey

stone. He was breaking another rule. 'I think you belong here too, Errol.'

The gardens are finished, but only time will reveal their full beauty. News of the book had spread by word of mouth, and other names were added to its pages, so that Sandy had to commission a second volume. Many of those who had written in one of the books are here today to complete the ritual with the laying of a stone.

The opening is to be simple. Sandy has staunchly fended off publicity-seeking politicians and numerous clergy who wanted to make a speech or say a prayer. He was adamant. 'All we need is some music and a simple dedication.'

Moss waits nervously. Remembering her panic before Linsey's funeral, Finn hovers nearby in case she needs support. He's dying for a smoke but will wait now until the formalities are over.

Helen pushes Sandy gently, and he moves to the front of the makeshift platform and takes the microphone.

'Ladies and gentlemen—and children, too, of course. Today we are opening the Opportunity Gardens, the gardens where we have all worked so hard for the past two years. What an effort! Congratulations, Opportunity.' Cheers and whistles from the crowd as Sandy pauses. 'For many of you, the gardens are simply a place of beauty and pleasure, a place to enjoy with family and friends. But for some, this is the day when you will complete the act of remembrance you began when you signed one of the books that we are keeping in our beautiful rotunda. Today is the day that you will lay your stones in the labyrinth.' His expansive gesture embraces the spiral path with the exquisite little structure at its centre. 'But before that . . .' He smiles fondly as Moss climbs the steps to the platform. 'Before that, I'm pleased and proud to introduce Opportunity's adopted daughter, and our dear friend, to sing for the loved ones we remember here today. Miranda Sinclair, with "An Eriskay Love Lilt".'

Moss is nervous, fearing that emotion will get the better of her. She catches Finn's eye. Hamish and Ana smile their encouragement. *All these people have faith in me*, she thinks. *I can do this.* She steps forward and sings.

Vair me oro van o,
Vair me oro van ee
Vair me oro o ho
Sad am I without thee.

When I'm lonely, dear white heart,
Black the night, or wild the sea,
By love's light my foot finds
The old pathway to thee.

Thou art the music of my heart,
Harp of joy, oh cruit mo chridh
Moon of guidance by night
Strength and light, thou art to me.

Vair me oro van o,
Vair me oro van ee
Vair me oro o ho
Sad am I without thee.

A shaft of sunlight pierces the clouds and strikes the stained-glass windows of the rotunda. Splinters of coloured light fragment the air as the clouds part. The garden is drowning in light; a light that pours comfort and grace over the patient lines of pilgrims waiting with their stones.

Helen and Sandy have invited Moss, Finn, Hamish and Ana back to the house for a private celebration. The wisteria is flowering early this year, and the long verandah is draped in a graceful blue curtain. Sandy and Helen smile a welcome at the door. The house has not forgotten the sadness it has witnessed. Houses never do. But it has woven this into its new story with such subtlety that it is transmuted into something softer, more bearable and, finally, hopeful. Moss, of course, knows this. She feels such things in her bones.

The rain is persistent now, and the sky has darkened, but the lamps are lit, revealing the good but slightly shabby furniture, the mellow beauty of the floorboards and the welcome of an open fire. A young kelpie has commandeered the armchair by the hearth. He wags his tail but stays curled up on the cushion. It's Sandy's chair and the dog doesn't want to push his luck.

'We're glad you could all come,' Sandy says. 'It's important to have everyone here.'

In the dining room, the heavy old table is set with a lace cloth, and Rosie's silver gleams beside her fine china.

'We'll open the champagne later,' says Sandy. 'Right now, I have a better idea for a toast.' Helen comes in and places a tray on the table. And quietly, respectfully, she fills each cup from an engraved silver teapot fitted with a hand-knitted tea cosy.

'A toast,' says Sandy. And they stand and raise their teacups to a world of possibilities.

Acknowledgements

Many thanks to:

My agent Gaby Naher who believed in my book and who steered me, so deftly, through the unfamiliar world of publishing.

Allen & Unwin editors Annette Barlow, Catherine Milne and Clara Finlay from whom I have learnt so much in these last few months.

The Stillbirth and Neonatal Death Support Group (SANDS) for permission to use their name and the inscription from the communal burial site. Special thanks to Anne Bower who facilitated the process, and who with Joan Noonan offered valuable advice regarding the services SANDS offers to the community.

Sadber Sanders, who helped me with details for the story of Ana and her family.

Jonathon Ferguson, former Assistant Curator, Military History, National Museum of Scotland, for facilitating my application to use the quotation from the Scottish War Memorial.

Janet Bristow of the Prayer Shawl Ministry for the use of the lines from her beautiful poem 'Ariadne's Blessing'.

Kerry Scuffins, poet and author, who was the first person to call me a writer and who, with Lauren Williams and members of the SPAN Writer's Group, has given me so much help and encouragement.

My teacher, novelist and poet Sallie Muirden, and class-mates, especially Les Zigomanis, from Novel 2 at NMIT for their thoughtful advice and criticism.

My daughter, Carolyn Evans, who generously gave so much of her valuable time, reading and critiquing my manu-script with such honesty and insight.

My husband (and research assistant), Terry, for his patience, his encouragement and belief in me as a writer.

My sons, Timothy and Julian, my mother Alice Websdale, and all of my extended family and friends, for their encourage-ment and delight in the publication of this novel.

Caitlin and Michael, who are already writing wonderful stories, and Charlotte, whose own story is just beginning.